FIC ASHLEY KRI
Ashley, Kristen,
Walk through fire /

BEA

NOV 0 9 2015

ath.

"[...] own, I set who you were [...] back then I'd do
th[...] wrong. And you gave [...] you thought I needed and
I'[...] grateful, Millie. But outta that over the years we both got
somethin' else. We're not young and stupid and so caught up
in love we're blind. We got life under our belts and we know
better now. So, what I'm sayin' is, in future, learn from what
we lost and don't ever do shit like that again."

In future.

Was he saying...

"In future?" I choked.

"In future," he stated plainly.

"I...you...we..." I shook my head in his hands. "Are you
saying we should start up where we left off?"

His comeback was instant.

"Did it ever end for you?"

Acclaim for Kristen Ashley and Her Novels

"A unique, not-to-be-missed voice in romance. Kristen Ashley is a star in the making!"

—Carly Phillips, *New York Times* bestselling author

"I adore Kristen Ashley's books. She writes engaging, romantic stories with intriguing, colorful, and larger-than-life characters. Her stories grab you by the throat from page one and don't let go until well after the last page. They continue to dwell in your mind days after you finish the story and you'll find yourself anxiously awaiting the next. Ashley is an addicting read no matter which of her stories you find yourself picking up."

—Maya Banks, *New York Times* bestselling author

"There is something about [Ashley's books] that I find crackalicious." —Kati Brown, DearAuthor.com

"Run, don't walk...to get [the Dream Man] series. I love [Kristen Ashley's] rough, tough, hard-loving men. And I love the cosmo-girl club!" —NocturneReads.com

"[*Law Man* is an] excellent addition to a phenomenal series!"
—ReadingBetweentheWinesBookclub.blogspot.com

"[*Law Man*] made me laugh out loud. Kristen Ashley is an amazing writer!" —TotallyBookedblog.com

"I felt all of the rushes, the adrenaline surges, the anger spikes...my heart pumping in fury. My eyes tearing up when my heart (I mean...*her* heart) would break."

—Maryse's Book Blog (Maryse.net) on *Motorcycle Man*

WALK
THROUGH
FIRE

Also by Kristen Ashley

The Chaos Series

Own the Wind
Fire Inside
Ride Steady

The Colorado Mountain Series

The Gamble
Sweet Dreams
Lady Luck
Breathe
Jagged
Kaleidoscope

The Dream Man Series

Mystery Man
Wild Man
Law Man
Motorcycle Man

WALK THROUGH FIRE

A CHAOS NOVEL

KRISTEN ASHLEY

FOREVER

NEW YORK   BOSTON

This book is a work of fiction. Names, characters, places, and incidents are the product of the author's imagination or are used fictitiously. Any resemblance to actual events, locales, or persons, living or dead, is coincidental.

Copyright © 2015 by Kristen Ashley
Excerpt from *Own the Wind* © 2013 by Kristen Ashley

All rights reserved. In accordance with the U.S. Copyright Act of 1976, the scanning, uploading, and electronic sharing of any part of this book without the permission of the publisher constitute unlawful piracy and theft of the author's intellectual property. If you would like to use material from the book (other than for review purposes), prior written permission must be obtained by contacting the publisher at permissions@hbgusa.com. Thank you for your support of the author's rights.

Forever
Hachette Book Group
1290 Avenue of the Americas
New York, NY 10104
www.HachetteBookGroup.com

Printed in the United States of America

First edition: October 2015
10 9 8 7 6 5 4 3 2 1

OPM

Forever is an imprint of Grand Central Publishing.
The Forever name and logo are trademarks of Hachette Book Group, Inc.

The Hachette Speakers Bureau provides a wide range of authors for speaking events. To find out more, go to www.hachettespeakersbureau.com or call (866) 376-6591.

The publisher is not responsible for websites (or their content) that are not owned by the publisher.

ISBN 978-1-4555-3325-1

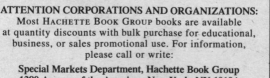

ATTENTION CORPORATIONS AND ORGANIZATIONS:
Most HACHETTE BOOK GROUP books are available at quantity discounts with bulk purchase for educational, business, or sales promotional use. For information, please call or write:

Special Markets Department, Hachette Book Group
1290 Avenue of the Americas, New York, NY 10104
Telephone: 1-800-222-6747 Fax: 1-800-477-5925

This book is dedicated to Beth Isenhour Ruble.
A woman who proves friendship lasts a lifetime...
And beyond.

WALK THROUGH FIRE

CHAPTER ONE

I Never Would

Millie

I SHOULD GET a salad.

I should have gone to Whole Foods and hit their salad bar (and thus been able to get a cookie from their bakery, a treat for being so good about getting a salad).

I didn't go to Whole Foods.

I went to Chipotle.

So, since I was at Chipotle, I should get a bowl, not a burrito.

I had no intention of getting a bowl.

I was going to get a burrito.

Therefore, I was standing in line at Chipotle, trying to decide on pinto or black beans for my burrito, telling myself I was going to have salad for dinner (this would not happen but I was telling myself that it would, something I did a lot).

And in the coming weeks, I would wish with all my heart that I'd gone to Whole Foods for the salad (and the cookie).

It was lunchtime. It was busy. There was noise.

But I heard it.

The deep, manly voice coming from ahead of me.

A voice that had matured. It was coarser, near to abrasive, but I knew that voice.

I'd never forget that voice.

"Yeah, I signed the papers. Sent 'em. Not a problem. That's done," the voice said.

I stood in line having trouble breathing, my body wanting to move, lean to the side, look forward, see the man attached to the voice, *needing* that, but I couldn't seem to make my body do what it was told.

"Not set up yet with a place, don't matter," the voice went on. "Got a condo in the mountains for the weekend. Takin' the girls up there. So I'll come get 'em like I said, four o'clock, Friday. I'll have 'em at school on Monday. I'll sort a place soon's I can."

I still couldn't move and now there was an even bigger reason why.

Takin' the girls up there.

I'll have 'em at school on Monday.

He had children.

Logan had kids.

Plural.

I felt a prickle in my nose as my breaths went unsteady, my heart hammering, my fingers tingling in a painful way, like they'd gone to sleep and were just now waking up.

The voice kept going.

"Right. You'd do that, it'd be cool. Tell 'em their dad loves 'em. I'll call 'em tonight and see them Friday." Pause, then, "Okay. Thanks. Later."

The line moved and I forced myself to move with it, and just then, Logan turned and became visible in front of the food counter at Chipotle.

I saw him and my world imploded.

"Burrito. Beef," he grated out. "Pinto. To go."

I stared, unmoving.

He looked good.

God, *God*, he looked so damned *good*.

I knew it. I knew he'd mature like that. Go from the cute but rough young man with that edge—that dangerous edge that drew you to him no matter how badly you wanted to pull away—but you couldn't stop it, that pull was too strong.

I knew he'd go from that to the man who was standing in front of the tortilla lady at Chipotle wearing his leather Chaos jacket.

Tall. His dark hair silvered, too long and unkempt. Shoulders broad. Jaw squared. I could see even in profile the skin of his face was no longer smooth but craggy in a way that every line told a story that you knew was interesting. Strong nose. High cheekbones. Whiskers (also silvered) that said he hadn't shaved in days, or perhaps weeks.

Beautiful.

So beautiful.

And he once was mine.

Then I'd let him go.

No, I'd pushed him away.

I turned and moved swiftly back through the line, not making a sound, not saying a word.

I didn't want him to hear me.

Out, I needed *out*.

I got out. Practically ran to my car. Got in and slammed the door.

I sat there, hands hovering over the steering wheel, shaking.

Takin' the girls up there.

I'll have 'em at school on Monday.

He had kids.

Plural.

Girls.

That made me happy. Ecstatic. Beside myself with glee.

I signed the papers. Sent 'em.

What did that mean?

So I'll come get 'em...I'll sort a place soon's I can.

Come and get them?

He didn't have them.

Signed the papers.

Oh God, he was getting a divorce.

No. Maybe he'd just gotten one.

I'll come and get 'em...

He was a father.

But was he free?

I shook out my hands, taking a deep breath.

It didn't matter. It wasn't my business. Logan Judd was no longer my business. He'd stopped being my business twenty years ago. My choice. I'd let him go.

And clearly it didn't happen—where he was heading, where that Club was heading, what I expected would happen didn't.

He was in line at Chipotle, not incarcerated.

I didn't see him top to toe from all sides but from what I saw, he didn't have any scars. He had that scratchy voice, so obviously he hadn't quit smoking when he should have (or not at all). But he seemed strong, tall, fit.

Maybe he had a beer gut.

But with what he'd been getting into then, what Chaos was into back in the day, I expected twenty years later Logan would be a lot different and not just having-a-scratchy-voice, having-a-craggy-but-still-immensely-attractive-face, maybe-having-a-beer-gut different.

Worst case, I expected he'd be dead.

Almost as worst case, I expected he'd be in prison.

Still almost as worst case, I expected him to be committing felonies that would eventually land him either of those two. Not in a Chipotle getting a burrito, talking on the phone with someone about picking up his kids, taking them to a condo in the mountains and getting them to school on Monday.

What I'd expected was one thing.

What I saw was what I'd hoped.

I'd hoped he'd find his way to happiness.

It struck me on that thought that he'd said his order was to go.

Oh God, I needed to get out of there. It wouldn't do for me

to escape him inside only for him to see me outside in my car, freaked out so bad I was shaking.

I pushed the button to start my car, carefully looked in all mirrors and checked my blind spots, reversed out, and headed home.

I had no food at home except for a bin of wilting baby spinach and some shredded carrots.

This was because I thought grocery shopping was akin to torture. I did it only when absolutely necessary, which was infrequently considering the number of options available for food in my neighborhood.

Conversely, I loved to cook.

I just didn't do it frequently because I hated to shop for food, and anyway, cooking for one always reminded me I was just that.

One.

Singular.

I had good intentions. Practically daily I thought I'd change in a variety of ways.

Say, go to the grocery store. Be one of those women who concocted delicious meals (even *if* they were only for me), doing this sipping wine in my fabulous kitchen while listening to Beethoven or something. There would be candles burning, of course. And I'd serve my meal on gorgeous china, treating myself like a princess (since there was no one else to do it).

After, I'd sip some fancy herbal tea, tucked up in my cuddle chair (candles still burning) reading Dostoyevsky. Or, if I was in the mood, watching something classy on TV, like *Downton Abbey*.

Not what I normally did, got fast food or nuked a ready-made meal, my expensive candles gathering dust because they'd been unlit for months and not bothering even to dirty a plate. I'd do this while I sat eating in front of *Sister Wives* or *True Tori* or some such, immersing myself in someone else's life because they were all a hell of a lot more interesting than mine.

Then I'd go to bed.

Alone.

To wake up the next morning.

Alone.

And spend the day thinking of all the ways I would change.

Like I'd start taking those walks I told myself I would take. Going to those Pilates classes at that studio just down the street that looked really cool and opened up two years ago (and yet, I had not stepped foot in it once). Driving up to the mountains and hiking a trail. Hitting the trendy shops on Broadway or in Highlands Square and spending a day roaming. Using that foot tub I bought but never took out of the box and giving myself a luxurious pedicure. Calling my friends to set up a girls' night out and putting on a little black dress (after I bought one, of course) and hitting the town to drink martinis or cosmopolitans or mojitos or whatever the cool drink was now.

Seeing a man looking at me and instead of looking away, smiling at him. Perhaps talking to him. Definitely speaking back if he spoke to me. Accepting a date if he asked. Going on that date.

Maybe not going to bed alone.

Every day I thought about it. I even journaled about it (on days when I'd talked myself into making a change and was together enough to journal).

But I never did it.

None of it.

I thought all this as I drove home, then into my driveway, down the side of my house, parked in the courtyard at the back, got out and went inside, stopping in my kitchen, realizing from all these thoughts something frightening in the extreme.

I was stuck in a rut.

Stuck in a rut that began twenty years ago on the front stoop of the row house I shared with Logan, watching him walk away because I'd sent him away.

Walk through fire.

The words assaulted me and the pain was too intense to bear. I had to move to my marble countertop, bend to it to rest my elbows on it and hold my head in my hands.

Then it all came and blasted through me in a way it felt my head was going to explode.

You love a man, Millie, you believe in him, you take him as he is. You go on his journey with him no matter what happens, even if that means you have to walk through fire.

His voice was not coarse back then. No abrasion to it. It was deep. It was manly. But it was smooth.

Except when he said those words to me. When he said them, they were rough. They were incredulous. They were infuriated.

They were hurt.

Walk through fire.

The tears came and damn it, *damn it*, they should have stopped years ago.

They didn't.

They came and came and came until I was choking on them.

I didn't make a salad with wilting spinach and the dregs of shredded carrots. I didn't hit my desk and get back to work.

I pulled my phone out of my bag, struggled to my couch, collapsed on it, and called my sister.

I couldn't even speak when she picked up.

But she heard the sobs.

"Millie, what on earth is happening?" she asked, sounding frantic.

"Dah-dah-Dottie," I stuttered between blubbers. "I sah-sah-sah-saw *Logan* at fu-fu-fucking *Chipotle*."

Not even a second elapsed before she replied, "I'll be over. Ten minutes."

Then she was over in ten minutes.

She took care of me, Dottie did.

Then again, my big sister always took care of me in a way I knew she always would.

The bad part about that was that I never did any of those things I said I was going to do.

I never pulled myself out of my rut.

I never fought my way to strong.

When I lost Logan, I lost any strength I might have had.

That being him.

He was my foundation. *He* was my backbone. *He* made me safe. *He* made life right.

Hell, *he* made life worth living.

Then he was gone, so I really had no life and commenced living half of one.

Or maybe a third.

Possibly a quarter.

Likely an eighth.

In other words, I was the kind of sister who would always need to be taken care of.

I knew I should wake up one day and change that.

I knew that just as I knew I never would.

At a party, in a house, twenty-three years earlier…

"Hey."

"Hey."

He started it. He'd been checking me out since he got there ten minutes ago and not hiding it. Then he'd come right to me and started it.

I liked that.

I also liked that he'd approached, not wasting a lot of time.

But mostly, I liked how incredibly cute he was.

Cute and edgy.

Holding my cup of beer in hand, I stared up at him.

God yes, he was cute. *So* cute.

But cute in a way that my mother would not curl up at night, safe in the knowledge her daughter had excellent taste in men.

In other words, I wasn't talking to a well-dressed guy who I would soon learn had a life mission he'd decided on when he was a boy, this being astronaut or curer of cancer.

He was cute in a way my mother would despair, pray, live in terror and my father would consider committing murder (one of the various reasons my mother would be living in terror).

But looking into his warm, brown eyes, for once in my life, I didn't care what my mother and father thought.

I just cared about the fact that he was standing close to me at Kellie's party, he'd come right up to me and he'd said, "Hey."

"Name's Logan," he told me.

God, he even had a cool name.

"Millie," I replied.

I watched his eyes widen a bit before he burst out laughing.

That wasn't very nice.

I swayed a little away from him, feeling hurt.

He kept chuckling but he noticed my movement and focused intently on me, asking, "Where you goin'?"

"I need a fresh beer," I lied.

He looked into my full cup.

Then he looked at me, smiling.

Oh God, *yes*. He was *so* cute.

But he was kinda mean.

I mean, my name wasn't funny. It was old-fashioned but it was my great-grandmother's name. My mother had adored her and Granny had lived long enough for me to adore her too.

I liked my name.

"You got Millie written all over you," he stated.

What a weird thing to say.

And more weird, it was like he knew what I was thinking.

"What?" I asked.

"Darlin', all that hair that doesn't know whether it wants to be red or blonde. Those big brown eyes." His smooth, deep voice dipped in a way that I felt in my belly. "That." He lifted his beer cup with one finger extended and pointed close to my mouth so I knew he was indicating the little mole that was just in from the right corner of my top lip. "Cute. Sweet. No better name for a girl that's all that but Millie."

Okay, that was nice.

"Well, thanks, I think," I mumbled.

"Trust me, it's a compliment," he assured.

I nodded.

"What're you doin' tomorrow night?"

I felt my head give a small jerk.

Holy crap, was he asking me out on a date?

"I... nothing," I answered.

"Good, then we're goin' out. You got a number?"

He was!

He was asking me out on a date!

My heartbeat quickened and my legs started to feel all tingly.

"I... yes," I replied, then went on stupidly, "I have a number."

"Give it to me."

I stared at him, then looked down his wide chest to his trim waist, then to his hands. One hand was holding his beer, the other one had the thumb hooked in his cool-as-heck, beaten up, black leather belt.

I looked back to his face. "Do you have something to write it down?"

He gave a slight shake of his head and an even slighter (but definitely hot) lip twitch before he stated, "Millie, *you* give me your number, do you think I'm gonna forget a single digit?"

Okay, wow. That was *really* nice.

I gave him my number.

He repeated it instantly and accurately.

"That's it," I confirmed.

He didn't reply.

I started to feel uncomfortable.

And nervous.

I'd just made a date with a guy I didn't know at all except I knew my parents wouldn't approve of him and then I gave him my number.

Now what did we do?

"You come with someone?" he asked.

It was weird that he asked that now, after he'd asked me out.

After I thought it was weird, I thought that maybe he thought I was on a date and then made a date with him *while* I was on a date and then he'd think I was a bitch!

"No, just some girlfriends," I told him quickly.

He gave me another smile. "That's comin' with someone, darlin'."

Oh.

Right.

I bit my lip.

"Who?" he asked.

"Justine," I answered, tipping my head toward the kitchen table where there were four guys and two girls sitting. When he turned his head to look, I expanded my answer, "The brunette."

And right then, Justine, my friend the pretty brunette, drunkenly bounced a quarter on the table toward a shot glass, missed, and grinned. Two of the guys and one of the girls immediately shouted, "Shot!" Thus, she unsteadily grabbed the glass and threw it back, some of the vodka in it dribbling down her chin.

She finished this still grinning.

"You ain't ridin' back with her," Logan growled, and my gaze shot back to him. "Fact, she ain't drivin' anywhere."

Oh man, I could love this guy.

Oh man!

That was crazy!

How could I possibly think I could love this guy just from him saying that?

"She isn't and I'm not," I shared. "We're staying the night here."

"Good," he muttered right before he got bumped by someone precariously making their way to the keg.

"You wanna get out of here?" I found myself asking, and got his swift attention. "I don't know. Sit out on the back deck or something?" I finished quickly so he didn't get any ideas.

"Fuck yeah," he whispered, his brown eyes locked to mine, and the way he said that, the way he was looking at me, I felt a shiver trail down my spine.

"Okay," I whispered back.

He leaned in and grabbed my hand. His was big and rough and felt warm and strong wrapped around mine.

Okay.

Oh God.

Seriously.

Seriously.

It was true. It was crazy and *totally* freaking true.

I could fall in love with this guy.

And I knew that just from him wanting me to be safe and the feel of his hand around mine.

Oh man.

He led me out to the deck, straight to the steps that led to the yard and we sat on the top one.

I was nervous in a way I'd never felt before but it felt good as I stared out into Kellie's parents' dark yard.

"So, Millie, tell me what we're doin' tomorrow night," he ordered.

I turned my head to look at him. "What?"

"Whatever you wanna do, we're doin' it," he stated. "So tell me what you wanna do."

I tipped my head to the side, intrigued with this offer.

"How about we fly to Paris?" I suggested on an attempt at a joke.

"You got a passport?" he asked immediately, not smiling, sounding serious.

My heart skipped a beat.

Though, he couldn't be serious.

I mean, Paris?

"Do you?" I returned.

"Nope, but that's what you wanna do, I'll get one."

I grinned at him. "Not sure you can get a passport in a day, Logan."

"You wanna go to Paris, I'll find a way."

I shook my head, looking away.

He was good at this. A master at delivering lines.

I liked it. It showed confidence.

But they were still just lines.

"And he says all the right things," I told the yard.

"Babe, I'm not jokin'."

My eyes flew back to him because he still sounded serious.

And when they flew back to him, the lights from the house illuminating his handsome face, he *looked* serious.

"I don't wanna go to Paris," I whispered. "Well, I do," I hastened to add. "Just not tomorrow night. I don't think I have the right thing to wear on a date in Paris."

He grinned at me. "Well, that's a relief. Coulda swung it by the skin of my teeth but it'd set me up for a fail on our second date. Not sure how I'd top Paris."

He was already thinking of a second date.

I liked that too.

But I liked his words better because it was cool to know he could be funny.

I couldn't help it and didn't know why I would try.

I laughed.

He kept grinning while I did it and scooted closer to me so our knees were touching.

"So tell me, Millie, what d'you wanna do?" he asked when I quit laughing.

"I wanna see what you wanna do," I told him.

"Then that's what we'll do."

I looked into his eyes through the dark and felt something strange. Not a bad strange. A happy one.

Comfortable. Safe.

Yes, both of those just looking into his eyes.

"So, do *you* wanna go to Paris?" I asked. "I mean, one day."

"Sure," he told me. "Though, not top on my list."

"What's top on your list?"

"Ridin' 'cross Australia."

"Riding?" I asked.

"On my bike."

I felt my eyes get big. "You mean, the motorcycle kind?"

He put pressure on my knee as he gave me another grin. "I'm the kinda guy, Millie, who doesn't acknowledge there *is* another kind of bike."

Absolutely for *sure*, my parents would not approve of this guy.

And absolutely for *sure*, I so totally *did*.

"So you have a bike?" I pushed.

"Harley," he told me.

"Do I get to ride on it tomorrow?" I went on, not bothering to filter the excitement out of my question.

He stared into my eyes.

"Absolutely," he answered.

I smiled at him and I knew it was big.

His gaze dropped to my mouth and when it did, my legs started tingling again. But this time, the tingles emanated from the insides of my thighs, out.

I looked away and took a sip of beer.

"Millie," he called.

I kept my gaze to the yard and replied with a, "Hmm?"

"Safe with me."

My attention cut back to him.

"Never won't be, babe," he went on softly. "Not ever. Hear?"

Again, it was like he read my thoughts.

And he knew. He knew he was exactly what he was. That guy parents would freak if their daughter ever said yes to a date with him.

But I knew something else, looking at him.

My parents were wrong.

"Hear?" he pushed when I just stared at him, not feeling tingly.

Feeling warm.

"Yeah," I answered.

He pressed his knee into mine again and looked to the yard.

"So, you wanna go to Paris," he noted. "What else you wanna do?"

I looked to the yard, too, and told him.

We stayed out there, sitting on the steps of the deck, our knees brushing, for what felt like minutes at the same time it felt like hours, talking about nothing that felt like everything before the guy he came to the party with stuck his head out the back door and called, "Low, ridin' out."

To that, he told me he had to go and we both got up.

He didn't kiss me.

He walked me into the house straight through to the front door.

There, he ordered somewhat severely, "Your girl is totally shitfaced, so you go nowhere with her and you let her go nowhere. Hear?"

I nodded. "Staying here, Logan."

He nodded.

Then he lifted a finger as his eyes dipped to my mouth and he touched my mole.

More thigh tingles.

He looked back at me. "Tomorrow, babe. Call you."

"Okay, Logan."

He grinned and walked away.

I watched him, feeling a crazy-giddy that had nothing to do with beer, strangely not disappointed he didn't kiss me.

He'd touched me in a way that felt way sweeter than a kiss.

And the next day, he called me.

CHAPTER TWO

Every Breath He Took

Millie

Present day…

WHAT I WAS about to do was ridiculous.

And possibly insane.

But there I was, about to do it.

It had been a week since I saw Logan at Chipotle.

I still had that bin of spinach and bag of shriveled carrots in my fridge and they were still the only things there. Except that bin of spinach was now not wilted but instead spoiled.

I should throw them out.

I didn't throw them out.

I worked.

I got fast food (or ready-mades, though no salads).

I slept.

I watched TV.

And I thought about Logan.

I couldn't get him out of my head. I even dreamed about him.

And these were not good dreams. They were dreams of him walking away. They were dreams of him shouting at me that I was a coward. That I'd thrown my life away. They were dreams where he was pushing a faceless little girl on a swing, smiling at a faceless woman who, even if faceless, I knew she was beautiful and she was definitely not me.

In other words, bad dreams.

Dreams that haunted me even when I was awake.

So now I was here and it was ridiculous, stupid, insane.

Dottie would be pissed if she knew I was here. Twenty years she'd been struggling to pull me out of Logan's snare, a snare I was caught in even if he didn't want me there and wasn't even in my life.

She wanted me to move on. She'd even *begged* me to move on. At first she'd wanted me to go back to Logan (and she'd begged me to do that too). When she realized that wasn't going to happen, she'd wanted me to go on a date, to go see a shrink, to go get a life, *any* life without Logan.

None of this had worked.

Now I couldn't get him out of my head.

So I was there.

"Shit, damn, damn," I whispered, looking at the façade of the roadhouse.

It was run-down, near to ramshackle. The paint peeling on the outside. The sign up top that said SCRUFF'S was barely discernable considering it was night and only the neon *u* and the apostrophe worked.

Strangely, Scruff's looked much the same as it had twenty years ago when Logan and I used to come here all the time.

Except back then the *c* also worked, though it had flickered.

There were bikes outside, less of them now than back when this was Logan and my place because it was Chaos's place, but it was still clearly a biker bar.

I just had no idea if one of those bikes was Logan's.

I hoped one was.

And I was terrified of the same thing.

"You should go home," I told myself.

I should.

But home was where I'd been nearly every night since I'd bought my house and moved in eleven years ago. It had changed since I'd renovated every inch of it (I had not done this myself—I'd paid people to do it—but it was all my vision).

I loved home. I never got sick of looking at what I'd created (or someone else had, obviously, through my vision).

But I was there nearly every night. And the only times I wasn't were when I was at Dottie's or babysitting a friend's kid or at one of the events I'd planned.

The last, being my work, didn't count.

Now I was not at home. I was back at Scruff's. A place I hadn't been in twenty years.

I was there because Logan might be in there.

And I couldn't stop thinking about him.

"God, this is crazy," I muttered, pushing open the car door and throwing out a leg.

I got out, slammed the door, and beeped the locks, keeping keys in hand and purse clamped securely under my arm.

I walked toward the building, worried about my car. I had a red Mazda CX-5 that was only a year old. I loved it. I hadn't upgraded cars in five years, so it was my baby. And not only was this bar not the safest spot in Denver, it was located in a neighborhood that also wasn't the safest in Denver.

I had to brave it. I was there. I was out of the car.

There was no going back.

Before I got to the door, a biker fell out of it, shouting behind him, "Fuck you too!" and I nearly turned back.

He stumbled the other way, so my path was clear.

I knew I should retreat.

I didn't.

I went in.

When my eyes adjusted to the dim, I saw the inside hadn't changed much either, except to get seedier. In fact, even the neon beer signs looked the same and on my second eye sweep after the quick, frantic one I did to see if Logan was there, I saw four of the plethora of them no longer worked at all. The vinyl on the barstools was worn, the furniture scattering the space was more mismatched. Even the felt on the pool table was more faded.

And there was no Logan.

Actually, there wasn't much of anybody. It wasn't vacant but back in the day the place was nearly always hopping. Logan and I would go on a Wednesday to find fun with the dozen people who were also there that we knew and partied with. Or we'd go on a Saturday and find mayhem with three dozen people we knew and partied with.

It was Chaos's place. It was where the boys went when they wanted to tie one on, tag fresh meat to bang, find trouble, or if none was to be found, make it.

However, looking around, I didn't see a member I knew from back in the day. I didn't even see a Chaos patch on any jacket.

This was a surprise. Chaos had been a fixture there in a way that there wasn't a night when at least a couple of brothers were at Scruff's.

This was also an excuse to leave.

I didn't go.

I walked to the bar and slid onto a stool, doing this with my eyes still scanning the space like Logan could materialize out of thin air.

"Well, fuck me. Millie freakin' Cross. Blast from the past and not a good one."

I turned my head and stared in shock at Reb.

Reb had been a bartender back then. One I would have suspected would have been long gone by now.

This was because she'd been sleeping with Scruff's son

who was set to inherit the place since Scruff was on his death-bed. Though, Scruff had been on that deathbed the entire three years I'd gone there (two of which I'd drank with a fake ID, not that Reb or any of the other bartenders cared).

Wade, her man and the next in line to own the establishment, was rarely there (or rarely there working). He was usually there drinking or alternately out cheating on Reb or fighting or dry-ing out in a jailhouse or on his bike wandering and leaving her behind to bitch about him and swear she was going to leave him.

Reb was tough. She was so unfriendly she was mean. And she didn't take a lot of shit (except from Wade).

I was sure she'd get fed up and go.

But she wasn't gone. She was behind the bar, looking as faded and worn as the rest of the joint, like she'd aged forty years in the last twenty.

I barely recognized her.

The life-is-shit-and-then-you-die look in her eyes was unforgettable, still there and even sharper, so I knew it was her.

"You're like a mullet," she stated, glaring at me from her side of the bar. "'Cept haven't seen you in forever and I see too many a' those every week. Though, you're here so just sayin', coulda used a longer forever when it comes to you."

That wasn't a warm welcome.

Reb wasn't big on handing those out. She never had been.

But this was more than her usual nasty.

I decided to ignore it.

"Hey, Reb," I greeted.

"Fuck off, Millie, and I mean that as in, you can get your ass off my stool and get the fuck outta my joint," she replied.

I stared.

Way nastier than her usual nasty.

"Like," she leaned in to me, "*now.*"

Because apparently I'd gone insane, I decided to ignore that too.

"Your stool? This is your place?" I asked.

She straightened and held my gaze like a threat as she stated, "Yeah. Was suckin' the wrong dick. Wade didn't own the place, don't know what I was thinkin', takin' his shit. The old man might not'a gotten around real good but he still had a dick and any man's got one of those, they like it sucked. Sucked my way to him changin' his will. Now Wade's gotta eat my pussy to get on *my* schedule to get *his* tips and actually *work* to get 'em. Like it better that way."

I knew she was sharing all of this information to shock me and she succeeded.

I tried not to let it show and replied, "Well, good for you, Reb. Glad you got what you wanted."

"Didn't get it," she returned. "Worked for it. Worked my ass off behind this bar for ten years. Sucked old man dick for two. Now it's mine, shit hole that it is, so not exactly doin' cartwheels 'cause it cost a fuckuva lot more than it's worth."

I couldn't agree more.

I didn't share that.

Instead, I asked, "Can I have a beer?"

"No."

This time, I held her eyes and started softly, "Reb—"

She leaned in again.

"This here's a *biker* bar, Millie," she snapped. "Chaos quit comin' years ago but it's still a biker bar and there aren't many people wanna show here but I'll pour a drink for any a' them, *'specially* if they're a biker 'cause that's the way it is; that's the way it's always been. Who I will *not* pour a drink for is some up-her-own-ass bitch who don't like bikers. I think you get I can use every dollar my boys spend on the rotgut that goes here. That don't mean I'm willin' to take yours."

"Reb, what happened was a long time—"

"What happened was you told one of *my* kind," she jabbed a thumb to her chest, "you're too fuckin' good for him. You're too fuckin' good for High, you're two fuckin' good to sit your ass on my stool. Now, Millie, not gonna say it again, get the fuck out."

High.

That was right. I'd forgotten. Logan had become High when he'd officially become Chaos. The joke was his name had been shortened by his parents to the nickname Low. But he liked to smoke back then and not only cigarettes, so he'd become High.

I'd hated that name mostly because I really wasn't that fond of how often he smoked pot. I'd hated that name enough I'd never used it.

I had to admit (just to myself) I still hated it.

"There are things that I—" I tried again.

"Don't give a fuck."

"I'm looking for Logan," I blurted.

Her face twisted in a way that scared the absolute shit out of me as she moved closer to the bar, put her hand on it, and leaned deep.

"And I hope like fuck you don't find him," she hissed. "He moved on but before he found it in him to do that, you *obliterated* him."

My heart constricted in a way I actually felt pain.

Excruciating pain.

"Christ, he was so into you, he *was* you," Reb spat. "He *lived* for you. Every breath he took, it was *for you*. Then you sunk the blade in and slashed it straight through, gutting him. Honest to fuck, Pete, Tack, Arlo, Brick, Boz, none a' us thought he'd survive. Ride off a cliff. Set himself swingin' in the Compound. Get himself in a fight he knew he couldn't win. He searched for it. It never came and you could *smell* the goddamned disappointment on him when he woke up to face another day without you in it. Every woman on this goddamned earth wants a man like that to feel like that about them and you had it and you fuckin' tossed it away like it was garbage."

I nearly fell off the barstool in my need to flee because I could take no more. The pain was so immense it was a wonder blood wasn't oozing from every pore.

"Yeah, bitch," she kept at me as she watched me move. "Get gone. Get *the fuck* gone. Don't ever come back." She lifted a hand and jabbed a finger at me. "And don't you go lookin' for High. He don't need your shit in his life. Not again."

I backed away two steps, unable to tear my eyes off her simply because I had no thoughts. It was actually a wonder I was moving.

All I could feel was the pain.

Eventually my body took flight and I got out of the bar. Into my car. I hit the button and reversed out of my spot without even looking to check if it was clear.

And I drove home.

It was late and even though I needed her, I wasn't going to call Dottie again. I wasn't going to call any of my other friends who knew about Logan and my inability to get over him. I wasn't going to go home and burst into uncontrollable tears that felt like they'd choke me and keep crying until I hoped they would so it would finally be over.

I got into my house and flipped the switch illuminating the kitchen.

I locked the farm door behind me.

I walked to my marble countertop that was white with gray veins and dropped my purse on it.

And then I stood still and stared unseeing into the living room.

Reb was right. I knew it. I knew I'd destroyed Logan.

We'd met when I was eighteen, nine weeks after I graduated high school.

He'd asked me out within minutes of the first words we spoke to each other.

I'd slept with him on our first date.

Not because I was easy.

Because I knew he was everything.

And he was.

He was a dream come true. A fantasy come to life. Every clichéd hope of every girl on the planet walking, talking, touching, kissing.

Except, perhaps, rougher and owning his own bike.

He'd treated me like gold.

No, like a princess.

No, both.

I was precious. Beloved. Treasured.

He looked at me and every single time he did it, I knew he thought what he saw was so beautiful he couldn't believe his luck.

The sex wasn't great.

It was explosive.

And we slept entwined and woke the same way, like we needed to be connected to each other to recharge in the night so we could take on the day. Like without that, we wouldn't be able to function.

To my parents' dismay and his parents' delight, we'd moved in with each other within six weeks of meeting.

We fought and every single time we did it, we ended it laughing like what we were fighting about was ridiculous because, mostly, it was.

We were together for three years that felt like fifty-three, all of them blissfully happy.

Then that time felt like three days the minute he walked away from me because I made him do it.

I looked around my kitchen with its marble countertops and butcher block island that had a vegetable sink. Its heavy, white ceramic farm sink under the window and white cupboards, the top ones with windows. Other cupboards specially designed for wine, cookbooks, spice racks. I took in the kitchen's stainless steel appliances and six-burner, two-oven stove, the wine fridge.

Then I moved.

My boots struck against my hardwood floors that had been

refinished four years ago and they still gleamed perfectly. I went to my living room with its multipaned windows at the front and on either side of the fireplace at the side.

I looked around the white walls and the brick of the fireplace (also painted white).

The sheers on the windows were white, too, and they were diaphanous. The furniture was slouchy and comfortable and all in soft taupe. The accents of toss pillows on couch, love seat, and cuddle chair as well as the vases spotted around surfaces were in muted pastels. The frames of pictures dotted on surfaces were all whitewashed or engraved mirror or intricate silver. And the pièce de résistance was a large circular peacock mirror over the fireplace.

The effect was cool and stylish, but not cold. Pretty and welcoming.

I walked down the hall with its walls filled with perfectly placed frames, all black with cream matting, holding black-and-white pictures of Dottie and her family. My parents. Grandparents. Cousins. Aunts and uncles. Friends.

I moved past the guestroom and guest bath into the extra bedroom that was a junk room. I flipped on the light, which set the ceiling fan to giving the room a gentle breeze it did not need in September.

I went right to the closet, slid the door open, and struggled through the wrapping paper, luggage, boxes, then hefted out the plastic crates that were stacked in the corner.

Four of them.

I wanted the bottom one.

I got to it and pulled it into the room. I fell to my behind on the floor and flipped down the latches on the sides of the crate, lifting the top away.

In there were albums, three of which I'd happily, but painstakingly, filled with photos.

One album for each year.

The rest of the crate was filled with those envelopes pictures came in with the front holding the film.

And last, there were loose photos tossed in in a frenzy to hide painful memories.

In the beginning, I'd pulled that crate out often.

But it had been years since I'd opened that box.

I grabbed an album, put it on my lap and opened it randomly.

My throat closed against the burn consuming my insides as I stared down at a photo of me standing by Logan, who was sitting on his bike.

We were outside Ride, the auto supply store with attached custom build garage that Chaos owned.

Logan was off to do something, I didn't remember what. I was saying good-bye to the man I loved, who I would see again within hours. He had one of his hands on the bike grip, the other on my hip. I was facing him but looking over my shoulder at Naomi, the wife of one of Logan's Chaos brothers.

My hair was long, down to my waist and unencumbered, like Logan liked it. Unrestrained and wild. A way I hadn't worn it in years.

Logan had on sunglasses that made him look cool and badass, jeans, a tee, and his Chaos cut.

We were close, like we were always close whenever we were together, touching, like we were always touching, and smiling.

Like we were always smiling.

The picture below that was of us stretched out on a couch in the common room of the Chaos Compound. I was mostly on top of Logan, partly tucked into the back of the couch. I had a hand on his chest and my head thrown back, the picture captured my profile and I was laughing.

Logan was on his back, head to the armrest, arm wrapped around my waist, holding me to him even though he didn't need to since I was lying on top of him. He was looking right at the camera, also laughing.

On the opposite page there was a picture of us at Scruff's. I had my booty up on the edge of the pool table (something I did a lot to be goofy because being goofy made Logan smile, but something that annoyed the hell out of Reb). Logan was leaning over the table with cue in hand, lined up ready to take a shot.

But his head was tilted back, his eyes were on me and mine were on him.

We weren't smiling. I was saying something to him and I had his full attention.

Like I always had his full attention.

I pressed my hands on the pages, palms flat, like I could soak in those times, like I could be thrown back years to relive them, like I could absorb the feelings I'd had back then of being safe and loved and living the life that was just right for me.

It didn't work.

I turned the page.

Then I turned another page.

And another.

I did it reliving memories I'd relived countless times. They were burned in my brain in a way they were always there, even when I wasn't calling them up. They were scars that tormented me in a way that changed the course of my life.

It wasn't simply that I was in a rut.

My life had been interrupted and I'd never restarted it.

Since Logan Judd, I had not had a boyfriend.

I had not had a lover.

Not in twenty years.

He was it for me and those pictures showed why.

I met my perfect man at age eighteen and I had him for three years.

Then I sent him away.

Could I right those wrongs?

Should I?

You obliterated him.

I had.

And I'd done the same to myself.

Every woman on this goddamned earth wants a man like that to feel like that about them and you had it and you fuckin' tossed it away like it was garbage.

I hadn't tossed him away.

Reb didn't know.

She'd never know.

But I hadn't done that.

I'd never do that.

Not to Logan.

Every breath he took, it was for you.

I turned the page and went still.

On the two pages before me were six pictures taken at what was known among the biker world as Wild Bill's Field.

What it was was a biker rally that happened on Bill McIntosh's farm every year.

I remembered those rallies, all three of them I went to.

The pictures on the page were from the second one.

Top left, Logan sitting on a log, me on a blanket in front of him on the ground between his legs. He was bent forward, arms around me, chin on my shoulder, the firelight was illuminating our faces as we laughed toward someone that, if memory serves, was Boz being his usual lovable idiot.

Center left picture, same, except my head was turned and tipped back and Logan's chin was off my shoulder and he was looking down at me.

Bottom left, my hand was up and curled around Logan's forearm and my head was still tipped back.

But Logan wasn't looking at me.

He was kissing me.

I shut the book.

The Field.

Wild Bill's biker rally.

Every biker from every club in the entire state of Colorado went to that rally every year. It was mayhem, bikes, tents, campers, RVs, sleeping bags, bonfires, a makeshift stage set up for local and not-so-local bands who played loud and deep into the night.

It was bring what you want or hit Wild Bill's kitchen that he set up in a massive tent at the edge of the makeshift campgrounds. He bragged that the proceeds sent him to Miami for Christmas and supported him throughout the year, except we all knew we hit his field just after he harvested the hay or corn he always grew in it, which was the way he really made his living.

First weekend of October.

Which was two and a half weeks away.

Every breath he took, it was for you.

You obliterated him.

I needed to right that wrong.

He needed to know.

And I was the only one who could tell him.

It was good now. It was safe. He was alive and well, ordering burritos and raising kids and not a fugitive from the law or worse.

And he needed to know.

So I was going to find him.

Then I was going to tell him.

On a blanket by a lake, twenty-three years earlier...

He was on me and in me.

He was done.

So was I.

Logan Judd had just given me my first orgasm.

And it was crazy-*great*.

We were on our date.

He'd picked me up on his bike.

I had been right. My parents had freaked.

But they did what they always did. They trusted me and didn't make a big deal of it.

They didn't like me hanging with Kellie either. She was considered a hood. Her dad had taken off when she was a little kid and never came back. Now her mom and stepdad partied more than Kellie did and didn't mind it when Kellie had all her many friends over (this was because, I suspected, Kellie, Justine, and I cleaned up afterward and they didn't have much worth anything to break).

But anyway, I got excellent grades. I was going to college in a few weeks. I'd gotten into a good one. University of Denver. This meant I was going to stay close to home, something my sister didn't do (she went to Purdue), so this was something my parents liked. I did my chores. I got along with my big sister. We were thick as thieves and I missed her like crazy since she'd gone to Indiana. I loved my family and showed it. I'd never been one of those bitchy, pain-in-the-ass kids who got in their parents' faces all the time.

Even so, I was a bit of a rebel. I drank and it was illegal. Kellie and Justine and I'd go joyriding. I'd lost my virginity at age seventeen (but it was to my boyfriend of two years, who had broken up with me in his first few months at University of Colorado).

I wasn't disrespectful. I loved my family.

I was just...me.

And the me I was wasn't stupid and *totally* irresponsible.

And the me I was put me on the back of Logan Judd's bike.

He'd driven us into the mountains and I'd loved the ride. Dad had a friend who had a bike, Dottie and I had been out on it and we'd both loved it.

This was better.

A *whole lot* better.

Riding wrapped around Logan.

The best.

He'd pulled off the highway and drove to a lake. We'd got-

ten off the bike and he hefted a backpack out of one of his sad-
dlebags, a blanket out of the other. He'd then taken my hand
and walked us down a trail that led to the lake. The sun was
just getting ready to set, so we had plenty of light to see the
beauty around us and I saw it.

But I felt the beauty of walking with Logan, his fingers
around mine, the backpack slung over one of his shoulders, the
blanket tucked under his arm, knowing this was already the best
date ever and feeling in my heart it was only going to get better.

I'd been right.

He moved us to the edge of the lake and threw out the blanket. We got on it and he pulled stuff from the backpack.

It was nothing fancy. He had four bottles of beer in there.
Homemade sandwiches (turkey and Swiss). Bags of chips (that
were a bit crushed). A package of Oreos (similarly crushed).

But sitting by a beautiful lake up in the foothills of the
Rocky Mountains with Logan, eating and watching the sun
set, it was the most delicious meal I'd ever had.

We'd talked.

From our conversation on the steps of Kellie's deck, he
knew my full name, my age, that I had a sister, what high
school I'd gone to, that I was heading to DU for the fall semester, and that Kellie and Justine were my best friends. I'd
learned his full name, that he was three years older than me,
he was a recruit for a motorcycle club called Chaos, and he
was close with his parents and younger sister, even if he'd left
them in Durango, where he'd grown up.

On the blanket, we'd talked more and it was cool because it
was like a rite of passage. The first real grown-up conversation
I'd ever had.

I wasn't some eighteen-year-old just-ex-high-schooler that
he'd met.

I wasn't a girl.

I was a woman.

A woman he liked.

We talked about the work he did at Ride, the garage and shop that was owned by the motorcycle club he belonged to. We talked about how, when he was finished being a recruit and he was a full member, he'd get a bigger cut of the money made there. We talked about his brothers and how he liked them. We talked about his brothers' "old ladies," or the wives and girlfriends, and which of them he liked...or didn't.

We also talked about how I was kind of worried that Justine was partying too much and getting blasted out of her mind when she did. We talked about the fact that I was worried about this because she'd screwed up on her SATs, refused to take them again, and she'd had a really bad couple of semesters, so her GPA was shot. Then, when the first two colleges she applied to didn't take her, she'd quit applying. And I'd told him I thought she was lost and freaked about her future and instead of finding her way, she was getting drunk a lot.

"One thing I know, darlin'," he'd said gently when we were talking about Justine. "You ain't ever gonna change a person. Stand by their side or be at their back. But do not push change or expect it. Just be there for them while they sort their shit out. But do it knowin' you might have to cut ties if their shit starts leakin' and becomin' yours."

Thus I'd learned on our date that Logan Judd was wise.

Conversation had while eating changed into conversation had while cuddling and talking and staring at the moon on the water.

Cuddling had gone from just talking to talking with some kissing.

My first kiss from Logan Judd had been a revelation. It, too, was my first adult kiss. No fumbling around. No inexperience. No desperation. None of that feel you'd get from a guy like he knew he was lucky he managed to get his mouth on you and the second he did, he was thinking about what else he could get.

Logan knew what he was doing. Logan took his time doing it. Logan liked what he was getting and Logan knew how to guide me to giving that back.

It was dreamy from beginning to end.

And then the talking stopped and it was just kissing until it turned into Logan making love to me on that blanket by a lake in the Rocky Mountains.

It was slow and sweet and exploratory until it got faster and more urgent and finished on totally *explosive*.

It was not only my first orgasm.

It was also the first time a *man* had made love to me.

And I lay under him, feeling his weight, smelling his hair, my body sluggish in a way I liked, at the same time I was crazy-giddy like the night before, except in a quieter way I liked better. All this because I was connected to Logan, feeling complete when I didn't know I was incomplete and it was crazy, totally nutso, but I knew it to be true.

I was complete with Logan.

And I also knew it was no longer that I *could* fall in love with Logan Judd.

It was that I'd started doing it at his first "hey."

No, when I first saw him walk into Kellie's house.

And I was still doing it and knew I'd keep doing it until the deed was done.

Which, with the rate I was going, would take another date.

This, for some reason, didn't freak me.

No.

It should. It should freak me. It should feel wrong.

But it only felt right—oh so right...

I...could not...*wait*.

He pulled his face from out of my neck and I instantly missed his heavy breaths there.

But when his eyes caught mine in the moonlight, I suddenly declared, "I'm not easy. You're my second. And if you think I am and this isn't about the fact that we're good together...if you've missed what's going on with us...if you take this, what just happened, and don't call again...all I can say is...your loss, Logan Judd."

I said this and I did it with attitude.

But I also did it completely terrified by the very idea that he might not call again.

He grinned and his body started shaking on mine.

"That it?" he asked, his words also shaking with humor.

"Yes," I answered, deciding from his amusement not to be freaked that I'd just blurted all that out.

"Just sayin', already got our second date scoped out," he replied.

I relaxed under him and did it biting back a whoop of glee.

"And the third," he continued.

I slid my hand up his spine.

"All the way to the sixth," he kept going. "And then it's your turn to decide what we do, so best start thinkin', Millie, 'cause that's gonna happen next week."

Man, oh man, he had our first *six* dates planned.

He was going to call me again.

And again.

And again.

And this made me unbelievably happy.

"I like you."

God, still blurting!

The grin he was still wearing got bigger.

"That's good seein' as you just let me have you as in *all* a' you. I liked it a fuckuva lot but even if you hadn't given me that, I also liked shootin' the shit with you so think it's safe to say I like you too."

I turned my head to the side, suddenly scared at how relieved I was that he liked all he'd gotten from me and wanted more.

"Millie," he called.

"Hmm?" I asked the tall grass at the side of the blanket.

"Beautiful, look at me."

At the "beautiful," my fingers clenched into his skin and my eyes went to his.

"No bullshit, baby," he whispered the second he got my gaze. "I am absolutely, one hundred percent *not* missin' what's goin' on."

It was then I suddenly wanted to cry because I'd just been made love to, had my first orgasm, and was still connected to a man I liked a lot, a lot, *a lot* in a way I knew I was falling in love.

"This is kinda crazy," I whispered back.

"This is all kinds of crazy," he agreed. "Crazy good. And we'd both be fools, we don't roll with it."

He was right. I knew it down deep.

I slid my hands up so they were both cupped, one over the other, at the back of his neck.

"I really liked that," I told him softly. "What we just did."

He dipped his face closer and gave me a hint more of his weight, replying quietly, "Got that when you came for me, darlin'."

"Does our second date involve more of that?" I asked, and watched his eyes begin to shine.

"Definitely."

"Good," I whispered.

More shining from his eyes before I lost that shine because I closed mine, seeing as he was kissing me.

In the end, our first date involved more of that.

I got home late.

I knew my parents worried even though they didn't say a word.

But Logan and I had plans to go out the next night.

So I was walking on air.

CHAPTER THREE

Thank You

Millie

Present day, two and a half weeks later...

I STOOD IN front of my bathroom mirror wearing my undies and bra and holding the handle of a large hand mirror.

I turned and lifted my free hand to my neck. Sweeping aside my hair and holding it at my opposite shoulder, I raised the mirror and looked.

I forced my eyes to stay open even when I wanted to squeeze them shut.

Unless I looked, I didn't see. And my hair was long enough that it was rare I caught a glimpse.

And if by chance I caught a glimpse, I'd pretend I didn't.

Now I was looking.

And there it was, as it would be since it was a tattoo.

Well done, the artist a master, not faded at all.

Then again, it was all in black.

Squat words that scrolled long in a beautiful, flowing script: *Only him...*

And I knew the second part of that tat started on Logan's hip bone and ran across his hip, in bold scripted black underlined with a flourish of barbed wire: *...only her.*

The words and memories burned through me as I dropped my hair, turned, set the mirror on the counter, and moved toward the walk-in closet in the bathroom.

It was time to get dressed and go.

It was time to find Logan.

It was time for him to know.

* * *

I stood removed, watching and feeling shock at all the changes I saw.

There was a blazing campfire like days gone by. Also as in years past, one of the brothers had hauled logs in his truck to the field so they were positioned around the fire. And there were tents dotted around with the requisite bikes.

But the tents were bigger, more expensive.

And there was not one but *three* tricked out RVs parked facing the campfire and two deluxe travel trailers set up as well.

When I knew Chaos, they did well and this well didn't entirely come from their custom car and bike garage and the automotive supply shop they ran but other not-as-legal enterprises.

Clearly, things had gotten even better and I knew part of that was Ride becoming outlandishly successful, something you couldn't miss even if you tried since everyone in Denver knew about it.

I just wondered if the other part also kept going.

We'd never had RVs.

Or, I should say, *they* never had.

I was no longer someone who could refer to Chaos as "we" and they were sticklers about that kind of thing, so I knew I shouldn't even think that way.

I stayed removed and watching, seeing brothers I knew. Even though they'd aged, I recognized them immediately. Boz, Hound, Big Petey. There were brothers missing, including Arlo, Dog, Brick, Hop, Black, Chew, Crank, and, most surprisingly, Tack, who was one of the more intense members of Chaos, but he seemed more Chaos than the average brother and considering they were all in—blood, guts, and glory—that was saying something.

Logan had been wary of Tack, telling me when I'd asked, "Good man, good brother. But Tack's got ideas and the way shit is, my best bet is to lay low, see if he decides to play 'em out, and if he does, how."

Logan had not shared these "ideas" with me. That was brother business and he'd gently but definitely firmly shared that brother business was not my business.

I was okay with that. My man was far from stupid and I knew the brothers that made up the brotherhood by then, so I knew why he was in it.

And I trusted him.

The last was the bottom line, really.

In the end, I'd needed a lot of trust.

But it had never wavered.

Not once.

Though, he didn't know that because I didn't share that.

I'd shared the opposite.

I set those thoughts aside and studied the rest of the Chaos crew. There were more than a few younger guys I didn't know, some of them with women I also (obviously) didn't know.

This shouldn't have been surprising, even though it was. The Club recruited and did it regularly. When I was with Logan, they were looking into opening another auto supply shop in Fort Collins and only brothers were involved in that (or anything to do with Chaos).

However, the sheer number of new, younger men shocked me. They outnumbered the members I knew and that made Chaos—something that was so familiar to me, once a part of my life with me being a part of their family—unfamiliar and that caused a pang of hurt I knew was not my right to feel.

Though, one of the girls I suspected I knew except when I knew her she was a whole lot younger.

Tabitha Allen. Tack's daughter.

Like she had back then, she looked just like her dad, except female. She was just as beautiful as he had been handsome. And she was clearly *with* one of the brothers, a tall, lanky, good-looking one who was also very *with* her.

But no Tack.

And no Logan.

This meant I had to go in search of him.

This was a daunting prospect. The rally had grown over the years. It appeared triple the size it used to be. And I knew by some of the flags flying or pinned to the sides of RVs that the clubs there were not just from around Colorado but from other states as well.

Wild Bill was likely raking it in.

But I had all weekend. Wild Bill opened it up for setup Thursday at noon with the rally officially beginning with a concert on Friday evening.

It was now Friday night, nearly ten o'clock, when all the brothers should have arrived and started kicking back and letting loose.

However, watching them around the campfire, although there were beer bottles, smoking of two kinds, whisky being passed around, this was not the Chaos letting loose I'd been used to way back when.

Chiefly, there wasn't a single outsider approaching them to buy weed.

On this thought, I moved away knowing from the prime location of their camp that they'd either sent a recruit in the early hours Thursday morning to camp out on the road and then move in to stake claim to their space or the recruit had actually *camped* out by the side of the road Wednesday night to do it.

And their spot was prime. They were far enough away from the music they could hear it but it didn't drown out conversation and you could bed down and it not bother you much, or perhaps in those RVs it was drowned out completely.

Also, they were on the other side from Wild Bill's kitchen tent (which I'd noted when driving in was now four big tents), so the smells of cooking—no matter how good they were, they were also constant—didn't permeate the air.

However, the Chaos camp wasn't too far you couldn't wander to what was known as the Trench.

The Trench was the area in the middle of the activity close to the stage where you went only if you didn't know better, were too drunk to care, you were so badass you could handle whatever was thrown at you, or you had your man with you who was so badass he could take care of whatever was thrown at you.

I'd loved being in the Trench. It was heaving. It was out of control. It was loud and crazy. And to be in it, you had to let go, give in to the flow or you'd panic and be lost because you didn't get out until the ripples of the Trench naturally spewed you out.

You could make instant friends with a look or instant enemies with the same.

But usually, it was friends. Although fights could (and did, regularly) break out, they never got (too) out of hand.

This was because everyone loved Wild Bill, so it was rare they disrespected him by doing something problematic that could mean the cops would show up.

In fact, in all the years since he'd been hosting the rally, which by now had to be at least thirty, the cops had only shown twice (that I knew of and even not going anymore, come early October, I paid attention to the news just in case).

The Trench was just a big, crazy party and it used to be every night for three nights Logan would guide me in and stick close to my side as we had the time of our lives until the undulations spat us out. Then we'd go back to Chaos, sit around the fire, shoot the breeze, drink, neck, and end up in our tent, where we'd fuck.

It had been awesome.

And being there again after all those years, it occurred to me just how narrow my life had become.

There was a day I was up for anything and with Logan at my side, safe to do it.

So I did.

Now I didn't.

I wandered away from the Chaos camp and edged the Trench, thinking I was glad that Logan hadn't been with them. I didn't want to make an approach with the guys around.

It wouldn't be awkward, making that approach to Chaos. It would be dangerous. Not to my body, to my mental health.

I knew the guys who'd been around back then would know and feel the same way about me that Reb did. I figured the younger ones had heard the history, perhaps without names, but a whisper would tell them who I was and they wouldn't be any more welcoming.

So it was find him elsewhere.

Which was good.

I scanned for Logan as I moved, skirting the edges of the Trench, careful not to get sucked in. As many good memories as I had in there, I couldn't go in. Not without being three sheets, not without someone to take my back, and not in the clothes I was wearing.

I didn't own biker chick attire anymore. I didn't live in jeans and cutoffs and tees and tanks and halters. Dripping with silver. Wrapping kickass beaded headbands around my forehead or covering my hair in a bandana and being able to get away with it. Wearing a tee of Logan's and belting it to make it a dress that was precariously close to showing ass cheek and not giving a damn.

I'd been all in. I'd embraced the biker life like I'd been born to it. I'd done it so thoroughly, at first my parents and Dottie were terrified, utterly, completely, so much they'd eventually broken down and shared it.

Then the weeks had passed into months and they got to know Logan.

Honestly it hadn't taken him much time to win them around.

He loved me. Was besotted with me. Treated me like porcelain. And he showed all that.

But it was more.

He was respectful. He didn't curse around them, smoke or drink (too much), or maul me when they were near. He called Dad "sir" and Mom "Mrs. Cross" until she sat him down and begged him not to do it because, "You're a part of our family now, Logan. It's time to call me 'Mom.'"

In the beginning, they'd hated me with Logan.

In the end, they'd been devastated when I'd sent him away.

They didn't understand. They'd both talked to me about it then, asking why I'd ever let go of a man who loved me that completely and wanted the things they wanted for me, a safe home, marriage, and a big family.

They didn't know.

Only Dottie knew.

Still, to this day, no one knew but Dottie.

And if I could find him, now Logan would know.

I just hoped I didn't have to brave the Trench to find him.

I moved around the Trench, watching the revelers, taking in their attire, and thinking about how I wore different clothes back then. I was in jeans, boots, a sweater, and a leather jacket but my whole ensemble didn't cost me fifty bucks because I'd scored kickass threads from some vintage shop or bought my tee at a concert or from a roaming vendor at a rally.

My ensemble cost over a thousand dollars (not including jewelry), and I might be among bikers, but they'd know it.

So I kept to myself, scanning faces, peering into the outskirts of the Trench, weaving around bodies and bonfires and tents and bikes.

I was nervous, most definitely. But I'd had two and a half weeks of practicing what I was going to say. Not only that, but also practicing how I was going to get Logan to listen to me.

I had the words down *pat*.

So I had that part covered.

What wasn't covered was the fact that I had no idea what his reaction would be (or what my reaction would be to his reaction, though, I'd run a few of those around in my head as well, about seven thousand of them).

I just hoped that when it was done, when I'd explained, some of the scars would heal. At least enough that I could move on. Know he understood and finally—way too late but not never—close the book on that chapter of my life, give Logan that closure, and let us both go forward without that wound damaging our souls.

On a mission, I kept looking and did it for hours. Sometimes finding a safe spot to stop and watch just in case being on the move was why I was missing him. I even hung close to Wild Bill's kitchen, thinking Logan might come to get a brat or a paper basket of late-night, drunken-eating gravy fries (Wild Bill's specialty).

I saw Wild Bill. He was now old as dirt and looked it, but even though it was past midnight, he was serving up fries to bikers and their babes, doing it smiling.

Finally, I realized it was time to give up. At least for that night. I was getting tired, things were getting rowdier (the Trench) or quieter (the outskirts), so people were settling in for the night one way or another, and if Logan was there, he'd be doing the same.

Therefore I needed to pack it in, go home, get some rest, and come back the next night.

I didn't think of finding Logan with a woman (which could be possible).

From the conversation I overheard at Chipotle, it seemed he was getting divorced or was finalizing but he could have moved on (though whatever ended that relationship was not him straying—he'd never do that, not in a million years, I knew that for certain).

But I'd deal with that if it happened and when I told myself I'd deal, I also told myself that it might even be good. He'd have someone and I wanted him to be happy.

And if he had someone, it might free me to find someone. Knowing Logan was with someone (and hopefully happy this time, as a possible divorce stated he hadn't been the last time—but I tried not to think about that) might release me from his snare and finally allow me to move on.

I thought this even knowing there would be consequences from seeing him with another woman.

But I'd deal with them if they happened too.

What I hoped was that in the next two days, I'd actually find him.

If I didn't, I'd have to go to Chaos. I'd have to go to Ride, the store or the garage, and look for him, ask after him.

Or, God I hoped not, the Compound.

But if that happened, it would.

And that, too, I'd deal with when it did.

Night one was a bust but I wouldn't give up.

I'd come back for night two.

This thought made me sigh as I made my way through the bikes, trucks, and other vehicles parked outside the camp areas. Apparently, going to Wild Bill's was like riding a bike since I remembered to make note of landmarks that would lead me back to my SUV in that sea of vehicles.

Back then, Logan had taught me to have that care.

Therefore, twenty years later, I had that care and walked right to my car.

I beeped the locks and had a hand to the handle when I heard, "Lookin' for me?"

When that deep, coarse voice came at me through the dark,

my body became paralyzed, my eyes glued to my hand on the handle.

Then it kept coming at me.

"Bitch, followed you the last forty-five minutes. Reb got in touch. Told me you hit Scruff's." On the next, the voice was nearer. "You're lookin' for me. So tell me what the fuck you want so you can quit lookin' and I can quit lookin' at you."

Slowly, I turned, my head going back automatically because I felt him close and I knew what close to Logan meant.

I was five-seven.

He was six-one.

He towered over me, or at least that's what it always felt like because he wasn't only tall, he was also a big guy with a big presence.

And right then, it felt like that, especially since his big presence was an angry one.

His face was in shadows, I could barely see it.

But I could feel him.

And I could smell him.

God, I could *smell* him.

He didn't wear cologne or aftershave. His scent was all his. And I remembered lying in our bed holding his pillow to me, my face shoved into the sheets, taking him in after I'd made him walk away.

His scent hadn't changed. Not even a nuance.

Smelling it without warning felt like walking unsuspecting into the street and having a truck slam into you. And that feeling was so strong it was a wonder my body didn't go careening through the trucks and bikes, slamming into them, shattering every bone.

He moved forward so he was in my space, the smell strengthened and my body tightened to guard against it.

"Woman, after all this time, whatever shit you gotta hand me, fuckin' do it," he ordered irately. "You got two seconds to spit it the fuck out. You don't, you won't get another chance, and you know I'll make it that way. So this is your only shot. Take it or get in your fuckin' car and get your ass outta my world."

I stared into the shadows of his face, wishing with everything that I could see it.

Apparently, I did this for two seconds because Logan bit out, "Right. See nothin's changed. Weak. Now get your ass..." he dipped his face to mine, "*gone*."

And when he did, I got up on my toes and kissed him.

It was totally crazy.

But I also totally couldn't help it.

He smelled so *fucking* good.

And he was Logan.

Close. Right there. His face in mine.

He jerked away, muttering a disgusted, "What the fuck?"

But the words or their tone didn't penetrate.

I smelled him and I'd had a taste.

I was gone.

I lifted both hands to either side of his head, yanked him down to me, and went back in, going for it, giving it my all. Even when his fingers clenched painfully into my hips pushing them back to set me away, I held on tighter and shoved my tongue between his lips.

It touched his, just that, just a touch, and then I cried out into his mouth when I found my back slammed into my SUV.

But it wasn't his way to get me to let him go.

No.

His head slanted and he forced my tongue out of his mouth when his invaded mine.

And that was when I was *gone*.

I was already gone but right then there was nothing to me. Nothing at all.

Except my hands on Logan's head, his body pressing mine

into my car, his smell all around us, his tongue plundering my mouth, all this exploding fire *everywhere*.

He drove a hand into my hair, twisting it, the pain bristling over my scalp and I cried out into his mouth again even as I arched deeper, pressed closer, willing, like it had always been, to give it all because he was Logan, he got it all.

But also because I knew I'd get it back a hundredfold.

He swayed us forward so his other arm could lock across my back and he kept at my mouth as I rolled way up on my toes, pushing deep, wrapping my arms around his neck, consumed by the kiss and not giving that first fuck.

I was ready to ride it out.

No, I *needed* to ride it out.

No matter where it went.

He broke away and that was when my hand went into his hair, fisting tight in protest.

"That what you want?" he growled, his voice lower, the abrasion physical, and I shivered with delight.

I wasn't entirely certain of the question but I answered a breathy, "Yes."

"That's what you want," he repeated, a statement this time, seeking confirmation.

"Yes, Logan."

He let me go but took my hand, his skin rough against my fingers. The feel of it back after all these years washed through me and I fancied I remembered every time, in quick succession, from the first night we met to the night before I broke it off when he'd taken my hand and guided me somewhere.

Lost in it like I'd always been lost in it, I followed blindly.

Attached to Logan, I'd go anywhere.

Even if we were walking through fire.

He wended his way through the vehicles, quickly, strides long, and I rushed to keep up, my fingers curled tight around his just in case he got any ideas of letting me go.

Finally, he pulled me down the side of an RV I knew was part of the Chaos zone, stopped at the side door, and didn't let me go as he dug some keys out of his pocket.

He inserted one, unlocked the door, yanked it open, and tugged me up the steps as he shoved the keys back in his pocket.

I had the barest moment to look around and be stunned at the utter opulence of the place as he stopped us inside and locked the door.

Total mega-platinum-rock-star-on-the-road-mobile, including manly mess, like he didn't give a shit about the opulence to the point it was in your face just how much he didn't care that this thing likely cost more than many people's homes.

I was unable to get over this because Logan finished with the door and was pulling me through the space to the back.

And the bed.

He hauled me in and around so I was back to the bed, facing him.

Then he tugged my jacket down my shoulders.

"Logan—" I began, my voice holding a tremor, saner thoughts seeping in and forcing themselves to be noticed.

I had no choice but to cry out yet again when his hand shot up and in my hair, cupping the base of my skull and jerking me to him so powerfully, I collided with him, unable even to get up a hand to cushion the impact.

"We do this, you don't talk except to say 'fuck me harder,'" he ordered roughly.

Those never-forgotten tingles shot out from my inner thighs.

I opened my mouth, my hand drifting up in order to force it between us when he bent his head slightly, his eyes—those brown eyes I loved so damned much—not warm but severe and piercing.

"And you do *not* fuckin' *ever* say my name again," he whispered sinisterly.

Yes, saner thoughts were prevailing.

And the biggest one of those was that this was *not* right.

His mouth crashed down on mine and his scent assaulted me and it again *was* right.

Absolutely.

I tore at his Chaos cut, forcing it down his arms.

He broke free of my mouth to yank off his thermal, then put a hand in my belly and shoved me onto the bed.

I took in the wall of his chest, its dark hair dusting across his pecs and down his six-pack, his upper body wide, his abs cut, his arms big and defined, all of it powerful, and I went for my belt.

He yanked off my boots.

Since I'd undone my belt and fly, he went after my jeans next and they were gone. My sweater went up as he put his hands to the hem at the same moment he put his knee to the bed beside me, joined me, and the sweater was gone.

I felt a moment of joy when the weight of his body hit mine and then felt something else that was still joy but a lot more of it when his mouth hit mine.

The years melted away and we went at each other like we always used to go at each other. Every day, sometimes more than once, sometimes if we had the time *all* day.

But there was a difference.

This was frantic.

Hungry.

No.

Starved.

Everything I could take I did with hands and mouth and teeth and tongue, rabid for it, pushing him to his back for better access and going all in. Eventually separating from him only enough to yank at his belt so urgently, his hips left the bed.

"Jesus, fuck," he muttered, but I knew that tone. I'd heard it before.

He was gone too.

And I was going to obliterate him a different way.

I tugged his jeans down until his hard, thick cock bounded free and God, *God*.

There were a lot of beautiful things about Logan Judd and one of them was the perfection of his dick.

I missed everything about Logan Judd.

Including that.

But there it was, inches away, so I wasted no further time.

I bent low and glided the tip of my tongue along the underside, hearing his groan, looking up and seeing nothing but the underside of his jaw, his head digging back into the pillow.

He liked that.

I quit fucking around and took him in.

All in.

"*Jesus...fuck,*" he groaned.

I blew him, just like he liked it, *exactly* like he liked it—definitely like riding a bike, I remembered it *all* and gave it to him.

I took him there, in woefully little time, and he communicated this to me by shifting away and taking over. Coming up on his knees, catching my eyes, his still severe and piercing but also fired and glorious, shoving a hand in my back and pushing me face-first into the pillows.

He moved and I felt my panties yanked down to my thighs. The tingles gone, my whole body was quivering in anticipation, my moans muffled against his soft sheets.

I moaned again when he shoved my legs apart and I felt my panties stretched tight, biting into my flesh.

Then he drove in and he was mine again.

Mine.

"Yes, baby," I whimpered, overwhelmed, undone, simultaneously feeling joy while burning with desire, my fingers clenched into the pillow and I reared back in welcome and demand.

His fingers grasped my hips and kept me stationary as he pounded in.

"Oh God, yes. Fuck me. Fuck me harder," I begged, fighting against his hold at my hips so I could participate as he rammed hard, fast, God...*God*...

Deep.

My chest stayed down but my head jerked back and I tipped my ass as high as I could, took it and kept taking it until I came apart, the pieces of me flying as I exploded with a succession of sharp cries that led to panting moans.

And he kept at me.

The pieces drifted back and I smelled him on the sheets, felt him thrusting inside, gloried in having him back, and tried to push up to my hands to help take him there.

"Down," he growled.

"But—" I started.

One of his hands left my hip and moved to my back, shoving in to keep me where I was.

"Stay the fuck down," he bit out.

I stayed down and stilled, the pieces of me drifting started shooting together as I took his thrusts and finally *felt* his thrusts.

A different burn assailed me as his noises came and I knew he was close.

Then he came, pouring himself inside me, holding me still and in position to be able to do nothing but take it.

He jerked into me as his orgasm had hold over him, then he buried himself to the root, staying there.

I remained still.

As I was beginning to fear, he wasted no time pulling out.

But even in my wildest imaginings, my worst nightmares, what he did next was not something I'd ever expect.

Not from Logan.

Not from the man who had my heart.

Not from the man who'd vowed to me the first time we met that there was never a time I wouldn't be safe with him.

Not even after what I'd done.

I felt him leave the bed and was dropping to my side, reaching blindly for the covers, listening to the sounds of his buckle being done up.

I just got the covers over my lower half, my torso up on my elbow, my head turned to him, when I felt the heavy weight of my jeans slap against my body.

My eyes shot to his.

"You got what you wanted, bitch. Now get the fuck out."

I stilled completely as horror and agony slashed through me.

Logan did not still.

He bent to snatch up his thermal, turned, and prowled out into the hall.

I stared at the space he'd occupied as it belatedly came to me what just happened.

He'd fucked available pussy.

I threw it at him.

He took it.

Now he was done.

This came with the territory for a biker. Groupies hanging around for that sole purpose. They didn't care who or where or how. They got off on it.

I'd known a few of them, hung with them, shot the shit with them, and it was my considered opinion that they enjoyed it more than the guys, the notches they earned on their proverbial belts. They didn't want commitment. They wanted fun and someone to let loose with and a fabulous orgasm (if they could get it).

I was not a biker groupie. I was an old lady. I wanted what the groupies had but I also wanted the whole package.

Though, I had to admit, I'd admired them. They didn't care what anyone thought. They lived their lives in the pursuit of what they wanted and anyone who looked down on that could go fuck themselves.

But, again, I was not a biker groupie.

Yet Logan had just fucked me like one.

No.

Worse.

And it was worse because he didn't even show me the respect of a cuddle or a kiss or offering me a shot after he'd done it.

What just happened was a revenge fuck.

And I'd walked right into it.

Mortified, shocked, wounded, I yanked up my panties and slid out of his bed slowly but I didn't take my time dressing.

I hurried.

I did this thinking the Logan Judd I knew didn't have that in him.

Men needed to earn his respect.

Women, that was another matter.

My mom, my sister, old ladies, biker groupies, whoever—he gave them respect. It wasn't earned. It was given. He did not judge. He was never a dick, much less a complete asshole.

As Reb said, I'd obliterated him.

And I knew I had.

But I didn't deserve *that*.

No woman deserved *that*.

But he'd treated me like that.

I pulled on my jacket and headed down the hall, moving swiftly, completely forgetting why I even came to the rally, needing to get out of there before the wound opened any further and I bled out on the floor of Logan's tricked out RV.

I knew he was still there when I made it to the front. I felt him but I also saw him out of the corner of my eye.

But I went right to the door.

"I don't see you again," he stated when I was lifting my hand to open the door. "Ever again. Hear?"

Hear?

Agony.

I turned to him and it felt like I was moving in slow motion, that simple movement taking *years*.

And then I saw him.

Yes, craggy.

No scars.

No beer gut.

Just beauty.

An older version of my Logan but with cold eyes and a curl of distaste on his full lips.

"You'll never see me again," I whispered.

His eyes stayed locked to mine as he clipped, "Good."

I felt my eyes brim with tears but I didn't move. I stood there staring at the man I'd loved and lost and mourned for twenty years but I did it knowing I hadn't even begun to mourn him.

Because my love for him had never died.

Now the mourning would start.

Because he'd just killed it.

"Thank you," I said.

"For what?" he bit out.

"For killing it," I replied.

I saw his heavy, dark brows shoot together but that's all I saw before I turned to the door, unlocked it, yanked it open, and raced down the steps, the tears flowing, the pain growing and spreading.

Blindly I ran in the direction of the Trench, turned the corner that would take me out of the Chaos zone and ran straight into something solid.

I stepped back, looked up, and stared in horror at Tack Allen.

He also stared at me before his face went hard and he growled, "Fuck me."

He hated me and even in those two seconds I knew it because he didn't hide it.

Not again.

I couldn't take this again.

I turned, nearly ran into the redhead at his side who I distractedly saw was not Naomi but was looking at me curiously right before her head jerked visibly, her eyes got wide, and her mouth opened.

I darted by her and raced into the night.

Tyra

"Do you know her?" I asked.

My husband didn't answer.

He started stalking (*stalking*, not walking) quickly toward High's RV.

"Tack!" I snapped, dashing after him. "Do you know that woman?"

Tack didn't get to the RV before the door was thrown open and High prowled out.

"Brother," Tack called.

High didn't even look at Tack. He marched right to his bike that was parked by his RV and threw his leg over.

"Brother!" Tack shouted over the roar of High's Harley that he'd fired up, my man quickening his steps, which meant I quickened my steps, now running behind my husband.

High revved his bike, his head turned to look behind him as he began to back it out.

"*Brother!*" Tack bellowed just as he stopped close to High's bike, and I skidded to a halt at his side.

Then I didn't move a muscle as High turned his head and looked to my man.

I also didn't breathe.

I was close with all of the brothers. Over the years, and there had now been many, through ups and downs, births and deaths, breakups, makeups, fuckups, we were tight.

But if I was forced to list which brother I was least close to, it would be High.

He was a good guy. He was a good brother. He was nice to

me. He respected me truly and did this in word and deed and not because I was the president of the Chaos MC's old lady but because he felt that for me.

But we weren't that tight.

And I'd noticed he wasn't close to any woman attached to the Club, not even, when he'd had her (which now he did not), his own wife.

I knew he'd bleed and die for his brothers. If it came down to it, he'd even do it for the old ladies.

That didn't mean he'd shoot the shit with us at a Chaos hog roast.

Thus he didn't.

And I had an idea that I'd just found out why.

Because that beautiful woman with tears streaming down her face who looked like she'd just been told the man she loved with every fiber of her being had been shot dead on the street had just come from High's RV.

A High who looked like he was off to wrestle the devil himself to take over hell and had enough fury in his belly to win.

He didn't address Tack. He backed out and roared away.

I stood next to my husband and looked into the darkness where High had last been.

When Tack moved, I shifted quickly, turning to face him.

"Who was that woman?" I asked.

He looked down at me and said the wrong thing.

"Do not get into this, Red."

There it was.

This was big.

This was why High was High.

So this was something that I needed to know.

"Who was that woman?" I repeated.

Tack turned fully to me, got close, and bent his neck to capture my gaze through the dark.

"Do not get into this, Tyra," he also repeated.

"Who . . . was . . . *that woman*?" I demanded.

I watched my husband's jaw grow tight as he studied me.

We'd had a decade together.

He knew me.

So it wasn't a surprise when he stated, "You know men got dream women, just like women got dream men, you bein' mine."

That was a good way to start, buttering me up, because I did know that.

He was my dream man.

I was his dream woman.

We didn't just wear each other's rings.

That was the truth of it.

And we'd shared that with each other in a myriad of ways over the years.

"Yeah," I answered.

"Her name is Millie Cross," he went on. "And 'bout twenty years ago, she used to be High's woman."

"I think I got that part," I informed him.

"No, Red," he said, getting closer, lifting a hand to curl it around the side of my neck. "She was his and she was *his*. As in, his dream woman."

Uh-oh.

"Crap," I muttered.

"Yep," he agreed. "And you know how High got himself addicted to the rush of doin' stupid shit that was also felonious in order to make a shitload of money for the Club?"

Uh-oh!

Now ancient history, the Club doing felonious shit, my man had seen to that, dragging his brothers along for the ride.

Though, truth be told, most of them were willing and invested every step of the way to the point they bled for the Club to be clean.

And one died for it.

High had been harder to convince that the Club needed a new direction.

"Yes," I replied slowly.

"When she gutted him, gettin' shot of his ass, tellin' him he had no ambition and she had graduated from college and had a golden life ahead of her so, since he was tainted with Chaos so deep, she knew he'd never get a real life. This meant he had to fuck off. Which he did. And that was when he went so deep into that shit, it took what happened to you years later to pull him out."

What happened to me was that I'd been kidnapped, and stabbed repeatedly, by an enemy that used to be an ally of Chaos. An enemy that High had wanted to reaffiliate with.

Until that enemy nearly killed me.

"Shit," I whispered.

"Yeah," Tack agreed. "That bitch is not a bitch. That bitch is a biker-hating cunt and I have no clue why the fuck she's here except to fuck with High's head 'cause she spent three years doin' that and got way the fuck off on it." He looked beyond me and muttered, "Probably got herself dumped. Maybe has kids to take care of. Lookin' for some fuckwad who's stupid enough to take on her shit and thinkin' wrongly with the way he fell for her that'd be High."

I stared up at my husband, the sharpest man I knew, wondering how, at least with one thing, he could be so dumb.

"Uh, I don't think so."

His gaze cut back to me. "Come again?"

"The woman we just saw was the female adult equivalent of a six-year-old who just learned there's no Santa Claus, no Easter Bunny, *and* she was adopted."

He looked to the heavens and muttered, "Fuck."

"Seriously," I snapped.

He looked back to me. "Red, I'm tellin' you," his fingers on my neck squeezed, "do *not* get involved."

I shook my head in disbelief. "As his brother, seeing him, seeing her, how could *you* not get involved?"

He dipped his face close to mine. "'Cause she was runnin'

away, which means I hope like fuck she *stays* away. And if she doesn't, I'll do everything in my power to set her away in a way she gets my goddamned message and stays... *the fuck*... away."

"Tack—"

"Tyra, do not get involved," he ground out.

"Whatever happened between them, she was devastated," I hissed.

"Good," he clipped. "She rained that shit on High, she deserves it and a fuckuva lot more."

Loved my man.

But I was right.

Like any man blinded by loyalty to a brother, about this shit he was so *dumb*.

"Has it occurred to you that a biker-hating woman would be nowhere near Wild Bill's field no matter what she might need unless what she needs is what she *needs*?" I asked.

"Nothin' occurs to me except takin' my brother's back, Tyra," he returned. "And you need to listen to this, baby, and let it sink way the fuck in. Every brother is gonna do the same and you do not wanna go against Chaos on shit like this. The ones who didn't live that with him will hear about it and we'll be all in in a way you've experienced *once*. When we all put our asses on the line to save your life."

I drew in a sharp breath.

He heard me do that and muttered, "You get me."

"Tack—"

"Let it go."

"Tack!"

"Red." He got super close. "Let... it... *go.*"

He stared into my eyes.

I stared into his.

Neither of us said a word.

Tack broke the silence.

"You gonna let it go?"

"I haven't decided yet," I snapped.

He drew back a bit and grinned.

"Take your mind off it."

I rolled my eyes.

He came back in and brushed my mouth with his. "Still riding the high of the Trench, baby. Now wantin' to ride something else."

It sucked but even after a decade with this man, I knew he was a very good rider, so even ticked at him, that did it for me.

I reached out and grabbed his hand, declaring, "We'll talk more about it later."

"No, we won't."

"We *so* will."

He shook his head, turned, and tugging my hand, grinning again, he led me to our tent.

We got in it and my husband took my mind off High and a woman called Millie Cross.

He did it thoroughly.

But even so, I was me.

So it was only temporarily.

Millie

Twenty-three years earlier...

"Five?" I asked incredulously.

"Five," he answered, grinning up at me.

I was naked on top of Logan in his bed in the two-bedroom apartment he shared with some guy who was not Chaos.

But, since Logan figured his time as a recruit was coming to an end, and his pay at work would increase, this meant he was planning to move into a different place that was only his.

He'd just made love to me after taking me to a fancy steak dinner at the Buckhorn Exchange.

It was fantastic. I got to dress up. I got to see Logan's version of dressed up (nice shirt, not-too-faded jeans, the ever-present leather cut declaring he was a motorcycle club recruit).

He'd not blinked an eye when I got carded after I ordered a beer and showed my fake ID (though he'd teased me about getting away with it when the waiter was gone).

He'd talked me into trying Rocky Mountain oysters (not my favorite) and elk (delicious).

We'd laughed, talked, held hands over the table, and played footsie under it.

In other words, this, our fourth date, was just as good as all three preceding it.

Now we were in his bed and Logan had just told me he wanted five kids.

Five.

My "Seriously?" was again incredulous.

He shrugged against the mattress, still grinning up at me, and explained, "Only got a sister and we're close. All a' us. Don't know why my parents didn't have more. They didn't share. Maybe by the time they made their own, they were worn out from the ones their folks had made. Though I think in the beginning it was money and not bein' able to afford havin' more. But my folks both came from big families. My dad's got two brothers and a sister. Ma's got two brothers and two sisters."

His arms wrapped tighter and he kept talking.

"Love my family, Millie. Love spendin' time with them. And I got a lot of that growin' up. The best times were holidays. Nearly all Dad and Ma's kin still lived around Durango and we'd get together all the time. Easter, Thanksgiving, Christmas. Lots of food. Loud. Wild. All the kids would go trick-or-treatin' together, big brood, terrorizin' the neighborhoods. Huge graduation parties. Big sweet-sixteen parties. We were tight and it was a blast."

I was no longer incredulous.

I was deeper in love.

"You miss it," I said softly.

"Yeah," he replied. "Think, later, my folks wished they didn't stop. All except for two of their brothers, the rest went whole hog with makin' babies and not many have moved away, so they still got that in Durango. Same goodness, gettin' bigger all the time. Fuck, my uncle had to put up a tent last Thanksgiving and heat it so he could put tables out there 'cause there was no room in the house. Which meant, all a' us out there got to be even louder and rowdier and he didn't give a fuck. Loved it. We all do."

I smiled at him. "Sounds like fun."

His arms around me gave me a squeeze. "Take you there next Thanksgiving."

That was a future date I was very much looking forward to.

Then again, four days, four dates, and I looked forward more and more to every one.

"I just have a sister," I told him, changing the subject because I didn't want to scare him with showing just how much that was true. "Always wanted a brother too."

He lifted a hand and touched his finger to my temple, trailing it down and back, over my ear until he cupped his hand around the back of my neck.

"You're young, baby, but you think about kids?" he asked.

"My sister is the absolute best and no way in hell I'm gonna live a life where I don't have two girls who can share a room and have bunk beds and giggle every night so much me and my man have to shout threats at them to shut up," I declared, and watched in wonder as his face got soft.

Seeing that, I decided I wasn't done.

"If this means I have to have three boys before I get my two girls, or five boys, I don't care. I'm going until I get two girls."

He started chuckling, his brown eyes lit with humor and warmth, but that soft look never left his face.

"So, you're prepared to push out seven kids," he remarked.

"That would not be the optimal scenario," I replied. "But, yes. To get what I want I'm prepared."

"Well, I want boys. I've got a sister, good friends back in Durango. Havin' that, not losin' it even leavin' town and leavin' them behind when I headed out to see what was up next in life meant I looked for it here in Denver. And that led me to Chaos. So I know what havin' a brother is but wish I had it all my life. Want my boys to have that."

"So, best case, two boys, two girls. Worst case, two boys, two girls, and various wildcards," I replied, and Logan chuckled again.

"Yeah, though, worst case don't sound too bad either."

He was right and I didn't care that we only had four dates and it was early.

Four dates had done it for me.

This was my guy.

So the thought of giving him as many babies as he wanted thrilled me to pieces.

I didn't want it the next day or week or month.

But when I got close to graduating from college, I wanted to start thinking about it because I wanted it early so I could be young and enjoy my kids and then be young and enjoy my grandkids.

"Start early," I whispered hesitantly.

"Oh yeah," he agreed instantly.

See?

This was my guy.

We agreed on everything. Not just everything that meant something, everything as in *everything*.

His gaze grew intense on me right before he rolled us so he was on top.

"Gotta get you home soon but want a little more of you before I hafta let you go," he told me.

Oh yes.

We agreed on *everything*.

I melted under him.

"Okay," I agreed.

His eyes warmed a different way before he slanted his head and kissed me.

Logan got a little more of me and I got a lot more of him.

Then he took me home.

I hated to say good-bye at my parents' front door.

But it wasn't that bad.

Because we had plans the next night.

CHAPTER FOUR

A Tragedy

Tyra

"Right," Elvira, sitting in my car next to me, stated. "I'm wired for sound. I go in, you listen in. Now, I'm likin' this 'cause for me, it kills three birds with one stone. It breaks up the tedium of herdin' commandos all day. It gets you intel on your girl. And, seein' as she's a party planner and I called all her references before I set up this gig, she and me do this sit-down, I get the prelims done for my wedding."

She then clapped her hands together and held them palm out in front of her, indicating *done*.

"Uh...don't you think it might be bad luck to start planning your wedding before Malik actually pops the question?" Lanie, crammed in my backseat, asked Elvira.

Elvira twisted around to glare at her. "Uh...*no*, seein' as

Malik'll be the one with the bad luck if that man don't put a ring on it *and soon*. He don't, I got two choices. Kick his black ass out or kill him. And, just sayin', I'm leanin' toward door number two."

She didn't have to "just say." She'd been ranting about this for months, so we already knew.

I didn't blame her. Elvira was my girl and Malik was her man and had been for a long time. He needed to make a move.

I felt for her because I loved her.

But this was not the time for that.

"Not to change the subject from one this important," I put in. "But I don't have a good feeling about our current mission."

It was only three days after Wild Bill's rally.

In that time, I had taken into consideration my husband's warnings to stay out of it.

Then I (and all the boys) had been treated to High's foul mood.

So I decided to go for it.

To that end I'd roped in Elvira, my friend who also worked for Hawk Delgado, who was a kind of private investigator, kind of commando, but mostly unsung superhero (in my mind). I'd also pulled in Lanie, my bestest bestie, who had traveled my path. She'd just done it years later when she, too, married a Chaos brother, Hopper "Hop" Kincaid.

Once she heard, being one to dive in to something like this with both feet, Elvira made short work of doing the legwork, utilizing Hawk's superhero resources at his command center.

Therefore we knew a fair amount about Millicent Cross.

We knew she was forty-one. We knew she'd never been married (something I found telling, and Lanie and Elvira agreed). We knew she also had never had children (again with the telling). We knew she'd lived in her house for eleven years.

But we also knew that, years ago, she'd shared a rental with High and they'd done that for three years.

Further, we knew she had one sister, who was married

with two kids and lived local, and two living parents who had moved to Arizona three years ago.

And last, we knew she owned her own business.

She planned parties.

All parties.

Weddings. Anniversaries. Bar mitzvahs. Bat mitzvahs. *Quinceañeras.* Corporate gatherings. You named it, she planned it, and after Elvira had called the references listed on her website, we'd found that she did it very well.

She also had an add-on to this business where she'd design the schemes, then decorate houses or offices, inside and out, for holidays. Any holiday (but mostly Christmas). And from the pictures in the gallery on her website, she was *really* good at that.

After learning all of this, Elvira had concocted a plan where she scheduled an appointment, ostensibly to plan her upcoming nuptials, this happening so we could get a "feel" for Millie and from that feel, decide for ourselves if we should officially wade in.

And without girl posse consensus, Elvira had put that plan into action.

Thus we were there, sitting in my Mustang on the street in front of Millie Cross's (very quaint and unbelievably pretty) little old house in Cheesman Park.

We were there because, at the back of the main house, there was a small mother-in-law cottage where Millie had a studio in which she ran her business. You got to this going up a drive that was two narrow strips of concrete between wider strips of tufted lawn. These were under an overhang that was, back in the day, probably to protect cars or even carriages and it had a wall of trellis covered in wisteria.

And Elvira's appointment was two minutes away.

Elvira turned her attention to me. "How can you not have a good idea about this? It's the perfect plan."

She would think that, it was her plan.

"Well, you might not have gone through the initiation ceremony, that being becoming an old lady, but you're still de facto Chaos," I stated. When Elvira opened her mouth to retort, I kept going. "And you know it. Which means, if Millie Cross is who I think Millie Cross is, and we can fix what's broken with her and High, which means she might come back in the fold, do you think the first thing we should do as her possible future Chaos sisters is pull a fast one?"

"What I think is you gotta know what you're dealin' with here and you got your man's strong words. *She's* got her man's strong words." Elvira jerked a thumb at Lanie. "And those two boys are far from dumb. Loyal, perhaps to a fault, but not dumb. So I think you gotta proceed with caution."

Elvira wasn't wrong. Lanie had gently probed Hop about his knowledge of the history of High and Millie.

Hop's response had been, "Heard she showed her face. I'll say what Tack said to Cherry. Bitch is not welcome anywhere near Chaos. So do not stick your nose in that, woman. You do, you won't be prepared for the extreme."

Lanie being married to a biker and the mother of one of his sons, getting this warning and sitting in the back of my Mustang with crazy Elvira on a mission was one of the many reasons she was my bestest bestie.

I still didn't have a good feeling about this.

"I hear you," I told Elvira. "But I think you should call her, reschedule, and we should talk this out further before—"

Her phone beeped before I finished. She held the screen out to me.

I saw the appointment alarm on the display just as she said, "Go time," turned to the door, tossed it open, threw out her Valentino pump, and hauled herself out.

The door was slammed and she was gone.

"Shit," I muttered.

"Shit is right," Lanie agreed, and I looked to the backseat.

"I can't help but feeling, one way or another, this is going to go south for us."

I had that feeling too.

I was worried Tack and Hop, who both knew Millie and had been around when whatever went down went down, were right.

I worried more seeing Millie Cross's neat, trim, pretty old house that obviously was lovingly restored and taken care of.

It did not say biker babe.

Nor did her clothes say it at Wild Bill's.

Then again, before I met Tack, mine didn't either and in many cases, at least with my clothes, they still didn't.

Lanie's didn't either. You took one look at her, you thought, *Retired Supermodel and Current Muse to Couture Designer.* You did not think, *Biker Bitch.*

So Millie's look and her house meant nothing.

Millie's expression that night meant everything.

And I was hanging a lot on that because the boys did not like meddling in their affairs and Tack was not wrong. If one of the guys got a hangnail, the rest of them would rally around staring balefully at the unfortunate who wielded the cuticle clippers until it was successfully clipped out.

Okay, so that was a slight exaggeration.

But there was a lot expected of earning the Chaos cut.

Loyalty was at the top of that list.

If High was done with this Millie woman, he was done.

The thing was, no man was in a foul mood for three days after he saw an ex unless he wasn't over that ex, if she was an ex for twenty minutes, but *especially* for twenty years.

Since it had been twenty years, something was going down.

And I intended to get to the bottom of it for High, who I might not be tight with but I liked him. I respected him. And he was the only Chaos brother I knew who wasn't happy.

He lived. He loved his brothers. He loved his kids. He put up with his recent ex-wife.

But down deep, the man was existing.

Joy came from his two girls.

That was it.

And I wanted more for him.

So did Lanie.

So did Elvira.

So we were here.

Elvira wasn't dumb but—as hard as it was to believe, it was true—she was even more loyal to the sisterhood than Chaos was to the brotherhood. If there was a sister in need, she was there, one hundred percent, and she didn't even need to know them to be there.

I knew this from experience.

So did Lanie.

And I worried in her zeal she was going to fuck it all up.

"I think we should go in, introduce ourselves, and come clean," I told Lanie, even though I was worried that Millie would recognize me from Wild Bill's.

"I don't know about that but I *do* know we should go in and stop Elvira from starting to plan a wedding before Malik proposes," Lanie replied, shaking her head, her tone turning dire. "That's bad juju and every girl knows it."

This was also true.

"Elvira?" We heard through the speaker Elvira had requisitioned from Hawk's equipment room that was right then in my car, connected to the mic that Elvira was wearing.

"Damn straight," Elvira answered. "Millie?"

I could actually hear her smile through the speaker as she replied, "That's me. Please come in. Do you want some coffee? Tea?"

"Let's go," Lanie said over Elvira's response on the speaker.

I nodded, turned off the speaker, threw open my door, and got out, lifting the seat so Lanie could curl herself out of the back.

Then, both of us coming from work to do this, thus both of

us in high heels, tight skirts, and fabulous blouses, we hurried up the concrete strips to Millie Cross's studio.

To get there, we hit a large back courtyard that was covered in attractive pavers, part of it overhung with a pergola that radiated out diagonally from an L in the house. The pergola was also covered in dormant wisteria. There was a shiny red Mazda SUV back there and enough room to park two more vehicles. There were also enormous, eye-catching pots dotted around that had been planted for autumn in purple-pink, lavender, and white cushion mums.

And beyond the courtyard, between the house and the studio, an area you got to under an arch, there was terraced garden, the grade going down. I couldn't see much of it, but I could see a gazebo.

This, the clothes Millie wore to Wild Bill's, and her website told me she was a single woman with not much in her life so she spent her money on herself and her house.

This also made me think we were doing the right thing because I knew what it was like to be a woman of a certain age who was doing the same.

There were good parts about it.

But there were also bad.

And the bad had been written all over Millie's face in the dark at Wild Bill's.

I stopped at the door to the studio and looked at Lanie.

She nodded.

I nodded back, took a deep breath, opened the door, and entered.

Two heads turned our way and two sets of eyes got huge.

I ignored Elvira, who looked pissed, and turned my full attention to Millie Cross.

Her hair color was too rich a red to be strawberry blonde, and yet it wasn't red either, more a deep-hued reddish gold. It had an amazing wave to it that wasn't kinky or curly, just pretty, and that wave looked natural. It was pulled into a soft, side ponytail that managed to look graceful at the same time professional. She had big, dark brown eyes and a pixie face with one of those moles by her mouth that defined why they were known as beauty marks.

She was wearing a pretty cream blouse that was both immensely feminine with some gentle ruffles down the front, but it, too, was professional. High-heeled, dark brown pumps that, at a glance, I pegged as Manolos.

And, like Lanie and me, she was wearing a pencil skirt, hers tight, brown tweed, and to die for.

Her face started to pale as she stared at me.

"You—" she began.

"I'm so sorry," I rushed out my words. "Really. Truly. I just…" Crap!

I hadn't planned this, so I didn't know what to say.

"You," she whispered, face now very pale and her eyes still huge.

"You screwed this pooch," Elvira hissed as Millie didn't say anything and I didn't either. "*Say something.*"

"I'm Kane Allen's wife," I stated. "Um…Tack."

Something moved over her face.

Not pain. Not fear.

Emptiness.

No.

Armor.

Shit.

"I know Tack," she stated coldly.

"Well, um…we ran into each other at—" I began.

Her voice was ice when she cut me off to say, "I remember."

I nodded and threw out my hand. "This is my friend, Elvira. And my other friend, Lanie." I indicated Lanie, who'd come in behind me. "Lanie's married to Hopper Kincaid. I think you might know Hop."

"Indeed I do," she replied, her words brittle.

Okay, this was not going too well.

I had to lay it out.

"We had a plan, the girl posse and me," I admitted. "Elvira actually *does* have a man she's been living with for a long time and they're close to…"

I didn't finish that just in case I'd hex her because Lanie was right about that bad juju.

However, unfortunately, I also didn't grab my friends and bail.

I struggled on.

"But, well, I saw your face at Wild Bill's and I talked with Tack about you and I thought that maybe…"

I trailed off when she continued to sit behind her tidy, pretty, delicate, white desk with its squat bunch of pale pink roses shoved tight with green hydrangea in a round vase at the corner, staring up at me emotionlessly.

I'd seen her once for maybe a second and that one time I'd seen her, there was so much emotion pouring off her, I could swear I could taste it.

Right now, void.

Nothing.

"We're here to help," Elvira chimed in.

Slowly, Millie Cross's eyes moved to Elvira, and even Elvira, who feared nothing and no one, not even any of the badass commandos she worked with or the badass bikers she hung with, I could see shiver when the frost of Millie's gaze touched her.

"You're here to help," Millie repeated.

"With High," Elvira went on.

That was when I saw it. I heard the noise Lanie made behind me and I knew she saw it too.

But I was too busy flinching at pain that wasn't mine but was visible to extremes. Pain that slashed through Millie's face before she hid it.

Oh yeah.

There was something going on and as awkward as this was,

we were right to come. I knew it. I sensed it with the surety of a woman, the certainty of a mother, the definitiveness of a sister.

"You're here to help with…" she paused strangely, then emphasized the word, "*High.*"

"Boy's in a foul mood," Elvira shared, either powering through the chill Millie was emanating or she'd put up her shields and was impervious to it. "Spreadin' that wide through Chaos. Somethin's gotta be done."

Again with the strange emphasis. "*High* is in a foul mood."

"That's what I said," Elvira replied.

"You," Millie started, then looked to me, "and you," her gaze went beyond me to Lanie, "and *you* all came to my place of business, which is also my home, to inform me that *High* is in a foul mood and you're here to help."

"Listen." I took a step forward. "I know this may seem strange. And we've obviously taken you off guard. But I saw High after whatever went down and the boys aren't really sharing much about your history but you should know that he—"

Millie interrupted me.

"Get out."

I saw Elvira straighten with a jerk in her seat even as I felt my own body jerk, not to mention the surprise coming from Lanie, who was now standing beside me.

"I think you may mistake me," I tried again. "We're sisters. We're—"

She interrupted me again.

"Get out."

"Girl, you don't get us. We're here 'cause—" Elvira tried.

Millie interrupted her too.

Except this time, she did it by straightening out of her chair and screeching, "*Get out!*"

We all went completely still.

There was no other reaction to have.

The mask had slipped.

The anguish had been bared.

And it was so immense, so impossible to process, witnessing it was paralyzing.

"My apologies," she said, her voice shaking, as was her body. Visibly.

"I was wrong," she went on. "You can help. Please follow me."

And then she started walking stiffly, rounding her desk, passing Lanie and me, and moving right out the door.

We looked at each other and then followed.

All our heels sounded against the pavers as we made our way across the courtyard to the steps that led up to a split farm door that had a window at the top. The steps were brick and formed a half circle into the pavers.

Definitely a cute house.

Millie went in the door.

We followed her into a kitchen that I would kill for just so I could look at it (since my husband did most of the cooking).

It wasn't cute.

It was *fabulous*.

"If you'd stay there," she requested, and we stopped.

She disappeared into a hall off the equally fabulous living room.

Honestly, it was amazing. Like out of a magazine.

"Bitch can decorate," Elvira muttered.

I gave her a look.

She raised her brows. "Do I lie?"

She didn't.

"Just shush," I hissed.

"Not me who blew our plan," she returned.

"It wasn't *our* plan," I shot back in an irate whisper. "It was *yours* and I think we all get it wasn't a good one."

"Okay, girls," Lanie cut in. "Before, we had to tread cautiously. Now we know we have a minefield to navigate. Look alive and don't do it bickering."

She had a good point, so I shut up.

It was a good call because Millie appeared carrying one of those large, lidded plastic crates, blue with an opaque white top.

It looked heavy.

Even so, she gave it a heave. It flew several inches through the air and was clearly weighted wrong because one side dipped, so when it hit her wood floor, it did it on an edge. The latch on the lid popped, the lid opened, and it landed on its side, its contents spilling and sliding across the floor right to our feet.

Photographs.

Hundreds of them.

And at a glance, they were all of a younger Millie Cross... with High.

All of them.

"Twenty years and I can't bring myself to get rid of that. So," Millie stated, "if you're here to help, if you'd be so kind as to take that away, that would be appreciated. Dump it. Burn it. Whatever. Just get it gone."

My eyes drifted from the abundance of evidence that Millie Cross was High's dream woman—and High was Millie's dream man—to Millie just in time to see her straighten her shoulders.

"I sense you're nice women, so I hope you'll do as you said you wanted to do and help me by leaving immediately and taking that with you." She pointed to the floor. "And I hope with all my *fucking* heart I never see it again."

Oh yes.

She hoped that.

And oh yes.

She needed our help.

Just not that kind.

She kept talking.

"I also hope you take no offense when I say I'm walking out of my house and going back to work and I never want to see any of you again either." She looked to Elvira. "Gayle Niedermeier is an excellent wedding planner. If I'm maxed with clients, I refer to her. If you do, indeed, need assistance, I'd contact Gayle. Mention my name. She'll take care of you." Her gaze swung to all of us. "Have a nice day."

She then stepped over the avalanche of photos carpeting her kitchen floor, walked by us and out of the house.

I stared at the door.

Lanie stared at the door.

Elvira squatted down to the floor.

"Shit," she mumbled.

I looked to her to see she'd picked up a photo and was studying it.

I looked at the photo she was studying.

Dream man.

Dream woman.

Happy.

Whoever took it wasn't a good photographer because half of High was not in shot.

But in it they were in each other's arms, Millie with her back to the camera. Her head was tipped and twisted to smile over her shoulder at the lens. She was doing this so big it wasn't hard to read she was laughing, her long, *long* hair hanging down over High's arms that were wrapped tight around her.

High was looking down at her, grinning, his face carefree and happy like I'd never seen it before.

Not once.

Not even when he was with his kids.

Not for the ten years I'd known him. I tore my eyes off High and looked at Millie.

She belonged in those arms and she knew it.

So what had happened?

I lost sight of the photo when Elvira straightened from her squat.

"This situation just went from code blue to code freakin' red," she declared.

Lanie reached and pulled the photo from Elvira's fingers, whispering, "Truth." She looked from the photo to me. "Have you ever seen him like that?"

I shook my head.

She looked back to the picture, murmuring, "God, High happy. Crazy."

"Crazy beautiful," Elvira stated. "We *were* on an assignment. Now we're on a *mission*. Regroup for tactical strategy meeting, tonight, cosmos and boards, my house," Elvira declared, then lifted a hand and wagged a long-rounded-gray-painted fingernail at us. "And don't tell me no shit about no kids. Saddle those biker boys of yours up with diapers and Tasers and get your ass to my house. Seven sharp. No excuses accepted."

Since Lanie's Nash was hardly a year old, when Elvira mentioned Tasers, she was talking about my Rider and Cutter.

My boys were hellions. I knew it. I figured they'd work it out or become bikers and it'd work out for them.

This was Tack's second round of kids, so he had more experience and more patience.

But my boys were who they were, so I wasn't going to give my husband any ideas about Tasers.

"I'm in," Lanie said.

"Me too," I added.

"You thinkin' Tabby on this or you thinkin' she knew Millie?" Elvira asked me about Tack's daughter, my stepdaughter. She was *the* Chaos princess and also an old lady since she was married to Tack's lieutenant, Shy Cage, and now pregnant with his baby.

"That's why she's not here. I'm thinking she knew her," I shared.

Elvira looked at Lanie. "Then, Lanie, softly-softly, but you get what you can outta Tabby and see where she's at with bein' pulled in on this. But we got our work cut out for us, and I can herd commandos in my sleep, but whatever that bitch in that studio," she jabbed her finger toward the door, "is dealin' with, it's all hands on deck."

I nodded.

Lanie nodded.

And all three of us squatted down to right the crate and gather photos.

Not one of us suggested we should leave well enough alone.

But even if it had crossed any of our minds, sifting through those photos to put them back into that crate, it would have been banished.

Whatever ended Logan "High" Judd's and Millie Cross's love affair was not a play or a betrayal.

It was a tragedy.

And if a sister had the power to right a wrong, it was her sworn duty to do it.

We were sisters.

So we were doing it.

Millie

Twenty-three years earlier, outside the Chaos Compound…

"I'm Tabby," the little girl declared.

She had a mass of thick, dark hair and deep blue eyes and she was wearing jeans and a pink T-shirt that had a glittery decal on the front that declared her *princess*.

I sat on top of the picnic table outside Logan's biker club head-quarters, looking down at the little girl who had to be no more than four or five while replying, "Hey there, Tabby. I'm Millie."

"Do you belong to Low?" she asked.

Belong.

She was certainly a princess.

A biker princess.

I grinned down at her.

"Yep," I answered, knowing this to be true even if this was only our sixth date.

But since our sixth date was coming to a cookout with his soon-to-be brothers, a date he had planned from the very beginning, a date that all the other dates led up to, regardless of how few there were, I figured I was right.

I was Low's.

And that made me happy.

"I like Low," little Tabby told me.

"I'm glad you do," I replied. "I do too."

"That's good," she said, her eyes going beyond me.

I felt him before I turned my head and saw him just as Logan settled in beside me, arm coming around my shoulders, leaning into the picnic table . . . and me.

But his eyes were on Tabby.

"Yo, Tab," he greeted.

"Your girlfriend's pretty," she declared.

"No, she ain't, little pea," Logan returned. "Lots a' things are pretty. Millie here's loads more than that."

Little pea.

Loads more than that.

God.

Seriously.

Even if I wasn't his, I would make him be mine.

But I was.

Which meant he was.

Oh yes.

Happy.

I grinned again and leaned in to him.

"She ride on the back of your bike?" Tabby asked.

"Yup," Logan answered.

"Rush says I can't ride on a bike," she announced, and looked from Logan to me. "That's my brother," she explained. "He's older than me and thinks he knows everything."

"I suspect most older brothers do," I shared ruefully, like I felt her pain.

"He's stupid," she proclaimed. "I'll ride what I want."

"How 'bout you wait about fifteen, twenty years before you do that?" Logan suggested, a smile deepening his voice.

"Well, *duh*!" she cried like the next word she wanted to use but knew better than to use on a biker was *silly*. "I can't do it now," she went on. "Even if I had an old man, I can't get my arms around his middle."

I swallowed laughter but Logan didn't bother. I heard his chuckle.

"You ever think of getting your own bike?" I asked her.

She tipped her head to the side and stated contemplatively, "Maybe. When I can reach the grips." She righted her head. "Do you have your own bike?"

"Nope," I answered.

"Want your own bike?" she asked.

"Nope," I repeated.

"You like ridin' with your old man," she proclaimed knowingly.

"Yep," I stated, and Logan's arm around me tightened.

"*Tabitha!*"

I tensed at the shrill noise, Tabby's body jerked and whirled, and Logan straightened but didn't let me go.

I looked up just when a redheaded woman, who was pretty but she had an ugly look on her face and it was directed at the little girl in front of me, shrieked, "*Get your ass over here!*"

"Gotta go," Tabby mumbled, and did it hightailing it over to the shrieking woman.

"Naomi," Logan said, and I looked up at him to see his eyes still directed to the redhead. "Woman'd be okay, 'cept she treats her daughter like shit. Kid's 'bout five years old." He shook his head. "Do not get that."

I didn't either and didn't get the chance to comment on it because something took my attention and I turned my head the other way.

There I saw a man Logan had introduced me to earlier called Tack.

He was looking at the redhead, too, and you could tell he didn't like the way she treated her daughter either.

Not at all.

"Naomi's Tack's old lady," Logan said, and I looked back to him to see he now was gazing down at me. "Loves his little girl like crazy so don't see that lastin'."

"What?" I asked. "Her treatment of their daughter?"

He nodded. "That and if he can't put an end to it, then what'll end is Naomi bein' his old lady."

"Good," I murmured, looking back to Naomi who was bent over Tabby, wagging a finger in her face, her own expression like thunder.

I watched, wondering what the kid had done. She was just talking to us, and I hadn't been keeping tabs on her, but before that, she was just talking to other people.

The finger wagging stopped when suddenly Tabby wasn't standing in front of her mother, head tipped back, face pale, lower lip quivering.

Instead she was in her father's arms, and without a word, he turned and walked away.

Watching it, I decided I liked Logan's brother Tack.

Naomi stared daggers at their backs, visibly huffed, and then stormed off in the other direction.

I decided I didn't like Tack's old lady, Naomi.

"She's it," Logan stated, and I looked to him again.

"What?"

"Naomi. She's it. Only bitch a' the bunch." He bent toward me. "All the rest, all good. Good folks. Good family."

He wanted me to like them.

I smiled, twisted, and leaned in to him so my breasts were brushing his stomach.

"There's always one."

He cupped my jaw, eyes to my mole, and muttered, "Yeah."

I'd learned what Logan's eyes to my mole meant and I liked what it meant.

But I had a few things to say.

"I like that there's kids here," I told him quietly, and earned his gaze.

His warm, happy gaze.

"Yeah," he agreed.

"This isn't what I expected of bikers," I admitted.

And it wasn't. Sunny day. Grill fired up. Table groaning with food. Coolers filled with ice and packed tight with bottles of beer and cans of pop. Loads of people around. Kids in the mix.

I didn't know what I expected, but something this laid back and friendly was not it.

"Lotsa different kinds of families, Millie."

I nodded.

He was right and it appeared, away from the one he left behind in Durango, he'd found a good one.

And the fact that was what he'd do, find a family, said a lot about him, all of it good.

I leaned deeper in to him and dropped my voice even more. "Thanks for bringing me here, Logan. I don't want this to sound corny because I mean it. But I'm honored you did."

The warm tunneled into his eyes, going deep.

"Means a lot, beautiful," he replied.

I grinned and lifted a hand to curl it around his wrist. "Good."

Finally, he bent, touched his mouth to mine, and I let him.

"Yo! Low, Millie!"

Logan lifted away and we turned our heads toward a brother I'd met called Black who was manning the grill.

"Burger. Dog. Brat," he shouted. "Call it now, they're goin' fast."

"What you want, darlin'?" Logan asked me.

"Brat!" I yelled to Black.

"Got it!" he yelled back. "Low?"

"Burger and a dog," Logan replied.

Black lifted his chin and turned back to the massive half-barrel grill.

"Fresh ones."

This was muttered from our sides and I looked to the man introduced to me as Big Petey, a guy probably in his forties, an older member of the Club, which was definitely multi-generational, just as he slid the warm bottle of beer out of my hand and put a cool one there.

He grinned at me and winked while he did it.

Then he, too, jerked up his chin to Logan as he did the same with Logan's beer.

"Black kicks ass with a brat, baby, good call," Logan said before lifting his fresh beer to take a draw and turning his attention back to the grill. "Then again, he kicks ass with everything."

I shifted so my side was pressed to his and lifted my own bottle, saying, "Awesome," before I took a sip.

"Gotcha!"

I looked to my left and saw the brother called Boz with a camera he was lowering after obviously just taking a picture of me and Logan.

I hoped, if I asked nice, he'd give me a copy.

Our first photo.

It had just been taken but I couldn't wait to see it.

"Too pretty for that brother, Millie," Boz declared as he gave Logan a joking take-that look and me a grin. He turned only to stop and lift his camera to take a picture of a dark-headed boy who was racing after a dog on the tarmac between the Ride store, the Ride garage, and the Chaos headquarters.

"Don't eat all those, Chew," snapped a woman I had not yet met, who was not too far from us at another picnic table, one that was laden with food. "They're Low's favorite."

"He's a grunt. He gets the dregs," the brother I *did* meet, called Chew, replied, doing it with a mouthful of deviled egg, two more of which he had in the palm of his big hand.

"He's got his girl with him, moron," she returned. "Grunt or not, all Chaos got manners." She planted a hand on her hip and challenged, "Or am I wrong?"

"You're not wrong but you *are* a pain in the ass," Chew shot back.

"My job," she muttered.

I giggled quietly.

"Dad! I want a puppy!" the dark-headed little boy shouted, and I looked that way.

He was now close to Tack, who had his daughter riding on his shoulders.

"You got it, bud," Tack replied with a grin.

That was easy.

"*Really?*" Tabby screeched.

Apparently, Tabby felt as I did.

Tack twisted his neck just as she leaned over and put both hands to his cheeks.

"Yeah, baby," he told her.

How sweet.

Yes, totally liked Tack.

"Puppy!" the little boy I suspected was Rush shouted as he pumped his arms with excitement.

"Pushover."

The word was muttered from behind us and when I twisted, I saw it was from Big Petey, who had his gaze to Tack and his kids, and even if his word sounded disapproving, his grin was not.

Oh yes. I liked Logan's whole Chaos family because it *was*

like family. Safe. Loving. And like any family, even having its flaws, it still felt good.

I sighed and melted sideways into my man.

"You okay?" he asked the top of my head.

I wrapped my arm around his waist and rested my head against the side of his chest.

"Yeah, Logan," I replied. "I'm definitely okay."

He gave me a squeeze.

I returned it.

"Millie!" Black called. "Brats are done, honey." He looked to Logan. "Low, come get your woman her food."

Your woman.

"Be back," Logan muttered, let me go, and walked toward the grill to get me my food.

I watched him move away thinking, *Yes, oh yes.*

Absolutely *yes.*

I was one hundred percent *okay.*

CHAPTER FIVE

Don't

High

"HEY! HIGH!"

Striding out from the back of the store toward the Compound, hearing Cherry's call, High looked toward the garage to see her quickly coming down the steps to the office in her high heels.

He changed directions and started moving her way.

"I'm in a bind," she called when she got to the bottom of the steps and started rushing to him. "The tires don't fit!"

High said nothing. He just kept walking across the expanse of tarmac to her.

"The buyer is coming on Monday and Joker's decided on different tires, not recutting the wheel wells," she went on, still hoofing her way to him. "I called the first two suppliers and they don't have what he wants. And I—"

They met. She stopped. He stopped, too, and lifted a hand so she'd also stop yapping.

"What you need, Cherry?" he asked.

"I need tires," she replied. "Which means I have to call around to everyone to find them and that means I can't go get the champagne."

His brows drew together. "Say again?"

She threw out a hand in agitation. "I can't get the champagne."

"What champagne?" he asked.

"For the event," she told him. "Tack and I are donating twelve cases of champagne to this fund-raising thing happening downtown. They called and needed underwriting. They were in a bind because something had happened and the champagne donation fell through. It's a good cause and a big event and any big event needs champagne. But there wasn't enough time to get the brothers together so they could vote on the donation so I decided Tack and I would donate it personally."

"Thinkin' the brothers would cover you, you thought it was worth the cake," High informed her of something she absolutely knew.

She shook her head and grinned at him. "Doesn't matter. Tack and I need write-offs too."

"Whatever," he muttered, and got to the point. "So what you need from me?"

She nodded. "Right. Well, it's ordered, the champagne that

is, and they need it because the event's tonight. They also need it in time so they can get it in the fridge to chill. I was supposed to go pick it up and take it there. The store can load it and they have guys at the event location to unload it. I just need the pickup. But now I can't—"

"Where's the booze and where's it gotta go?" he asked.

Cherry smiled big and shouted, "You're the greatest!" before she shocked the shit out of him by leaning in, putting a hand to his chest, and getting on her toes to press her cheek to his.

Fuck.

She'd never touched him.

A decade he'd known the woman and she'd not touched him.

Not once.

She moved away, still smiling but also giving him the info he needed.

He nodded. "On it."

"You're my savior today, or you're King's Shelter's savior."

King's Shelter. They took care of runaways.

Yeah, a good cause the brothers would totally vote to support.

He didn't get into that again with her.

He told her, "You can keep talkin' to me or I can go get your shit and get it to the hotel."

She kept smiling. "Then I'll shut up. Thanks, High. You're the best."

She continued to smile as she lifted her hand and then the woman touched him again, squeezing his biceps before letting him go, turning on her heel, and sashaying toward the garage like she had all day and wasn't in a rush to find some tires.

He didn't think of that. Not when he was watching her ass move in her tight skirt, an ass that was beyond fine even after popping out two kids and being firm in her forties.

Tack was a lucky man, seeing as Cherry was his woman.

High stopped watching her ass and went to his bike, which he rode to Boz's place so he could switch it out for his truck.

Then he went to the liquor store, got that booze, and drove to the location, stopping behind it at the loading area where Cherry told him to go.

A kid came running out as High angled down from the truck.

"Got a delivery," he told the kid. "From Tyra Allen. Donation. Champagne."

"Right." The kid nodded, not looking into High's eyes, something High didn't like all that much because there was no reason why he wouldn't. Before High could get a lock on that, the kid muttered, "Be right back."

Then he turned and sprinted into the building.

Fuck.

He hoped this didn't take forever. He didn't have anything to do that morning but he had to go view more houses early in the afternoon. Something he wasn't looking forward to. Something he didn't like doing and not only because he'd already seen eighteen of the fuckers, none of which was right for him and his girls. But also he'd started that mission not liking moving through other people's houses trying to visualize their shit gone and new shit in it so he could make it a decent place for him and his babies.

On that thought he caught movement, focused his attention on the door, and felt his body snap tight.

Millie.

Fucking *Millie* walking out, her hair back from her face in twists and pinned at the base of her neck in a big bun, her body encased in a turtleneck sweater dress the color of toffee, a dress that skimmed every fuckin' curve—and she had a lot of them—her feet in shiny, fancy, sexy-as-fuck high-heeled boots.

The bitch had worn her hair down to get his dick at Bill's field.

This time, she was using the dress.

His body tightened further.

He'd been played.

Worse, he'd been played and he didn't even know what game was being forced on him. He hadn't seen her in twenty years, now she was everywhere.

Goddamned fucking *shit*.

Instantly pissed beyond reason, High didn't catch the look on her face as he took two steps toward her, growling, "You're shittin' me."

Tack had warned him. He'd said that he and Cherry had run into Millie and Cherry was getting a mind to stick her nose into High's business.

Obviously, she did and Millie went all in.

Goddamned Millie.

Fucking bitch.

"What are you doing here?" she asked, and, no less pissed, High missed the tone of her voice and still didn't take in the expression on her face.

"Was a long time ago, woman, but lesson you taught me I learned," he clipped. "Can't imagine how you'd think you could play me again."

"How I could...*play* you?"

Christ, she was good at what she did. If he was a dumb fuck thinking with his dick like he did back in his twenties, he'd actually believe her confusion.

"Donation from Tyra Allen?" he bit back.

He noticed her face pale and didn't give a fuck.

"Tyra *Allen*?" she asked.

"Jesus, bitch," he gritted, taking another step toward her, also noticing she stiffened even as she took a step back. "You and Tack's old lady maneuvered this bullshit."

"I...I was told the champagne was here," she said, her voice shaky, and it would be. She was a player, the female kind, which meant the worst kind, but she wasn't stupid. She couldn't miss he was pissed.

"Yeah," he returned. "The donation from Tyra Allen."

"A family called Masters donated it," she told him.

"Right," he gritted. "And Masters is Tyra's maiden name."

Her eyes got big and fuck him, the bitch was forty-one years old and that was still cute.

Cute and false and total bullshit.

He took three more steps toward her, which took him right in her space.

"Told you I did not wanna see you again," he reminded her tightly.

She stared up at him, unmoving, like she was frozen.

"I meant it," he kept at her. "You got this one time. You pull this shit again, you will *not* like the consequences."

"What shit?" she asked like she wasn't following. Fuck, like she was so lost, she barely knew English.

"This shit you got goin' with Tyra," he bit out. "Not that you'll give a fuck but you keep this up, you won't just piss me off, you'll twist shit with Tyra and Tack. Those two started out with the worst kinda rough patch you can go through. They earned smooth sailin'. Do not be the bitch who makes trouble for them."

"Tyra," she whispered like something was dawning on her.

He bent closer to her and smelled her like he had that night at Bill's.

She smelled different from before, when he thought she was his. Her hair. Her skin. All different.

Probably expensive shampoo and definitely expensive perfume.

He wasn't into that crap.

But fuck it if he didn't like it on her.

"Never again, woman," he stated. "Hear?"

"She ... she came to me and—"

Done with her, he lifted a hand to grab her elbow in order to get her attention and say words to make that clear.

He intended to make a point, not hurt her.

And he didn't hurt her. He barely touched her.

But she pulled away, taking two quick steps back, stumbling on her heels and righting herself, all of this like he'd grabbed hold, twisted, and caused agony.

"Don't touch me," she hissed, and it finally hit him that her expression had seemed dazed.

Now she was pissed.

What the bitch had to be pissed about, he did not know.

What he did know was her being pissed made him *more* pissed.

"Now you're gonna play *that* game?" he asked low.

"I'm not playing any game, *High*," she snapped, and fuck…
Fuck.

She'd never called him High. Not once when they were together.

Why did that feel like a punch to the gut now?

"Take your champagne and go," she ordered.

"Get your boys out here to come and get it," he countered.

"We don't need it," she returned, lifting her chin. "I'll figure something out. Now just take it and go."

"You talked Tyra into shellin' out for it, don't be stupid. It's here, take it."

"Regardless of what you think, *High*, I am not in cahoots with Tyra. She's in cahoots with some women called Elvira and Lanie. They have the wrong idea. So I'd suggest you get in that truck, take yourself and the champagne back to Tyra, and explain to her that you don't want to see me as I've already explained to her I don't want to see you."

"Right," he sneered. "Like I believe that."

"I don't really give a fuck what you believe," she returned, cold as ice. "But at this moment, I have an event that's happening in T minus six hours and forty-four minutes, so I also don't have time for your crap."

He went from being extremely pissed to being fucking *ticked*.

"My *crap*?" he ground out.

"Your…" she leaned toward him, "*crap*." She leaned back and continued. "You won't go, I will."

And on that, she started to turn.

So High got back into her space, rounding her and stopping close enough to halt her progress.

"Don't you fuckin' walk away from me," he growled.

"Don't *you* tell me what to do," she fired back.

He ignored that and ordered, "Get your boys to come get this shit so I can get gone."

"You're so fired up to help the kids at King's Shelter, *you* find some guys to help you unload," she returned.

"Not gonna say it again," he informed her.

"I'm not either," she retorted.

"Bitch—" he started on a growl but stopped when she rolled up to her toes so she was an inch from his face and everything about her assaulted him so—fuck him, goddamned weak—he actually *couldn't* go on.

"If you call me a bitch one more time, *High*, I swear to God, you'll regret it," she threatened.

"What you gonna do?" he asked cuttingly. "Suck my dick clean off?"

Hurt slashed through her features, reciprocating pain he fucking hated that he felt ripping through his gut, before her eyes fired.

"God, you're an asshole," she hissed.

"Bet I get you on your knees and I get my cock in you, one end or the other, you'll stop thinkin' that," he replied.

"That's never gonna happen again," she announced acidly.

"Right, like this whole scheme isn't your play to get more of my cock." He tipped his head to the side and asked sarcastically, "What happened, baby? The well run dry?"

"Move away," she demanded.

"You get your boys to unload, fuck your face in the back of my truck," he offered.

"*Move away,*" she bit.

He shrugged. "All the same to me, you want me to take your pussy."

She again rolled up on her toes. "Move . . . *away.*"

He lifted his brows in false shock. "Up the ass?"

She glared at him, trying to stare him down, entering a new game she couldn't win.

And she didn't.

So she tried a different tactic. He knew it when he saw the wet hit her eyes.

Another game she couldn't win.

"Prettiest crier I ever knew," he whispered, and heard her breath catch, her gaze turning searching.

Stupid bitch thought she got in there.

But he was not lying. Back in the day, anytime anything moved her to tears, she didn't ugly cry, getting all red and making faces. She wept like the practiced actress she was.

"Okay, baby," he kept at her. "I'll give you what you want since you didn't get it last time and I know how much you love it. Eat you before I fuck you. Just get your boys to *move* the fuckin' *booze.*"

Her head snapped sharply like he'd struck her and he felt that in his gut too.

"I think I hate you," she declared, sounding genuinely rocked, not to mention looking the same damned thing.

Good at this.

A master.

"No thinkin' about it on my part," he replied.

She sniffed, getting control, then squared her shoulders.

"Fine, High. You win. I'll ask Scott to round up some boys to unload the truck. Now," she tipped her head but held his gaze, "will you move out of my way?"

He immediately stepped to the side.

She didn't hesitate moving her round ass to the door, through it, disappearing in the shadows.

He stood there, looking into those shadows for far too long before he lifted his hand, tore his fingers through his hair, and moved to his truck.

He had eight of the twelve cases out and stacked by the door before the kid came back out with a bud.

They'd barely cleared the last box before he slammed the back down and moved to the cab.

He drove straight to Chaos, parked at the foot of the steps to the office of the garage, got out of his truck, and took the stairs two at a time.

Cherry's head snapped his way the minute he opened the door.

He saw hope there.

Then he saw her shut it down, assume a neutral expression, and lift her brows.

Oh yeah, he'd been played.

"Everything go okay?" she asked on a small smile.

"Don't," he replied, not even having come all the way in, standing in the open door.

This wouldn't take long but his message would be clear.

She looked uneasy before she asked, "Don't what?"

"Respect," he said softly. "You got it, Cherry. You know it. Don't lose it. Just don't. Hear?"

She swiveled her chair his way, starting, "High—"

"Don't," he repeated. "Hear?"

She stood. "I don't think you understand."

"No, babe. *You* don't understand. And I'm askin', Tyra, listen to me. I'm askin' for you to stop. No matter what she said to you. Stop."

He watched her brows knit and she asked, "What she said to me?"

He wasn't going there.

"Done with this," he told her. "And you're done with this. Then we're good. You're not done, we're not good, Cherry. And honest to fuck, I don't want that so don't make it that way."

Then he moved out of the door and kept moving even when he heard her call, "High!"

He jogged down the steps, got in his truck, and turned around in the forecourt even as he saw Cherry moving down the stairs.

He then drove out of Ride and didn't look back.

*   *   *

"You think she'll let it go?" Boz asked.

High and his brother were sitting at Boz's kitchen table, vodka bottle and glasses in front of them, no ice or mixers.

It wasn't that kind of night.

They were talking about Cherry.

And Millie.

Fucking Millie.

She was back.

Twenty years of her as a ghost in his head, haunting his memories, plaguing him, making him wonder how the fuck he was so goddamned stupid that he read it so fucking wrong.

And she was back.

Not a ghost.

Looking for him at Bill's.

Throwing herself at him.

Christ, when the bitch had pulled at his belt so she could get to his dick... *Christ.*

Shit like that, he could talk himself into forgetting.

He could talk himself into letting her have whatever the fuck she wanted... again.

Giving it all... again.

Just to have it back even if it was a lie.

Hell, he could talk himself into taking the pain, twenty more years of it, just so he could have it back.

Even if it was only for a day.

He poured more vodka in his glass, looked to Boz, and answered his question, "She's Cherry. No tellin' what she'll do."

Boz took up his own glass and threw back a slug, dropping it to the table, saying, "Tack'll talk some sense into her."

"Boz, brother, you been ridin' the Tack and Tyra train with the rest of us for almost a decade. Woman does what she does. He gets off on it. It's the way it is."

Boz leveled his gaze on High.

"It is," he said quietly, "in any other thing. But this is you, High. You and Tack got your history but this is you, a brother, *and* this is you and that cunt. He knows. He knows that bitch. Cherry does *not* know." His voice lowered further. "He'll talk some sense into her."

High tasted sour in his mouth, listening to Boz calling Millie those names.

He'd long since stopped wondering when that reaction would leave him. The automatic need to defend her. He was used to it now, and at least he no longer wanted to shove his fist down the throat of any man who referred to her that way. And in the beginning when the brothers had been so ticked at what she'd done, that had been a serious struggle.

High didn't reply to Boz mostly because there was nothing to say. With Cherry, especially if she and Millie had roped in Elvira and Lanie—the first crazier than the last, but not by much—there was no telling what would happen.

He just hoped none of those women pushed him too far. He liked them all. They were Chaos, even Elvira, who held no claim to a brother. Family was family and they were family, the kind that earned a thick thicker than blood.

But too far for a man like him was just too far.

He also didn't reply because he was done for the night.

So he took up his glass, threw back the vodka, then put it to the table.

"I'm turnin' in," he muttered, shoving his chair back.

"Right," Boz replied. "Later."

"Later, brother," High returned as he moved to the back

door, out it, down the long fence at the side of Boz's house and into the big space where Boz was letting him keep his RV.

This was where he was staying since he'd given the house to his recently made ex-wife, Deb. And this was something he'd done because he didn't want his girls' lives fucked any more than they already were.

Cleo, his oldest, was hanging in there. She was tough, like her dad. She was also smart. And she was his girl. She loved him completely. She loved her ma, too, but she was her dad's girl. And no matter how hard he and Deb tried to hide it, she'd sensed they weren't happy and now he sensed she was relieved it was over.

Which sucked.

Zadie was having problems. His baby girl had her head in the clouds in a way he could look back and see her in her crib, staring up at the mobile, not seeing that shit but seeing her tiny baby dreams. She didn't sense anything. His baby was ten years old and she believed she was going to marry a prince in a way that scared the fuck out of High because it was a way where she wasn't going to let go of that dream.

She never let go of any dream.

Like having a happy home with Mom and Dad together.

So she wasn't hanging in there. She hated that they'd split.

Which also sucked.

He needed to get them settled. Get in a house so the change didn't seem temporary. Get them their own room, a space that was theirs in a place that was his.

At twelve and ten, they needed their mom now, so he didn't go for half custody. They needed stability. They got their dad every other weekend.

He and Deb had made a deal. They weren't at each other's throats. They'd just lucked out and came to the conclusion at the same time that enough was enough. They didn't love each other, never did. He'd knocked her up and he was not the kind of man to let that responsibility slide when she said she was going to keep it and she'd needed him financially. So they got married.

But they liked each other and they both figured it would be better to end it still doing that than it turning bad, something, as both their lives slipped away in a marriage neither enjoyed, that was happening.

So Deb was good with him coming over for dinner. Going to the girls' recitals and sitting with her. Picking them up and having them at the Compound or taking them out for pizza or ice cream when it wasn't his time to have them.

He didn't get to see them every day, which didn't suck.

It totally blew.

But he needed to give them what they needed.

And when they needed their dad, when he had a place, when they felt safe there, when they got in a zone (or close to it) where they would become women and they'd have their mom right there when they did, a time Deb and he agreed would be when Cleo was fourteen and Zadie was twelve, they'd have their dad. So after two years that he knew would be two long years, they'd do half custody.

It was all in the agreement.

He just needed to find a fucking house and he didn't want to wait two years to do it.

His RV was the shit. Even Deb, who didn't agree with hardly anything he did the last thirteen years, dug that RV and she did this even knowing how much that fucker cost.

But he'd been living in it off Boz's house for nine months.

He needed to find a fucking house.

He got to the side door, unlocked it, went in, and powered her up.

He turned on one of the TVs (the thing had four, including one built into the outside) and sat to pull off his boots.

He didn't get the first one off before something caught his eye and he tensed.

Then instead of taking off his boot, he pulled the knife out of the side.

Slowly, he got up and moved to the cupboard, alert while opening it, reaching high, pushing aside the bag of flour that was there just to hide what was behind it. He reached in, grabbed his gun, and moved carefully down the hall, stopping in front of the bathroom.

Standing outside, cautiously, he curled his hand around the door and flipped on the light. Even more cautiously, he looked in.

And saw nothing.

He proceeded until he hit the bedroom.

He did the same thing as with the bathroom.

But no one was there.

Chaos didn't have many problems these days, not like back in the day when they had their allies . . . but they also had their enemies.

They did still have one problem, though. A big one. A psychopath with power called Benito Valenzuela who wanted to undo all the work Chaos had done to get clean and get their turf clean, work they'd kept strong now for years.

Things with Valenzuela had been quiet. But things had been coasting too long, the men were getting antsy and players in Denver weren't taking the Club seriously, so Chaos recently stepped up their maneuvers to warn him off, which meant all the brothers were on edge.

And these days with Millie back, High was on edge about a variety of things, not just Valenzuela.

He clenched his teeth and stared at the big blue plastic crate on his bed with its white top.

Then he made an annoyed noise in his throat when he saw a folded piece of paper on top with *High* written on it in Cherry's handwriting.

He'd loaned Tack and her the RV more than once for them to take the boys to stay at state parks and do other shit.

She had a key.

"Fuck," he muttered.

Shoving his gun in his back waistband, tossing the knife to the bed, he reached to the paper.

He unfolded it and read:

High,

Millie gave Lanie, Elvira, and me this crate. She said she couldn't bring herself to get rid of what's in it so she asked us to do it for her. When we saw what it was, we couldn't bring ourselves to do it either. I'm guessing, from our conversation today that you can.

So go for it.

I'm really sorry I stepped into it with you and Millie. I upset you and Millie was in a really bad way. Clearly, she also just wants to move on. I should have left it alone.

Now I'll leave it alone and I'll talk to Lanie and Elvira so they will too.

Sorry again, High.

xCherryx

Not wanting to but not able to stop himself, he flipped the latches, tossed back the lid, and sucked in breath at what he saw.

"Fuck," he whispered. "That fuckin' bitch."

He didn't waste time reaching beyond the crate, nabbing the lid to put it back on, and refastening it.

Then he stared at the crate.

Jesus, but she knew how to play the game. What was in that crate would have Cherry and her crew panting to dig in, do it deep and not quit until the job they wanted done got done.

He just did not get what she wanted. He didn't put it past her to come after him just because she was rabid for his cock. The lie they'd lived didn't include sex being fucking spectacular.

It was.

Every time.

And she'd panted for it.

Every time.

Maybe she'd hit a dry patch.

Maybe she was just bored.

He didn't give a fuck.

Whatever it was, he had to shut it down.

Why she kept those pictures, he had no clue, except she kept everything. Concert stubs. Half-ripped movie tickets. Ribbons from gifts. Plastic cups with their names written on them from parties. Strings of Christmas lights that didn't work that she was *sure* she could fix if she could find the blown bulb (then she never found the blown bulb, but the woman tried, sitting on the floor pulling out one and sticking in another for fucking hours).

And every picture taken of them together, even if it was out of focus or one of their faces was cut off or half the shot was obscured by a finger.

Those didn't make her albums but she didn't get rid of them.

She kept them.

All of them.

For twenty years.

And she'd found a use for them.

He lifted the crate, hauled it through the RV, set it down to open the door, and then tossed it out into the cold. He heard it land with a thud but paid it no more mind as he shut the door and locked it.

Then he went back to taking off his boots, doing it thinking again that he had no idea why she'd come back. He had no idea what she wanted from him. He didn't even fucking care.

He just knew she was all in to get it.

And no man could fight a war and win without information.

He thought he knew Millie Cross twenty years ago, but he didn't.

He didn't know dick about her now.

So he reached into his back pocket, pulled out his phone, went to his contacts, and touched the screen to connect.

He put the phone to his ear.

"Tell me you're callin' to set up a game," Shirleen Jackson said into his ear.

"Take your money anytime you want," he replied.

She drew out her, "Please."

But she was all bluff. This was why she was always losing. That and the fact he could read her hand by looking at her face.

Hell, the woman used to run poker games in Denver and she was the worst player he'd known.

But now she was also the receptionist at Nightingale Investigations, the premier private investigation firm in the entire Rocky Mountain region.

And she was a friend.

Shirleen and High had history. She'd do anything for him and he'd return the favor.

It wasn't about markers.

It was about bond. The kind circumstances in life can make that can't be broken.

She'd been dirty.

He had too.

But she'd been dirty when she'd had only her nephew at her back.

He'd been dirty when he'd had all his brothers at his, but the Club was broken.

He still had his brothers and she'd only had Darius.

Darius was loyal and he was smart but he was only one man, one man Shirleen felt the need to protect.

So there was a time when there was no one to protect Shirleen.

Except High.

He'd done it.

She'd never forgotten it.

And she was the kind of woman who never would.

"Need somethin'," he told her.

"Hit me," she invited like he knew she would.

"Anything and everything you can dig up on Millicent Anna Cross. Female. Forty-one. Lives in Denver. I'll text you what else I got on her that'll make it easier on you. But first, I'll need an address."

"You got it," she replied.

"Boys aren't in this, Shirleen," he told her. "Nightingale or any of them. You keep this on the down low. Only you know. Yeah?"

"Yeah, High," she agreed, then asked probingly, "You good?"

He didn't hesitate to give it to her.

"In a game I don't wanna be in but I'm in it, and this time, I intend to win."

"Right," she said quietly. Then, quieter, "Met you after it was over, boy, but anyone who was a player in Denver back then knew you had a girl named Millie."

He drew in a deep breath.

Then he said, "Just get me what you can get."

"Okay, High."

He rested back against the cushions of the couch. "We'll set up a game soon."

"Just don't bring Hound. Sure that boy's a cheat," she muttered.

With anyone else, that kind of slur against a brother would invite retribution.

But for High, Shirleen was family, so nothing invited retribution.

"Hound sniffs out a game, no stoppin' him from showin'."

"Whatever," she muttered. "Now, we gonna shoot the shit or you gonna let me get my beauty rest?"

"Wouldn't dream of disturbin' your beauty rest."

"Already did, boy."

After delivering that, she hung up.

High took the phone from his ear and grinned at it.

Then he tossed it on the cushion beside him and saw the stack of dishes in the sink where he'd left them that morning telling himself he'd take care of them that night.

He wasn't going to wash dishes.

He was going to hit the sack.

This he didn't delay in doing.

The RV was a mess.

But his sheets were clean. He'd made sure of that in order to wash Millie's scent away.

Unfortunately, in the dark, lying in the bed where he'd had her ass in his hands, his tat on her back inescapable so he'd eventually had to cover it with his hand so he could concentrate on coming instead of fucking her for as long as he could, even if he managed to do it until his last breath, he couldn't keep his mind off her.

Cleo and Zadie.

Deb had picked his oldest girl's name, High had picked his baby's.

Neither of them were anywhere near the ten names he and Millie had picked out.

Five for boys. Five for girls. That way they were sure to be covered whatever happened.

Her two top picks for girls were her two grandmothers' names.

Katherine and Ruth.

Katy and Ruthy.

He wondered if her girls were with her now or with some ex.

He clenched his teeth at that idea but that didn't stop the thoughts, which included wondering, if she'd instead had boys, if she'd picked the top names they'd decided. Flynn and Chance.

He wouldn't put it past her, even though giving another man's kids his boys' names would be beyond the pale, even for her.

But she'd been rabid about picking the right names. Three fucking years they went over it. It was like a game, one they both enjoyed, going from the bizarre to the sublime in choices, trying to make each other laugh, but also being serious, settling in on some, rearranging favorites, until they were sure.

But they never quit talking about it, running a name by the other just to see if it'd make the cut.

Until a couple months before she sent him packing.

Then she'd quit doing it and any discussion they had about it when he did was stiff and forced, like she wanted him to think she was still into it when she absolutely wasn't.

He hadn't really noticed at the time.

Like Zadie, he was living in a dreamworld.

Then Millie booted him out.

And now here he was, forty-four years old and he'd fucked up huge along the way. He'd had a loveless marriage that lasted for thirteen years. He'd had so many close calls of so many different varieties that could have bought him a different life, or an early death, it wasn't fucking funny.

But out of his life he still had his brothers and he had his two girls.

And he'd had three years living a dream.

A dream that was a lie.

But at least it felt like a dream before he found out it was a lie and he'd take that.

In High's life since he'd lost Millie, he'd take it.

And be glad for it.

Twenty-three years earlier, Chaos Compound common room…

"She's it for you, ain't she, High?"

At Black's words, Logan tore his eyes off Millie, who was across the room with Chew, giggling as Chew's tarantula crawled all over her.

Chew's tarantula and the fact he had seven of those fuckers and had always had one—by his word even since he was a little kid—being why the brother was called "Chew."

"So light!" Millie cried. "And furry. She tickles!"

Chew grinned at her in a way Logan didn't like but he didn't do anything about it because he knew, even though Chew clearly had a thing for his girl, she was Logan's girl and Chew was his brother. Not only would Millie not act on it, Chew wouldn't either.

Millie looked to him. "Logan! We need a tarantula!"

He did not want a fucking tarantula.

But if she wanted one, he'd get it for her.

He did not say this.

He just grinned.

She turned back to the spider crawling up the arm she had lifted in front of her face.

Logan turned to Black, who was standing with him, as was Tack.

"Yep," he answered.

"Moved in fast," Tack muttered, eyeing him, friendly but there was concern.

Logan liked Tack but the brother freaked him because he was like a genius or something. He saw shit others did not see. And he thought not a step ahead, or two, or five, but fifty.

There was trouble brewing because of that.

A man like Tack was not a soldier.

A man like Tack was a leader.

All the men knew it.

Including their current president, Crank, who didn't like it.

"Yep," Logan repeated, answering Tack's question, because he was right.

Millie and him were living together and had been for a couple of weeks. She was in school and had a part-time job. He'd been initiated into the Club officially and had a brother's cut of Club profits.

So it was all good, by his way of thinking.

That said, her parents had been ticked they'd moved in together. They'd agreed to cover her tuition, pay for books, but because she'd moved in with him, done it quick and done it without a ring on her finger, they were giving nothing else.

This meant Logan was covering her even though she was working her ass off, both at school and at the shit job she had at a store in the mall that she took so she wouldn't have to lean on him too much.

He didn't give a fuck.

He went to bed beside her, he woke up beside her, she was his. She could quit and sit around watching television and eating M&M's all day for all he cared. As long as she smiled at him like she smiled at him, like no other man breathed on the planet, he'd take care of her.

"Good choice," Black noted, and Logan gave him his attention to see Black had eyes on Millie. "Face of it, she ain't no old lady." His gaze slid to Logan. "Deep down, where that shit needs to be, she's all about it."

"Yep," Logan said again because this was true.

She was all about family. Hers. His. The one they were going to make one day.

So, yes. Definitely.

She was all about it.

Old lady through and through.

But only because he was a biker. She'd be what he needed her to be.

That was Millie.

"Happy for you, brother," Tack said. "Your age, men don't find the right one." He clapped Logan on the shoulder. "You did."

Logan jerked up his chin.

"Yeah, I did," he agreed.

Another giggle erupted from Millie and all the men's eyes went to her.

She now had two of Chew's tarantulas crawling all over her.

And she loved it.

And Logan loved her. He didn't give a fuck what it said,

how impossible it was that was the case since they'd only been together a couple of months. He fell in love the minute he laid eyes on her. More in love at her first "hey." Then more when she told him her name. And more when she looked so adorably hurt when she thought he was laughing at it.

And then more.

And even more.

It'd go on forever, he knew it.

Every day until he died, he'd fall more in love with her.

He'd been a lucky fuck and he knew it. He had a good family. Left that, had some fun, caused some trouble, found Chaos, and earned himself a new family.

Then he found Millie.

Yeah, he was a lucky fuck.

And staring at Millie with her tarantulas, feeling his lips twitch, he knew it.

CHAPTER SIX

You'll Give

Millie

AFTER I PLOPPED the sour cream into the bubbling contents of the skillet, my phone rang.

I looked to it, saw it was Dottie calling, and snatched it up. I put the phone to my ear as I reached for the Dijon mustard.

"Hey, babe," I greeted.

"You rang," my sister replied as I squirted mustard into the bubbling sauce.

I had earlier that day, leaving a voicemail.

"Yeah," I said. "Listen, I need a favor."

"You know the drill," she replied instantly. "You need it, free babysitting and that's gonna happen soon, seeing as Alan and I are *really* in need of a date night."

Two kids, both young, I knew that to be true.

Then again, it was always true. Dottie and Alan had been dating for years, pre-marriage, post-marriage, that's the way they were.

I liked that for my sister.

My sister liked it too. And she wanted it for me.

"Done," I told her, stirring my brew, talking to my sister, listening to Macy Gray from the new dock I'd bought, my candles burning, the steak and mushrooms already done and set to go in when the sauce was complete, the noodles resting in their water, ready to drain.

Then it was all a go.

Homemade beef Stroganoff.

It was smelling divine.

I just hoped it tasted the same way.

"What do you need?" Dottie asked.

"Okay, listen," I began. "I went to that Pilates place and don't let the pictures of people sitting on their asses bending around fool you. That shit is *hard*. But I got a wild hair, bought a five-session pass. I will not go again...*ever*...if you aren't here in workout clothes, guilting me into doing it. So the favor is, I need you to bring the guilt. Don't make me waste four sessions."

I finished talking, asking this favor knowing it wouldn't be hard. Dottie was a mother. Guilt, I suspected, for women was a specialty that was latent until you birthed your first baby. Then it kicked in full-force. I suspected this because it had happened with Dot.

But even though I stopped talking, Dottie didn't start.

"Dot?" I called, pinching some salt and pepper into my sauce.

"You went to that Pilates place?" she asked softly.

I stopped moving and stared at my counter.

"Yeah," I replied softly.

"I…" I heard her clear her throat. "Sure, I'll do Pilates with you."

Her tone was hesitant. Hopeful, but hesitant.

She knew what Pilates meant.

She knew what anything outside of me snarfing down fast food and watching reality TV meant.

"I'm done, Dot," I told her.

"Done?" she asked, still hesitant, still hopeful.

Damn, but I'd put her through the wringer.

I needed to stop doing that.

And finally, I was going to.

"It's time to move on."

She said nothing.

I was sure she was shocked. This had never happened. I might have talked about it. I definitely thought about it (daily).

But I'd never done a thing about it.

"Did… something happen?" she queried.

"Yeah," I gave her the truth. "A lot, actually. And I'll explain it later. I don't…" I shook my head even if she couldn't see me. "I don't wanna get into it. I'll share it one day but in the end, it doesn't really matter. In the end, it's just time. Long past time. So there it is."

In that speech, I'd lied.

It mattered.

Logan using me, taking advantage for his revenge fuck, then speaking to me the way he did, killing what we had, turning love to hate.

That mattered.

But it was done.

He hated me and there was nothing I could say that would change that. And the way he'd treated me—like what we had never happened, like what we shared wasn't everything, like all of that didn't buy me some kindness or at least some patience or at the *very* least some silence so I could share what I needed to share—it was inexcusable.

So it was over.

I was done walking through fire for that man.

And I wasn't wasting another moment of my life on him.

I was going to change.

Finally.

I'd made that decision after the debacle at Wild Bill's and that decision was cemented after what happened Saturday morning before the King's Shelter event.

I was all in.

My larder was stocked.

I'd gone to the mall and bought clothes for inside and outside workouts.

I'd also bought a little black dress.

And the aforementioned speaker dock.

And the night before, I'd given myself a luxurious pedicure, unearthing my foot tub out of its box to do it.

My five-session pass for the Pilates center was purchased.

My first session was under my belt.

I was making fabulous-smelling, and I hoped would be fabulous-tasting, beef Stroganoff.

And I was thinking of getting a cat (or two) for company.

Yes, I was all in.

New life.

New me.

New beginning.

All to write a new future.

Out of the rut.

And on to something good.

(I hoped.)

"I don't know what to say," Dottie said in my ear.

"Nothing to say anymore." I dropped my voice and kept stirring my sauce. "You've said it all, babe. I just never listened. Or if I did, it just didn't sink in. It's sunk in."

"It's seeing Logan," she guessed.

"Yes."

I did not lie about that, just my answer encompassed a whole truth she didn't know.

Her voice was stronger when she said, "Then it's good that happened. It didn't seem good at the time but every woman has her limits. Every woman finds her time. You seeing him, hearing him, knowing he moved on, has kids, is doing okay, that was it for you. So that's good."

She was right. That *part* was good.

For Logan.

But I didn't care or, more aptly, was determined to move toward not caring.

However, that thought was a good one to have.

I'd think of him that way, rather than the total asshole he'd been.

I'd think of him doing okay. Enjoying his kids. Being with his brothers.

And I'd find my things to enjoy.

Like beef Stroganoff.

"You're right, Dottie," I replied. "Now, I gotta add the mushrooms and steak to the sauce before it gets too thick."

"You're cooking?" She sounded shocked.

"New leaf, haven't you heard?" I teased. "I mean, I *did* just mention it two seconds ago."

"Kiss my butt," she retorted, as she'd done since I was six and she was eight.

"Show it, I'll kiss it," I replied, as I'd done since she was eight and I was six.

"Whatever. If that stuff you're making is good, then you're making it for Alan, the kids, and me."

"You're on."

"Awesome. Later, Mill."

"Later, Dot. Love you."

"Love you too, babe."

She rang off.

I set my phone aside and picked up the platter with the seared beef and sautéed mushrooms.

I added it to the sauce.

I stirred.

I tipped it over the drained noodles and ate it with a delicious glass of red wine poured into one of my fabulous red wineglasses that I hadn't pulled out in probably three years.

And it was divine.

*   *   *

"Holy crap, this is *Dynasty* except British with a better wardrobe and set in the early 1900s," I whispered to the TV.

My kitchen was clean. My candles still burning. Only one lamp was lit, along with my gas fireplace, giving the room a warm, cozy glow.

And I was sitting, curled up on my couch, wineglass in hand, into my third episode of *Downton Abbey*.

Violet was a stitch.

And I was *so* organizing a party where people had to wear clothes from the early 1900s.

The costumes were amazing!

Violet had just drolly let out another humdinger and I was giggling at it when my doorbell rang.

I turned and looked over my shoulder toward the hall that led to the rest of my house, including my foyer.

It was late but I was not surprised my bell had sounded.

This happened. It happened when Dottie got fed up with

Alan thinking that being a stay-at-home mom was a cushy job so he could come home, watch TV, scratch his crotch, and leave her on duty. She'd teach him by coming to my place, bitching, leaving him home on duty with the kids.

He'd learn.

Then he'd forget.

As was, according to Dottie, her lot since he was a man. They forgot stuff like that.

Repeatedly.

It also could be Justine, who worked but only part-time and her partner, Veronica, had a higher paying, higher stress, full-time job and Veronica felt the same way about Justine taking care of their son.

Thus she also had that lesson to teach, did it on occasion, Veronica learned and Veronica had a vagina but apparently she also had a short memory because she often forgot too.

Further, it could be Kellie, who did not have a partner (at the moment). However, she did have a life motto to have a good time *all the time* and even after all these years of shutting myself away, she never gave up. If she got a wild hair to try to drag me into her good time, she swung around my place in an effort to do just that.

Or it could be Claire, my assistant, who was a serial dater and seemed surprised when the men in her life found out about the other men in her life and didn't like it and then dumped her and broke her heart (ish). Claire also had a short memory since this happened frequently and she hadn't learned to come clean early that none of her relationships were exclusive.

As I set my wine aside and got up, I was guessing Kellie or Claire. It was way too late for it to be Dottie or Justine. My niece and nephew were nine and four. Justine and Veronica's little boy was eight months.

With the kids down, they'd totally be in bed by now doing one thing or the other.

I moved to the foyer, walked down it, and stared at my door, which was mostly a window covered in a beautiful sheer gathered at the top and bottom.

But I did this with my heart beginning to pump faster.

This was because the motion sensor light outside had lit and there was an unmistakable man's body silhouetted through the sheer.

I didn't stop moving toward the door, however, because I could not believe this.

It was past ten o'clock on a Monday night and he'd been a total asshole to me the last two times he'd seen me in a way I couldn't decide which time was worse since they both were *the worst*.

And here he was.

Logan.

Standing at my front door!

No, I absolutely did not stop moving.

I was too angry for that.

I went right to the door, unlocked it, and hauled it open.

I instantly looked up at him and demanded, "Are you serious?"

"Your door is a fuckin' window," he replied in an irate growl.

I blinked, my anger tamped down with confusion at his unexpected words.

"What?" I asked.

"Your *door* is a *goddamned window*," he bit off.

"So?" I asked.

His head tipped to the side in an intimidating way. "So?"

"Yeah," I snapped, back to angry, thus totally unintimidated. "So?"

"You know how easy it is to break into a house with a window in the goddamned front door?" he asked.

"No," I answered. "But I'm certain you do," I finished nastily.

"Yeah," he clipped, leaning slightly toward me. "I do. It's

fuckin' easy, which means this shit," he threw a hand toward my open door, "is unsafe."

"Are you telling me that you've shown up at my home after ten at night when you said you never wanted to see me again to tell me my front door is unsafe?" I asked incredulously.

"No," he stated. "I came for another reason."

Before I could ask what that was, he turned, bent, I got a view of his ass in his jeans I did *not* want because it was too good for words, then he straightened, hefting something up and turning back to me.

Dear Lord in heaven, he had that *stupid* crate.

Those crazy women who came to visit me gave him that *stupid* crate.

Damn it!

"You've got to be kidding me," I said on an annoyed snap.

"Nope," High replied, and pushed in, *right* in, doing it so I had no choice but to leap out of his way as he angled sideways to get him and the crate through the front door. And then, when he was through, he kept on walking.

"I did not ask you into my home," I called after him as he stopped at the hall, looked right, looked left, then turned left, toward the living room.

"Don't give a fuck," he replied as he disappeared.

I made a frustrated noise, closed the door, and stomped after him.

By the time I hit the living room, he was standing in it, box at his feet and he was looking around.

I rounded him angrily, opening my mouth to tell him to get the fuck out, when his eyes cut to me and he spoke.

"Christ, you live on a movie set," he noted with disgust.

"It's pretty," I snapped.

"It's perfect," he returned, like that was a bad thing.

"Yes, it is, utterly," I agreed. "Now—"

"And what's that smell?" He looked around and sniffed and

I got even *more* annoyed because only Logan could sniff and do it looking manly and yummy. "It smells like flowers and onions."

"Not onions," I kept snapping. "*Shallots*," I stated like any fool could tell the difference and his eyes came back to me. "And the flower smell is coming from my candles. Lavender. It's soothing."

"It's sickening," he replied.

"It...is...*not*," I shot back indignantly.

"It fucking is," he retorted.

"God!" I shouted, throwing out my hands. "Why are we talking about how my house smells?" I narrowed my eyes and swiftly kept speaking so he wouldn't answer since I didn't care about his answer. I cared about another answer. So I asked *that* question. "And why are you *here*?"

"Here to return this shit." He toed the box with his boot but didn't take his eyes off me. "And to warn you *again* to stop pullin' this shit."

"Then I'll say *again* I'm not pulling *any* shit," I declared.

"And I'll repeat, I don't believe you," he stated.

"And *I'll* repeat, I don't care," I returned.

He took a step toward me and I took a step back, eyes locked to his.

He hesitated, his head again tilting in that strangely intimidating way, then he kept coming at me.

I kept retreating.

He started speaking as we moved.

"It was a good play, usin' that crate. What's inside guaranteeing good women will go all out to have your back. But it's still a play. You know it. I know it."

I hit wall.

He invaded my space, tipping his chin way down to keep my gaze.

And he kept talking, lower, rougher, and his tone was more intimidating than any head tilt.

"You need to release Tyra before your shit causes Club shit, which you know, Millie, will be seriously uncool."

"And, again, High, I am *not* playing some game where I pulled Tyra or her friends in to help me do *anything*," I told him. "So you can repeat that until the cows come home but I can't control her. Hell, I don't even *know* her."

"You knew her enough to give her that box."

"*She* came *here*," I shared. "I did not ask her. I barely spoke to her. I asked her to get *rid* of that crate. Not give it to *you*."

"You knew what she'd do when she saw what was inside," he derided. "She's a sister." His face dipped closer and his voice went quiet. "You got a pussy, baby, know that pussy, tasted it, fucked it, so know you definitely got a pussy. That means you knew what she'd do."

God, he was *such* an asshole.

"You're disgusting," I announced bitingly.

"You didn't think I was disgusting when you were on your knees for me," he returned, still quiet, still close.

But it was the wrong thing to say, reminding me how he'd used me for his revenge fuck.

Very wrong.

And so I was done.

Done.

"Move back," I snapped.

His eyes dropped to my mole and, *damn it*, the insides of my thighs started tingling, even though I was *done*.

"Got a mind to change yours about how disgusting you think I am," he murmured distractedly.

"Move back, High," I warned, and on his name, his eyes sliced to mine.

"That name's not yours to use," he grated.

"If you leave, I won't use it," I fired back.

"Got a lesson to teach," he returned, and my belly curled.

Oh God.

What did that mean?

"Move back," I repeated, my voice weakening with fear and something else a whole lot different.

"Give you what you want," he said, his gaze again dropping to my mole, his voice again going soft. "Give you what you want so you'll give up the game."

"This is no game," I whispered what I knew for certain to be the truth, and he looked into my eyes again.

"Oh yeah it is, Millie. And this time, *I'm* gonna get what *I* want when *I win*."

Oh God!

This was not happening.

And suddenly, his mouth was on mine.

God.

It was happening.

I twisted my head away, lifted my hands to his chest, and pushed hard, shouting, "Move back!"

His torso swung away at my shove but then it swung right back in as the rest of his big body got closer, pinning me to the wall at the same time his hand came up and fisted in my ponytail, giving it a gentle-rough jerk that caught my attention.

It also caught my body's attention and more than my inner thighs started tingling.

"Do not pull away from me," he growled.

"Please leave," I begged, not above that.

Oh no, I was not above begging at all.

I had to stop this.

Immediately.

And I'd do anything.

"Not until I make my play."

"High—" I started another plea but stopped when his eyes fired, his hand in my hair pulled my head back, and his mouth came back down on mine, crushing it, pushing my lips against my teeth so I had a funny taste in my mouth.

But I felt High.

And I *smelled* him.

His body to mine, his hand in my hair, his lips on mine, his scent, all this permeated my anger and fear and when it did, it weakened my resolve.

But it didn't kill it.

I had enough left to twist away so his lips slid up to my cheekbone.

"You're hurting me."

He positioned me to facing him using my hair and went back in, not for a kiss, to nip my bottom lip with his teeth.

I went still.

Because it wasn't hurtful.

It was *playful*.

Logan was playful a lot when we'd been together.

A lot.

Especially sexually.

I loved it. I missed it when it was gone in a way that I craved it.

And there it was.

Oh...

Fuck.

"Then I'll quit doin' that," he whispered, and went back in.

He quit doing that. His mouth on mine was hard, it was demanding, but it wasn't painful.

It was coaxing.

Oh man.

"Logan," I murmured against his lips, unable to stop it.

"And she gives it," he muttered against mine, then swept his tongue into my mouth.

I tasted him and when I did, it hit me.

He wanted this. He'd come for it. No matter what it was for him, he'd found out where I lived and he'd come for it.

Teaching a lesson.

Playing a game.

It didn't matter.

Because for me, outside those I gave myself, I'd had only one orgasm in twenty years and Logan had given it to me.

He was intent on giving me another one?

Fuck it.

I'd take it.

But this time, I'd go in knowing what this was.

He'd used me before.

I'd use him now.

There were worse ways to end a brilliant evening of delicious food, fine wine, and Britain's classy version of soap opera.

Right?

My decision made, I slid my hands up to the sides of his neck, held on, and kissed him back.

He growled into my mouth and pressed me deeper into the wall.

I glided a hand up into his hair and pressed myself farther into his body.

He pulled my hair again so he'd broken the kiss and twisted my head to the side.

Lips to the skin right below my ear, his words caused shivers when he asked, "You want this?"

"You gonna give it?" I dared.

He nipped my earlobe with his teeth and right in my ear, he snarled, "Fuck yeah."

"Then do it," I challenged.

He righted my head, catching my eyes, his glittering with fury and heat.

"Bedroom," he grunted.

"Last door at the end of the hall."

He instantly let me go but grabbed my hand and I fought the bittersweet memories of the feel of his fingers around mine as he moved away and did it tugging me after him.

Like he'd been there before, the minute we entered my

room, he flipped the light switch and the crystal-based lights on the nightstands on either side of my bed came on, casting an intimate glow to my bedroom.

This was not good.

The last time, heat of the moment, I didn't even think of my body or, more importantly, what Logan would think of my body.

This time, I was turned on, I wanted this, but I was not out of my mind with want.

So I thought that my body was not twenty-one anymore. It was forty-one.

I had no idea how it had changed since then because I didn't pay a lot of attention.

I just knew a single session of Pilates kicked its ass.

"Lights off," I ordered as he kept tugging me, straight to my bed.

He pulled me around so we were facing each other, sides to the bed, and he shook his head.

"No, baby. I make you come, I'm gonna watch."

Fuck.

"High—" I started but got no further.

He released my hand so he could catch me at the side of my neck and yank me to him.

I fell into his body as his mouth crashed back to mine.

And it was on.

I didn't care about the lights anymore.

He wanted to see me?

Well, I wanted to see him.

All of him.

So I went after that, tugging his cut down his arms, then tearing at his clothes.

He copped feels, took bites, licked tastes as he let me at the same time he tore at mine.

We fell to the bed, him only in jeans, belt, and first two buttons on his fly undone, me in nothing but panties and a bra.

The second we hit mattress, I went after him.

God, I couldn't get enough.

The feel of his chest hair against my lips, his nipples tightening against my tongue, the ridges of his abs contracting at my touch.

He had new tattoos, several of them, and I wanted to discover them in a variety of ways.

But at that moment, other things took precedence.

In no time, I needed more of those particular things and went for it, fingers to the final buttons of his fly.

"Fuck no," he rumbled, his hand catching my wrist and my eyes flew to him. "This time I get to eat."

Ripples shot over my thighs.

I wanted that.

But I *needed* what I was going after.

"Me first," I returned.

"No way," he shot back.

"Way," I snapped.

He used his hand at my wrist to lift it, then when I locked my arm, he shoved it, successfully taking me to my back.

Before he could move over and pin me, I planted a foot in the bed and heaved, putting all my weight and strength into it, rolling him to his back with me on top.

He began to buck his powerful body to roll me again, something he'd achieve if I didn't stop it, so I shot up, straddling him and clamping my thighs to his hips.

He angled up with me, catching both my wrists and rolling his hips, pushing up farther, until he made his knees.

"*Fuck*," I hissed, grappling against his fingers wrapped around my wrists, catching his triumphant, hot-as-hell grin as he fell forward.

I hit the bed on my back with him on me, his hips between my legs and my head dangling off the end of the bed.

With his superior strength, he forced my hands to the bed at my shoulders as his lips hit my neck.

"Stop fighting it," he murmured.

Then he ran his tongue along my jugular.

So nice.

"Kiss off," I spat.

I heard and felt his chuckle.

So nice.

"God!" I snapped.

Logan nipped my collarbone, hands still holding my wrists to the bed.

I pushed against them, bucking my lower body, succeeding only in lifting us both off the bed an inch until his weight bearing mine down forced me to give up and we collapsed back to the mattress.

He slid his lips (and tongue) down my chest.

Destination: breast.

Knowing that, my body wanted to still, quit fighting, feel Logan's mouth on me again like that. He was good at that. He'd given me a lot of that back in the day because he liked it but more, because I *loved* it.

The problem with that was, I couldn't quit fighting and not only because something I didn't get was at stake and whatever that was, I couldn't lose.

But because this whole thing was a massive turn-on.

Unable to fight him any other way, I demanded, "My bra stays on."

"Whatever," he muttered, necessarily his hands having to move down as his body did, but they took mine with them.

Then I felt him nudge my nipple with his lips.

That was when I stilled.

"Oh yeah," he whispered, feeling it, hunger and victory in his tone.

I forced another buck, but that one was feeble.

I wanted his mouth on me.

I felt his tongue lap my nipple through my bra.

Yes.

I made a soft noise in my throat.

"Fuck *yeah*," he growled, and went in, sucking my nipple into his mouth over my bra.

That was when I arched, unintentionally (or perhaps not) forcing it in farther and he sucked harder.

"Logan," I moaned.

He let my hands go and shoved his under me, pushing up so I was compelled to remain arched, offering my chest to him.

I didn't fight it.

I drove my fingers into his hair.

He took one hand from around me and used it to pull down my bra.

And he had me, nothing in between.

"*Logan*," I gasped.

He went at me and kept doing it until I had fingers clutched in his hair. Then he moved to the other nipple and kept at me until I was squirming.

When he had me that way, he let go and lifted away.

I raised my head from where it was dangling off the end of the mattress and looked into his heated face right before he clamped his hands on my hips and dragged me down the bed so my head was no longer hanging.

Then, watching my face, he hauled my panties down my legs.

I closed my eyes in happy anticipation.

Logan opened my thighs.

He positioned in between and I tensed, waiting, ready, so *fucking* ready.

"Want it?" he asked.

God, he was going to make me say it.

Whatever.

Who cared?

I did want it and I'd get it, so what did it matter?

"Yes," I breathed.

He dragged his tongue through my pulsing wet.

Oh yes.

"More?" he asked.

God, this was hot.

"Yes, Logan," I whispered.

He lapped at me.

Yes.

"More, baby?" he asked.

Hot.

"Yes, Logan. *Please*," I begged.

He dipped in and went at me.

I lifted my knees, spread my legs wide, drove my pussy into his mouth and gloried in it.

He took his mouth from me, nipped my inner thigh with his teeth, and asked warningly, "Where should your legs be?"

So.

So.

So.

Hot.

I shifted them over his shoulders where he liked them so he could feel from the tension in my legs, my heels digging in his back, how much I liked what he was doing to me.

He cupped my ass, murmured, "Damn straight," pulled me to him, and went back in.

That time, he didn't stop.

He ate and he licked and he sucked and he darted his tongue inside until it built so high, it scared me.

"No more," I begged, squirming under him like I was trying to get away at the same time push closer.

"Take it," he growled into my pussy, and kept at me.

I slid my fingers into his hair. "Baby," I whispered, the word trembling as my body did the same, top to toe.

He latched on to my clit with his mouth, dragged his tongue tight over it, then sucked hard.

I was right.

Too much.

And perfect.

I dug my heels into his back, fisted my fingers in his hair, and exploded on a sharp cry that rang through the room.

He kept sucking and I kept flying.

He added fingers, driving them inside and my cries came again but softer, in pants, my heels plowing into his back, my head twisted to the side, my hand clutching his hair.

Then he stopped and I desperately drew in air, gathering up the pieces to pull myself together only to lose hold as his cock slammed deep.

"Look at me while I fuck you," he rumbled, his hand going into my hair to force me to do as told.

I caught his fired eyes, took his thick, hard cock, panting and whimpering as he fucked me.

"What you want?" he asked roughly.

"More," I forced out through harsh breaths.

He kept thrusting, hitching a knee to put more power into it, holding me in place with his hand in my hair, his weight on me, and I put a foot to the bed to plant myself to take him at the same time I wrapped my other leg around his thigh to anchor myself to him.

I began gasping.

"What you want?" he repeated, and it sounded like a groan.

It took a lot but I managed a breathless, "Harder."

His hips drove into mine and it was so beautiful, my eyes shut so I could focus on nothing but the feeling of Logan and me connecting, deep, brutal, driven.

"You kiss me before you come, Millie," he ordered, his voice so rough, it scored my skin like sandpaper.

And I fucking loved it.

"I—" I gasped, forcing my eyes open and looking into his,

seeing it was close for him, too, feeling him getting closer, this taking me over the edge. "Okay," I breathed, lifted my head, and pressed my mouth to his.

My whimper slid down his throat as his tongue drove inside.

I took that and the latest orgasm he gave me before his drives turned to pounds. He released my mouth, yanked my hair back, my neck arched, and he shoved his face in the side where he groaned while he bucked inside me and shot deep.

I closed my eyes and took it, loving it, my head turning, lips tipping up into a smile.

I gloried in his uneven breaths wisping across my skin, his cock buried, his chest hair gently scratching my breasts, his weight on me.

Then he asked my neck, "You covered with birth control?"

Was I ever.

But he'd come inside.

The last time, after that night at Wild Bill's, it had been another agony, coming home and washing him away from me.

This night, it wouldn't be.

He might have come to win this bizarre battle we'd somehow gotten locked into.

But no way was he the victor.

No *fucking* way.

"Yeah," I answered. "You covered with STDs?" I asked.

It was nasty but even if it was too late, it was necessary.

He lifted his head and I rearranged my features before I righted mine and caught his guarded eyes with my own.

"Could ask the same," he stated.

I gave a slight shrug. "No worries here."

"Same," he grunted, staring down at me, not moving.

I stared up at him and this went on for a while before I let my lips curve and I taunted quietly, "Feel like a winner, baby?"

He pressed his hips deep and involuntarily my lips parted, this driving his return taunt home. "Absolutely, darlin'."

I gathered my shit together and stated coldly, "Then I suppose we're done...for now."

Without a word or any hesitation, he pulled out and rolled off.

I immediately pushed up, catching him on his back, lifting his hips to pull up his jeans.

God, Logan in my bed doing that?

That was hot too.

I tore my eyes away from his beautiful cock, still hard and glistening with him and me.

Sitting on the bed, I righted my bra and reached under my pillow to get my pj's, thrilled they were a good set. A shimmery green, silky knit with scads and scads of fancy teal lace. Pants and a cami. The lace on the pants around the hems and cutting up the outsides of the legs all the way up to my upper thighs.

I pulled on the cami, then got out of bed and yanked on the pants.

Not looking at him, I strolled as casually as I could muster into my bathroom.

I hurriedly found what I was looking for and strolled back to find him sitting on the end of my bed, jeans done up, pulling on his boots.

I bent at the knees in a ladylike squat, capturing his wrist, and tugged his arm to me.

I also got his gaze.

I ignored it, pulled the top off my lipstick with my lips, spit it out, and rolled up the tube.

Then I wrote my cell phone number down the inside of his forearm.

I let him go, nabbed the top from the floor, and rolled the stick down, capping it as I turned my eyes to him.

"Anytime you want more, tiger, you know how to get me," I whispered.

"I'll take it," he rumbled.

"Good," I continued whispering, playing a game I didn't understand, terrified of it but not about to let him get the best of me.

Not again.

Not *ever* again.

"Use you up," he promised, a threat that was also a turn-on.

"Can't wait," I replied.

"You'll give," he declared.

I faked misunderstanding. "Oh yeah, I will."

"You'll give, Millie," he growled.

It was my turn to promise.

"Until you can't take any more."

He made a noise that sounded like it came from deep in his chest, a roll of fury and hunger.

My win.

I smiled, straightened, and wandered back to the bathroom, saying, "I'll lock up after you leave."

I stopped in the bathroom door and turned back to him.

He was still sitting on the end of my bed, shirtless, his elbows to his knees, eyes to me, looking sated at the same time pissed.

And beautiful.

"And take that fucking crate with you," I ordered. "I don't want that shit in my house."

Then I walked into the bathroom and shut the door.

I waited a long time, cleaning him from me, then listening to see if I could hear him leave.

I couldn't hear anything.

So I took a chance when I left the bathroom.

Logan was gone.

I walked to the foyer and locked the front door.

Then I walked to the living room to blow out the candles and turn off the fire and the lights.

The crate was still there.

"Shit," I whispered, staring at it, displeased.

I left it there, did what I had to do, and went to bed.

I slept like a baby.

But I still woke up, remembering the dreams.

More dreams of Logan that were really nightmares.

Twenty-two and a half years ago...

"Smile!"

I was sitting on Logan's lap on our futon in our living room. When the demand came, we both looked to Keely, Black's fiancée, which meant old lady, who had her camera up, pointed our way.

The minute she got our attention, the flash blew.

"Fuck, Keely," Logan growled as I tensed and blinked the residue of the bright light out of my eyes.

"Trust me, you two are so cute together, that'll be worth the pain," Keely blithely replied, grinning at us and sauntering into our dining room where bikers were gathered around the table, drinking, smoking, snacking, and playing some game.

An impromptu party at our pad. Without warning, they'd shown three hours ago.

I was all for it like I was always all for it since it happened a lot, not to mention Logan and I dropped in on his brothers a lot.

But tonight I had a problem.

I had a paper that I had to get done.

"You okay?"

I turned my distracted attention from our secondhand dining room table to focus on my man.

When I caught his gaze, I cuddled closer and said, "Happy that you broke from the game to give me a snuggle, Low. Also happy to entertain the biker babes while you boys do your thing at the table. But I have that paper—"

I didn't finish because Logan's expression turned from curious to mildly annoyed and he muttered, "Fuck, I forgot."

"It's okay," I told him hurriedly. "I'll talk to the girls, explain things. They can entertain themselves, I'm sure, and I'll go upstairs, get to it."

"Paper's a quarter of your grade," he told me something I'd told him. "You don't need distractions."

"It's okay, Low," I assured him.

"It's not," he returned.

I opened my mouth to speak but before I could, he looked beyond me to the dining room and called loudly, "Millie's got a paper she's gotta do. Party's over."

"Shit, Millie," Black called back. "Why didn't you say anything?"

I was moving because Logan was rising, taking me with him, putting my feet to the ground, and he did this while I talked.

"Because I needed a break and you boys give good break," I said on a smile.

Black shook his head and pushed his chair back. This commenced everyone doing the same and while they did it I was reminded why I liked Logan's family.

They didn't complain, give shit, ask to finish their beers or their game.

No. I needed peace and quiet, Logan made that clear, so they gave us what we needed and didn't mess around taking off.

Keely and Black were the last to go, Keely giving me a kiss on the cheek, pulling back and saying, "Good luck on your paper, babe. We'll go to Scruff's and celebrate when you kick its ass."

I grinned. "You're on."

"Later, Mill," Black muttered after doing a forearm clasp with Logan.

"Later, Black."

They took off.

Logan closed and locked the door, then turned to me.

I went back to our earlier subject.

"Really, I could have gone upstairs while you guys communed down here."

"Babe, give you what you need," he replied.

"I need to study and I could have—"

I stopped talking that time because he lifted a hand and ran his fingers into the side of my hair, pulling it away from my face, then curling his fingers around my skull and dipping close.

"Give you what you need, Millie, even if you don't know you need it and even when we're at cross purposes, me doin' that, you thinkin' you're givin' me what I need by lettin' my brothers stay."

I stared into his beautiful brown eyes, so in love with Logan Judd, I knew I couldn't fall any deeper.

Until he proved me wrong.

This happened frequently.

"Thanks, baby," I whispered.

And I fell.

"Anytime, Millie," he replied. "Every time."

Every time.

We'd been together for five months and he'd proved that to be true repeatedly.

I smiled.

He dipped even closer to brush his mouth against mine.

When he pulled away, his eyes went up the stairs behind me, back to me, and he ordered, "Now get to work."

"Right, boss," I returned.

His lips twitched before he went on, "You want a Coke or should I make a pot of coffee?"

He knew me. He lived with me. He got my study habits.

It was past nine. The paper was important. The night would be late. I needed caffeine.

And, like everything else, he was going to give it to me.

"I think it's a pot of coffee night," I told him.

"Fuck," he murmured, sliding his hand out of my hair and dropping it. "Am I gonna sleep alone again?"

I shook my head but said, "Not if we don't keep standing here talking and I get to work."

"Then get to work," he repeated his order.

I lifted my hand to my forehead and gave him a salute.

His lips twitched again and he turned to walk into the living room that would take him to the kitchen and his errand of making me coffee.

I put a foot to the bottom step and called his name.

He turned back.

"Love you, Low," I said quietly when he caught my eyes.

His warmed, he tipped his chin to me, and he replied, "Work, baby."

He loved me too.

I grinned and skipped up the steps.

Logan made me a pot of coffee.

In the end, after coming in and kissing my neck, he went to bed without me.

I didn't like him doing that, so I didn't mess around, got my paper done and joined him as soon as I could.

We slept entwined and I woke up, even after only five hours of sleep, charged up to take on the day.

I got an A on the paper and Logan and I celebrated with Black, Keely, Chew, Boz, Kellie, Justine, and half a dozen other friends at Scruff's.

It was awesome.

Life was awesome.

I was eighteen years old and it was crazy. I knew it. But I didn't question it.

No one in their right mind would question it, no matter what their age.

So I didn't.

Because I had it all.

CHAPTER SEVEN

Release Me

High

"THAT'S IT?" HE asked.

Shirleen studied him closely as she replied, "That's it."

High was standing with her among the shelves of Fort-num's Used Books, a store owned by Shirleen's boss's wife, Indy Nightingale. Shirleen had a paper cup in her hand seeing as, at the front of the store, a lunatic named Tex made coffee.

The man might be lunatic, but he made good coffee.

But High wasn't in the mood for coffee and he definitely wasn't in the mood to put up with Tex.

She'd given him the preliminaries of Millie's details the day before: address, phone number, place of business.

She'd just given the rest of it to him.

Never been married, no kids. Successful business. From what Shirleen could find, with her limited capabilities since High had not allowed her to pull in any of Nightingale's boys, Millie lived quiet and was married to her job.

This shit did not jibe.

At all.

She'd liked to party. She'd liked to go out. She'd liked hitting bars to listen to music, going to rallies, shooting pool. She was social, friendly, vibrant. She'd wanted kids.

Actually, she'd wanted kids in a big way.

No, it did not fucking jibe.

None of it.

Like his discovery the night before of what her house was like did not jibe.

"Lovers?" he growled, not wanting to know but needing more than this. Needing anything he could use to win, however he had to do that.

"Boy, no clue," she replied. "What I gave you is what I got. *All* I got. You want deeper intel, you gotta let me go into the field or get one of the boys on it for you," Shirleen stated, still studying him. "Least let me set Brody on it. Get him to do some hacks."

Brody was Nightingale's geek. The guy was a wizard with a computer.

He also had a big mouth.

High didn't need anyone else in his business.

Shirleen hadn't come up with much and if she went further, he'd court that.

It was going to be up to him.

"No on Brody," he told her. "I'll get what I need."

She continued her study of him even as she nodded.

"Thanks for what you got, Shirleen," he muttered, turning to leave.

"High?" she called.

He turned back.

"You know what you're doin'?" she asked.

He knew what he was doing.

Getting laid, phenomenally. Angry sex that melted into hungry sex that ended explosive.

Fuck yeah, he knew what he was doing and he liked it a fuckuva lot. He'd found this was a game he didn't mind playing seeing as he had no intention of losing, and the way it was going, he'd be a winner repeatedly along the way.

Millie thought she had him and he had to admit, sitting on the end of her bed last night, watching her strut around in her classy, sexy pajamas he wanted to rip right off her, the pants clinging to her ass, the lace at the sides exposing her long legs, the material tight at her tits, he thought she had him.

The move with her lipstick was smooth.

But he saw it in her eyes even if she tried to hide it.

She was scared.

She was in too deep and she was in denial.

It had been his win.

So he'd take what she had to give until she went under and he'd make sure that was in a way she wouldn't try to surface again.

Then she'd be in his rearview.

"Absolutely," he answered Shirleen.

She didn't nod again. She pierced him with a look he knew she was using to try to read him.

He didn't give her much of a shot.

He lifted his chin and took off.

He left the store, went to his bike, got on, and rode right to Millie's.

He'd cased the place the day before. But he'd chosen his time to approach last night with premeditation, when she'd be close to bedding down and had nothing else on her mind, so no distractions. Then he'd gone back.

Now it was early afternoon the next day. She'd be working in her studio at the back of her house.

So he'd be free to do what he needed to do in her house.

If she was there or came in while he was doing what needed to get done, he was good with that. He had two objectives that day and if she walked in on him, he'd instigate the second one.

He did a slow drive-by at the front of her house, seeing the rear of her SUV in the courtyard at the back, again taking in the tidy attractiveness of her pad.

Not a blade of grass out of place.

It set his teeth on edge because, again, it did not jibe.

He turned left at the end of the block, then left again into her alley. He rode down to the back of her house, stopped, and idled.

There was a garage back there built a long time ago. Unlike the house, it was not in good shape. Dilapidated, some of the glass in the windows of the swing-out doors broken. He cut the ignition of his bike, swung his leg over, and walked to the garage, looking into the windows.

Smartly, she hadn't put anything in there worth anything. There were some paint cans on shelves. A broken broom in the corner. Other than that, nothing.

He stepped away, eyes still to the window, and rolled his neck against the tension building there.

He went back to his bike, got on, started up, and began to roll but halted when he caught sight of it.

He'd stopped by the Dumpster.

"Fuck," he muttered, staring at the crate he'd brought back to her last night, which was sitting at the side of the Dumpster. "Fuck," he whispered, not able to tear his eyes off it.

She'd tossed it. Maybe it was too heavy to get up and in the Dumpster or the thing was full, but there was no mistaking the fact that it was set out to be hauled away.

She'd dumped it.

She'd dumped *them*.

"Fuck," he snarled, rolled off, turned out of the alley, and circled back to her house.

He parked two doors down and walked to her place, up her drive, under the overhang, eyes to the studio.

The door didn't open and he couldn't see inside any of her windows.

He moved to the back door of her house, noting there were no other cars but her own.

He squatted at her door, pulled out his tools, picked the lock, and let himself in.

He closed the door behind him and took in a kitchen that

looked like it was from a magazine. Even the plates, pitchers, glasses, bowls, and other shit that he could see through the glass-fronted cupboards were what she said they were last night.

Utter perfection.

And not Millie.

Or not the Millie he thought he knew.

Time had gone by, she made money now, wasn't a student, but this was a turnabout that shook him.

She had been into comfort and that was pretty much it. She had too much life to live to worry about decorating.

She hadn't shopped with the girls. She'd cackled in the Chaos common room with them, drinking beer and shooting the shit.

She also hadn't hounded him to paint walls or look at toss pillows like Deb had done when they started setting up house. If they were together, he and Millie were eating, cuddling in front of the TV, fucking, or tangled up in bed, whispering to each other.

Toss pillows never entered her mind. At their place they had cheap shit, secondhand shit.

And she didn't care.

High took in more of the kitchen.

There was a bowl in the sink soaking, a spoon in the bowl.

Other than that, nothing out of place. No mail stacked on counters. No breadcrumbs not wiped up. No wine bottle recorked to reopen that night. No dishes in a drainer drying. Fuck, there wasn't even a drainer out to mar the flawlessness.

Nothing.

He moved into the living room and found the same thing. Her wineglass from last night was gone. There wasn't even an afghan pushed aside, but instead a fluffy one was draped artfully over the corner of a big chair.

He started to look at pictures and felt his jaw set.

At least that hadn't changed. Millie liked happy memories around her. Back when they were young, it wasn't about fancy frames all over the place. Instead, she'd tacked shit she wanted to remember on cheap corkboards she'd bought or stuck them on the fridge with magnets. Hell, the fridge had had at least two layers of the stuff (something he'd teased her about). And he should have bought stock in Blu Tack, the woman went through so much of it, building collages of memories on the walls.

Now she had money to buy frames.

So she did.

As he studied the pictures, he saw she was still tight with Justine. If the pictures were anything to go by, it looked like Justine was gay, which would explain a lot. It also looked like she was happy and, since he'd always liked her, he was glad she'd come to terms with what was fucking with her head, gone for it, and found what she needed.

He also saw Dottie was married to a good-looking guy, the man kind of rough but not edgy. And clearly they'd had two kids, boy and a girl.

Then there was Kellie, no man he could see, but it was obvious those three, Millie, Justine, and Kellie, were still tight.

He got more of that as he moved out of the living room, into the hall.

First door to the left, a bathroom, elegant, clean, meticulously decorated.

Second left, a guest bedroom, same as the bath.

First right after the foyer, he found it.

A room with not much in it. Some weights resting on the floor, a treadmill with a towel folded precisely and draped over the bar on it, an attractive, cream media center with a small TV. Books in the shelves. CDs placed in holders that he saw when he looked were arranged in alphabetical order. Same with movie DVDs. Some yoga workout DVDs stacked by the TV.

But it was the closet where it would be.

He opened it and thought he hit pay dirt.

Until he sifted through it and found not one fucking thing.

Tax and other documents carefully organized and crated. Photos of family and friends not frame worthy but methodically packed away. Wrapping paper and other shit like that in easy reach and even that was organized, kid paper, female adult paper, male adult paper, Christmas paper, different colored bows, ribbons. There was luggage stored in that closet and empty boxes for kitchen appliances, breakables, computer equipment she was keeping for reasons unknown since she'd lived there eleven years and probably wouldn't be moving.

But nothing else. No mess. No keepsakes. Not a fucking thing.

High moved out of that room and into her bedroom, a huge room that took the whole end of the house. It had a small sitting area right through the door with one of those fancy, cushy lounge chairs in a plush, deep pink, a table and lamp, a silver frame with a picture of Millie, Dot, and their parents on the table.

To the left, deeper into the room, a king-sized bed he was now well acquainted with. Feminine ivory covers and sheets with hints of deep pink in its pattern, tons of pillows on the bed. Crystal-based lamps on the side. Carved, expensive-looking bureau. Wood floors with thick rugs.

Picture perfect.

High stood still and took it all in.

Nothing out of place. Bed made. No clothes or shoes thrown around. Hell, even the books and the tubs and bottles on her nightstand were carefully arranged.

Millie, the one he thought was his, was clean.

But she was not tidy.

She didn't have time to be. She went to school. She worked. She heaped love and attention on him, her family, her friends, his friends.

She walked to bed taking off clothes (if he didn't take them off for her) in a trail and she didn't pick that shit up for days.

She'd use something and set it aside when she was done with it, necessitating her asking him where it was and both of them searching for it until they found it—keys, hand lotion, hair brushes, pads of paper with jotted grocery lists.

She was what she called a "soaker," that being she left the dishes in hot soapy water and came back to them whenever she felt like doing them, saying, "They're easier to clean that way, wipe right up!"

And she was two steps down from a hoarder. Anything that had the slightest use or meaning to her, she didn't give it up. She kept it, boxed it away, put it in a basket or bowl or box to come back to it, tacked it up on the wall or put it on the fridge.

She couldn't live like she'd lived with High if this was how she needed to live. Living like that would drive a person insane if they needed this order and immaculateness. There was no way for three years she could live that lie.

High had to admit, he liked the look of her place in a removed way. He had a dick, so it wasn't his gig, but it looked good.

It just didn't look real. It didn't look like anyone lived here. It looked like a showroom, not a home.

There was no personality.

There was no *Millie*.

There was nothing and also nothing to go on. It was clear everyone in her life (except Kellie) had moved on, found husbands, lovers, had kids.

But not Millie.

He moved around the room and her master bathroom, opening doors, stepping into her closet.

She was a woman, she had shit, a lot of it.

But it was nothing a million other women wouldn't have, clothes, shoes, bags, scarves, makeup, jewelry. Even the vibrator in her nightstand was normal and lonely. No other toys. Not that they'd had that shit back in the day, but they'd been young. He hadn't introduced it to their play even if he'd been thinking about it just to give her something new he knew she'd get off on since she got off on everything he did.

Lost in his thoughts, he wandered down the hall, looking at the walls.

There were pictures of her cuddling her niece and nephew, smiling huge, looking happy at the same time disturbingly sad. Standing with her folks by a Christmas tree.

But not with her crew at a concert. Hanging at a party or a bar. Off on vacation. Goofing around.

He was feeling uneasy when he went through her living room, opening the drawers on her coffee table, exposing nothing but emery boards, tucked away remotes, pens and paper.

He was more uneasy going through her kitchen.

An appropriate amount of wine bottles in her rack. A bottle of vodka in her freezer, mostly full. A very good bottle of tequila and an excellent bottle of scotch in her pantry, the tequila not even opened, the scotch half drunk.

But not much food. There was stuff but it looked like enough for a day or two of consumption. It wasn't stocked for a person who liked to cook and Millie had loved to cook. She'd also loved to bake. She was adventurous with it, skilled because her momma taught her well, and successful. They'd had spices. All different kinds of oils. Everything you could possibly need at the ready to make chocolate chip cookies, brownies, cake.

In her kitchen now, there were odds and ends, but nothing like what they'd had.

He stood at the back door, his eyes drifting through the space, his mind consumed with uncomfortable thoughts that Millie had not only been a ghost plaguing him the past twenty years.

She'd *lived* like one.

She didn't exist.

Not even in her own fucking house.

Making a decision, he pulled out his phone and made his call.

"Yo," Shirleen answered.

"Dig deeper," High ordered.

"Say what?" she asked.

"Millie," he replied. "Get Brody on her and you tell that guy he says one fuckin' word, I'll break all his fingers."

"What happened?" she asked.

"Nothin'," he answered. "And that ain't no blow-off," he shared. "Just did a walkthrough of her house and not even sure she's been breathin' the past twenty years."

"What does that mean?"

"It means what I said," High returned. "Nothin'. There's nothin' to the bitch."

There was a moment of silence before, "High, gotta ask again, you know what you're doin'?"

"I know what I'm doin', just don't know what I'm gettin'."

"Now what does *that* mean?" Shirleen asked.

"If I knew, I'd say." He turned and looked out the window of the back door, and Christ, windows in both doors. She was asking to get fucked. His eyes hit the studio. "Got shit to do, Shirleen. Call me when you got somethin'."

"Am I gonna find something?"

More than he wanted to admit, he sure as fuck hoped so.

"No one can live twenty years this quiet, Shirleen," he told her. "You'll find something. Just wanna know what it is."

"And we're talkin' . . . ?" she prompted.

It pained him to start it the way he did, but he had to.

"Who she's fucked. If she's lived with anyone. What she spends her money on. Where she goes. What vacations she's taken. Piece together her life for twenty years and give that to me. Yeah?"

"Yeah, High."

"Right, later."

"Later, and, High?"

"What?" he asked, hand on the door handle.

"You say you know what you're doin'. Just sayin', I sure hope you do."

He had no response to that except a repeated, but firmer, "Later."

"Later."

He shoved the phone in his pocket, walked out, used his tools to lock up behind him, and then moved across the courtyard to the studio.

It was time to get to phase two of today's mission and he was looking forward to it.

He didn't even pause before he opened the door and stepped in. Eyes to her sitting behind her desk, he closed the door behind him and locked it.

High didn't pay a lot of mind to the office. What he saw was like the house—pretty, feminine, but professional.

And again perfect.

What he saw of her was the same. Tricked out for work even if she was doing it in a little house behind her home.

He also saw her eyes were big and her lips were parted.

"Up," he ordered.

She did not stand up.

She asked, "What are you doing here?"

"Up, Millie, and panties down."

At that, her mouth dropped open but he saw the flush hit her cheeks.

Then he saw her eyes flare before they narrowed.

"Are you crazy?" she asked.

He moved into the space and repeated, "Up, babe."

"You *are* crazy," she whispered, still eyeing him.

He rounded her desk and she swiveled her chair to face him as he did, stubbornly not rising and still glaring at him.

"Not gonna say it again," he told her.

"This is my place of work," she snapped.

"And?" he asked, stopping close so she had to tip her head back deep to keep his eyes, something she did.

"And you can't stroll into my place of work and order me around," she bit out.

"Can, seein' as I just did. Now, up, Millie. As I'm right here, I'll take off your panties."

Again her eyes got round, her cheeks got pinker, but her gaze got angrier.

"You're not to be believed," she hissed. "I have *work*. I have things *to do*. One of which is needing to leave in ten minutes to meet a client at the florist but I have three emails I have to reply to before I can do that."

"They'll have to wait."

She squinted up at him, even more pissed off, before she ordered, "Get out."

He put his hands on his hips. "Millie, get *up*."

She pushed her chair away, gaining a foot, leaned back, and crossed her arms on her chest.

"Okay, we've got this bizarre game going on. You know I'm in. But there need to be rules," she declared.

He shook his head. "No rules."

"I have a mortgage, High," she told him sharply.

Fuck, why did he hate it when she called him High? It wasn't the name given to him, but it was still his goddamned name.

He ignored his reaction to that and replied, "You're worried about your work, you best get up so I can fuck you and do it fast."

And he'd give her that.

He knew this was a low play but he also didn't give a fuck. He'd make any play he deemed necessary, especially if it meant burying his cock inside her, hearing her pant, and feeling her clutch him in all the ways she did that while he was doing it. And he was already hard thinking about it, looking down at her in her frilly blouse, tight skirt, and high heels.

But if she had things to do, he'd take what he wanted fast so she wasn't too late doing them.

"God, you're *infuriating*," she snapped.

"Score one for me," he returned. "Now, *up*."

"Fuck you, High," she shot back. "And get the fuck *out*."

He took a step toward her and stopped her from pushing back farther by leaning in, hands to the arms of her chair, holding it stationary, face in her face.

"Gonna fuck you on your desk," he whispered. "Gonna do it fast and hard and you're gonna come like you come for me, *loud*. Now quit fuckin' around and get the fuck *up* or I'm gonna put you where I want you so I can get on with takin' what I want from you."

He knew he had her seeing the heat in her eyes, feeling her breath come faster, noting her tits moving up and down quick with her breaths as she fought the feeling.

But her lips declared, "That is not gonna happen."

Then she cried out when he made it happen, lifting her clean out of her seat with one arm, twisting, using his other arm to sweep off whatever was on her desk and planting her ass-first on it.

He leaned in, taking her to her back, and she helped out by breathing, "High," which meant her mouth was open when he kissed her.

She didn't fight this time. She didn't twist away. She didn't push at him.

She accepted his tongue with a moan.

She'd been fighting the feeling.

And she'd lost.

Fuck yeah.

He ran a hand from her knee up, taking her skirt with it, then feeling his dick throb when he encountered the lace top of a thigh-high.

Feeling that, he knew it was time to quit fucking around.

So he did.

Tearing his mouth from hers, he watched as her eyelids lowered and a puff of breath escaped her lips when he used both hands to yank up her skirt.

She immediately locked onto his hips with both thighs.

She wanted this.

Panting for it.

Literally.

He twisted to see her leg in her thigh-high clasped against his jeans at his hip and the sight was such a turn-on, he had to fight against grinding his hard crotch between her legs.

Fuck, now he had to fuck her more than he'd had to fuck her.

Immediately.

He plunged a hand in, pushing aside the gusset of her panties.

The soaked gusset of her panties.

And Millie needed to be fucked.

Immediately.

"High," she whispered, that throbbing through his dick, too, as she rubbed her wet pussy against his hand and started shoving up his shirt with her fingers.

"You want it?" he asked, toying with her wet as he went after his belt and fly.

"Yes," she breathed.

"Hard?"

"Yes. Hurry."

To give her something, he started finger-fucking her.

She pressed into his fingers and arched her neck even as she begged. "Your cock, baby. *Hurry.*"

He pulled his cock free, slid his fingers from her wet, held her panties aside, positioned, and drove deep.

Christ.

Magnificent.

Her fingers curled into his shirt under his jacket, yanked up uncontrollably, then she set her nails into the flesh of his back and dragged down.

High grunted against the gratification of that as he thrust into her sleek, feeling her knees come up so he could drive deeper and she could get more.

When she got it, she raked her nails back up and that felt so fucking phenomenal, he groaned, burying himself to the root and grinding.

When he didn't stop and go back to fucking her, she righted her head and begged, "Move."

He wanted more of that wet.

But there was another score he was after.

"You gonna give it all?" he asked.

No hesitation. "Yes, High."

"Gonna take it, baby," he warned.

"Okay," she whispered.

He kept grinding. "Gonna play with this body."

Her breaths started coming hard as she shifted her hips to try to rub up and down his cock and her nails dug into his back.

"No rules, Millie."

"No rules," she gasped, desperate, swinging her calves in, trying to find purchase.

He had her.

And he totally fucking didn't.

"Am I even here?" he sneered. "Or am I just dick?"

And again, like last night, thinking he had her before she'd turned the tables on him, she did it again.

She opened her eyes, stared fixed into his, and replied, "You're always here, Logan. Even when you were gone. But since you're *here* and you got what you wanted," she lifted her head, putting her lips to his and scoring his back with her nails as she finished, "stop fucking around and *take it*."

Powerless to do anything else, he thrust his tongue in her mouth and took it.

It didn't take her long to give it all.

When she did, he let go and gave it all.

He was nibbling her lips and using her pussy to milk his cock after they'd both found it when she drew her hands out of his shirt and unclasped her legs from around his back.

He lifted his head and stared down at her.

In her pretty brown eyes, sex and fear.

Fuck yeah, he got what he was after. All of it.

He didn't smile, even if he wanted to.

She moved her gaze to his ear, mumbling, "I have to go."

He pulled out and shoved a hand between them. He shifted her panties back in place, then tucked his dick in his jeans before he pulled her up and set her on her feet, pinning her to the desk so she had it and him to support her. He kept her there, her eyes to his shoulder, one of her hands to the desk behind her, not touching him, as he did up his jeans and she used her other hand to yank down her skirt.

She was closing down but it didn't matter.

He got what he wanted.

"No rules, Millie," he reiterated, like a warning.

"I need to clean up," she told his shoulder.

He lifted a fist to her jaw and gently forced her eyes to him.

"No rules," he stated.

"I got that, High," she replied, a thread of defeat in her tone that, fuck it all, he did not like.

"You can end this, you give it up," he reminded her. "Tell me what the fuck you want so I can say no and we both can move on."

Determination stole into her gaze as she replied, "You don't get this but I don't want anything. And this will end, *High*, when I finally convince you of that."

He dipped closer. "Got my hand between your legs, you were soaked for me, Millie."

"Is that a surprise?" she returned.

"For a woman who wants nothin' from me, yeah," he answered.

She scored another hit when she whispered, "You're beautiful."

Jesus.

She did not just say that like she meant it.

He stared down at her, the words still ringing in his ears.

Fuck him, she did.

"Mill—" he started to growl.

She cut him off, her tone stronger, "And you're good at it. You were always good at it. So again, is that a surprise?"

"You want me gone, you're not gonna pant and beg for it," he informed her.

"I want you gone but if you're gonna give it until I can get you gone, it's that good, I'm gonna take it," she stated, and finally touched him only to lift a hand, put it to his chest, and put pressure on. "Now, move back. I'm already late. I don't need to be later."

Sensing he was going to get nothing more out of this, but having gotten what he wanted anyway, High stepped back.

She quickly moved away from him, toward a door he saw led to a bathroom.

He watched her do it, eyes to her ass, and doing that he decided he was going to go for more and he didn't care how late she was.

So he told her back, "It wasn't lost on you, what you did to me."

She turned and he saw her cheeks still flushed from sex, but the rest of her face was pale and her eyes were guarded.

"'Preciate the orgasms, Millie," he continued. "But cannot get a lock on how any woman could do that to a man, and no matter it's ten days or twenty years, come back for more. Release me. Tell me your fuckin' game. If it isn't as twisted as the last one, you need to get off, I'll give that to you until I find better."

The guard went down as anger flashed. "Well, thanks, High. What a sweet offer."

He lost patience. "Millie, ain't dickin' around."

Then he braced when her expression changed again. It was fast, the suffering that slashed through it before she hid it. But it didn't leave her and he knew it because it colored her tone.

"You're released."

He searched her expression.

Fuck, she meant that.

He felt his shoulders constrict.

"Just like that?" he asked.

"I made a mistake," she said quietly. "A big one, as it turned out. But it's been made. There's no rectifying it."

"The mistake?" he pushed.

"Coming to see you," she told him.

Jesus, were they getting somewhere?

"And you did that because ... ?" he prompted.

She shook her head. "It doesn't matter now."

Fucking shit.

More games.

"Millie, this is the fuckin' game I been talkin' about," he clipped.

She flinched, not a communication of discomfort or pain, one of frustration.

But he again didn't give a fuck.

She was frustrated?

He was too and the woman had started this bullshit.

"Christ, if you'd just spit it out, we'd be done with this," he reminded her.

She locked eyes with him. "Release me."

"Jesus, Millie—"

"You're coming to me," she pointed out. "Stop it. Release me."

He threw an arm out to indicate the desk and the shit he swept all over the floor and asked, "Gonna be hard for you to convince me that isn't the goal you wanna achieve, wrap me up tight in that wet pussy of yours and play with me however you want. I know that game, caught up in it before, so I also know you're good at it."

She attempted to instigate another score.

"It's almost impossible to believe, looking at you, knowing who you are, knowing who you *were*, and listening to you speak to me like that."

But that was taking it too far.

And High was not a man who allowed that shit.

Not anymore.

Not since Millie taught him not to do it.

"Fuck, bitch," he snarled, "you cannot seriously be standing there tryin' the guilt game on me when you fucked up my whole goddamned life, and like that wasn't enough, waltzed back into it, *you* lookin' for *me*, to try to do it again."

And apparently, what he said took it too far for Millie.

He knew it when she leaned forward, her beautiful face twisted in pain, and hissed, "I've been walking through fire for you for *twenty years*, Logan. Do *not* stand in *my* office that *you* walked into without an invitation and feed me your *shit*. This is revenge. This is your way of hurting me after I hurt you. I'm not *stupid*. You want it?" She leaned back and tossed out both arms. "Take it. But I'm not gonna get on my knees and let you shove my face down so you can't see it but you *can* fuck faceless pussy knowing *exactly* how much you're humiliating me. You need to take from me, I'll give it but only because I'm giving to *get*."

"Don't tell me you didn't *get* when you were on your knees for me at Bill's," he sneered.

"Don't tell me you didn't know *exactly* the insult you were delivering," she fired back. "You knew, High. *You knew*. You knew you were delivering the worst insult a man could give to a woman. You *knew it* and do not tell me you didn't."

He couldn't tell her that because she was right.

And she'd deserved it.

At least he'd thought that at the time.

Staring into her face, a face saturated with fury and hurt, he was thinking twice.

"Tell me how you walked through fire for me," he ordered.

"No," she whispered, the word soft but it held so much power, it left a gash in the air of the room and he felt his chest burning like he was struggling for breath. "Never," she went on. "I was gonna give that to you but then you lost the right to it."

"So it's still game on," he noted.

"Not if you release me," she replied.

He decided to lay it out.

"Clue in, Millie. I'm comin' to you, so who's got a hold on who?"

"You've got the power to let this be over," she told him.

"How's that when I don't even have to fuckin' kiss you to make you drenched for me?" he returned.

"God!" she cried, looking to the ceiling.

He ignored that and shared, "This isn't done, we both know it and I'm guessin' from this irritatin' conversation we got no choice but to ride whatever the fuck this is out, but it's me who's gotta do it hopin' you don't rip me up in the process."

She tipped her head down and again locked eyes on him. "If you think that, then you aren't paying attention."

"Baby," he drawled, "trust me, you got my *complete* attention."

It was then she landed the hammer.

"No, I don't and from the way you're treating me, it's clear I never did."

With that, she ended their conversation by turning, entering the bathroom, and slamming the door and he heard the lock go.

He could bust down the door but enough was enough.

The bitch told him she walked through fire for him, insinuating that there was something he fucking didn't catch back in the day.

Bullshit.

Total bullshit Millie games.

And High slammed out of her office thinking precisely that.

But the blow had been delivered.

And he'd walked through her house and he'd seen how she'd changed, how she lived like a ghost, how she was nothing like the woman he thought he knew her to be.

So he couldn't stop the nagging at the edge of his mind that Millie hadn't cut him out but instead he'd lost her and he hadn't only done it back then but he'd done it again now.

His Millie was gone.

In every way she could be.

* * *

Later that night, when High had switched out his bike for his truck, he went back to Millie's.

Not her house.

The alley.

He knew it was stupid.

He didn't care.

He told himself he needed every bit of ammunition he could get in this war and that crate was full of ammunition.

He wouldn't allow himself to believe he went back for a different reason.

But when he got to the Dumpster and got out of his truck, he saw the crate was gone.

He lifted the lid on the Dumpster and saw that it hadn't been emptied nor had the crate been thrown into it.

It was a decent crate, could be used for a lot of shit.

Someone had stolen it and stolen High and Millie with it.

Likely they'd toss all the photos. Three years of living a dream, gone.

He got back into his truck, his gut roiling, his hands clenching the steering wheel with fury.

She'd dumped *them*.

And now they were gone.

And as he drove away, High decided the bitch would pay for that too.

Twenty-two years ago...

Logan woke to an empty bed.

He blinked away sleep, looked to Millie's nightstand and caught the time on her alarm clock.

Then he threw back the covers, got out of bed, and walked out of their bedroom.

He didn't find her in the second bedroom, a room she'd set up as a place she could study.

He knew why he didn't find her there. When she did late nights like that, she did them at the dining room table downstairs so any noise she made wouldn't disturb him.

Unsurprisingly, he found her where he knew she'd be but he found her slumped over, cheek to a notepad, books open everywhere, dead asleep.

He moved around the room, shutting off lights, before he moved to his girl.

Gently, he lifted her away from the table, then up in his arms.

As gently as he did it, she roused.

"Wha...oh man," she muttered drowsily. "Did I crash?"

"Yeah, baby," he replied, moving from the living room into the foyer to the stairs.

"I can walk, Snooks."

Logan felt his lips curve up.

Snooks.

The boys called him High.

Millie didn't call him High.

She called him Logan, Low, and Snooks when they were in company and when they weren't.

But she called him Snook'ums when no one was around.

It was goofy and it was cute and it was all Millie.

He loved it.

Halfway up the steps, he stopped and put her to her feet but he didn't take his arm from around her.

She slid hers around him and they walked up the rest of the stairs together.

"You get done what you needed?" he asked.

"No clue. I don't remember when I crashed, but I'm guessing...no," she answered.

Logan's lips didn't curve up at that.

They tightened.

It was finals. She was taking a heavy second semester schedule in hopes of graduating in three and a half years rather than four so they could start their life and their family and do it without delay.

She was also still working part-time at the mall. She made dick but no matter how often he told her she should do it, she wouldn't give up the job.

She also wouldn't give up on him, the Club, their life.

She was all in with everything. She never missed a class. She studied between classes. She was never late for work. She studied when she got home. They went to movies. They went to bars. They went to parties. They went to concerts. They went to rallies. She cooked for him. She cleaned the house for him. And she studied more whenever she had the chance.

Business. That was her major.

"Don't know what I'm gonna do with it," she'd told him on a grin. "Just know I'm gonna kick ass whatever it is I do."

He believed that. She didn't do anything in half measures. She sucked life dry, setting her teeth in deep, straight to the bone and pulling out the marrow.

But this shit had to end. She was about to finish her first year of college and she wasn't going to take a break. She was going to take two classes during the summer and go full-time at the store in the mall until her sophomore year started.

Which meant more of this. All-nighters where he went to bed alone, woke up alone, saw her faking it and drained dry but giving him a grin and the cute when he knew she was about ready to pass out.

He watched her pull off her clothes, dropping them to the floor as she wandered to their bed, and he decided it was time for this shit to stop.

She got in and Logan got in with her. Pulling her into his

arms, he tangled himself up in her as she returned the favor and snuggled deep.

"Babe, you gotta quit that job," he told the top of her head.

"Need the money," she muttered sleepily.

"You don't," he replied. "I can cover us."

And he could. Chaos business, the garage and shop called Ride, and the other shit they did, he could totally cover her and him. He could even do more. Get them nicer furniture, new shit that looked good. After a year or two put money down on a house. Take her on vacation to get her away from her work. Take her to Paris and kiss her under the Eiffel Tower.

He could give them better than what they had.

He could give his girl everything.

He could do that.

Absolutely.

"Can't do that," she mumbled, sounding very close to sleep.

"Millie," he gave her a squeeze, "you're gonna burn out, you keep this shit up."

"Only two more years," she replied. "Most...two and a half."

"Babe—" he started but didn't go on when she suddenly tipped her head back.

"No, Logan," she whispered, her voice still sounding tired but it was also strong. "I do my bit."

"You'll do your bit when you got your degree and you get a fancy-ass job that makes us a lotta cake," he returned.

"I do my bit now. I do my bit every day," she shot back stubbornly.

He dragged her up his body so they were eye to eye in the dark. "You know it's no hardship, me takin' care of you. You also know that's my job, one I get off on, so stop bein' so stubborn and let me do it."

"If I can do my part, I will, and I can, Low," she retorted.

"Millie, this is the third night in a row you crashed at the dining room table," he reminded her. "When it's finals, it's worse, but it's bad all the time and that shit's not good for you."

"I have to."

Logan went silent at the fierce tone in her voice.

"I have to, Logan." She slid a hand up his chest to curve it around the side of his neck. "I know you can take care of me. I love how you take care of me. But I have to do this. For you. For us. To prove something to myself. My parents. You. I have to. And if you wanna take care of me, that's how you can take care of me. By letting me do it."

"I know what you need, baby," he whispered back. "And you gotta know I don't need that. I'm in. I know you're in. We're both in. *All* in. There's times I gotta have your back. There'll be times you'll hafta have mine. Let me have your back now, Millie. It'll mean a lot you got the time to do what you gotta do and I can go to bed beside you."

She was silent a minute and he thought he had her, then she shook her head against the pillow.

"Please understand," she said softly. "I just need to do my part. I need you to know I'm going to. No, that I'm *able* to. Life's gonna throw a lot at us, Snook'ums. I need you to know I'm ready to do my bit when it does."

She needed that. He knew it. He heard it. Fuck, he even felt it.

And he knew why she needed to give it to him. They were young. They were starting early. They were both all in. And they both wanted the same out of life. To be together, to build a family, to build a life. Neither wanted to delay.

So she needed to prove she could stick it, through thick and thin.

He didn't like it but if his girl needed it, he was going to give it.

So he gave in.

"Okay, Millie."

She snuggled even closer, pushing in to kiss his throat.

Then she took her hand from his neck, trailed it down his chest so she could wrap her arm around him.

"Thanks, Low," she murmured. It was again sleepy but there was feeling behind it.

Yeah, she needed it.

So he settled in, his girl cuddled close, and he gave it.

CHAPTER EIGHT

Going Through the Motions

Millie

My ALARM WENT.

I opened my eyes, looked at the time, sleepily went through the magnitude of things I had to do to get ready to face the day, decided on one I could not do in order to buy more sleep, and I hit snooze.

I settled back in, closing my eyes, exhausted.

Because of all that was going on with Logan, I hadn't found sleep easy the night before and I didn't sleep great when I found it.

And it was getting on my busy season. I had a wedding coming up in two weeks and the bride was still changing her mind about practically everything. I also had a fiftieth anniversary party that should go off like clockwork, but it was happening that coming weekend, so I had to dot all the *i*'s and cross all the *t*'s.

But it wasn't just the holiday season coming making things

crazy. I was also reconnoitering clients' homes and offices to create design schemes I would present, then I'd need to make sure I had everything to put my designs into action. Sometimes this took months. And it was taking those months, starting about two weeks ago.

I usually worked nine- to ten-hour days and nearly always put in time during the weekends. But it was getting to my six-day-a-week, ten- to twelve-hour-a-day season.

And to do that and be able to do it well I needed sleep, something I wouldn't get if Logan remained in my life.

I should never have let this game with him go on.

It wasn't just stupid.

It was unhealthy.

When he'd showed at my house Monday night, I should have done everything in my power to get him gone. Then I should have gone to Ride, talked to that Tyra woman, told her to stay out of my business and also told her to tell Tack to keep Logan out of it. And to do that, I should have threatened to call the cops.

Chaos did not like cops.

There were a variety of reasons why, including the fact that they grew and sold weed back in the day (and maybe still did).

I knew there was more to it than that but Logan had never shared any of it. And I knew whatever that more was was becoming a bigger part of Club business.

I knew this because, in the time I spent with Logan, Chaos's antipathy toward police had grown to paranoia.

I also knew it because Logan would often need to go off and do "Club business," business he did not share when he got back to me, business that could happen at any hour of the day and night, and the longer we were together, the more often that happened.

Not to mention, the more wired he got when he got home, agitation mixed with adrenaline that might translate to good things, like fabulous sex, but it was nevertheless concerning.

As concerning as it was, it was also Logan and I trusted

him. I trusted him to do right by me, himself, *us*, so I didn't question it. Not ever.

Until I could use it to be a means to an end.

So threatening getting the police involved would make my point and I should have done that.

But I didn't because I was weak and needy and Logan was Logan. True he was a new, asshole Logan who cut me to the quick, didn't mind doing it, and thus did it repeatedly. In fact, he got off on it in a way I knew it was his sole purpose to come back and dish out more.

But he was still Logan, older, wiser, and even better with his hands, mouth, and cock.

And as fucked up as it was, I had to admit I was getting off on the game in my own way. I was not in control of it as I was in control of every millimeter of space around me, every aspect of my work, every second of my life. I had no idea when he'd show and when he showed, what he'd do.

I just knew what I'd get.

His attention. As damaging as it was, it was still Logan in my space, eyes on me, mouth talking to me (and doing other things), hands touching me.

And I'd get all that as well as the orgasm he'd give me and the orgasm he'd have that I gave him.

Of course, thinking all of this, I did not snooze, so when the alarm went off again, I was wide awake and had so much to do that day I couldn't take the eight more minutes another snooze would give me.

I hit the Off button on the alarm and threw the covers back, hauling myself out of bed. I went right to the bathroom, doing this again thinking I needed cats. Another presence in the house. Someone to talk to. Someone to take care of. Someone to love.

Sure, feeding them would add time to my morning routine but to have all that, to cut through the loneliness I'd been deny-ing was weighing on me, I'd do it.

I scratched searching for kittens on my mental list of things to add to my physical list written on a pad on my desk in my studio as I did my preliminary bathroom business and walked out to put coffee on.

I did this thinking about my desk and the time it had taken to right everything after Logan left the day before.

I told myself it was annoying, especially since he'd destroyed my weekly delivery of flowers, got water everywhere, decimated several blooms, thus it took more time to clean up and the arrangement looked like crap after I put it back together and I was good with flowers.

But it wasn't annoying.

It was hot.

God, I was crazy.

No, I was fucked up.

And I was fucking myself up, letting this go on when I was supposed to be sorting myself out.

I sighed as I moved to the end of my kitchen counter that delineated the living room from the kitchen.

It was then I felt it.

No, I felt *him*.

I stopped dead, my head came up, and I stared at Logan leaning against the counter by the sink, mug of coffee in his hand, his Chaos cut thrown on the marble beside him, wearing his uniform of jeans, motorcycle boots, and black thermal Henley, looking gorgeous.

"Mornin'," he greeted casually, then lifted the mug and took a sip.

"Are you kidding me?" I asked.

"Nope," he answered after lowering the mug.

I looked to the back door, then to him. "You broke in?"

"Yup."

He broke in.

To my house!

I didn't have time for this.

Further, it was time to *end* this.

Now.

Intent on doing just that, I tossed my hair, feeling the loose bunch of it wrapped around a ponytail holder at the top back of my head wobble around and Logan's eyes went to it.

I felt my thighs start tingling.

Damn it!

"You need to leave," I informed him.

He looked from my hair down my body, then back up to my eyes.

His were grinning when he noted, "Nice jammies," before he took another sip of coffee, his gaze never leaving mine.

Rough, edgy, biker, bad boy, hot guy Logan "High" Judd saying the word *jammies* was both hilarious and a total turn-on.

Though he was right. They were nice jammies. Petal pink with ivory lace, another cami and pants that were so awesome, they should be illegal. This pair had lace edging the hem and sides of the pants—sides that were cut in overlapping slits all the way to my upper hips.

Sometimes I got tangled in them when I was sleeping, but they looked crazy-awesome on, especially when I was walking around, so I put up with the tangling.

I'd never had anyone to appreciate them.

Until now.

And Logan's appreciation worked, as it always did.

However, I told myself firmly, I would be happy with just my own appreciation.

And maybe the detached, feline approval of a Burmese cat.

Perhaps a Persian.

Yes, a Persian. A Persian would go better with my house.

I tore my thoughts off Persian cats and focused again on Logan, repeating, "You need to leave."

He didn't leave.

He stayed right where he was, lounging against my kitchen counter like he did it every morning, and asked, "What's the gig with your house?"

Even though I didn't quite understand his question, I did know he wasn't going to catch me in this again.

"Please leave," I requested politely.

He ignored me and threw out his hand holding the coffee mug toward my kitchen/living room.

"Babe, this place looks nice, but it's not you."

"It's one hundred percent me," I retorted, doing it wanting to kick myself because I should not engage. I should instead ask him to leave (again).

I knew this to be even more true when he took in the length of me again before catching my eyes.

"New you, that getup, this house," he muttered. "Old you, I got my dick inside you."

That did it, the dirty talk that was not all about dirty talk, the good kind that was sweet and fun and had one objective that was also sweet but mostly it was fun. Instead, it was dirty talk that was only partly the good kind but not intentionally so. Mostly it was meant to wound by taking more than it was giving and leaving bruises with the blows.

Therefore I stomped to the island, put my hands on it, and didn't share I had a busy day and I needed to prepare for it because he'd proved yesterday he didn't care about that, which was another indication he didn't care, at all, about me.

Instead I stated, "I'm not doing this again. This is over, this game we're playing. You need to leave. And I'm being serious, High."

Humor lit his brown eyes when he returned, "You're bein' serious?"

I tried to tamp down my annoyance, something else that didn't work, in fact, the effort only fanned the flames, and I replied, "*Very.*"

He lost none of his humor and actually looked more amused when he rejoined, "You're cute when you're *very* serious. 'Specially bein' *very* serious in those jammies."

I stared at him as panic hit me.

He was changing the game and the way he was changing it this time, teasing me like that, I knew I was going to lose.

And if I lost to that, I'd lose it all.

Again.

Oh yes.

Panic.

And staring into his playful eyes, that panic went extreme.

"Please leave," I whispered.

He heard my tone, maybe read my panic, the amusement fled and he got serious and I knew it was deadly serious even though he didn't move a muscle.

"What's the gig with your pad, Millie?" he whispered back.

"It's my home," I answered, hoping an answer might get him moving on. "It's how I like it. I worked hard on it. It's perfect. Now, I answered you. Will you please go?"

"It's not you," he told me.

"It's all me," I told him.

"It's not the you I know."

"You knew me twenty years ago, Logan," I reminded him. "Things have changed."

"Yeah they have," he readily agreed.

I leaned into my hands on the counter, my body tipping his way, my hope that he'd read that body language and see my sincerity.

"While we're like this, not angry, not being stupid and crazy, I hope you'll listen to me," I began. "I need you to leave, Logan. I *need* it. This isn't healthy. Not for either of us. We have to stop."

"Crate's gone," he shared, and my head twitched in confusion when he did.

"Crate?" I asked.

"Photos of us," he told me.

He'd searched my house.

Not a surprise.

Invasive and annoying but with no rules to this game, not a surprise.

"I took it out to the Dumpster," I told him.

And I had in a moment of fury.

The garbage men didn't come until the next day. I still had time to go out and drag it back in.

I was fighting the urge and hated the fact that part of me knew I'd lose that fight. But that crate totally would be back inside, tucked in my closet by day's end no matter how busy I was.

"Crate's gone," he repeated, and when I started to say something, he went on, "Someone took it."

I snapped my mouth shut against a pain that felt like someone had punched me in the throat.

"Rode around your house," he told me. "Saw it yesterday afternoon by the Dumpster. It's gone now."

Oh God.

It was a nice crate. They didn't cost a fortune but they also didn't cost pennies.

And crates like that were useful for a variety of things.

I could see someone taking it. I hadn't thought about it when I'd dragged it out there and set it beside the Dumpster, not too puny or lazy to throw it in, just knowing I'd never dig it out if I actually did that, so I'd set it by the side because I knew I was weak and I'd be back for it. Still, I was making a statement to myself even if I knew it was lame and I'd take it back.

"It's gone?" I asked, my voice husky.

"Nice crate, you dumped it, someone can use it. They'll do that and to do that, they'll dump the pictures."

Oh God, that hurt.

God, it killed.

Why had I taken it out to the Dumpster?

Why?

"Threw us away, Millie," he told me conversationally, then took a sip of coffee, his gaze still on me. When he was done swallowing, he continued. "My count, this is twice."

That blow was so true, it caved in my throat and I had to fight for breath.

I struggled past the pain, dragged in air, and begged, "Please don't do this. Just let it go and then *go*. If not for me, for you, High. This isn't healthy for either of us."

"Man's gotta get off and works for me I do that with a guar-anteed good lay. Seems healthy to me, and when I'm buried deep, definitely *feels* healthy."

I didn't hide my wince and he didn't show he cared even minutely that he'd caused it.

In fact, he didn't show that he cared much anytime I made it clear he'd wounded me.

No, he didn't care at all.

He was playing with me to cause hurt to get back at me for what I'd done.

But he'd already done that, in spades, and the more I took, the more I allowed him to dish out, the more I made it so I deserved it.

In other words, if only for the sake of self-preservation, if not self-respect, this had to end. I knew it even before it began. I never should have gone to look for him in the first place.

I should have let it lie.

Now it was in my power to make it be over and I was going to do that.

He was not going to get it all.

Oh no.

But I would give him enough to get him gone so I could try to find it in me to stitch up the new lacerations I'd given my own damned self and get on with my life without him in it.

"I saw you at Chipotle," I announced.

That got me something. I watched his body visibly tighten.

"I heard you on the phone. I heard what you said." My voice dropped. "I know you have girls."

His stare intensified but he didn't say a word.

I did.

"You looked..." I threw a hand his way, "good. Healthy." I shook my head, knowing my lips were curving in a sad smile but I didn't try to stop it. "And as ever, handsome. You were wearing your Chaos cut, so I knew you still had your brothers. I saw you, heard you, and I knew you had it all. So I knew it was time to say I was sorry. To find you and say I was sorry for ending things the way I did. I know I hurt you and I thought, you having everything you need, all you ever wanted, your brothers, a family, I should find you and give you that closure. I should give you the words I should have given you years ago and didn't. So I went looking for you." I drew in breath and finished, "And I found you but it didn't go as planned."

"You don't know shit," he stated the minute I quit talking.

"I—" I started, then stopped, letting out a sharp cry of surprise and jumping away from the island when he all of a sudden swung an arm out and let his coffee mug fly, the mug shattering against the cupboards across the room, the coffee spattering cabinets, countertop, and floor.

"You don't know *shit*," he snarled, and my eyes flew back to him.

"You...you..." I licked my lips nervously, taking another step back to retreat from the wrath pouring from him and pounding into me but stopping when his eyes narrowed in warning at my movements, "don't have girls?"

"Cleo and Zadie."

Oh *God*.

Cleo and Zadie.

Cute names.

Probably cute girls. I could picture them in my head, female versions of him.

Beautiful.

"Lights of my life," he bit out.

"I . . . that's good, High," I told him quickly. "I'm happy for you."

"Knocked up their ma. Didn't love her," he shared, and with each word he said, I sustained new wounds. "Fuck, didn't even really like her at the time. But she got pregnant and didn't wanna take care of it, so she gave me Cleo. I gave her a ring. We both didn't want Cleo to grow up with no brothers or sisters, so we gave her Zadie. Then we gave them both a crap home with two parents that didn't give much of a shit about each other until we decided we were doin' more harm than good and we ended it."

Outside of the fact that he had two daughters he loved, none of the rest of that sounded good.

I didn't want that for him. I'd wanted so much more for him. So, *so* much more.

I'd walked through fire to give it to him.

And I felt a new gash opening, knowing he'd never had it.

"I'm sorry, High," I whispered.

"I don't want you to feel sorry for me, Millie," he clipped.

"Okay," I said immediately.

"Lived thirteen years with that woman and our babies knowin' each day . . ." He shook his head. "Fuck, each fuckin' *second* what I wanted outta my life, what I wanted for my babies, what I thought I'd have with you, what I'd have to *give* to our kids, doin' that with you, and knowin' you tore that away. And you saw me and thought I wanted *closure*? You thought I wanted your ass back in my life so you could say you were *sorry* for takin' away the only thing that gave me joy? To tell me you were fuckin' *sorry* for takin' away the only shot I had at givin' that joy to the babies I made?" His eyes narrowed dangerously. "What the fuck's the matter with you?"

"I told you I fucked up," I reminded him carefully.

"Yeah," he growled. "You fuckin' did."

"Now you know how," I went on.

"Now I know how," he ground out.

We stared at each other, me anxiously, him angrily.

When I could take no more, I assured him, "When you walk out of my house, I promise, High, swear, you'll never see me again."

"You lied to me," he declared.

I shook my head in confusion. "I—"

"I got Cleo and Zadie. Where're your kids, Millie?"

I took another step back and did it wondering how I managed it. Truthfully, his words caused so much damage it was actually a wonder I was still standing.

Breathing.

Living.

"Told me," he continued. "We talked about it all the time, you told me you were all about family. Worked your ass off to finish school early so we could start. And I know you got no kids. So that was a lie too. Like your love. Like your commitment to us. Like everything that had shit to do with *you*."

"I made a mistake back then," I forced out, the words weak, pained.

"You sure as fuck did," he returned, and threw out a hand. "Payin' for it, in your perfect house with your fancy-ass pajamas and killer investment portfolio."

Killer investment portfolio?

Shit, he'd looked into me.

"Got money, babe," he sneered. "And you think you got it all. Worked your ass off to get it. Gave *me* up to get it all. That's what you wanted, not a life with a biker who had no future. You wanted *it all*."

He took a step toward me, his eyes locked to mine, and it took all I had left (which wasn't much) not to shrink from him.

And then he kept at me, inflicting his last wound.

A mortal wound.

Slaying me.

"But I'll tell you, bitch, what you don't got, what you won't ever get, what you lost when you lost me, is the most beautiful thing you can have. Your kid sayin' your name. Every fuckin' time Cleo or Zadie say the word 'Daddy,' even if they're whinin' or pissed about somethin', it lights up my world. So keep warm in this fuckin' joint." He threw out a hand again, then used it to indicate me. "In your sexy threads. But you'll never get warm to the bone, knowin' you changed the world, created a miracle, bringing beauty from between your legs that's got fuck-all to do with an orgasm."

On that, he grabbed his cut and walked right out of my house, slamming the door behind him.

And I stood still, staring at the door, the curtain over the window still swaying with the power of his slam, eviscerated, the life force flowing out of me, streaming across my gleaming wood floors, evaporating into nothing.

It took some time, a good deal of it, before I moved. Got myself a cup of coffee. Cleaned up the mess Logan left of his. Went to my bathroom to take a shower and get ready for the day.

But I did it knowing I was back to going through the motions.

Oh, I'd pretend.

For Dot.

And Mom and Dad. Justine. Kellie. Claire.

And I'd breathe until there was no breath left.

But that was all life would be for me.

I knew it because it had happened twenty years earlier, my life leaking away as Logan walked out of it. Then I went through the motions.

Now I'd do it again. But with practice, I'd do it better so those left who cared about me didn't worry.

That's all I'd give.

That's all I'd get.

Until the day I died.

And I was good with that because once I had it all with the promise of even more.

So I'd take that because I knew that was all I'd ever get.

And because I also knew I had no choice.

Elvira

"Yo."

Elvira looked up and saw the commando standing in her office door. His name was Mo.

"Shirleen Jackson just walked in the building," Mo told her. "Checked his schedule. Hawk's not got her on it and anyway, he's out. She here for you?"

Elvira wasn't expecting her but knew Shirleen must be there for her.

"Yep," she answered.

He jerked up his chin commando style, which meant Elvira had no idea how he didn't dislocate something while doing it. He then prowled off into command central, Hawk's theater-style space with workstations that were wired to take over NATO or the United Nations or Cheyenne Mountain or whatever struck his fancy to play with on any given day.

She took the time it took Shirleen to make the office to clear her desk of anything sensitive and she stood when Mo showed Shirleen to her door.

"Gotta talk," Shirleen said as greeting.

Elvira nodded, indicated the two seats opposite her desk with a hand, and invited, "Sit your ass down."

Shirleen sat her ass down.

Mo gave Elvira a look, then took off again and Elvira turned her eyes to her wall of windows that showed command central. It also showed none of the four boys out there manning stations were paying them any mind.

But she still knew they were paying attention.

She looked back to Shirleen, a woman she'd known a long time, a woman she'd worked jobs with, a colleague and also a friend.

"This is a surprise," she noted.

"You're lookin' into Millie Cross," Shirleen announced.

Another surprise.

Elvira said nothing.

But she'd been doing her homework and that included the enjoyable task of pumping information from her man, Malik.

Malik was a Denver cop. He'd been a cop for fifteen years, worked vice the last eight. Malik knew everything about the street.

So when Elvira and the girls instigated Operation MAC (Millicent Anna Cross), she'd gone to a source she knew would be a font of information.

This meant she knew about Logan "High" Judd and Shirleen Jackson. Primarily, she knew about their bond.

"Don't know how that shit began," Malik had told her after the good stuff was done, he was mellow, and they had entered the pillow talk stage that Elvira used for more than one purpose on more than one occasion.

Not that Malik minded. Her man was not stupid. He knew she always had a reason. He also knew she had a certain kind of job. So he filtered as necessary. Which was irritating as hell but it went with the territory when you had the po-po in your bed.

"Just know they're tight," Malik had gone on. "Word was, back when they were both dirty, if Shirleen had a mess she didn't wanna call Darius in to handle, pile more filth on her nephew than he already had, she'd call Judd. And Judd would do cleanup. She called. He came. Not in a way she had something on him and not in a way they were partners. So I don't get it. No one ever did. But it happened. She left the life. The Club got clean. And through all that, whatever they had did not die."

In other words, although this was a surprise visit, Shirleen being up in High's business, business that was getting interesting lately, was no surprise.

"We're joinin' forces," Shirleen announced. "And our first move is Kellie Cliffe."

Kellie Cliffe.

One of Millie's two besties.

The one who was up for anything.

"Joinin' forces with what?" Elvira asked, not playing dumb...exactly.

It was just that Tyra had put the kibosh on further maneuvers. After their last play went south, they'd decided they had to bide their time and find the right in to instigate their next one.

"On reunitin' a love gone bad," Shirleen replied.

"Listen, girl—" Elvira started, leaning across her desk, but she stopped talking when Shirleen's face changed.

Elvira could read faces and Shirleen's face stated loudly that the woman was serious and she was not about to waste any time.

"High would lose his mind, but he said I could put Brody on it, and I did. He did *not* say I could put Vance on it, but I did that too," she shared. "My boys at work, look at 'em, you'd say badass motherfucker. But I know how they are. They'll go the distance for true love, proved that again and again. Gave Vance what I knew, he ran with it. Boy has his ways and what he learned, High likes it or not on the road he's gonna be travelin', I know he'll like it when he gets to his destination. If I gotta club the man and put him on the train, I'm doin' it. And the game you and your girls are playin' that Vance shared with me with that King's Shelter business, I know you're with me. So we're joinin' forces."

Another non-surprise. Vance Crowe was one of Lee Nightingale's boys. He was good at what he did, finding information and fast with little to no muss and fuss.

But also, Vance's wife, Jules, was a social worker who worked at King's Shelter. So he probably knew, or suspected, before Shirleen asked that Tyra, Lanie, and Elvira were up to something.

As Elvira thought this, Shirleen kept talking.

"Vance had a chat with this Kellie girl. She knows the history and it ain't no surprise she's all in. So she's up next. And I got the plan."

Elvira studied her and she did this awhile.

Then she got impatient with doing it, so she said, "Well, lay it on me. Time's wastin', girl."

Shirleen smiled.

Then she talked.

Elvira listened.

Then she smiled.

After that, she grabbed her cell.

She made two calls.

When she was done, they were all agreed.

Kellie Cliffe was up next.

Millie

Twenty-two years ago…

I walked by our futon, Logan flat out on it, eyes to the TV, and I smiled down at him when those eyes came to me.

But I didn't get by the futon on my way to the kitchen to get a drink.

I got my hand caught by my man and pulled so I landed on him.

I stretched out even as I lifted up and looked down at him.

He was feeling good, I could tell by the mellow look in his eyes. I could also tell by the sweet smell in the air.

"How you doin', Snook'ums?" I murmured, and he grinned.

"Excellent grass," he murmured back. "And got my girl on me. So it's all good." He ran his hand over my ass and tilted his head on the arm of the couch. "Though, she's got too many clothes on."

Stoned sex with Logan.

That meant he'd take his time. Even hours.

The best.

Or the best when I got it but it was always the best when I got it, no matter how it came.

Unfortunately, even if it was the best, we didn't have hours.

"You do remember that Dot and my folks are coming for dinner?" I asked.

He rolled so I was pressed to the back of the couch and his face was in my neck. "I didn't forget," he said into my skin. "Come down by then."

"I know you will, Low," I told him, and I did know because he was careful like that. He never disrespected my parents. It was part of what won them over. I ran my hands up the muscle of his back over his tee and continued, "But we should probably not be having sex on the couch when my parents knock on the door."

He lifted his head out of my neck and grinned at me.

Stoned, not stoned, alert, drowsy, preoccupied, focused, I didn't care. Whenever Logan grinned at me, I loved it.

And this was no exception.

"Babe, it's just past two," he informed me.

"And I'm making a roast," I informed him.

"It take four hours to make a roast?" he asked.

"No, but when you're in a certain *mood*, it takes you four hours to get me off."

He burst out laughing, his arms convulsing around me so he was squeezing me to his body.

I watched him do it, smiling and loving that too.

While he was still chuckling, he moved in, nipping my lower lip before gliding his lips against my jaw to my ear.

"How 'bout two hours?" he asked there. "Can my girl give me two hours to have fun before she worries about her roast?"

"I suppose I can give you two hours," I said on a sigh, faking that it was a hardship when it absolutely wasn't.

He lifted his head again and smiled at me.

His smile faded as he moved in to brush his lips against mine.

He kept them there and held my gaze as he said, "Smokin' again and doin' it while I watch you blow me."

Oh God.

Total turn-on.

I *loved* his cock any way I could get it.

Including that way.

My legs moved with agitation.

His eyes started smoldering. "See you like that idea."

"Yeah, baby," I whispered.

"On the floor between my legs or on the couch..." humor mingled with the heat in his eyes when he finished, "between my legs?"

I wasn't feeling in a funny mood.

I was feeling in the mood to give my man a blowjob while he smoked a joint.

"What do you want?" I asked.

At my question, Logan got in my mood.

I knew this when he growled, "Floor."

"Whatever you want, Snooks," I whispered.

I gave him those words. Logan gave me a kiss.

When he ended it, I couldn't wait to give back and do it going down on him.

So I didn't mess around.

I sucked while he smoked until he set the joint aside and let his head loll on the back of the couch so he could concentrate on what I was doing.

His head didn't loll when I stopped sucking, climbed on, and started riding. His attention was all on me.

We were done in time for me to get the roast in and we had a great time with my family as we always did after they'd realized Logan was it for me and believed in it, believed in him and let him in.

Then, after we ate, played board games and they left, Logan and I had another great time.

But this time when we did, he took his four hours.

And another one besides.

Falling asleep twined up in my man, I thought it was what it always was.

The best.

And I slept sound, knowing I had the best, got it early, and also understanding to the heart of me that I would have a lifetime of it, a lifetime of Logan.

A lifetime of the best.

CHAPTER NINE

"Far Behind"

Millie

MY PHONE ON my nightstand rang. I opened my eyes, rolled, looked at the clock to see it was six after eleven, then pushed up to look at the display on my phone.

Kellie.

This happened, not frequently, but it happened.

Usually, I ignored it. She held no grudges. She knew me.

She knew it was a long shot but she never gave up on wanting me to have a life.

However, I'd spent the day making sure an anniversary party would go off without a hitch (it did), so I was even *less* inclined than normal (when I was *never* inclined) to pick up and do the Kellie thing.

But I was also committed to living my lie for the ones I loved.

Logan had walked out two days earlier and he had not come back.

For my part, since then, I had not faltered in continuing the charade.

Tomorrow night, Dot, Alan, and the kids were coming over for beef Stroganoff.

Further, Justine and Veronica were looking for a babysitter so we could plan a night where we could all put on our LBDs, go out, and drink cocktails. Claire was all in for that one, and without a kid or a steady who was truly a *steady*, she was ready when we were set to roll.

In other words, full steam ahead on the charade.

Now it was time to prove to Kellie I'd turned a new leaf and intended to go back to living my life.

So I snatched up the phone, took the call, and put it to my ear.

"'Lo, babe," I greeted, still shaking away sleep.

"*She answers!*" Kellie hooted in a shriek in my ear, so I had to pull the phone away an inch. "*Right on!*" she kept shrieking.

I put my phone back to my ear and said, "Love you, you know it, but don't love you phoning me and shouting in my ear in the middle of the night."

"Three o'clock in the morning is the middle of the night, Mill. Eleven o'clock is *not*," she informed me.

"Whatever," I muttered. "Why are you calling?"

"'Cause there is this *kickass* band you *have to see* playing *right now* at The Roll. They just finished their first set, bitch, and they *brought down the house*. Get your ass outta bed and get it over here, *pronto*, or I'm never speakin' to you again *in my life*."

The last twelve, thirteen years, I'd quit answering Kellie's late-night calls.

The years between being with Logan and not answering her calls, I did take her calls but would then engage in a long conversation about how I needed sleep, how I had work the next day, how I was no longer into live music or doing shots or whatever, this taking time and getting frustrating (hence my quitting answering).

But undoubtedly she'd spoken to Dot and/or Justine, so she'd know about LBDs and beef Stroganoff. She'd hear about *Downton Abbey* or come over and see my candles lit and me using my wineglasses.

So in order to prove to her I was living my life at the same time hiding that I was dead inside, I replied, "I'll be there in an hour."

Silence that wasn't silence, exactly, since I heard the crowd in the background as well as the music they were playing between the live sets.

Then I heard, "Say again?"

I threw back the covers and reached for my light. "Give me an hour and I'll see you there."

I had to take the phone away from my ear again when she screeched, "*Right on!*"

That made me grin and grinning made me realize I was doing the right thing because no matter how I felt down deep, I was giving the people I loved what they needed.

I should have done it a long time ago.

It was too late for that now but better late than never.

And anyway, I *did* like live music and it had been ages since I'd seen a band play.

Not to mention, my little black dress was killer. So I was also going to be sure to find some time to go out with Justine and Veronica. They needed excuses to pretty up and remember why they fell in love in the first place, that being they were both hot, funny, got a kick out of each other, and post-baby that Justine carried, they were still *way* into each other.

Last, I had decided I was totally getting cats. I had it all, lost it all, and knew I'd never get it back. But lonely was lonely and lonely sucked, so I was going to cut the lonely with kitties.

I pushed up from bed and headed to the bathroom, ordering, "Now, hang up so I can slap some makeup on and head out."

"You got it, bitch. Get that ass in gear. See you soon! *Yee ha!*" Kellie cried before I heard her disconnect.

I got my ass in gear and started going through the motions.

When I got a look at myself in the bathroom mirror, I saw that I'd not been in bed long enough for my hair to go wonky, so that was good. Therefore, I slapped on a fair amount of makeup because good rock 'n' roll demanded sacrifice and it had been a while but I knew the depletion of your makeup collection was an acceptable offering.

I no longer had rock 'n' roll clothes but I did my best, throwing on a pair of faded jeans, high-heeled booties, a thick belt, and a thin mulberry sweater that looked torn up and misshapen but it did this with intent, clinging in the right places, flowing and keeping you guessing in better places.

I wrapped a narrow rock 'n' roll (ish) scarf around my neck and stuck long, silver hoops in my ears, piling on the rings and jingling bracelets before shoving lip gloss and wallet into an envelope clutch, grabbing my suede jacket, and heading out.

I hit The Roll, a place that was half bar, half club and had live music on the weekends and some weeknights (this being the club part) but mostly it was a watering hole that I'd heard was a hip place (via Kellie). Therefore, I knew where it was, but it had started up after Logan and I were over, so I'd never been there.

And I hit it not liking what I saw, considering the parking lot was jammed and there was a line out the door.

I parked on the street two blocks away, got out, and started toward the bar even knowing this effort to convince Kellie I was moving out of years of grieving a life gone bad was going to fail. I'd have to pick another night to do that because no way was I standing out in thc cold in a line by myself for God knew how long in order to have a few drinks and listen to music.

And as I walked toward the bar, I had my phone to my ear to tell Kellie precisely that.

This dccision took a hit when she answered and I heard the unmistakable truth that the band was back onstage and they were rocking it even through a cell phone.

"Yo!" she shouted.

"Babe, there's a line," I told her. "It's cold and the line's long. I probably wouldn't get in until the final set and no way I'm standing outside for hours for that."

"Leave it to me. Just go to the door," she replied on another shout.

"Kellie—" I started, but I was talking to dead air. She was gone. "Fuck," I hissed, deciding the next time she called that I'd prove my new leaf by ignoring the call, phoning her the next day, and having her over for Stroganoff or some other brilliant meal I taught myself how to make.

I then hoofed it to the door, knowing no way with this crowd they were going to let in a forty-one-year-old woman who might have good hair, a great suede jacket, and fabulous high-heeled booties because she was still forty-one and no one in line looked over twenty-three.

However, when I got to the door, the bouncer gave me a top to toe, grinned, and then turned to look behind him when he heard shouted, "She's with me!"

Kellie was head and shoulders out the door. The bouncer nodded to her, turned to me, lifted a hand, and did a "get your ass in there" gesture to which someone at the head of the line groused, "Seriously, dude? Been standing out here an hour. What the fuck?"

I ignored the discontent coming from the line, muttered, "Thanks," to the bouncer as I moved swiftly past him, got a, "No problem, sweetheart," which was nice but probably had more to do with Kellie being a regular than me having good hair (or a great jacket). But I still turned my head and gave him a smile.

He gave me a wink.

He couldn't be more than thirty-two, so that felt nice.

I let it feel nice, then let it go and moved to Kellie.

"This'll be *so* worth it," she declared before I could even say hello, her words strangely heavy with meaning.

She reached out a hand and nabbed mine as she spoke.

Before I could reply or figure out the weight of her words, she tugged me inside, the door closing the cold behind us, leaving us in the warm that wasn't just the inside of a building but the inside of a bar heaving with people.

And this was when I realized my mistake.

I'd gone cold turkey on life when I'd ended things with Logan, so I hadn't been to a place like this since then, except my brief visit to Scruff's a few weeks earlier.

That didn't count.

This was it.

This was where it was at.

This was one of a bevy of things back in the day that filled me up and kept life beautiful.

The sights. The lights. The people. The sounds. The vibe.

Electric.

Alive.

Not me.

So, so not me.

Not anymore.

I was there, feeling it, immune to it and missing it all at the same time, the last like an ache because when I'd had it, I'd had it with Logan.

Yes.

Big mistake.

Huge.

I had to get out of here.

I couldn't go.

Dragging me with her, Kellie wended her way expertly through the crowd to a table back in the jumble around a stage where music was blasting.

Good music.

The band was excellent.

I didn't look at the band. I concentrated on getting where Kellie was guiding me without slamming into someone in a chair or a waitress negotiating tables and bodies.

Kellie got us to her table, which was populated by two men and another woman, none of whom I knew, all of whom looked to us as we got there.

"These are my best friends for the night since they let me sit at their table," she shouted, Kellie being one who could make friends anywhere (and did) and thus could go out without a girl posse (and did). She threw her arm out their way. "Jeff, Mark, and Helen."

"Hey," I yelled.

"Yo," Jeff or Mark yelled back.

Mark or Jeff threw up his chin.

Helen smiled, gave a slight wave, then looked back at the stage.

Kellie tugged my hand again until I was sitting in one of the two vacant chairs.

She sat in the other one and expertly snagged a passing waitress.

"Twelve shots of tequila!" she shouted at her, and I felt my eyes get big. "Two for all, and four for my girl here so she can catch up!"

Four shots?

"Gotcha," the waitress yelled back, and took off before I could stop her.

I leaned into Kellie.

"Babe, I'm driving!" I shouted.

"You're also gonna be here awhile and my new buds got popcorn to soak up the booze!" she shouted back, tipping her head to the table.

I looked to the wax-paper-lined red basket on the table that had, on a quick count, seven popped pieces of corn and a plethora of unexploded kernels left in it. Then I looked back to Kellie, who was now eyes to the stage.

"Babe!" I yelled. She kept staring at the stage, bobbing her head and not turning to me, so I yelled again, "Kellie!"

She leaned back my way, attention never leaving the band, and yelled back, "They *so* need a dance floor here. This band makes you wanna *move*."

She was not wrong. They were currently kicking the Black Crowes' "Hard to Handle" and doing it so brilliantly, if Chris Robinson was standing at the bar, he'd be smiling.

My eyes started to move to the stage but stopped when someone slammed into my chair and my entire body jerked as my chair moved three inches toward Kellie's.

"Whoa!" a man shouted, and I looked up at him. "Sorry!"

I smiled. "That's okay!"

He grinned back and moved on.

I again was about to look at the stage when I heard, "Rumor was true! They get their old front man back whenever they come to Denver. And fuck if he doesn't *rock*!"

This was shouted by Helen and I looked to her just as the band ended the song and she jumped up, as did everyone else at our table, at other tables, all the people obscuring my view of the stage, and the crowd roared its approval.

I started clapping and kept smiling because this wasn't so

bad. I'd do a shot, maybe two, order a Coke and listen to good music, sitting with my girl and her new friends. I'd be tired tomorrow but it wouldn't kill me, Kellie would be happy and that was all that mattered.

Slower notes to a song I recognized started. The folks around drifted their asses back to their chairs and a familiar voice sounded over the microphone.

"This song is dedicated to a bitch named Millie."

My eyes shot to a stage I now could see and my heart shriveled to dust when I saw Hopper Kincaid, back in the day a new Chaos brother, and by his words undoubtedly still a Chaos brother, standing front and center. His flame-tattooed arms were moving on the guitar he held. His eyes filled with hate were aimed at me.

"*Not* good to see you again," he growled directly to me, the dust of my heart floating away on his words. Then he played a few more notes and launched into the lyrics of Candlebox's "Far Behind."

I heard Kellie's totally pissed-off, "What the fuck?" but I couldn't tear my eyes from Hop lacerating the bloody pulp of my soul with every word of a sad, angry song.

It was a fantastic song but I'd never really listened to the lyrics.

I listened to them then.

And I knew they might mean one thing to Candlebox.

They meant another to Hopper Kincaid and the family I once had that I loved called Chaos.

Last, they meant something else entirely to me.

And as he tore through me with that song, intentionally lashing wounds that already were laid bare and never would heal, I heard Kellie snap, "I didn't buy into *this shit*," and I knew.

I.

Fucking.

Knew.

I was not there because Kellie got a wild hair to drag me back to life.

I was there because of something else.

I ripped my stare off Hop and looked through the bar knowing what I'd find before I found it.

Then I found it.

Off to the side of the stage, at their own table with a RESERVED sign on it, sat Tack Allen.

With him was his woman, Tyra.

Also the one they referred to as Lanie.

Worse.

Boz. Hound. Big Petey.

And Logan.

The men were aiming their loathing at me. It hit true, the toxin coating my skin and sinking deep.

The women were looking shocked.

They got to Kellie.

They got to *my girl*.

And she'd jumped on board being fed promises of healing wounds that had no cure not having any clue their play would end me.

I shot out of my chair, tucking my purse under my arm, and rounded the table, winding my way their way, eyes to my guess at the ringleader.

Tack's new woman.

"*Millie!*" Kellie screamed.

I ignored her and kept going, brushing people, twisting past chairs. Well before I got to the Chaos table, all were standing, the men in aggressive defensive postures, the women uncertain.

I stopped at their table, Hound stepping mostly in front of me, but I kept my eyes pinned to Tyra.

"Stop!" I shouted, knowing my face was twisted, certain it was ugly, but not caring, only needing one last thing before I ceased to exist.

And that was to get my message across.

"I—" she began, but I cut my gaze to Tack.

"Make her stop!" I demanded.

"Millie—"

That was Logan. He was close. I could hear it and I could feel it.

But I had eyes to Tack, who was injecting my bloodstream with the venom of his gaze at the same time opening his mouth to speak.

Kellie got there before him. "You *motherfuckers*!" she screeched. "Total fuckin' *bitches*. You played me! You goddamned *fuckin'* bitches. Got me to play *my own girl*!" she shrieked.

Tack looked from me to Kellie, then down to his woman.

"Tell me you did not," he growled.

She looked up at him, face pale. "Kane, honey—"

"Millie."

That was Logan again and I felt his hand on me.

It burned.

God, it burned.

Seared.

Scorched my flesh to *nothing*.

I twisted my arm viciously, yanking away, slamming into Kellie and tipping my head back to look up at him.

I lifted my hand, pointing a finger an inch from his face.

I couldn't shroud the agony and I didn't care about that either when I shouted, "Make them *stop*!"

"Babe—" he began, lifting his hand but before he could get to mine I tore it away.

"I'm done walking through fire for you, High!" I yelled. "I'm done not because I'm done but because there's nothing left of me to *burn*. You have it *all*! You've always had it *all*! I gave up *everything* so you could have it *all*! Please! God! Leave me to my nothing!" I swung an arm out to their table.

"And if you gave one single *shit* about me, *ever*, make *them* let me have my *nothing*!"

On that, I pushed, shoved, desperate to get to a place where I could completely fade away and do it alone. Having been given too much too soon and paying the price by having it ripped away so that was all I'd ever have. Nothing. All I'd ever be. Alone. With all that, I made my final dash through the flames, making my way through the bar, out, and I ran to my car on my high heels.

Destined to fade away.

Ready to fade away.

Needing nothing but to leave it all far behind.

High

"Woman, I fuckin' told you." High heard Tack snarl.

But he couldn't pay any mind to what was unraveling because Cherry couldn't keep herself to herself.

He was moving.

Moving to get to Millie, her words battering his brain.

I gave up everything so you could have it all!

And then he was not moving because Kellie was in his space, in his face.

"You fucking *motherfucker*!" she screamed, shoving at his chest.

His body locked, his jaw tightened, and both were good because they stopped him from reciprocating in any way when she shoved him again.

"You *ruined* her!" she shrieked, and his locked body strung tight. "Wasn't that enough?" she asked. "Do you and your bitches gotta get your jollies by fucking her up *again*?" She looked beyond him in the direction of the table. "Newsflash, assholes, there was nothing to fuck up. She was *gone*. You didn't need to make the effort. But *awesome*," she snapped sarcastically, "you hit it just right, bringing back the *only* fuckin' thing on this earth that would tear her shreds into *tatters*."

And on the last, she jerked a thumb High's way.

"Memory serves, bitch, someone else was in shreds after your gash laid him to waste," Boz returned.

"Oh yeah?" Kellie asked, eyes narrowed dangerously on his brother.

"Yeah," Boz shot back.

"You didn't see."

Hop was now at their table, the band still playing onstage, but the players embroiled in the current mindfuck could be anywhere, their attention completely on what was happening right there, right then.

Especially when Kellie whispered those three words.

And how she did it.

They all heard it; High could sense how they heard it.

But he *felt* it.

Each word.

"What didn't we see?" Pete asked.

High watched Kellie's body twitch, then she shook her head. "You don't deserve to know that. You don't deserve," she looked to High, "*dick*." She raised a hand to point a finger in his face. "Keep the fuck out of her life, asshole. Leave her alone."

"She left me," High growled.

"Wasn't her who walked away," Kellie returned.

High's shoulders strained taut in a way it felt any movement would make them snap.

Jesus.

Fuck.

Jesus.

"Was her told him to get gone," Boz pointed out angrily.

"Wasn't her who walked away and didn't come back," Kellie replied to Boz, but the words were for High and he knew it from more than the fact that she didn't take her eyes from him. She was whispering in a heaving bar with a rock band playing but he heard every word clear. "You didn't come back." She repeated, got up on her toes, her gaze locked to his, and sneered, "So who left who behind, asshole?"

On that, she rolled back on her heels, sent a poison look through them all, turned, and stormed through the tables.

High watched her go, frozen.

You love a man, Millie, you believe in him, you take him as he is. You go on his journey with him no matter what happens, even if that means you have to walk through fire.

He'd said that.

Twenty years ago, he'd said that, looking into her eyes, feeling so much, he didn't see shit.

He didn't see what was in her eyes.

I'm done walking through fire for you, High!

Jesus.

Newsflash, assholes, there was nothing to fuck up. She was gone.

Fuck.

She was gone.

He knew it. He saw it. Her house. Her clothes. Her office.

The only time she was back was when he had her in his arms.

So who left who behind, asshole?

Fuck!

He came unstuck just as a hand landed on his shoulder.

He turned to it.

"Brother," Tack said low.

"Control. Your. *Woman*," High ground out, shrugged off his brother's hand, and pushed through the bar to the door.

He got to his bike, swung on, and took off.

He hit every red light, every *fucking* one, before he parked right in front of Millie's house.

He saw it was dark.

He found this concerning.

Jesus, her face at the bar.

That was not anger. It wasn't frustration.

It was anguish.

Etched there.

Hidden until then.

It had leaked out. He'd seen it in her office.

But he'd still refused to see.

Fuck.

He prowled up to her house, pounded on her door, and kept doing it.

Nothing. No lights coming on, he sensed no movement through the sheer.

He continued pounding.

She could be ignoring him.

The look on her face in that bar, she could be in there doing something else.

He didn't have his picking kit and he didn't have time to go get it. Furthermore, upon testing it, she had a deadbolt, so a credit card didn't work.

That meant he had to take off his cut, wrap it around his fist, and punch through her glass.

He did it, unlocked the door, pushed it open, and went in, his boots crunching through the shards.

He went right to her bedroom switched on the light, and his lungs expanded so sharp, he thought they'd explode.

Shit was everywhere. Clothes, shoes, drawers open, stuff hanging out.

He jogged to the bathroom and found more of a mess.

Fuck, did she do this or was someone waiting for her?

Was this a struggle or a frenzy?

Was someone paying attention to what High was doing, where he was going, *who* he was doing, and they targeted Millie to get to High? To Chaos?

Shit, had Valenzuela finally lost patience and made his play?

With Millie?

Fuck, could their luck suck *that* bad?

He jogged out of the bathroom, her bedroom, into the house, finding switches, turning on lights.

Everything in the rest of the house was as it should be.

Immaculate.

He moved to the back door, pulled the curtain aside, and looked through.

No red SUV.

He swiftly moved back through the house to the unused bedroom, going straight to the closet.

Her luggage was gone.

It was frenzy.

It was Millie.

It was Millie packing in a rush to get away from him and to get away from Tyra and her crew's bullshit.

"Goddamned...fucking...*shit*," he bit out, yanking out his phone.

It was then High made the call he'd not made in twenty years.

It rang five times and then he heard, "Hello, you've reached the voicemail of Millie Cross of Cross Events. I'm unable to take your call right now but leave a—"

He hung up and tried again.

Voicemail again.

He went to the email with the file Shirleen sent and pulled it up.

He stared at it, scrolling through with his thumb to get the number he needed.

He decided to start with phoning. He'd see where that got him and make his next move.

So he punched in Dottie's number.

It was picked up on the second ring and High got a pissed male voice who didn't bother with a greeting.

"I know who the fuck this is and I know your shit is done," the man stated. "She's gone. Let her be gone and stop dicking with her head."

High studied his boots and ordered, "Listen to me—"

The man cut him off, "You got nothin' to say I wanna hear. Nothin' Dot wants to hear. Sure as fuck nothin' Millie wants to hear. It's over, man, and it's that in a way you got no choice. So let it go."

"I don't know you, bud," High started. "But I know you weren't around then, so you don't know dick about what's happening, so you don't know I gotta speak to Millie and you don't know *how* I gotta speak to Millie. You got no call to trust me but I'm askin' you to trust this, it's urgent."

"Only chance you got of gettin' your *urgent* message to her is if you can send smoke signals, she can read them, and she sees them before she gets her ass on a plane. Dot and her are on their way to the airport. She'll be gone before you can get your bike parked out there."

Fuck!

"DIA?" High prompted.

"Far away from you," the man replied. "First hit, red-eye to New York. Second hit, Paris. Think that's far enough she can get her head together and sort out her life. But, man, I'm tellin' you this for the sole purpose that you'll get the message. She's not comin' back. She's puttin' distance between her and here, which means her and *you*, and she's gonna keep that up one way or another and I mean physically. Denver is a memory for her because *you* need to be a memory for her. And while I got you, *bud*, thanks," he spat the last word. "Thanks for takin' our girl away from us. The aunt my kids fuckin' love, the sister my wife adores, the woman I met who's got no light in her but she's still got enough love in her to light up the worlds of the people who matter. That's lost to us now 'cause a' you. Thanks for that, asshole. Thanks a fuckin' lot."

And with that he hung up.

High dropped his hand to his hip, fingers still curled around his phone, and he studied the toes of his boots.

Not sure you can get a passport in a day, Logan.

You wanna go to Paris, I'll find a way.

She went to Paris.

He knew from what Shirleen and Brody found that Millie had never left the country but she did have a passport.

And she was using it to go to Paris.

Without him.

Leave me to my nothing!

High had a choice.

Lead with his heart and get an emergency passport, get Brody on finding her, and get his ass to France so he could find out what in *the fuck* was going on.

Or lead with his gut, knowing a woman could not change her entire life from Paris. She had a business. She had a home.

She'd be back.

And when she was back, she'd be calmer. She'd have taken the time to get herself together.

And he'd know when she was back because he'd have Brody on that too.

Then he'd talk to her right there in that fucked-up, immaculate house and *then* he'd finally find out what in *the fuck* was going on.

He wanted to lead with his heart. All he could see was her face at The Roll. All he could hear were her words clawing at his soul.

But he'd gone with his heart with Millie before. He'd sustained the blows she was delivering, not paying a lick of attention, walking away in an effort to end the pain.

If he'd gone with his gut back then, he'd have paid attention. He'd have seen. He'd have heard.

He wouldn't have left her behind.

He would have known all she spewed was shit and he would have gone back.

"Fuck," he muttered. "Gut," he decided.

It cost him but High went with that decision.

But before he did, he went to get his truck, drove to Ride, got some plywood, and went back to Millie's to board up her door.

Tyra

I followed Tack into our bedroom.

He turned on the light, moved to the bed, sat on it, and bent to his boots.

I closed the door behind me and stood leaning against it.

The drive up the mountain was silent and uncomfortable.

My man was mad.

"Kane—" I started.

He lifted his head to look at me and I shut my mouth.

"I told you," he rumbled.

"You don't understand, honey," I said softly.

"No," he bit, standing. "You don't understand, Tyra." He planted his hands on his hips. "Fuck, woman, can you honest to God stand there and fight your corner after witnessing how your fucked-up shit played out tonight?"

"There can't be that much feeling unless there's *that much feeling*, Kane," I pointed out.

"Tell me, Red, when we were gettin' together, you gutted me and I walked away from you, made it clear I wanted nothin' more to do with you even if you sorted your head out. Some bitch you didn't fuckin' know got up in your business, shovin' you at me only for you to take the hit of gettin' shot down again and again and again, the brothers at my back delivering the same kind of blows. You'd want that?"

"If I got you back, yes," I whispered. "I'd take any hit over and over and over again until I got you back."

He stared at me.

I held his stare and let the silence stretch.

Then I ended it.

"Tell me you saw her tonight," I said.

He looked away, tearing his hand through his hair.

He saw.

"She's in pain." I told him something he now knew.

He looked back at me. "None of our business."

"Honey—"

His next came as a warning whisper.

"None of our business, Red." He drew in breath and kept his eyes locked to mine. "You know it. You know how it is. Those boys, my brothers, *your* brothers, they fuckin' love you, babe. Totally fuckin' love you. But you know men like us. You fuckin' know down to your soul men like us. You know this shit is not on. Your purpose is compassionate. But men like us, your methods are unacceptable." He kept hold of my eyes and dropped his voice to gentle. "And you know it, baby. So you know this is none of our business."

"She might do something—" I started.

He cut me off. "I'll keep an eye."

I nodded. I'd take that because I had to but also because I knew he would.

"You done now?" he asked.

I shook my head and saw his jaw grow hard.

But I told him, "I don't like it. But I think I have to be."

His face relaxed and his order was quiet and coaxing. "Get ready for bed, darlin'."

I nodded again and went about doing that.

I joined my man in bed.

I didn't sleep.

My husband felt it.

"You need to relax," he said.

"Do you think that High's going to—?"

"I think it's none of our business."

I lifted my head. "Tack—"

"Babe. No." Two words, firm. And he went on just like that. "You are who you are and I'm with you because a' that. I am who I am and you're with me because a' that. What we got, it works. Phenomenally. We do what we do, we are what we are and we get off on it, no holding back. But this is us. *That's* the Club. That's a brother. The same does not hold true with the brothers. You got your place in the Club. I got mine. We know our places, Red, and we don't deviate. So until a brother makes somethin' our business, it's none of our business, yeah?"

"I'm worried," I shared.

There was a vein of amusement in his gravelly voice when he muttered, "No shit?"

"Tack." It was a lame snap.

He pulled me deeper into his arms and held me close.

"High and me have not seen eye to eye on numerous occasions over the years but that don't mean he isn't Chaos. He's Chaos, down to the bone. He's a brother of my soul. So what do you think he's gonna do?"

There it was.

Exactly what I needed.

"Take care of Millie," I whispered.

"Yeah," Tack whispered back, starting to stroke my hair. "Now, you gonna relax and go to sleep?"

"I'll try."

He sighed.

Then he rolled into me.

Once there, he muttered, "Know a way to make you relax."

He knew about seven thousand of them.

Before I could say a word, he dipped his head to me, took my mouth, and set about making me relax.

High

The next day, High was back at Millie's to be there when the men he called replaced the glass with another thick, bevel-edged sheet.

Due to the fact that he swiped an extra key, he was also there three days later when the men he called installed the alarm system, which meant all the glass, windows, and doors throughout her house were wired for break-ins.

And he took the call when Brody told him what hotel she was staying at in Paris. He also took more calls when she used a card so Brody could tell him where she had breakfast, lunch, dinner, got money, what tours she went on, where she shopped and what she bought.

Last, Brody told High when she'd be back.

Two weeks.

He had to depend on his gut for two weeks.

He applied for an emergency passport anyway.

Just in case.

Millie

Twenty-one years ago...

"Brother's bummed," Dog stated.

I looked from the recruit behind the bar at the Chaos compound—a recruit who was no longer a recruit and that was why we were all partying since he and his new brother Brick had been fully initiated into the fold the day before—to the couch where Dog's eyes were aimed.

Boz was slouched there, deep in the seat, legs splayed wide, eyes aimed across the room.

Dog was right.

Boz looked bummed.

Someone had to do something about that and I decided that someone would be me.

I turned back to Dog and grinned. "This is a party, so *that* can't happen."

He looked to me and winked. "Go get 'im, girl."

I slid off my barstool, grabbed my beer, and said, "Tequila. Stat."

Dog turned, nabbed a bottle of tequila from the back of the bar, and handed it to me.

I lifted it. "Perfect medicine."

At that, he smiled and muttered, "No doubt."

I tipped my head and smiled back, then moved through the room, past the pool tables, toward Boz, my feet in biker boots, my ass covered in cutoffs, my top barely covered in a halter.

As I approached Boz, he didn't even look at me.

The guys looked. They hugged. They even touched, a hand or a waist, sometimes a tug of the hair. I was a girl. I was showing skin. They were men in the sense they were *men*. This happened.

But I was an old lady, so it happened in a certain way that would not communicate anything that Logan wouldn't like.

It was respect to him.

It was also respect to me.

It was Chaos.

I finally got Boz's attention when I threw myself onto the couch beside him and declared, "Know a boy who looks like he needs a buzz."

He smiled a smile that didn't reach his eyes, then tipped his head to the bottle. "You gonna take care of that for me?"

I extended the tequila. "Absolutely."

He grabbed it, murmuring, "Gratitude, sister."

Sister.

I sighed happily and slouched next to him, our bodies touching from shoulders to knees.

He uncapped the bottle, flicked the top, and it flew then skidded across the floor, unheeded, several feet away.

I watched as he took a healthy tug.

When he dropped the bottle, I asked, "You okay?"

"I'm good, Millie," he told the room.

And he lied.

I looked from him to the room and I saw the party.

I also saw something else.

I was an old lady, so I wasn't let in on a number of things. If the boys were at our place and conversation turned to something that wasn't mine to know, Logan gave me a look I knew and acted on without question. I then would get out of earshot, going upstairs to listen to music in our bedroom or going to the second bedroom to study.

That didn't mean I didn't hear things or see things.

And right then I saw things.

What I saw was Tack, Brick, Hop, and Black standing in one corner, huddled and talking, beers in their hands, none of this happening in a way that seemed they were at a party.

I also saw Naomi, Tack's old lady, sitting at a table with Keely, Big Petey, and Bev, a new girl who was hanging around that Boz normally, if he wasn't in a crappy mood, would be paying attention to. Keely, Bev, and Big Petey were shooting the shit. Naomi had all her attention focused on her old man and she didn't look happy.

The woman rarely looked happy but in this instance, she looked less happy.

And last, in another corner, I saw Chew and Arlo talking with my man.

They stood with Crank.

Crank was Chaos's president. Crank was a decent guy but he was also the only one who kind of freaked me out.

I couldn't put my finger on it but every brother I knew was genuine. They were who they were and showed it, no bullshit.

I got a weird feeling that what made Crank went deeper, possibly darker. That feeling told me he didn't share it all. And it was so stark compared to how all the other brothers were it freaked me.

I watched and saw that Crank right then was not paying attention to Chew, Arlo, or Logan, who were also huddled and talking.

He was staring at Tack in a way I found chilling.

I didn't know what this meant. All I knew was that Brick and Dog were fresh brothers. Hop too.

And they'd all been recruited by Tack.

All the brothers could put forward a man to become a recruit but Tack had been busy the last few years.

I also knew Chew, Arlo, Boz, and Logan had all been recruited by Crank.

So had Black.

But Black was standing with Tack.

There was a split. I felt it. It wasn't tension, nothing with the brothers was that perceptible.

But there was a vibe.

Things were changing in the Club in a lot of ways. The store and garage were getting busier, the Club pushing for that, which meant Logan was working more. It also meant, since the brothers split any profits equally, he (which translated to *we*) was making more money.

Like, *a lot* more money.

Though there was more and that more meant Logan was busy far more than he'd ever been before on Club business that had nothing to do with the store or the garage.

I got the sense he liked it at the same time I got the contradictory sense that it troubled him. I also got a sense that whatever this was was a moneymaking venture that had nothing to do with selling auto supplies and building custom bikes and cars or even growing and selling pot.

Logan didn't talk about it and I knew he wouldn't so I didn't ask so I couldn't know.

This troubled me.

That concern didn't run deep. I wasn't out and out worried. I wasn't questioning things. I knew these men. I knew this family.

I also knew they were bikers, lived in their own world, had their own rules and did things their own way and those things were whatever the hell they wanted to do.

Last, I knew that if they stayed solid and strong, they could get away with doing whatever the hell they wanted to do. In fact, their bond was so powerful, if they stuck together, they could achieve anything.

This was the part that troubled me.

Because I sensed a split. I sensed that Boz didn't know which way he was leaning. And I saw that it seemed that Logan had cast his lot with Crank and I didn't know if that was the right choice.

I sipped my beer, staring at my man, watching him nod at something Arlo was saying, lost in these thoughts until I felt my knee nudged by Boz.

I looked to him and at what I saw in his eyes, I held my breath.

"It's always gonna be good," he said quietly.

"Okay," I replied just as quiet.

"High will make it that way for you, babe. You know it. Yeah?"

Something was wrong in the Club.

But I knew what Boz said was right.

And that was all that I needed.

"Yeah," I whispered.

He grinned at me and it again didn't reach his eyes.

Then he kept doing it and finally committing to it when he offered the bottle of tequila to me.

"Time for us to get smashed, gorgeous," he declared.

I took the bottle from him and replied, "No truer words were spoken."

Then I threw back a healthy slug.

"That's my girl," Boz stated, and when I looked at him, he had humor and approval gleaming in his eyes. His earlier look of uncertainty and disquiet was gone.

I'd done my job.

So I handed him the bottle and slouched deeper into the couch, slouching into Boz as he shifted to curl an arm around me and I shifted to curl my legs on the seat, resting my head on his shoulder.

"Don't get comfortable," he warned, giving me a squeeze. "After another coupla shots, I'm kicking your ass at pool."

"The hell you are," I returned. "We're fifteen and twelve with *me* being the fifteen and about to make it sixteen."

"Bullshit."

"You'll see," I muttered, sucking back more beer.

When I was done, the tequila was in front of my face and I took the bottle from Boz.

I also threw back another slug.

When I was done with that, my eyes hit on my man.

He was smiling at me, his smile content and not troubled.

I knew it before but I knew it even more then.

Boz was right.

Whatever was happening in the Club would happen.

But Logan would keep it good for me. It'd never touch me.

Not ever.

Not *ever*.

CHAPTER TEN

Finally

Millie

I SAT IN the back of the taxi, exhausted beyond comprehension, my phone to my ear.

"No, I'm good, Dot," I told my sister, a complete and total lie since travel and jet lag were kicking my ass. "Is my car at my house?"

"Alan and I took it there yesterday, babe. Also straightened up a bit," she shared cautiously, giving me the information and doing it not wanting to remind me why my place was left the way it was. "But do you think you should stay there?" she asked, then suggested, "Maybe you should stay over here."

I wanted to stay with my sister and Alan and the kids for as long as I could stay with my sister and Alan and the kids since I intended to move as soon as I could to Arizona, and I wouldn't be able to see them whenever I wanted to see them.

But I was wiped and being wiped and needing sleep and clear headspace to get on with doing what I needed to do were not conducive to having two kids under the age of ten in the house.

"I'm gonna crash at my place," I told her. "And I'll be fine," I assured hurriedly, hoping she'd believe me even knowing she wouldn't. "I just need to get my head together, start getting other things together, and maybe tomorrow night I can come and stay with you?"

"You can stay with us anytime, you know that," she replied.

I did.

And I would.

For as long as it took me to sort things out with work, get my house on the market, and get the hell out of Denver.

"Right," I said. "I'm almost home. When I get there, I'm going right to bed. When I can think straight, I'll call you and we'll plan. Okay?"

"Okay, Mill. Whatever you need."

That was what it had always been from Dottie.

Whatever I needed.

And nearly two weeks ago, after I'd driven like a lunatic to get home after what happened at The Roll, packing like a crazy person, only grabbing the things I needed, all this so I could get out of there and fast just in case Logan got a wild hair and followed me, she'd again done just that.

Given me what I needed.

I'd woken them up when I'd made it to their house. Then I'd blathered and bawled, letting it all hang out, everything from what happened in Logan's RV to Hop singing "Far Behind" and all the rest.

As he listened, Alan, a good man, a good husband, a guy who loved his wife like crazy and loved her sister, too, had kept it together by the skin of his teeth. I knew he was close to ballistic. That ballistic being hunting Logan down and giving it his all to beat the crap out of him (which would be an interesting scenario, as Alan was a badass so it would be a close match, though I suspected Logan would fight dirty).

But he didn't lose it because at that moment he needed to be all about me and doing what he could to help his woman help her sister.

And that he did.

Dottie had kept it totally together, as usual, and got online to get me covered.

She'd also let me borrow things to take with me. Once

sorted, something that at Dottie's hand didn't take long, we got in the car and she stole me away to the airport.

It had taken ages but I'd eventually landed in France. I'd then had my first vacation since...*ever*...doing it the first week communicating liberally with Claire, Justine, Dottie, and various clients. I did this with the girls so they had my work covered (it took all of them pitching in...and they all did, *loved* my girls and owed them *huge*).

I'd also phoned my parents in Arizona and sorted that out.

Then I'd found a real estate agent.

Last, I'd had several in-depth conversations with Claire, who had been with me a long time, who knew what she was doing, demonstrated this repeatedly over the years but did it more by covering my shit while I took off to another country and had a mini nervous breakdown.

She was considering buying me out. It'd take her years. She'd have to do it in installments. And she didn't much like the idea. She liked working with me and actually preferred being an assistant and not having the headaches of being the boss.

But she knew she was good at what she did, the clients knew her and trusted her, she could keep Cross Events functioning and successful, and she could make a whole lot more as the boss.

So she was considering it.

That was all I'd managed to do while I was away, partly because I was in a different time zone on a different continent, so there wasn't much more I could do.

But mostly it was because I was taking my first vacation... *ever*...and I was in *Paris*.

And I was in Paris at the perfect time because it was November, the place wasn't overrun with tourists, and there were actually Parisians in the city (Parisians, I was told while I was there, did their best to take off when the place was covered in tourists). Thus I decided my experience was more authentic.

It was chilly but it was amazing. So beautiful it almost seemed unreal.

So I ate. I drank. I roamed. I shopped. I got on tour buses, rode, took pictures, and listened to not very good tapes telling me what things were. I got out of the city and saw Versailles. I sat in spectacular gardens and people watched. I spoke broken French to French people who were a lot friendlier than I'd expected them to be.

I had intended to spend two full weeks there but it finally occurred to me I was hemorrhaging money having a Parisian getaway/breakdown when my future was uncertain. Therefore, I cut my visit two days short, thus necessitating a variety of flight changes that were not the greatest.

But they got me home.

And I got what I needed from Paris.

I'd come to terms with what was left of my life.

And what I came to terms with was that I was not beaten.

I was angry.

Twenty years ago, I'd broken up with Logan. Yes, we were in love, *deeply* in love. Yes, we were happy. Yes, we had it all.

Because I gave it all to him.

Sure, he gave it back but I was the best old lady *ever*. Keely absolutely adored Black, she had old lady down *pat*, but I was even better than *her*.

And I was totally better than Naomi, who, frankly, was mostly a bitch (so I was glad Tack had moved on, though I was not admitting it since I was also ticked at Tack *and* his new woman).

And most importantly, I'd ended it for *him*.

For Logan.

Logan didn't know that but I did, damn it.

What I didn't do was cheat on him. Steal from him.

Stick him with a knife while he was sleeping because he didn't buy me a diamond bracelet I wanted (since I didn't want any diamond bracelet, just him). Burn down the house in a fit of pique to make a point about him not doing the dishes.

We were together.

We broke up.

Twenty years ago.

People broke up all the time!

He had to get over himself.

But he'd have to do it without me.

He thought I had to pay? Well, maybe he was right and I knew he didn't know (and I wasn't going to tell him, not *ever*), so being the man he was, he would think that.

And I'd paid.

Now I was done.

No more.

I hoped I communicated that to him and the rest of them that horrible night at The Roll. I'd also spoken to Kellie and she told me what she'd told them, so if I didn't communicate it to them, I hoped what she said did.

But it didn't matter. I had set my course and it was time for massive change. A new life away from any possibility of seeing Logan at my home, having his people mess with my life, or even seeing him at a Chipotle ordering a burrito.

I just hoped I could avoid any of that kind of thing before I was able to get myself gone. There was a lot to do. It would probably take weeks.

During that time, after I got preliminary stuff sorted, I'd stay at Dottie and Alan's. I could work from there, too, unless I had to see a client, which meant going to my studio. And being at Dot and Alan's, I would hope, would mean Logan wouldn't mess with me.

But if anything happened, if *any* of them did *one single thing*, I was calling the cops.

Fuck them.

All of them.

Especially Logan.

He was dead to me.

All of Chaos were.

They had to be so I could get on with what was left of my life.

This was what I was intent on doing (after I slept for three days) when the taxi dropped me off behind my house. The driver took my luggage out of the trunk and put it inside the back door. I gave him a good tip. He smiled and I didn't watch as he got in his cab and rolled away.

I knew Dot had been in to turn up the furnace, straighten up, return my car, and make sure I had some food.

So all I had to do was take off my clothes and drop in my bed.

Which was what I was going to do.

I locked the door behind me and wandered into the living room, sliding the purse from my shoulder to toss on my couch, my feet set on a course for my bed.

"Millicent Anna Cross."

I stopped dead as my body coated in ice when I heard a voice that shouldn't be coming at me from my living room. I looked and saw the man sitting in my cuddle chair, facing me, two men standing behind him.

I'd never seen him before.

He was dressed well. Hispanic. Good-looking. And he seemed laid back.

But he scared the holy shit out of me because I didn't know him, he knew me, and *he was in my living room*!

I tensed to flee but stopped as my head shot to the side when I felt movement there.

Another man was coming close.

And he had a gun pointed at me.

I felt the blood drain from my face and my eyes drifted

back to the man in my cuddle chair against their will because I thought it pertinent to keep an eye on the guy with the gun.

But the man in my chair spoke again and he seemed the type of guy who liked to have people's attention when he talked. He also seemed the type of guy you didn't piss off, seeing as he was cool with breaking into a woman's home with his minions, one of whom pointed a gun at her.

"You should know who I am, of course," he stated. "I'm Benito Valenzuela. Perhaps your man has mentioned me."

I stared at him, fighting my body quaking, so aware there was an actual *gun* pointed at me and scary people *I did not know* in my living room that both these things felt like physical touches slithering against my skin, making the fight to stop shaking an extremely difficult one.

"Has he?" the man asked.

I kept staring and did it awhile before it hit me he'd asked me a question.

"Sorry?" I croaked. "Has who what?"

"Has High mentioned me?"

Oh fuck.

Fuck, fuck, FUCK!

This guy was here because of Chaos.

This man was in my house with his minions, one of them training a gun on me, *because of High.*

It was then I belatedly saw the crate sitting next to my cuddle chair.

The crate I thought was lost.

The crate with the pictures in it that I'd mourned.

Until two weeks ago.

Now, like a bad penny, it was back.

But now I knew this man had taken it.

Which meant he had an eye on my house. High coming. High going. Pictures of High and me in that crate.

He had the wrong idea.

Fuck.

Fuck, fuck, *fuck*!

"I see he hasn't," the man muttered, and my attention sliced back to him. "Chaos. The only thing we agree on is keeping gash out of our business."

I felt my mouth get dry.

He tipped his head to the side. "You've taken a lot of resources."

"I...what?" I asked when he didn't say anything further.

"Having a man at the airport waiting for you," he told me. "Two weeks. That's a lot of man hours."

More cold slinked over my skin.

Why would he do that?

"Weak link," he said softly, something in his eyes changing, and I didn't like him or this situation before, but that change made me like it even less. "With Arlo out west and the situation here deteriorating, I had to find the weak link. The one with the hot head. The one who understands how the game is played. The last bastion of a lost empire. The one I could nudge to set things in motion." He lifted his finger, wagged it up and down my way, and whispered, "I'm nudging."

"I don't know..." I cleared my throat quickly when the words came out choked. "I don't know what you think but I don't have anything to do with Chaos."

He shook his head, moved a hand, tapped the top of the crate beside him, and said, "High Judd fucking you on your desk in that pretty little house out back says different."

Oh God!

"You watched?" I wheezed.

He shook his head again. "Not me, I missed that show. But I heard it was a good one."

Oh *God*!

Now I was terrified *and* humiliated.

"Now," he went on, "I've waited some time for your return

and I'd rather not wait anymore. You're home, so you can deliver a message for me."

Since delivering a message usually included being capable of doing that, this gave me hope that perhaps this scenario was not going to end how I feared it would. In other words, culminating in a variety of horrible, degrading, painful, and possibly deadly ways.

So quickly I asked, "What message?"

Eyes on me, slowly, he stood.

I braced, doing it fearing my body would splinter into pieces, my attention keen on him.

I experienced that sensation for far too long as he just stood there, staring at me.

When I thought I'd scream, he said one word.

"Nudge."

Then, just with that, he gave me a weird, frightening smile, looked to the men in the room, jerked his head, and they all walked to my hall and disappeared.

I heard my front door open and close.

I stood frozen to the spot, breaths coming in rasps, torn between running the other way and running their way to make sure they were gone.

I heard a car start up outside and I also heard it drive away.

When I heard it no more, I moved.

I did it fast and I did it without thinking.

My movements took me to the drawer in my kitchen that held a variety of things, all of it meticulously organized in trays.

I grabbed my car keys and dashed out the back door.

I didn't lock it.

I ran to my car, got in, tossed my purse to the passenger seat, started up, turned the SUV around in my courtyard, and headed down my drive.

I then took a trek I had not taken in twenty years.

I drove to Broadway, down Broadway, direct to Ride Auto Supply.

Direct to Chaos.

I pulled in, drove down the side of the store, and saw the big garage in the back where they built their bikes and cars. I headed into the massive forecourt of the garage, turned left, and parked outside the long building that ran the length of the space from the back of the store to the end of their property.

The Chaos Compound.

I parked, got out, and ran into the Compound.

I skidded to a halt in a place I knew like the back of my hand, hadn't seen in decades, and with the little I took in, noticed it hadn't changed a bit.

I'd skidded to a stop at the curve of the bar that ran along the front of the room.

There I saw Big Petey on a stool and seeing a man I once cared about deeply, I couldn't hack it.

So I looked behind the bar to a good-looking, young, blond guy I didn't know and snapped, "Who's your president?"

I was holding on by a thread. I was drained from travel, my body in a different time zone, and I'd had my home invaded by a man I knew was the worst news there could be.

"Say what?" the blond asked.

"Millie—" Pete started, and I sensed him getting off his stool.

I whipped up a hand, palm out his way, not looking from the blond but declaring to Pete, "You don't exist." Then I used my hand to jab a finger at the blond and demanded, "You. Tell me *immediately*. Who's your president?"

The blond didn't look happy some strange woman was barking at him but I didn't give that first fuck. I'd stand there and scream my question until I was hoarse in order to get an answer.

The blond opened his mouth to speak when I heard from behind me, "I am."

I turned at the rough voice I knew all too well and watched Tack sauntering into the Compound.

He'd taken over.

His side had won.

And Logan was still Chaos.

This didn't surprise me in the least.

Bottom line no matter who held the gavel, Logan would be Chaos.

It was what he was.

It was *all* he was.

That filtered through me but as it did I didn't lose hold on my mission.

I turned to Tack.

"You have this one shot," I declared. "It happens again and I survive it, I'm going straight to the cops. I know Chaos doesn't like cops and this is *the...final...respect* I pay the Club. It happens again, I don't care if it brings down the brotherhood. I'm going to the police."

Tack didn't look from me when he ordered, "Snap, get High. Now."

"No!" I yelled, panic leaking in, me beating it back, and I looked toward the bar to see the blond moving the length of it. "Don't you move!" I cried. "This is not about High. I do *not* wanna see High."

"Go," Tack commanded. "Fast."

The blond jogged out.

Fuck.

Focus. I had to focus.

"Millie, sweetheart, you're riled up," Big Petey said from behind me. "Come sit down, girl."

I didn't look away from Tack.

"You get him to back off," I demanded. "You tell him I am *not* Chaos. You tell him to keep *the fuck* away from me."

"You need to talk straight to High, Millie," Tack returned, weirdly gentle, like he was handling me with care. "You know how it is, darlin'," he finished.

"Why?" I asked. "He's not president."

"It's his business, not mine," Tack replied.

"It *is* yours. It's," I whirled a finger in the air, "*all* of yours."

Tack started to say something but I felt a hand light on the small of my back so I whirled, then I scampered four steps deeper into the room, running into a chair and stopping.

"Do *not* touch me," I hissed at Big Petey.

He flinched, his face turning haggard with worry, then he looked at Tack.

I also looked at Tack and saw him watching me closely.

"High's at the store, Millie. He'll be here soon," Tack said.

"I don't give a fuck where he is," I retorted. "You're the president. You deal with shit like this. I know. I know this is your shit because he told me. Benito Valenzuela sat in *my*," I jerked a thumb toward myself, "*cuddle chair* while one of his minions pointed a gun at me and *he told me*!"

The room, on alert, went wired but I didn't give that first shit.

"Keep him away from me," I snapped. "You don't, I call the cops. Your shit stopped infesting my life at The Roll while Hop sang a Candlebox song."

"Valenzuela visited you?" Tack asked, and I heard it.

I heard the menace.

Hell, I even felt it since it was clogging the room.

"He told me to tell you *nudge*," I shared. "I don't know what that means. I don't care. Just keep that asshole *out of my life*."

"Millie, honey, you need to take a breath and take a seat. Let me get you a drink," Pete offered, and I cut my eyes to him.

"I don't want a drink. I want nothing from Chaos except for them to get *the fuck* out of *my life*!" I ended this screaming and I ended it right before a door closed.

I looked that way and saw the blond.

I also saw Hop.

And further, I saw Logan.

He looked surprised. He looked watchful. He also looked guarded. And he looked all of these as his attention was focused entirely on me.

But the brutal beauty of the vision of him burned. Burned straight into my eye sockets, searing right into my brain.

I'd let him go to give him everything.

I'd searched for him to explain and say how sorry I was it had to be that way.

And he'd used me, abused me, and torn me to shreds.

Then his shit invaded my home, not the bad shit that was him and his brotherhood, the stinking pile of shit that was whatever mess Chaos was involved in with Benito Valenzuela, something they were clearly failing to control.

"This is the last time I see you," I told Logan.

"Millie," he said quietly, moving my way slowly. "Let's go back to my room so we can—"

It happened then.

There was no way to hold it back.

I no longer had it in me.

So I leaned his way and lost it.

Completely.

"This is the last time I see you!" I screeched.

He rocked to a halt as my emotion scored jagged through the room.

I looked to Tack and jabbed a finger his way again. "You keep your business out of my business." I jabbed my finger toward Logan but kept my gaze to Tack. "And you keep *him* out of *my life*."

"Millie, baby," Logan, now talking gently, said as the door opened and Hound and Boz came in, eyes instantly darting around to take in the players. "Come with me to my room—"

"Fuck you!" I spat at him, and looked back to Tack. "Deal with it. You don't, *I* will."

And I was done.

Even as the door opened again and Tyra and the tall, lanky, dark-haired guy that was with Tabby at Wild Bill's moved in, I started to make my way hurriedly toward the exit.

I was stopped when Logan moved quickly to the side and caught my elbow.

I twisted it out of his hold and scuttled away again, this time running into a table.

"Don't you ever again put your hand on me," I bit out.

"Mill—"

"*You never again touch me!*" I shrieked.

"Baby," he said softly. "We gotta talk."

My body snapped straight and my mouth moved.

"Yes, we do," I bit out. "We absolutely do. While Tack deals with your little problem that's leaking into *my* life," I declared. Logan shot a quick glance at Tack, then back to me when I continued speaking, "*I'll* talk."

Then I kept right on going.

Right on going.

It was time.

Time to fucking *end this*.

He was going to get it all so I could do what he said he was going to do.

Once and for always.

Put him in my fucking, *fucking* rearview.

My love for him.

My longing for him.

My grief for all we'd lost.

My sorrow for all we'd never have.

The burden I'd borne as I'd walked through fire for him and he'd *thrown it all away*, knocking up some bitch and making all I'd sacrificed not . . . worth . . . *shit*.

"I'm as good as gone, *High*," I stated. "I'm leaving Denver. But before I go, you get it. You get *it all*. So you'll know and I can be *done with you*."

"Millie, darlin', fuck, *please* come with me to my—"

"I'm not going with you anywhere." I pointed a finger to the floor. "This is happening here."

He moved toward me. "Babe, I'm beggin' you, *please*—"

I retreated, bumping into things and scurrying out of the way, warning, "Don't get any closer."

"You don't go with me there, I'm takin' you there," he warned.

He'd do that. I knew it. These men got what they wanted.

They always got what they wanted.

However they had to do that.

The panic I was holding back started breaking through.

"Don't get near me!" I yelled, still scurrying, needing to get this done, get out, get gone and *not* needing to be alone with Logan.

"Baby—"

"Don't call me that," I snapped, changing direction, watching him change direction with me, stalking me.

"Fuck," he clipped. "*Please*—"

"Stop moving," I demanded.

"Millie—"

He was getting closer.

And I hit wall.

I slithered along it, shouting, "Don't get near me!"

"Goddamn it, Millie—"

"*I can't have children!*" I shrieked.

Logan froze.

I did too.

All of me.

Except my mouth.

"There, Logan! There! *You have it all!*" I screamed. "I'm infertile. *Barren.* No go. No way. *Never.* And I knew you wouldn't let me go. You'd *never* let me go. And you wanted kids so bad." I shook my head, not even feeling the tears filling my eyes. "So *fucking* bad. You wanted to build a family. A big, fat, loud, crazy, wonderful family. I couldn't give you that. I could *never* give you that. And you were *mine.* You were *my* Logan. You had to have it all. You were *mine.*" My voice cracked and I didn't hear it, didn't even feel it. I was beyond feeling anything but the need to get this done and *go.* "It was *my job* to make sure you had it all. It was *my job* to make sure you had everything. But you wouldn't let me go. You'd never let me go. So *I made you let me go so you could have it all!*"

My throat was burning. My eyes were leaking.

But I saw the look on his face.

Ravaged.

Wasted.

That wasn't giving him it all.

That was killing it.

And that wasn't my job.

I'd failed.

Failed *again.*

So I had to escape.

And thus I ran.

Ripping viciously through unseen hands that tried to grab me, I got to the door of my car, hand on the handle, but I didn't get it open.

Suddenly, I was pressed to the door, Logan's hard body pushing in behind me, his arms like steel bands clamping around me.

"*Let me go!*" I shrieked.

He didn't let me go.

He shoved his face in the side of my neck.

"Let me go! Let me go!" I jerked unsuccessfully in his arms. "Let me go, go, *go!*"

"Why didn't you tell me?"

Quiet.

So quiet.

But each word was a new wound.

I stilled in his arms.

"You wouldn't let me go," I whispered.

"No." His arms tightened. "No, Millie. I would never let you go."

I again pushed against his hold.

"Now you need to let me go," I kept whispering.

He didn't let me go.

He held me so tight I felt the air leaking out of my lungs.

Then he moved, violently, brutally. He took one arm from around me, drew it back, and slammed his fist into the steel at the side of my car, making a dent, his face coming out of my neck.

"*Why didn't you tell me?*" he roared.

My body went still but my soul shattered.

"High, brother."

I heard this like it was from far away.

Tack.

"You are not in this," High growled.

"Get your woman inside," Tack said quietly. "It's cold and starting to snow."

I stood still.

So did High.

For a nanosecond.

Then he moved me from the car.

For the next however long I did not know I had very little recollection of anything that happened except in that first moment, me arching my back so hard my feet left the ground as High kept hold of me and turned us toward the Compound while I screeched, "*No!*"

Faintly, I remember struggling. Clawing. Screaming. Kicking. Pushing. Getting loose when he got me back in the Compound and seeing all the brothers of Chaos fanned out in the common room, sentries for Logan, soldiers of their brother, fencing me in.

I made a frantic choice, running toward the blond guy to get through him. I failed. He got hold of me and dragged me right back to Logan.

Logan again took control and I fought it but eventually found myself behind the closed door in his room and it went on.

Me fighting him. Fighting him like I was fighting for my life.

And Logan defending himself against my attacks, doing it gently, doing it in a way he wouldn't hurt me and helped me not hurt himself, and doing it continuing to contain me as he murmured over and over again, soothingly, "Calm," and, "Relax, baby," and, "Stop it, beautiful."

At my end, reaching it somehow on the bed with Logan, I grunted as I gave one final, colossal buck to pull out of the ironclad hold of his arms, attempting to jerk my legs away from the heavy weight of his clamped to mine.

Then I went slack.

When I did, he slid his hand in my hair.

"That's it, Millie," he whispered to the top of my head. "Settle. It's over, darlin'. It's done."

"Are Cleo and Zadie beautiful?" I asked his throat in an uncontrolled utterance because even if I already knew, I still had to know, and felt his fingers bunch my hair reflexively.

"They are," he rumbled. "So, *so* beautiful, baby."

"I gave you them," I told him, fading, finally fucking fading.

"You did, Millie," he agreed softly.

"I gave you them. I gave you that Daddy they call you that warms you to your bones."

He pulled me deeper into his arms, shifting into me, taking me to my back, smothering me with his weight and heat, drowning me with his scent, but he said nothing.

Still fading, I murmured, "I gave you them. I gave them you."

"Baby," he whispered, the word tortured.

"I gave you up, walking through fire to do it but I did it," I told him. "I did it in the end. I gave you everything," I finished, finally, *finally* fading.

Fading away.

Into nothing.

High

High waited, holding his girl, making sure she was in a place where there was no pain and taking his time doing it.

When he was certain she was resting, gently he pulled away.

Then carefully, he took off her boots, more carefully tugging off her jacket, and he pulled the covers out from under her, dragged them over her, and tucked her in tight all around.

After he did that, he didn't look at her.

He couldn't.

He'd climb back in bed with her, which meant he wouldn't do what he had to do.

So instead, he walked out of the room.

They were all there. Word had gotten out. It did that in times like these. So all the brothers were there. Even Lanie, Elvira, Shy's wife, Tabby, and Joker's woman, Carissa, were there.

He looked right to Tack, not missing a step on his stalk to the door.

"She does not leave," he stated.

"High, you shouldn't leave either. Not if your shit's not tight. Snow's gettin' bad," Tack replied.

He stopped, hand on the handle, and looked back to his brother.

"Then do me a solid and get food in 'cause if I get back and it's too bad to get her to my RV, we're workin' the rest of our shit out here and considerin' what just went down, that's gonna take some time."

On that, he walked out into the snow.

He'd taken his truck that morning, knowing the weather was moving in.

So he swung in the cab, started her up, and rolled out of Ride.

The snow was heavy, sticking, but the roads weren't bad as he made his way to where he needed to go.

He parked out front, prowled up the walk, and pressed his finger to the bell, not pounding on the door like he wanted to and taking his finger off the button only because there could be kids inside.

The door opened, not much, a crack, but she moved into the space and looked up at him.

"Holy crap, Lo—" Dottie started to breathe, eyes wide.

"You didn't tell me," he growled, watched her face pale and knew his guess was right.

Millie had shared with her sister.

And her sister did not share with him.

"Logan," she whispered.

"I wouldn't give a fuck and you know, woman." He lifted a hand to stab a finger her way. "*You know* I wouldn't give a fuck and you let her do it anyway."

She opened the door only to wedge herself in it and asked, "Did something happen?"

"Millie's in my bed at the Compound, passed out, fucked up, *gone*. She shared, Dot. She told me why she got shot of me. She did it and she unraveled right in front of my goddamned eyes, finally givin' me that fuckin' shit and you fuckin' *knew* and you said *shit*."

Her pale face went white and pain entered her eyes.

"She wouldn't be swayed," she said carefully.

"So the fuck what?" High shot back. "*You* knew and *you* could have told me and stopped her pain because I sure as fuck would have stopped her pain and *you know it*."

She shook her head. "I couldn't, Logan. She's my sister. I love her. You don't know how she was. I couldn't—"

"I know how she was," High growled. "Twenty years it's been and I got that pain passed out in my bed, Dot."

"No," she said harshly. "You don't know. It was bad, Logan. So bad. I couldn't go against her wishes."

"You could have and you *should have*. And you *fuckin'* know it," he fired back.

"You both wanted kids so bad," she whispered.

"No," he grunted. "I wanted Millie. You knew it. You *fuckin'* knew."

"Low—"

He leaned away but kept her skewered with his stare. "She live a good life, Dot? Hunh? She move on and find her happy?"

Dottie's eyes got wet.

High's gut burned.

She didn't.

Just like him, his girl lived twenty years blistering in the fire.

"Yeah," he snarled.

"You don't know how she was."

"No, I didn't. But I found out half an hour ago, woman, which was twenty years too late."

She flinched.

He liked her, once loved her like the sister she was supposed to be for the rest of his life, but more, he had shit he had to see to.

So he relented.

"I'll fix it."

Her eyes got big again.

"Wh-what?" she stammered.

He didn't repeat himself.

He ordered, "And while I'm doin' that, you take my back. You get that man of yours to take my back. You get Justine and Kellie to take my back. And you work with me however I gotta maneuver it to guide my girl back to happy."

A tear slid down her cheek as she stared up at him, lips parted.

When she seemed unable to speak, he prompted, "Hear?"

Her head jolted.

"I hear, Low," she said quietly.

"Do not fuck up again, Dot," he warned, then went on, "First up for you, you put the brakes on whatever moves she's made to get outta Denver."

Another tear escaped but her lips quirked as she muttered, "Seems we Cross women have a type. Bossy."

Was she fucking serious?

"I'm not thinkin' anything at this juncture is funny," he growled.

She pressed her lips together before she nodded and said, "Right. Of course. Consider the brakes put on." She tipped her head to the side. "Do you wanna get out of the snow and come inside where it's warm to boss me around? You do that, I'll make cocoa and introduce you to my kids."

He didn't want cocoa.

He did want to meet her kids.

And fuck him, he was pissed as all hell at her but at the same time he forgot how much he liked the bitch.

"You got an important job, focus and don't fuck up," he said as reply.

"Aye, aye, Captain."

Fuck, the Cross sisters.

Pains in the asses and too goddamned cute for their own good.

Dottie was demonstrating mostly the first part and he was screwed because he was ticked beyond reason and he still liked it.

Christ.

"Get on that," he muttered, turning. "I got shit to do."

He moved off her stoop but stopped and twisted back to her when she called his name.

"Missed you," she said, face soft, voice soft, words easing a nasty sting he'd been living with so long it had become a part of him. "You let go me fucking up, I'll let go the shit you've been pulling the last coupla months. And I'll start all that by saying I'm glad to have you back, Logan."

He stared at her a beat and said nothing.

Then he turned from her and walked away, that sting still there, but suddenly it didn't hurt so goddamned much.

Not looking back at her house, he got in his truck, started up, made a decision, and took his chance before the snow got worse.

He drove to his RV.

Once there, he packed a bag.

Then he drove to the Compound.

He moved through the space crowded with people who gave a shit and were worried.

As he moved, he asked Tack, "Food in?"

"Yep," Tack answered.

"Out in my truck," High ordered.

Tack's lips twitched.

High ignored that and went to his room, which meant he moved back through the space crowded with people carrying a totally out of it Millie.

Big Petey lumbered in front of him, right there to open the door to the backseat of the cab so High could move in and carefully lay her there.

He shut the door quietly, turned and saw Pete in his space, Tack several feet back, Cherry standing at her man's side.

"Get home," he ordered them as the snow fell heavy all around them.

"You good?" Pete asked.

High looked down at Pete.

"I will be," he stated, and turned, brushing against Big Petey when he did.

He opened his door, climbed in, and drove on roads getting bad to Millie's house.

He carried her inside, put her in her own bed in a room that had been straightened, probably by Dot, sometime while she was away.

It was picture perfect again.

She was going to have to kiss that good-bye.

High didn't live immaculate.

And neither did his Millie.

High moved back out to his truck, got his bag and the groceries, and brought them in.

He put the shit that needed to go into the fridge away. He left the other shit wherever he found a place for it on the counters.

Before he took his boots off, sitting on the ottoman to her big chair, he stared at the crate, wondering how she got it back and deciding he'd learn that after they waded through twenty years of colossal fuckups.

He was just glad it wasn't gone.

He left his boots on the floor where he took them off.

He tossed his cut on her couch.

Then he walked back to her room, climbed under the covers with her, pulled her in his arms, and tangled himself up in Millie.

She felt so good sleeping woven up in him it was like he'd lost a limb and it had miraculously grown back.

He tipped his chin so his face was in the top of her hair.

I gave you up, walking through fire to do it but I did it. I did it in the end. I gave you everything.

He'd fucked up, the stunt he pulled at Wild Bill's field and everything after, the penance he made her pay for a sin she never committed.

But he'd fix it.

Then it was his turn.

Finally, fucking *finally*.

It was his turn to give her everything.

Twenty years ago…

Logan stood in his and Millie's bathroom, the little pink, flat, round case in his hand.

It was opened.

It was empty.

He knew her cycle so he knew that wasn't right.

She was close to graduating.

His girl worked for it. She worked her ass off for it. She worked to get it, to give it to him, and she'd succeeded.

Three years and she was going to graduate.

And he knew by the empty pill case in his hand that she didn't fuck around getting her degree, she wasn't going to fuck around about other stuff that was even more important.

He grinned down at that pill case, remembering their conversation from a week before.

"You want it to be a surprise?" she'd asked.

"Want what to be a surprise?" he'd asked back.

She was on him, naked in their bed, and she pulled herself up so they were face to face.

"When I get pregnant," she whispered, and he felt his gut get warm, so fucking warm it felt like mush at the thought of his Millie with his baby growing inside her. "Do you want to plan for it or do you want it to come as a surprise?"

He slid a hand up her back and into her hair. "What you want, beautiful?"

"A surprise," she whispered.

"Then that's what we'll have."

She grinned a happy, triumphant grin and he knew then what he knew standing in the bathroom a week later.

His Millie did not fuck around.

He flipped the case closed and tossed it back into the medicine cabinet.

Then Logan moved out of the bathroom in order to find his woman and aid her in her efforts of not fucking around.

But he intended to do it by fucking around *a lot*.

He was going to enjoy this. He knew it from a shitload of practice they'd already had.

He was also going to enjoy watching her grow heavy with his kid. He was going to enjoy helping her fill their home with babies. He was going to enjoy being at her side watching them grow up.

And she was going to be a fucking brilliant mom. She had a good one. Her sister was the shit. Her father was solid. She was the best woman a man could find.

She'd kick motherhood's ass.

He found her in the kitchen cooking.

He fucked her on the floor.

Dinner was ruined.

Neither cared. They just hopped on his bike and went out for food.

Logan never mentioned he saw she'd dumped her pills.

Then, for six months, he watched her try to hide the slowly increasing changes in her manner, to shield him from the worry that he sometimes caught leaking into her eyes as all else remained the same.

Including them fucking like rabbits anytime they could and his girl never coming up pregnant.

He did it not knowing that he'd live for twenty years before he found out she fed him bullshit as to what all that meant.

He did it not knowing, through all that, he should have mentioned those fucking pills.

CHAPTER ELEVEN

Hole in My Soul

Millie

I OPENED MY eyes feeling disoriented and not knowing where I was.

But I smelled bacon.

I shoved up a bit and saw I was in my bedroom.

I'd come home.

Right, I'd come home.

But what was with the bacon?

Suddenly, it hit me like I was at the bottom of an avalanche, covering me, smothering me, and in a flurry, I threw back the covers and launched myself out of bed.

I stood there and looked down at myself.

I was in the clothes I'd worn to travel. No boots. No jacket.

I looked around.

My room had been tidied.

However, the last thing I remembered, I was fading away in Logan's arms in Logan's bed at Chaos.

How did I get here?

On that thought I spied a beat-up black leather bag on my chaise, gaping open, clothes hanging out, some in puddles on the floor.

Cautiously, I moved to the bag.

I pawed through the clothes. Heathered gray thermal Henley. Faded black thermal Henley. Midnight blue thermal

Henley. Two pairs of exceptionally faded jeans. A belt. Black socks. Black boxer briefs.

Slowly, I turned my head to look down the hall.

It was empty.

But the bacon smell was assailing me.

Without thought, my stocking feet took me in that direction, soundless against the wood floors.

I made it to the end of the hall and stopped, peeking around the corner.

And there I saw Logan moving around my kitchen, hair wet and slicked back, unshaven.

What on earth was he doing here?

No.

Unh-unh.

I didn't care.

Not right then.

He wanted to be in my house cooking bacon after the extreme of the day before?

Whatever.

One thing I'd learned the past few weeks, I needed to look after *me*.

And what I needed was to get out of these clothes. I needed a shower. Both of these things would make me feel tons better and (maybe) able to face whatever Logan had in store for me next.

Bacon, of course, the universal cure-all, would probably do that even better.

However, since Logan was cooking it, I wasn't going there.

I retraced my steps and locked myself in my bathroom.

Or, more aptly, I locked Logan out of it.

There I saw on the double sink vanity (at the sink I didn't use) a can of Barbasol (though why he had that and put it in the bathroom since he clearly didn't use it, I did not know). Ditto these thoughts on the opened pack of razors and the electric shaver. There was also a comb.

And as I approached the shower, I saw a bottle of shampoo that wasn't mine and a bar of green veined soap.

Who used bars of soap anymore?

I knew who.

Bikers.

Fabulous.

It appeared Logan had moved in.

I decided for my own peace of mind, considering how fuzzy that mind was and how unable I was to use it at that current juncture, to ignore that too.

I kept ignoring things when I saw that Logan had thoughtfully brought all my luggage from the back door and set it in the walk-in closet in the bathroom.

I busted open my luggage, dug out what I needed, made a decision that was based on what was happening with my head and the strange, nagging but not alarming nausea I was feeling, and selected my apparel for the day.

I then took a long, hot shower, shampooed, conditioned, exfoliated (face and body), shaved, and got out to towel off, lotion, gunk up my hair, tone and moisturize my face, then put on my undies and pajamas. The pj's were a soft gray-green, no lace, long tight sleeves, a fair amount of chest (if not cleavage) bared, and lounge-y, loose-fitting pants.

Unfortunately, through this, I learned that the healing powers of a shower didn't extend to jet lag.

In other words, it was time to crash again, snooze away the fuzziness in my head, the weird feeling in my belly, and wake up, hopefully to Logan having consumed his bacon and being the hell out of my house.

I unlocked the door, opened it, and stopped dead.

This was because Logan was standing there, arm up high, hand to the jamb, leaning his weight into it. His ankles were crossed, his other hand was fisted and to his hip, and, until I opened the door, his head was bent to contemplate his socks.

But when I opened the door, his eyes came to mine.

They were warm. They were concerned.

They were *Logan*.

"Hey, baby," he said softly.

I thought I was dead inside.

Gone.

Faded away.

So how could he keep killing me?

I didn't respond to him. I skirted him and went directly to the bed.

I climbed in, pulled the covers up to my ears, and closed my eyes.

He wasn't there.

This wasn't happening.

Yesterday didn't happen.

I was experiencing a very weird, long, crazy dream.

The bed moved and I knew he'd sat on it.

Shit.

He was there.

I gritted my teeth and fought back screaming in frustration.

"You still tired?" he asked.

"Go away," I answered.

He said nothing to that but the bed moved again as he shifted to pull the covers down to my shoulder; then he locked them in place when he leaned over me, putting his weight into the covers by my chest.

"Think it's best you're awake when it's day here, Millie. You need to get used to bein' back on Denver time. And you gotta get some food in you."

I needed to get used to being back on Denver time?

How did he know I wasn't on Denver time?

I didn't ask that because I didn't care about his answer (I told myself).

"I'll do all that when you go away," I audibly told the insides of my eyelids.

"Not goin' away, beautiful," he said gently.

Why?

Then again, these days, why did Logan do anything?

"Of course not," I sighed.

"Sit up," he ordered. "I'll bring you some food."

Weirdly, even though I felt kind of queasy, I also felt hungry.

And there obviously was bacon.

That decided it.

I pushed back, avoiding his body that was sitting on the bed behind me, and sat up.

"Be right back," he muttered.

I didn't say anything. I arranged the covers precisely folded over my lap.

It took him longer to get back to me with food than it did for me to arrange the covers but at least in that time I was able to come up with a strategy.

I was tired. I was nauseous. I was jet-lagged. I'd had a massive drama the day before. I had a lot of reasons to be quiet that he'd likely get and therefore not question and thus I'd eat. Then, if I didn't actually pass out, I'd *pretend* to pass out.

While I was pretending (or actually unconscious), I'd hope Logan would go away.

If he didn't, I'd use that time to come up with a strategy to *make* him go away.

With this plan in place, I felt better when he got back, carrying a plate in one hand, a coffee mug in the other.

No tray.

"You didn't bring a tray," I blurted.

He was eyes to me as he walked my way and he didn't falter a single step when he asked, "A tray?"

"If I have breakfast in bed, it should be on a tray."

He stopped by the side of the bed and stared down at me.

God, he was tall.

And his shoulders were really broad.

And he'd made the perfect winter fashion selection, even if it was singular with the only variety being color and the nuance of fade to his jeans. Snug-fitting thermal Henleys were *perfect* on him. Including the wine-colored one he was currently wearing.

"Never brought breakfast to anyone in bed, didn't know the protocol," he muttered.

My eyes went from his thermal at his chest to his face to see his lips curved up.

That was perfect too.

"I could get bacon grease on my sheets," I informed him haughtily.

"They'll wash," he returned, bending to put my coffee cup on my nightstand (without a coaster!) at the same time offering me a plate that had four slices of bacon, a huge pile of fluffy eggs, and two slices of bread liberally slathered with butter and grape jelly.

More disasters waiting to happen to my sheets.

I took it from him automatically, telling him, "Bacon grease isn't easy to get out. And what if it gets on the duvet cover? That could be cataclysmic."

He raised his brows.

Also perfect.

Why oh why when it felt like I was fading away I…just… *didn't*?

"Grease on your sheets is cataclysmic?" he asked.

"Have you ever tried to get grease out of *anything*?" I asked back.

His lips curved up again on his, "No."

"Then you don't understand. Further, this bed set is seasons old. And it's perfect. If something happened, I'd never be able to replace it."

"Fuck, you're right," he stated. "That *is* cataclysmic."

I felt my chest depress.

He was being sweet, gentle, thoughtful, and teasing.

In other words, speaking to him was totally fucking with my strategy of eating then fake–passing out and coming up with a new strategy to get him gone.

So I had to stop speaking to him.

I moved and set my plate on the nightstand so I could get out of the bed and I did it mumbling, "I'll eat in the kitchen."

A hand landed firm on my shoulder, pressing in, and I tipped my head back.

When I caught his eyes, he said, "I'll get the fuckin' tray. Where is it?"

Logan was going to get me a tray.

I stared up at him.

Apparently I did this too long because he straightened and turned, saying, "Whatever. I'll find it."

Then he walked out of my room.

Something came to me the instant he disappeared and I yelled, "Bring a coaster! They're in the drawers of the coffee table in the living room!"

I heard a faraway, "Jesus," then nothing.

It was then I had thoughts of climbing out the window.

I was in jammies, had wet hair, and my mind wasn't all there, likely for more reasons than just that I was jet-lagged, so I didn't think being in my jammies with wet hair on the run in the cold would be a good idea.

So instead, I reached for my coffee and sipped it.

After that, I stared at the breakfast and hoped he didn't dawdle. It looked delicious and food like that was a lot more delicious when it was warm.

I didn't think about the fact that he cooked it.

When we were together, Logan cooked, but not much. This was because I loved cooking and he loved letting me do what

I loved. But part of loving it was doing something for my man, doing my bit to take care of him.

When he cooked, it wasn't bad, it wasn't great, though by the end he was really getting good at the grill and he could make any kind of potato fabulous.

He'd obviously gotten better, at least at eggs.

He came back with a tray that I'd bought with the idea of putting out hors d'oeuvres and serving fabulous cocktails on it during the parties that I eventually never gave.

It appeared there was more food on it, definitely another mug of coffee.

He came right to me, plopped the tray on my lap, took a coaster from it, and tossed it on my nightstand, then grabbed the plate of food and mug of coffee off it and moved away.

I watched apprehensively as he rounded the bed and put his coffee mug (*not* on a coaster) on my other nightstand. Then he climbed in bed with me, settled back to the headboard, legs stretched out, stocking feet crossed at the ankles, and he forked up some eggs.

I sat motionless, staring at him eating in my bed.

With me.

What was going on?

With mouth still full, he turned to me and asked, "Hand me the other coaster, would you, babe?"

My brain having stopped functioning altogether, I looked down at the tray, saw another coaster there, mutely picked it up, and handed it to him.

He took it, twisted, I was treated to his thermal stretching across his ribs and lateral muscles and doing this tight as he put his mug on the coaster. Then he sat back, his eyes sliding to me.

"Eat," he ordered low.

"What's happening?" I asked.

"Eat," he repeated.

I turned more fully to him. "What's happening, High? Why are you here? Why are you making bacon? Why are you eating my food?"

"Dot stocked you up but she didn't buy eggs and bacon, Millie. That's from Chaos," he told me. "Now this shit is fuckin' good, so grab it before it gets cold and *eat*."

It was from Chaos.

I turned and looked at my food like a woman who'd just been informed her meal was laced with arsenic.

From beside me came a warning, "Eat or I feed you, Millie."

I wasn't in the mood to test that.

Hell, I'd probably *never* be in the mood to test that.

So I didn't test it.

I grabbed the plate, put it on my tray, slid the fork out from under the food, and stabbed at the eggs.

I put them in my mouth.

There was cheese, a sharp cheddar. There was garlic, not too much. Fresh ground pepper, which was nice. And something else savory and flavorful that I couldn't put my finger on.

Then I did.

A hint of oregano providing a pleasant surprise.

Damn, Logan put oregano in his eggs.

God.

The food was still warm. The bacon crisped to perfection. The toast lightly and expertly toasted. And my coffee had a splash of creamer, no sugar, very strong, like I liked it.

Like I'd always liked it.

I forced down the food, enjoying it too much, but doing it telling myself I was *not* going to cry.

I was going to eat and pass out and wake up with my head clear and then I was going to find the words to communicate to Logan that our game had been played, he won, and I was leaving him to his life in Denver.

Logan cut into my thoughts. "How many pairs of those jammies you got?"

"Several," I muttered, biting into a slice of bacon, ignoring him using the word *jammies* again, or more accurately, how cute I thought it was.

"Mmm," he murmured. It was rough and growly, which was not cute in the slightest, and I felt tingles hit my thighs.

I did not need tingles.

Ever.

I focused on my bacon, deciding to speed things up, so I took a bite and chewed fast.

"Dumped snow last night," Logan stated. "Serious. Snowed all yesterday and all night and it's still goin'. Two feet and we're gonna get more. They say you don't gotta go anywhere, don't."

Oh no.

Was I going to be shut in my house with Logan during a blizzard?

That could not happen.

I turned to him. "Then you need to eat and leave."

He took a bite of toast and looked to me, speaking and chewing. "Say it one more time, babe. Not leavin'."

"Why?" I asked.

"Why?" he asked back.

"Yes, High. Why?"

He tipped his head to the side, opened his mouth, and shut it.

He studied me and he did this for some time.

Then he looked back at the plate he was holding in front of him and said, "We'll talk after we eat."

"If it's snowing that bad, you need to get going," I pointed out.

He looked back to me and his voice was quiet when he replied, "Let that go. That fight you ain't gonna win. We'll talk after we eat but I'm not goin' anywhere, Millie. And I mean that in a lotta ways, so you best start gettin' used to it now."

Panic assailed me and I twisted farther his way. "High—"

"*Eat,*" he ordered inflexibly. "Then we'll talk."

I stared at him, fear beginning to infuse my bloodstream, then I turned back to my plate and ate.

Fast.

Forking it in, swallowing it down, cleaning my plate in no time.

I then turned back.

"Done," I announced, mouth still holding half-chewed toast.

His lips were curled up as he replied, "Christ."

I swallowed with difficulty and declared, "We'll talk in the living room."

Before I could move, he dumped his plate on mine on the tray and took the tray off my lap. He then leaned so deep into me his stomach was pressed to my thighs and he did this so he could drop the tray to the floor with a clatter.

Before I knew what he was about, he arched up, took hold of me, shifted, hitched, twisted, and hauled so he was under the covers with me. He'd pulled me over his body in a roll and pinned me to my back in the bed with him on me.

Panic gripping me, I started panting.

Then I caught the look on his face and started gasping for air.

"I get it," he whispered.

"Y-yes," I stammered. "You did. I gave it to you. And now it's supposed to be over."

"I get it," he strangely repeated.

"Logan, I told you so this would be *done.*"

"I get it and I'da done the same thing."

I stared up at him.

He lifted his hand, the tips of his fingers tracing my hairline along the side of my face and he kept talking.

"Found out it was me, found out I couldn't give it all to you, I woulda done the same thing, Millie. I would have made it so you got it all and I would have done it ugly so you'd walk away from me and never look back so you could have it." He dipped his face closer to mine. "So I get it. I get why you did what you did. I totally fuckin' get it."

Okay.

That felt good. Better than good. It loosened the grip that took hold of my heart the second he turned and walked away from me, letting it pump again, almost like normal.

But no.

It was good he knew. It was great he understood.

But this was over.

"I'm glad you understand," I replied. "And thank you for sharing that with me," I went on. "However, what I don't understand is why you feel the need to do that lying on top of me in my bed."

His head jerked back a few inches.

"Say what?" he asked.

"It's all out there, High, the game has been played. There are no more moves to make. So it's over and it's time we both put it behind us and move on."

"Put it behind us and move on," he parroted incredulously.

"Yes. What we have is damaging and unhealthy and we have to put a stop to it and get on with our lives."

He stared down at me and I tensed when his expression started to turn stormy.

I tensed even further when his face suddenly cleared and he roared with laughter, his weight bearing into me, his head dropping so his forehead rested on my cheekbone, his hair tickling the skin of my face.

"High." I pushed at him.

He kept laughing.

"High!" I snapped, pushing harder at him.

He lifted his head, eyes dancing, lines radiating out the sides creasing, body trembling with the chuckles that still had control over him and there it was again.

Perfection.

Enough!

"Get off me," I demanded.

"Babe," he replied.

I listened.

He said nothing else, just rode the wave of his amusement until it naturally died.

Then it hit me. The memory. The memory that there were a variety of occasions where Logan spoke Badass.

There were only a few words in the Vocabulary of Badass but each one had a number of meanings. They included *beautiful*, *Christ*, *fuck*, *Jesus*, and *shit*.

But the one used most was *babe*.

I was out of practice. I had no idea what that particular *babe* meant.

And I wasn't going to find out.

"Nothing about this is funny," I bit out. "Let us not forget, I *came to you* to *tell you* what I told you yesterday and in your fancy-ass RV, *you humiliated me*."

There was no amusement in his expression when I quit talking.

No.

Instead he shifted over me so he was fully covering me. I was taking a fair amount of his hefty weight, and he lifted his other hand so he could use both of them to hold either side of my head.

In other words, there was no escape.

"Yeah," he growled. "I did. I did it with intent. I was a dick and I was a dick on purpose. Because what you did to us fuckin' *destroyed* me and I never put the pieces back together. But, Millie, I did it for more reasons than that. I did it for self-preservation. I did it 'cause you were back in a way you were *back*, in my bed, ass in the air for me, takin' my dick and I felt you, I smelled you, I heard you, and I saw the ink on your back permanently declarin' you were mine when you made that a lie for reasons *I did not get*. And all I could think was that I wanted to keep fuckin' you, listenin' to how much you loved takin' me, feelin' my cock sink inside you, and I wanted that until I stopped breathing. If I had you on your back, woulda seen your face, which would have fucked with me more. I picked the lesser of two evils. So I had to cover that shit on your back so I didn't let go and let you lead me to the brink again and convince me to jump."

Oh my God.

"High," I whispered, and he dragged his thumb along my cheek, pressing it into my bottom lip until it hooked on the edge of my teeth and he moved in so we were so close, I could see nothing but him.

"I'm Logan to you." His voice scratched out, chafing my skin.

Against his hold on my mouth, I forced out, "I—"

That was all I was able to do.

"You feel sweet. You feel scared. You feel happy. You feel sad. You feel *anything* you use your name for me. You can call me High. But not times like now. Times like now, I'm Logan."

I wasn't entirely certain I understood precisely the different occasions I could use his different names but I felt in his current mood I should agree.

So I said, "Okay."

He swept his thumb from my mouth to the flesh under my cheek and pressed in lightly.

Then he went on.

"I held you down for that," he continued to explain. "I held you down, coverin' that ink. You were not faceless pussy, Millie. You could never be that and you fuckin' know it. Even if you forgot, what came after woulda told you that shit couldn't be true."

"What came after wasn't much healthier," I shared hesitantly.

He moved back an inch and tilted his head slightly. "Yeah? You think?"

What?

He didn't?

"Of course," I said quietly. "You were there. You have to think the same thing too."

"Three weeks ago when I didn't have it all, maybe. Now. Fuck no."

"It wasn't healthy, Logan."

"I couldn't get enough of you, Millie."

I drew in a sharp breath.

"Couldn't get you outta my head. Didn't rest until I found a new reason to get in your space. Found those reasons, got in your space. If I didn't give a fuck about you, I wouldn't have followed you for forty-five fuckin' minutes, from the second I laid eyes on you at Bill's rally, and found my shot to get in your face. If you didn't mean shit to me, I'da seen you and put you out of my head. I didn't. I got in your face. You kissed me. I fucked you. And I kept comin' back for more."

Okay.

Damn.

Okay.

Shit.

That made sense.

"And you," he continued. "If you didn't give a shit about me, you moved on, you would not have seen me buyin' a burrito and come lookin' for me. You woulda heard what I said, felt what that meant, and went on with your life. You didn't. You found me. *You* kissed *me.* You took my cock. And even with how I took that from you, when I kept comin' back for more, you kept takin' it. You didn't want it, you know you made that clear, I woulda been gone. You did not make that clear. You entered that fucked-up game we were playin' because you needed what you got, unhealthy or not. Just like me when it comes to you, you'd take what you could get."

You'd take what you could get.

I would. With Logan, I would.

Until the day I died.

I tried to turn my face away, to get some sort of privacy to process his words, but he put pressure on to keep my focus on him.

"I need you to get off me, Logan," I whispered.

"You did wrong," he replied.

I stared up at him.

"You did wrong and only hindsight makes that clear. No way in fuck, baby, *no way in fuck* you shoulda made the decision you made to end us all on your own. You shoulda told me."

My heart started hammering with a different kind of panic and my words were still whispers when I said, "But you told me you got it."

"You were twenty-one, way too fuckin' young to have what we had, feel what that meant, know we had a lot of life before us, and have enough of it under your belt to make the right choice. I remember bein' twenty-four and feelin' you put an end to us so I can go back there and know where you were at and why you did what you did. But it still was wrong."

"Please, Logan—"

"You should have told me."

I shut my mouth and pressed my lips together so they wouldn't quiver.

He slid his thumb back to them, gentle this time, and rested the pad against my lips.

"You should have told me," he whispered. "'Cause now I can't prove to you you were all I wanted. You were all I needed. You took that shot away from me and it was as important then as it is now that you know that to your bones, Millie.

You gave me what you thought I had to have and I'm grateful, so fuckin' grateful, baby. When you meet Cleo and Zadie, you'll get just how grateful that is. I love my girls. Fuckin' love 'em, the lights of my life. But it's the goddamned, motherfuckin' truth that I would have had all I needed. I would have had everything if all I had in life was you. And you took away my shot to show you that. You also took away any shot I had of helpin' you through gettin' the knowledge we couldn't have a family and buildin' a new dream together and that cuts just as deep. You made those decisions on your own without sharing with me. And that was wrong."

When you meet Cleo and Zadie.

My voice was trembling when I demanded, "You have to get off me."

He put pressure on my head.

"You are not gettin' me," he growled.

I thought he had all my attention but the way he said that, I found myself giving him more.

"This is not me layin' the guilt on you," he carried on. "This is not me plantin' more shit in your head to fuck with it. I told you I got it, I get it. Back then, twenty-four, knowin' how bad you wanted kids, knowin' how bad we both wanted to build a family, findin' out it was me who'd take that from you, I love you so goddamned much, I couldn't bear it. I wouldn't be able to live with that burden for a lifetime with you. And I woulda done everything I could to make myself a man unworthy of you, make sure you knew it. It'd kill me. But I'd live life dead inside knowin' I gave that to you."

His face got close again and I held my breath.

"So I get it. I get what you did for me 'cause back then I'd do the same. And you gave me what you thought I needed and I'm grateful, Millie. But outta that over the years we both got somethin' else. We're not young and stupid and so caught up in love we're blind. We got life under our belts and we know better now. So, what I'm sayin' is, in future, learn from what we lost and don't ever do shit like that again."

In future.

Was he saying . . . ?

"In future?" I choked.

"In future," he stated plainly.

"I . . . you . . . we . . ." I shook my head in his hands. "Are you saying we should start up where we left off?"

His comeback was instant.

"Did it ever end for you?"

My body jerked under him and my fingers formed fists on the bed at my sides.

He might not have seen my hands but he felt my reaction and he read it.

"No," he stated. "You're a ghost and I lived life haunted by your ghost so there's no takin' up where we left off because we never left off. We're still back there. Now we just gotta find a way to put the shit in between behind us and keep on goin'."

I started to say something but he kept talking before I could get it out.

"And the way we're doin' that, coasters *do not* factor."

My body jerked again in surprise at his bizarre declaration.

And for a variety of reasons, all of them having to do with self-preservation, I focused only on that.

"I have nice things, Logan," I informed him of something he could absolutely see.

"And you make a mint, got a mint invested, and I'm not hurtin'. You get bacon grease on your sheets, babe, we buy new and who gives a fuck?"

"I do," I snapped. "These sheets are perfection. It took me two years to find these sheets. I don't need to spend two more years finding new sheets that are perfect."

"I'm in bed beside you, I'll make it so you don't think about sheets."

He was beside me, I'd sleep on a bed of broken glass and not give a damn.

This was not something I intended to share at that juncture.

So instead, I shared, "I have a lock on two Himalayan kitties from a local breeder and they match these bedclothes. I've put deposits down on them. Cats can live fifteen, twenty years. And honestly, the last time I went looking, it *felt* like it'd take twenty years to find the right sheets. Put cats in the mix, these sheets have to last a long time."

"You're gettin' cats to match your house?" he asked in open, badass, hot guy, biker astonishment.

"Of course," I answered, like that was a perfectly sane thing to do. "The house *and* the sheets. It's all going with me to Arizona. Including the cats, which my mother is ecstatic about, she loves animals. And I'm good to pick them up any day now."

I'd clearly said the wrong thing because the storm that threatened his expression earlier in the conversation clouded his features and this time it did not clear.

Again with his voice chafing, he declared, "You're not goin' to Arizona."

"It's all sorted," I returned.

"Babe, have you been listening *at all*?"

I shut up.

He didn't.

"You're leavin' town to get away from me and shit has *changed* in a *big* fuckin' way."

Oh God.

It appeared that it had.

"Oh, right," I muttered.

"Right," he ground out.

"I'm seriously jet-lagged," I explained.

"You're lucky you got that excuse or about now you'd seriously be gettin' a tanned ass."

I felt my eyes get big.

"Are you joking?" I demanded to know.

"Babe," he clipped. "Twenty years apart, haunted by you, walkin' around with a hole in my soul, we're back and we're talkin' about cats and you goin' to Arizona? No, I'm not fuckin' jokin'."

Walkin' around with a hole in my soul.

I stared up at him.

I stared up at *Logan* lying on top of me.

He was back.

Lying on me.

He knew it all.

He got it.

He wasn't angry with me.

I'd laid it out and had a drama and woke up the next day to Logan making bacon and telling me we were back.

We're back.

"I don't know, but I think I'm either gonna be sick, start crying, or lapse into catatonia," I whispered, way, way too out of it to be able to process all I was experiencing.

I felt his body relax on mine.

"It's the first one, do me a favor and give me a heads-up so I can get you to the toilet. Bacon grease on sheets I can live with. Puke, not so much."

I felt the weird sensation of hysterical laughter fizzing inside me and it didn't feel bad in the slightest.

Tentatively, I put my hands to his sides, feeling his thermal, the heat and hardness of Logan under it.

We're back.

"Millie."

I focused on him and not the irrefutable evidence of all Logan was saying weighing down on me, heating me through his thermal, and saw his eyes searching mine, like he looked standing outside the bathroom earlier.

Warmth and concern.

Logan.

My Logan.

He was back.

My fingers fisted in his shirt.

"I missed you."

It wasn't a whisper.

It was a breath.

Barely audible, each word weighed down by heartache and history.

But he heard it and then I heard his groan, felt it tearing through him, tearing through me.

Pain.

A sound filled with pain.

A sound made releasing pain.

Then his face was in my neck, we were on our sides, and his arms were locked around me.

I slid my hands up his back and fisted them again in the material there, latching on like I should have twenty years ago.

Like I'd never let go.

I turned my head, my lips seeking his ear.

"Please kiss me."

No hesitation, Logan obliged. His hand sliding up to curve around the base of my head where it met my neck, he held tight, took my mouth, and kissed me, deep and hard and wet.

It hurt, God, it hurt. The pain was unbearable.

And it felt utterly, impossibly, magnificently beautiful.

He ended it, shifting his head so his temple was pressed tight to mine.

"Missed you, too, beautiful."

I closed my eyes and clutched harder at him, pushing into his body, holding him to me and attempting to meld myself to him.

The hiccup I involuntary gave to hold back the tears was an unpleasant one.

"Oh shit," I whispered, and his head came up.

"You gonna get sick?" he asked.

"I…" I swallowed, the wave passing so I went on, "Don't think so."

"Fuck, Millie," he clipped.

I slid a hand to his chest. "I'm so sorry, Logan. I…this… it's…" I shook my head. No words had been created to communicate it, how significant this was, how happy it made me. So I finished, "I'm ruining our reunion."

"Don't give a shit about that. You're not feelin' you, whatever. You'll get past it and I'll give you a reunion you won't forget. But you not feelin' you reminds me I'm pissed at you."

My chin jerked back and my body locked.

"I thought—" I began.

"You went to Paris without me."

My mouth dropped open.

"That shit ain't right," he growled.

I stared into his annoyed eyes, thinking about all that had transpired, twenty years of it, the intensity of the last weeks, the conversation we just had (well, mostly he had because he did all the talking but I was there), and I could just not believe in all that he was pissed *about Paris*.

"It's still there, Logan," I pointed out.

"I know that, Millie, doesn't make it any better."

"It's been there hundreds of years, Logan," I kept going.

"I know that, too, Millie," he bit out. "Doesn't make it any better."

"What I'm saying is we can still go."

"You seen the Eiffel Tower all lit up at night?"

I shifted my eyeballs to the ceiling.

"Right," he stated irritably. "First time you got that it was without me and it was supposed to be *with* me."

I had to admit, seeing the Eiffel Tower blinking into the night was absolutely magnificent but would have been much better shared with Logan.

And I had to admit that he was right. It was *totally* supposed to be with him.

Although I had to admit both those things, I didn't do it out loud.

I looked back to him and requested, "Can we not fight when I'm jet-lagged and we've just reunited?"

"Yeah, we can not fight now. We'll discuss that shit when you're feelin' better and after I instigate the official reunion."

My thighs started tingling.

"The official reunion?" I asked.

"Like you don't know I'm gonna fuck you breathless in a way you're gonna remember every second of it for the rest of your life."

I got breathless at that.

"But now, since you hauled your ass to Paris without me," he went on, "and you're fucked up because of it, I'm haulin' your TV in here and we're gonna hang and watch it. You're gonna stay up the best you can so you can get over that shit. Then I'm gonna give you that reunion and after, we're gonna sort the rest."

Oh man.

"The rest?" I prompted.

"Babe, got kids. Kids who're gonna be in your life. Got shit happening we need to make decisions on. And you're gonna undo whatever you did to make plans to get outta Denver."

Luckily, none of that last was set in stone.

Logan, however, wasn't finished.

"And apparently, we got some cats to pick up."

Tentatively, I grinned at him, ignoring the onset of anxiety at his *kids who're gonna be in your life* comment.

"I saw pictures of the kitties on the Internet," I told him. "A boy and a girl. They're very cute."

"Whatever," he muttered, his eyes to my mouth. "The girls'll love 'em."

At that, it was harder to ignore the onset of anxiety since

it was growing swiftly, even though I was pleased to learn his daughters liked animals.

"Now, I got dishes to get in the sink and a TV to haul," he muttered, and when he did, something stole over me.

It was heavy, warm, frightening, comforting, so much of all that my hands clutched at his shirt again and he stilled.

"Babe."

I stared at his chin. The whiskers there were long and I could feel just how long as the skin on my face felt the ghost of them from his kiss.

"Millie," he called sharply.

I lifted my eyes to his.

"Are you really here?" I whispered.

"Fuck," he groaned, moved in, and kissed me again. And again it was wet, it was deep.

But it was not hard.

He pulled away but not too far.

"You gotta put a damper on the cute and sweet, baby," he said quietly. "I'm a big fan of your mouth, big fan of havin' it back, big fan of finally havin' it available to me again. Not a big fan of courtin' you needin' to puke durin' a kiss. So help a man out. Hear?"

Hear?

I didn't believe it.

Not until then.

Not until that.

Something that was so Logan. He was the only person I knew who said that like he said it.

Hear?

He'd said that the first time I met him. He'd said it a million times after.

And he'd just given it to me again.

Not like he did when we were playing our crazy game.

Like he used to give it to me.

Wars were fought for things that had no meaning. Hearts

were broken. Betrayals were committed. Fortunes were paid. Sacrifices were made.

All for nothing. All for shit.

But I'd give anything, battle to the death, break hearts, tell lies, pay every penny I owned, sell my soul to have back Logan's *hear?* just like that. Something that meant the world because it meant I had him.

And I had it back.

Him back.

I drew in breath through my nose as my sinuses started tingling at the same time I nodded.

Then I said, "I hear, Logan."

"This is the last you're gonna get, Millie, before we settle in so you can get sorted," he said unceremoniously, like he was just carrying on our conversation.

Not like he was about to change my whole world.

Then he changed my whole world.

No, he didn't change it.

He gave it back to me.

"I love you," he declared. "Loved you then. Love you now. Never quit lovin' you in a way I know I never will. You were it for me, the only one, the only woman I ever loved, and you never quit bein' it. So I think you can get how I cannot find words to explain how fuckin' pleased I am that you're back."

"I..." I hiccupped, deep breathed, clutched his shirt, and he waited through all that. "Ditto," I pushed out.

Totally lame.

But it bought me his eyes smiling and a brush of his lips.

His lips stayed where they were, his eyes looking into mine, when he whispered, "You always sucked at that shit."

I did.

I could tell him I loved him and I did. I could show it and I did.

But I didn't do flowery.

Logan did biker, badass flowery and he did it really good.

And I had that back too.

I started deep breathing again.

"Baby, eggs are gonna dry on those plates you don't let me go," he told me.

I hiccupped, nodded, and slowly, very, very slowly, I let him go.

He slid away but I felt his hair wisp across my face, his lips along my jaw while he did it.

When he was gone, I curled up, pulling up the covers, and watched as he moved around the bed, collecting all our stuff.

I heard from far away the sink going as he set the dishes to soak.

And I watched him haul the TV in, setting it up on a nightstand he brought in from the guest bedroom, watching him plug it into the cable jack I'd had installed but never used.

Then I felt him gather me up after he got into bed with me.

I also heard him order, "Don't fuckin' fall asleep. You gotta make it until eight o'clock, then you can crash."

I had not forgotten how bossy he was.

It was just that I never minded it.

It was him.

And I never minded anything about Logan.

Though, now it was kind of annoying. But it was mature, badass biker—*my* mature, badass biker who was *back* annoying. So even if it was annoying, it wasn't *that* annoying.

I didn't share that.

Instead, I watched a movie and a half with Logan.

Then I did whatever the hell I wanted, which was what I'd always done when he was bossy.

Or, I should say, I did what my body wanted.

I crashed.

In my bed.

Tangled up with my man.

CHAPTER TWELVE

We're Found

Millie

I WOKE UP and it was dark.

But I woke up and I was *awake*.

I also woke up in the middle of my bed, tangled up in Logan.

I lay there. I did it a long time. I did it happy to do it forever.

Then I couldn't do it anymore because I had to go to the bathroom.

So the last thing I wanted to do, I did. Sliding out of his arms, unwinding my limbs from his, I got out of bed and went to the bathroom, closing the door, not turning on the light until it was shut so it wouldn't disturb him and going about my business.

I turned off the light before I left the bathroom but I only took one step into the room.

The curtains were opened, so the room was very lit even if it was still night.

And I could see Logan, sheets to his lat, body curved on the bed, one arm under my pillow, the other arm thrown out to where I lay minutes before, the dark of him against the light of my sheets more beautiful than the Eiffel Tower at night.

And the Eiffel Tower at night was spectacular.

Weirdly, even with Logan in my bed, the light beckoned me and I moved to the front of the room right to the window.

Logan should have closed the curtains. Anyone could see in.

And someone could be looking.

I didn't care when I made it there and looked out.

The snow had stopped. The sky was clear. The moon was shining bright on gazillions of tiny crystals, the streetlights casting an unnecessary glow.

The snow had been heavy and long. It coated everything and there was a lot of it. Cars parked on the street, the snow was up to the middle of the doors.

The street had not been cleared. That much snow, they'd concentrate on the heavily trafficked areas. If we were lucky, they'd get to my street sometime that day.

But cars had tried to navigate it, the snow not dirty and brown, it just had tire tracks cut through.

Not many.

Too much snow to take that risk.

People would stay home. Warm. Safe. With their loved ones around them.

I looked back at the bed where Logan was, and clear-headed, it all came to me.

So I looked back to the peace of the snow and filtered through all of it.

It had occurred to me frequently through the years that there was a good possibility I'd made a mistake. That I should have told Logan, once he'd given me the go-ahead to get pregnant whenever, that I'd pushed my birth control pills into the toilet and flushed them away. I should have told him that I'd been trying for the surprise of a baby for months. And when that didn't happen, I should have told him I'd gone to the doctor and sustained the crushing blow, alone, that with one simple test I found out it wasn't going to happen.

There was nothing we could do. No hoops to jump through. No surgeries to be had. No treatments to try.

It just wasn't going to happen.

But when these thoughts occurred to me, I couldn't bear it. I couldn't even consider I'd made such a massive mistake. And even if my brain pushed through that idea, I couldn't think about finding him, telling him, and courting the possibility he'd be even angrier at me and wouldn't take me back.

But I'd found him.

I'd told him.

And it didn't even take twenty-four hours before he told me he got it and took me back.

But now...

What?

He said we should put twenty years of being apart behind us and keep on going.

He clearly thought it was that easy.

He loved me like I loved him and that had never died, for either of us.

But it wasn't going to be that easy. Twenty years had passed. We weren't the same people.

Sure, he was still Chaos, but he had daughters, an ex, and Chaos had changed with Tack being at the helm and I'd noted not only the new recruits but brothers were gone. I hadn't seen Chew, Crank, Arlo, Dog, Black, men who'd be around. Men who would go watch Hop play. Men who'd be at Wild Bill's field. Men who'd be at the Compound.

And I had changed. I was nothing like the Millie he knew and wasn't sure I could make my way back. No way in hell I was ever putting on another pair of cutoffs and a halter top. And if Logan tried to light up a joint in my house, I'd lose my mind.

You didn't chase after bikers telling them to crush out their marijuana cigarettes and forcing them to put their beer bottles on coasters.

Coasters do not factor.

Oh man.

What if we made it to this point only to find out we could go no further?

What if I got him back only for him to get to know me again and not like what he gets to know?

I mean, I was totally boring!

And his girls. He had girls. They had a mom as well as a dad. What if they didn't like a new woman in their dad's life? What if they wanted their mom and dad back together? What if they plain just didn't like me?

I was, as noted, boring.

No one liked boring.

Not even little girls.

I jumped when two arms closed around me and I felt a face in my neck.

I lifted my hands and curled them around Logan's forearm at my chest.

"Logan."

"Know you'd be up in Paris," he said to my neck. "But you're gonna be down in Denver."

He then started shuffling me back.

That day, I'd done okay. I'd crashed but not for long.

When I woke, Logan fed me again. He moved us out to the living room (hauling the TV back) because he didn't think it was good I was in bed, too easy to slip away. We chatted about nothing, him resolutely keeping things light. Likely because things had been so heavy, we both needed it. I continued to have the mild but nagging nausea, though after my nap, I was more clearheaded. We'd watched more TV. We'd snuggled, which felt oh so good to have back. Logan had turned on the fire.

I lost it again around nine thirty, totally unable to keep my eyes open. When that happened, Logan helped me stumble to my room and went to bed with me.

I thought I'd done okay.

But right then, my body clearly thought I was in France because I was wide awake.

He turned us, keeping his arms around me, shuffling me toward the bed.

"I'll come back to bed with you, Logan, but I'm wide awake," I told him. "You sleep. I'll see if I can drift."

"Who said shit about sleepin'?"

My inner thighs quivered, my breasts swelled, and Logan got me to my side of the bed, where he took us both down on our sides, then immediately moved back so he could shift me around and up, head to the pillows, and he followed me.

Then he dipped close and I stared up into his shadowed face.

"Reunion time, Millie," he murmured.

Oh man.

He tilted his head and kissed me.

I didn't fight it. There was no reason to fight it.

Words needed to be spoken. A conversation needed to be had. Several of them.

But I was taking this.

I'd earned it.

I'd forced him to earn it.

So I was taking it and I was giving it.

With no anger, no game playing, it was different. The kissing. The touching. It was hungry but it wasn't desperate. It also wasn't tentative but it was slow, exploratory, like we were getting to know each other. Like we'd never done this before.

Then when we found the years hadn't changed this—my sensitive spots, the things I liked, the things I loved, his sensitive spots, the things he liked, the things that made him start to lose control—we slid into it.

I found myself wishing I could turn on the light, see him, all of him, discover with my eyes any ways he'd changed that I hadn't had it in me to discover the times before.

But once we were into it, it wasn't about light. It wasn't about anything but each other's bodies. Him going for the moan. Me going for the groan. Him pulling off my pajamas. Me yanking down his briefs. Taking in the familiar taste of him that had smoothed out and mellowed in a way I loved. Giving him tastes of me and glorying in the noises he made that told me he liked it, the urgency he built because he liked it a lot.

We stroked and we petted and licked, sucked, dragged, nipped, until the urgency he built took over because Logan took over and all I could take in was his scent, all I could do was clutch him to me, my face in his neck, my hips riding his fingers thrusting into me, rolling against the thumb he was using to work my clit.

"Baby," I panted.

"You breathless?" he asked.

God, was I.

We were again on our sides and Logan threw a thigh over my legs, pinning me, hindering my movements so I couldn't help. What he was doing to me was all him.

Better.

Oh God.

So...much...*better*.

"*Logan*," I whimpered.

"Breathless, Millie?"

"Yes," I breathed.

He drove his fingers deep and pressed hard with his thumb.

I shoved my face deeper into his neck and dragged my nails down his back.

"*Logan*," I wheezed.

"Now I got it," he growled, rolled into me, his fingers gliding out.

I opened my legs and felt his cock glide in.

"Oh yes," I whispered as he rode me, slow and gentle. I slid a hand up his spine into his hair and wrapped my other arm at an angle across his back. "More, Low."

He kissed me, long and wet, but that was all the more he gave.

So when he broke the kiss, I lifted my knees and begged, "Please, more, baby."

He buried his face in my neck and worked his mouth there,

still thrusting his cock deep, rhythmic, but slow, his hand gliding up my side and in. His finger and thumb finding my nipple and rolling gently.

Torture.

I'd take it.

I'd kill for it.

Die for it.

Anything for a million more moments like this or anything I could get with Logan.

But still, I needed *more*.

"Snooks." I swung my feet in, digging my heels in his ass and using him to lift up. "*More*."

I didn't need my second word.

On my first, he went faster, pounding, like he'd lost control.

Then he took my mouth and I knew he'd lost control.

And there it was. What we'd had while playing our game. What we'd always had. Never going through the motions. Connecting fiercely, even savagely, with a hunger that couldn't be quenched. Clutching, thrusting, gasping, grunting, scratching, clamping, *joining*.

"Logan!" I cried, and felt his hand in my hair tug sharply, yanking my head back and it began to move over me.

"Never forget, Millie." His voice scratched the words into the skin at my throat. "Never forget this *ever*."

I would have given him my assurances that forgetting what we were sharing was an impossibility, but I couldn't.

The best orgasm I'd had in my life was rocking through me, shaking me to my core, embedding itself into my soul so there was no way I *could* forget.

I endured it gladly, gripping his hair, clenching him to me every way I could, *every* way, and heard his grunts of exertion as I felt him pound deep, God, straight through me. Like his cock drove through my gut, my heart, right to my throat before he lodged himself inside. His head jerked back, his body shuddering, rooted in mine, covering mine, wrapped in mine, and I absorbed his orgasm with every part of me.

Finally, he collapsed on me and I took his weight, all of it, and I did it knowing he could never move and I'd be happy. He could squeeze the breath out of me and I'd be happy.

I had him back, *really* back, and if it was only just this once, I'd be happy.

His hand relaxed in my hair so I could right my head and he slid his mouth to my ear.

"You love me, Millie?" he whispered there.

I closed my eyes and clenched him tight to me.

"Yes," I answered.

"You always loved me?" he asked.

I clutched him so tight it was like I was trying to fuse with him.

"Yes, Low."

"You wake up every day knowin' you'll love no other man but me?"

A tear I couldn't control slid out of the side of my eye.

He'd done that for me.

And I'd done it for him.

And he deserved to know it.

"Yes, baby."

He lifted his head and looked at me through the moonlight.

"Then whatever you were thinkin' starin' at the snow, stop it. We lost each other. Now we're found. And nothin' else matters."

He believed that.

Me?

God.

I just hoped it was that easy.

"Okay, Logan," I whispered.

"Okay," he whispered back, moved in and kissed me.

He took his time, it was long and deep and wet and sweet. And even if he hadn't given me all the words he'd given me just then and during our day together, that kiss would have said it all.

So no, oh no.

I'd never forget this.

Not in my life.

And when he broke the kiss, he swept his thumb across my lips like he was trying to seal the memory of it there.

He didn't have to.

Then he asked, "You wanna clean up?"

I wasn't leaving his arms until I had to.

"You can sleep in the wet spot," I teased.

I heard humor in his voice when he muttered, "I'll get a cloth."

He hated the wet spot.

Crazy, but I loved having that back.

"It's late, or super early. You'll crash. You won't even know it," I told him, holding on even when he was trying to separate.

"Won't take a second," he muttered in reply.

All teasing was gone when I declared, "Logan, you leave me, I'll shoot you."

He stilled.

"Though, I don't have a gun but metaphorically I'll shoot you," I went on stupidly.

He didn't move or speak.

"I'll sleep in the wet spot," I gave in.

He rolled us to our sides, his cock sliding out but he kept his hips between my legs so his weight was resting on my thigh.

I didn't care. My leg could fall asleep, all blood circulation curtailed, and I'd deal to keep him wrapped in me.

He reached out and jerked up the covers.

He was settling in.

I wanted him where he was but this was a surprise. And I might want him where he was but I wanted him to want to be where he was more.

"We sleep like this, I'm gonna leak on you," I pointed out.

"Don't care."

What?

He'd always cared.

"You find the drip irritating." I told him something he knew because he always dealt with these matters for precisely that reason.

"Right now, don't care," he returned.

I sighed. "I'll go clean up."

His arms around me tightened. "Babe, you leave me, I'll shoot you and I *do* have a gun."

I stilled.

"Christ, it's ten your body clock's time, middle of the night my time," he declared. "I fucked you hard, gonna crash in 'bout three seconds you shut up. I crash, I won't feel shit."

"Oh," I mumbled. "Okay."

"So shut up and drift," he ordered.

Yes, years ago, I found the bossy hot.

Now it was kind of annoying.

Hmm.

At first I shut up because I didn't have anything to say.

Then I had something to say so I stopped shutting up.

"You own a gun?"

"Own five, only got one with me. And you know I own guns, Millie. Owned three when we lived together."

This was true.

"You have one with you?"

"Millie."

"What?"

"How about we talk about this tomorrow when my cum isn't drippin' on me, irritatin' as fuck?"

"I *can* go clean up, Logan," I noted again.

He sighed, heavy and deep.

I shut up again.

It was then, with the reference to him having a gun, it occurred to me in all that happened, he didn't know Benito Valenzuela visited me.

"Logan?" I called.

"I'd stop her talkin' by fuckin' her face but fuck if I don't have that in me right now so do I stick a sock in her trap or listen to her babble?" he asked no one because he certainly didn't say that shit to me.

I forgot about Benito and snapped, "Stick a sock in my trap?"

"Millie, it's two in the mornin'. Even when I was twenty-four, after fuckin' you hard, I needed some shut-eye before I had another go at you."

This was true. Though those were catnaps and I usually stirred him from them with blowjobs.

A point to ponder.

"No clue how," he muttered grouchily. "But forgot how much you liked my dick."

"I'm not angling for more sex, Logan."

"You pushed my buttons back in the day, babe, what'd you get?"

Oh man.

I got fucked.

Logan used sex for a variety of purposes, including ending fights, getting me out of bad moods, or turning the tables on a discussion he found aggravating.

I shut up.

Logan was silent.

I was the same.

Then the bed started shaking and it wasn't me doing it.

"Logan?" I called.

He pulled me deeper into him and his voice was unsteady with his laughter when he said, "Fuck, it's so good to have my girl back, it's not fuckin' funny."

God.

I loved that.

Loved it.

Maybe we could do this. Maybe it *was* going to be that easy.

I melted in his arms and started to stroke his shoulders.

"Go to sleep, Low," I whispered.

He found my mouth, touched his to it, then settled back in.

"'Night, beautiful. Drift good."

I smiled, pushing in closer, my face at the base of his throat where I kissed him.

"'Night," I whispered against his skin. "Sleep well."

"Tangled in you, only good sleep I've had for twenty years."

It was no surprise I felt the same, which made it even more unfortunate mine was messed up with jet lag.

I closed my eyes and snuggled deeper, shifting my hand to play with the ends of his hair.

I felt him enter dreamland and he did it rolling into me so I was to my back, his weight was partly to my side, but his hips were still between mine, his face in my neck.

I pulled the covers up over his shoulders, then kept playing with the ends of his hair, feeling him, smelling him, holding him...

And lying in the wet spot.

I tamped down my giggles.

Then, later, I finally fell asleep.

High

When he heard his phone ring, High opened his eyes, seeing, smelling, and feeling Millie.

This meant for the first time in two decades, Logan "High" Judd woke up smiling.

He heard his phone stop ringing, and although he wanted to stay right where he was, he couldn't.

He had to get up, check his phone, and if it wasn't who he thought it was, he had to make a call and do it while his girl was asleep.

It wasn't that he wanted to hide that from Millie. It was just that he needed to introduce it to her slow-like.

One thing was certain from the last two days. He had to handle Millie with care. He had to pay attention. As they rode out their reunion, he had to have total focus on her even when he had other important things in his life that needed his focus.

This was because he needed to take care of her.

It was also because he was not about to let anything spook her so she slipped through his fingers again.

So he carefully extricated himself from her, exited the bed, made sure she was covered, and found his briefs. He yanked them on, and his jeans, pulling his phone out of his back pocket.

He checked the screen.

The call didn't come from who he thought it came from.

It came from Tack.

Tack could wait. The call he needed to make couldn't.

He went to the bathroom, took a piss, washed his hands, brushed his teeth, and came back out to the bedroom. Eyes to Millie curled up in bed looking peaceful, his lips curved up. Then he nabbed the Henley he wore the day before off the floor and tugged it on as he walked out of the room, closing the door behind him.

He started to make coffee at the same time he hit the buttons on the phone and put it to his ear.

He'd called her yesterday, before Millie got up and again after Millie crashed the first time.

And he'd learned from Deb that his girls were disappointed the snow came right before a weekend so they were shut in but not shut out of school.

Though, Deb reported they had plenty of food and all was good.

The second time he phoned, he'd talked to his girls, both now ecstatic about the snow, both wanting him to come over so they could go out and do shit in it.

He couldn't and he lucked out when he heard Deb say in the background, "I know you want to see your dad but I also know you don't want him driving in this snow. It's dangerous. You can see him after the roads are cleared."

With her doing it, he didn't have to say no to his babies, something he found difficult to do, which in turn didn't make Deb happy.

On this thought, after pouring the water in the coffee-maker, he was shoving the pot under when she picked up.

"Hey, High," Deb greeted.

She'd always called him High. Not once did she call him Logan. She knew his name—it was on their marriage certificate, their kids' birth certificates—but he'd introduced himself to her at the bar where they met as High and he'd never been anything but all the time they were together.

Truth be told, not many people called him Logan anymore. Even his mom and dad had reverted to using High most of the time.

So that had become Millie's.

And now he had her back so he had Logan back.

There was something significant about that that he wasn't going to sift through while on the phone with Deb.

But he understood it. He remembered the man he was before her, with her.

He also knew the man he became when he lost her.

Having that name back was like having that man back. Washing away the shit of his life without Millie and starting clean.

It would take more than that but that didn't mean it didn't feel fucking *great*.

"Hey, Deb," he replied. "The girls good?"

"They're hoping for more snow so school will be canceled tomorrow," she told him. "But it's good. They're clearing the roads. Company sent us home on Friday, so I'll probably need to go in this afternoon to do some catch-up so I'm not swamped on Monday. But Mom said she could come around and look after the girls when I do."

Deb had a great job, made good money as the manager of the shipping department of a computer parts factory in town. They had five factories all over the world and were corporate through and through, but they weren't assholes, which was good in times like these since they did shit like send her home when a storm got bad.

And he knew Deb's mom, Connie, would look after the girls. Her son had taken a job in Idaho, married a woman there, had kids there. Her other daughter had moved to Alabama when her husband had been transferred, and obviously their kids went with them. So Connie only had Cleo and Zadie to shower with love and attention and she had a lot of both for her grandbabies and she did it as often as she could.

High liked Connie. She was a good woman. Her husband had walked out on her when her kids were young and then did only the minimum of what a father should do for his kids financially and to be in their lives, so it was all on her to raise them and do it right.

This had been one of the reasons why Deb had accepted his ring. It wasn't lost on her how hard it was for her mother to do what she did for her children. She didn't want that for herself or her own kids.

So she took his ring and the only way that didn't end as a massive fuckup was that they had Zadie and they both loved their girls.

"Cool," he muttered, pouring beans into the grinder, then setting the bag aside. "Got somethin' goin' down but would like to see 'em tomorrow."

"That works, High," she replied.

He drew in breath and looked out the window over Millie's sink that showed a view of her courtyard and his truck, all covered in snow.

It was gorgeous.

And looking at it, it struck him some of the changes in his Millie, some of the things she'd built along the way, absolutely did not suck.

And looking at it, after what had happened the last two days, what they'd lost, he knew he couldn't dick around.

So he lowered his voice when he went on.

"Also need for us to have a conversation, private. You and me, not the girls. Nothin' bad. Just need to talk to you about something."

There was barely a beat of pause before she stated, "You're with someone."

He felt his head jerk in surprise at her jumping right to that.

Then he asked, "You talk to an old lady?"

He heard her laugh. It wasn't filled with humor. It wasn't bitter either. Deb was and always had been no-nonsense. Almost emotionless. Definitely passionless. She didn't get bitter.

She loved her girls. Like any good mother, like her mother taught her, she showered love and attention (and when it was needed, discipline) on her daughters.

Other than that, there was nothing there.

"A Chaos old lady phoning me to gossip?" she asked, then continued, "I don't think so."

He should have known.

She was not a fan of Chaos. Therefore, Chaos were not fans of Deb.

He turned his back to the window and rested his hips against the counter. "Well, I can confirm it's that."

"You're a free agent, High," she pointed out.

Yeah.

Passionless.

She was the same kind of lay. She got the job done. But there was nothing else to it.

She did her wifely duties. It wasn't good, it wasn't shit, it was never close to what he had with Millie back in the day and now, but he'd never stepped out on her. No one caught his eye to push him even to considering it.

But even if it had, he wouldn't have done that to Deb. A man was any man at all, no matter what was going down at home, he didn't fuck over the mother of his children in any way, but especially not that way.

So he didn't.

Another reason why they finished things. Not because she wanted to find something good. Not because she gave enough of a shit about him that she wanted him to find that for himself.

Because the longer she gave him nothing much, the more she figured she courted a betrayal that was not hers to claim—a betrayal of the heart—but as his wife it *was* hers to claim...legally.

"I know, Deb," he replied to her free agent comment. "And we'll talk more when I got you face to face."

"You want to introduce her to the girls," she surmised.

"Yeah," he confirmed.

"Okay," she stated. "We'll talk. But it's not like I didn't know this would happen and I trust you. You wouldn't bring just any woman into the girls' lives. And anyway, I think this would be good for Cleo. She worries about you. It might even be good for Zadie. She needs to get her head wrapped around the end of us and if you're moving on, that might happen."

High wasn't surprised at her reaction to him having a woman in his life. She wasn't about jealousy. She wasn't about anything but her daughters. It was like she knew from what her father taught her that she'd never have that kind of love in her life, so she convinced herself early she could live without it.

And she did a bang-up job.

He didn't try. That was never what they were about. He was hung up on Millie and that was the way it was.

He'd never shared about Millie. Even as his wife, as fucked up as it was, that wasn't Deb's to have, partly because she wouldn't have wanted it.

But even if he had tried, he wouldn't have gotten in there. She'd closed that part of her up so tight, he often wondered if it wasn't her dad but instead was just her.

"Right, we'll set something up," he muttered.

"Okay," she agreed.

"The girls up?" he asked.

"Not yet," she told him, and he smiled.

They wouldn't be. His girls liked their sleep. Since they shared a room, they also liked giggling into the night. Their sharing a room was something that he demanded, wanting them to have that together time to bond as sisters. It was also something he never told Deb he wanted because Millie had it with Dottie and remembered it fondly.

"I'll call later and talk with 'em," he said.

"That's cool," she replied. "Later, High."

"Later, Deb."

They disconnected and he put the phone down on the counter, reaching to the coffee grinder and hoping him using it couldn't be heard through Millie's bedroom door.

As far as he could tell, it couldn't. He had the coffee brewing and was unearthing a waffle iron that looked like it'd never been used when his phone rang again.

He looked to the display and saw it was Tack.

He didn't answer. If Millie wasn't up soon, he'd be waking her up, feeding her, fucking her, then talking to her about what was next up for them.

That was important.

Whatever Tack needed could wait.

Since Millie didn't have Bisquick, something High couldn't fathom of the old Millie but something that he could (and it set his teeth on edge) about the new, he looked up a recipe on his phone. And since she had the ingredients for homemade, he was mixing the waffle batter when he saw a flash of motion.

He lifted his head and caught Millie entering the living room teetering to a stop sideways, pajama bottoms on, still yanking down the top, her face a mix of sleep and panic.

He felt his shoulders string taut as he went alert at her actions and expression.

His shoulders relaxed and he felt warmth steel through him when her eyes hit him and visible relief hit her frame.

She woke up alone, maybe disoriented because of jet lag, and thought he was gone, panicked, pulled on her clothes on the run, and came looking for him.

His voice sounded strange even to him, low and smooth, when he called, "Come here, Millie."

She didn't move for a beat, staring at him across the living room.

"Babe," he prompted.

He lost her expression when she looked to her feet but those feet moved her toward him.

They kept doing it and he turned so she was able to collide with his front, head still down, the top of it hitting his chest, her arms immediately moving to wrap around his waist.

He slid his around her and pulled her closer—a lot closer—so she had to turn her head and press her cheek to his chest as he tucked the rest of her tight.

He didn't get in to how she'd made her entrance. He was there. He was going to make her waffles. It was all good and he didn't need to take her there.

Instead, he bent his neck and asked the top of her hair, "How you feelin'?"

"Normal," she muttered.

"Good," he replied.

"Are we having waffles?" she asked.

He grinned and answered, "Yeah."

"Awesome," she said softly. "I love waffles."

She might love waffles, something he knew since she'd loved them before, but she liked it more where she was because she didn't move.

High wanted breakfast but he preferred holding Millie in her kitchen, so he let that go on for a while, giving it to himself, to her, before he decided it was time to take care of both of them.

That was when he stated, "Not easy to make waffles for my girl with her wedged up against me."

She tipped her head back and he lifted his to catch her eyes.

"Figure it out," she bossed, and having moved her head, she didn't move another inch.

He grinned again and replied, "You feel like stayin' close, not gonna complain, but you're also gonna hafta help."

"I can do that," she told him. "Though, I don't smell bacon cooking."

He lifted his brows. "You want bacon with your waffles?"

"Is bacon bacon?" she asked ridiculously.

He felt his grin get bigger. "It's a lot of things, including being bacon."

"Then, yes, I want bacon with my waffles."

She finished what she was saying but she did it talking through the doorbell ringing.

Both of them looked to it but High suspected only he knew who it was.

All the brothers and their women had left him and Millie alone yesterday but Tack had called twice that morning. The sun was shining. The crews would have been at work on the roads, but Tack would never let snow stop him doing anything.

Especially if his woman was up in his shit about making sure High and Millie were okay.

Something that Cherry totally would be.

"Who's out on these roads?" Millie asked.

"Don't matter," High answered. "Two seconds, they're

gonna be gone." He gave her a squeeze before separating from her and then he looked down at her. "You start the bacon. I'll deal with the door."

She nodded.

He moved.

He saw who it was through the filmy curtain on the door and he wanted to turn right back around.

He didn't.

He sighed, moved to the door, unlocked it, and opened it.

Two kids, one a little girl, one a little boy who was holding his mom's hand, Millie's sister and her man.

Before he could open his mouth, both kids started to make a dash inside but stopped dead when they saw who had opened the door.

They also both stood staring up at him, mouths wide open, eyes big.

But High was frozen.

Solid.

And he was this to fight the pain.

It wasn't the boy. The boy was cute. Dark hair. Brown eyes. Maybe three, four years old.

It was the girl.

She had her aunt's eyes.

She had her aunt's hair.

She had her aunt's mole.

All this something he wasn't able to see fully when he took her in in the candid, but black-and-white photos Millie had around her pad.

She was the vision of what he thought he'd have when he gave a girl to Millie.

Exactly.

She was adorable, top to toe, and the beauty of her carved out his insides.

"Well, I see you weathered the storm," Dottie stated, and

he tore his gaze from the little girl to look at her mother. "So, let's get this started," she went on. "Katy, Freddie, this is your uncle Low. Logan, these are my kids, Katy and Freddie. I think you can figure out which is which."

Katy.

She'd named her daughter what Millie and him were going to name theirs.

This wasn't a surprise. It was her grandmother's name too.

And she'd do that kind of thing, Dot would, giving that to her sister when her sister couldn't give it to the world.

He forced his eyes back to the kids and rumbled, "Yo."

Their eyes got even bigger and their mouths opened even wider.

That was cuter.

And more painful.

Then his world suspended completely when their attention was taken with something, they looked away from High and their faces lit with pure happiness.

They forgot their amazement that a man had opened their aunt's door and the girl shouted, "Auntie Millie! You're back from France!"

The boy just tore his hand from his mother's and started running, hands up in the air waving.

High turned to look and saw Millie in the hall, beaming at her niece and nephew, her hands up in the air waving like Freddie's before she dropped to a squat and they both hit her, dead-on, taking her right to her ass.

She didn't care.

Fuck no.

Her laughter rang through the room, filled with joy, her face saturated with it—the first hint he had of his old Millie since he'd seen her again—as they crawled all over her and she wrapped herself in them, hugging them, holding them, tickling them.

Loving on them.

Christ.

Christ.

He thought he got it. He was sure he understood what she did to tear them apart.

He didn't get it.

Not until then. Not until he watched that. Not until he felt the memories of a million moments just like that he'd had with his own girls.

It was only then he got it.

She'd saved him from this. She'd saved him from having to watch her never having this with their kids. She'd saved him from having to watch her only getting it when she got her hit of Dot's kids.

And she'd given him his own.

It was all the same as what he thought he got but witnessing it made it more acute.

So yeah, now he really fucking got it.

And it killed.

"Kids! For goodness' sake! Get off your aunt Millie! You've got her pinned to the floor in her pajamas!" Dottie demanded, shoving in.

"Jesus." He heard a man mutter, and he slowly turned back to the door as Dot's husband stood outside it, not moving, and went on critically, "Knew you were a biker but you're *rough*."

High took in the big man with dark hair clipped short, undoubtedly due to that making it zero maintenance. He was wearing a white thermal under a padded flannel shirt, faded jeans, scuffed, worn work boots, and the whiskers on his face said he hadn't used a razor in, High's guess, at least three weeks.

High then extended his hand and replied, "Right. You're pot. Nice ta meet you. I'm kettle."

The man's eyes narrowed.

Dot burst out laughing.

High dropped his hand that was ignored.

"Auntie Millie!" the little girl cried in despair. "Your boyfriend's name is *kettle*?"

"*Boyfriend*?" the boy asked in disgust, his attention coming back to High and it was not difficult to see the kid found him lacking.

"Alan, honey, do me a big favor and shut the door on that cold," Dottie called. "And, no, I told you. That's your uncle Logan," she said to her kids. Then she kept talking. "So okay, how about we take this into the house where there's coffee?" She looked at her sister, who was pulling herself up from the floor. "Alan insisted we come, not call, to check in on you. Sorry we're interrupting but whatever. We're here now and I'm two cups down since it took us twice as long as it normally does to get here on those blasted roads."

"I—" Millie started, but her attention came back to High when he had to shift back, something he did only slightly, to let in her brother-in-law.

When the man was in, High shut the door while the little girl asked her aunt, "Did you bring us presents from France?"

"Did I bring you presents from France," Millie replied. Not a question, a scoffing astonishment. "I can barely go to the drugstore and not get you presents."

"*Yay!*" the girl screeched.

All this went on while High and Dot's husband faced off in the hall.

Dot had caved when he'd confronted her. As she would. She'd been there. She knew.

This guy, High had his work cut out for him.

Their face-off continued until the little boy announced, "You're not Auntie Millie's boyfriend. *I am*."

High looked down at the kid whose face was now twisted with dislike and outrage and, fuck him, but he couldn't beat back the smile.

"You're not my boyfriend, sweetheart," Millie said. "You're my nephew."

The boy looked to his aunt and snapped, "Same thing."

If High didn't know they were already close, what happened next would prove it.

"We're making waffles," Millie announced, adeptly dealing with the kid's attitude by offering food. "Who wants waffles?"

The kid's stomach was obviously more important than his claim on his aunt because he forgot about his issue with High and yelled, "*Me*!"

The girl started jumping around, also yelling, "Me too! I *love* waffles."

"You guys had oatmeal at home," Dottie said, herding her kids into the house.

"That wore off like *ages* ago," the boy replied, pulling away from his mother and dashing into the living room, following his aunt, so intent on doing it that his arms were pumping in an effort to give him more speed.

They disappeared.

With that distraction gone, High turned back to Alan and was again confronted with a wall of attitude, the adult kind he didn't like all that much.

It didn't sit well with him because this guy didn't get it and was making judgments that weren't his to make.

But that didn't matter.

It was High who was going to have to make the effort.

"It means a lot you give a shit," he said low. "And as you can see, she's doin' good. And so you know, I get it may take time and I'll put in the time but in the end, you'll know I got this."

"You fuckin' better," Alan replied, and High had to remind himself it was good Millie had people who cared in her life, as that was all the guy gave him before he prowled away.

He looked to his feet, sighed, then looked up again when he heard little Freddie shout, "*Bacon*! Yee ha!"

And High steeled himself against what he knew would be all good at the same time it was pure torture as he walked out of the foyer toward the living room, hearing Millie ask, "Okay, who's going to help man the waffle iron and who's gonna help fry the bacon?"

She got two, "Waffle irons!"

When he hit the living room, he felt slightly better seeing Dottie's eyes come to him with a soft look of understanding and a definite communication that it was all going to be okay.

He felt a fuckuva lot better when Millie's eyes came to him and she gave him a smile that said she was happy her house was filled with people she loved.

Then it was High who ended up frying the bacon.

CHAPTER THIRTEEN

Gonna Be My Throat

Millie

"ALAN WILL COME around," I whispered against Logan's neck.

We were in my bed, Logan in his clothes, me in my pj's, Logan on his back, me on top of him.

My sister and her family had left five minutes ago. The snowplow had gone down our street thirty minutes before that but it didn't matter. Alan told us it was going to get near sixty degrees that day, so Denver was going to thaw.

When they'd left, I'd wanted to do the dishes.

Logan had firmly led me right where I was.

"I know, Millie," he whispered back.

I lifted my head to look up at him. "How did Dot know about us?"

Conversation had not been heavy during our surprise visit with my family. We made waffles. We ate them. We talked about France. I gave out presents. The kids took most of the attention but that didn't mean Dot didn't go out of her way to communicate to her children and her husband that Logan was welcome and accepted. This meant she went out of her way to communicate the same to Logan.

Alan, on the other hand, resolutely refused to heed this communication and spent a lot of his time scowling at Logan and being very loving and familiar to me. He did this last bit by centering anything he said around things Logan couldn't know or hadn't been a part of, leaving him out.

Logan appeared not to give a shit about this.

But he was human and he was back with me. Family was all important to him.

He'd give a shit.

This was one concern.

The other concern was the fact that they'd come at all, not to see me after France, but obviously to check I was okay since they knew Logan was there.

"After you passed out in my bed in the Compound," Logan began, "I went to her. We had words."

I felt myself go tense as I felt my eyes go wide.

"Uh . . . *what*?" I asked.

His arms were already around me, loose but warm.

At my question, he started stroking my back with one hand.

"Babe, she's Dot," he declared. "She was more worried about you than me showin' up at her door pissed off she didn't share with me back then. Then she showed her usual spunk, and side note, glad to see she hasn't lost that, it can be irritatin' as fuck, but just like you, mostly it's cute. In the end, she asked me in for cocoa and welcomed me back."

I felt better at his words.

I also felt amused at the cocoa bit.

"Did you have cocoa?" I asked.

"Fuck no. Had you back in my bed. Said what I had to say and got the fuck outta there." His hand stroked up my spine and curled around the back of my neck. "And seein' as I'm sharin' this, even if you weren't already pullin' out of that Arizona thing, Dottie's probably been manipulatin' that since I was at her place so you would be pullin' out of it, seein' as I gave her that assignment and, like her little sister, when she's in, she's *all* in."

That didn't surprise me either. Dottie, like my parents, had loved Logan. They'd missed him. Dot had tried repeatedly (and failed miserably) to talk me out of ending things with him.

However, Logan going to get in her face wasn't fair.

He didn't know that.

But it wasn't.

I bent closer to him and shared carefully, "You should know, she didn't agree with what I did. She tried—"

He slid his hand to cup my cheek in his palm. "Babe, you don't gotta say no more. She told me you were in a state. I told you I get the state you were in. We've talked that through. Let's not go back there."

I stared at him.

I knew I missed him. I lived with that pain every day.

But now I was remembering all the reasons *why* I missed him.

One of these being that he was understanding. He listened. He did it with focus. He heard what you were saying and if it meant something to you, he found a way to get it so it wasn't an issue. Alternatively, if he didn't get it, he eventually found a way to accept it. That didn't mean there weren't arguments or out and out fights, but that was usually about unimportant stuff.

The important stuff Logan treated as important.

Another of these things was the fact that once an issue was put to bed, it was done. Not only did Logan not dredge it up again, hold a grudge, use it as an example, reopen discussions, he also didn't let me do it either.

If we found ourselves at a hurdle in life, once we cleared it, we kept going.

No turning back.

These thoughts were profound and made me an alarming mixture of happy, hopeful, and sad, thus they made me drop my head so I hit his collarbone with my forehead. I turned so my cheek was pressed to him and his fingers were forced to glide into my hair. To get more of him, I then slid my hand down his stomach and up so I could shove it under his shirt, skin against skin, around to his back.

"What's on your mind?" he rumbled.

"I never forgot why I loved you so much, missed you so much. But having you back, I find that I still forgot."

"Baby," he said softly.

"I'll get over it," I told him, hoping that was true and I didn't live with new wounds, wounds reminding me of all I'd missed over the years.

"Yeah," he murmured, gave me more soothing strokes, then moved us along. "Now we should take a shower. You got shit to sort bein' back and we got shit just to sort and we should get on with that."

I didn't want to.

The day was sunny and warm. The snow was thawing. And this time we had together would be at an end.

Logan was intent we'd have more times together and no matter how bumpy that ride got, this time I was going to hold on tight along the way.

But now we had this moment. This final stretch of time in our reunion before we had to get on with life.

And I wanted more.

Even if it was just a little bit, I was going to finagle it.

In order to do that, I lifted my head and shifted so I took some of my weight off him as I slid my hand into the other side of his shirt.

"How about we sort out life in a little bit?" I asked quietly, watched his eyes fire, and I not only got my answer to my question, I got tingles.

"Works for me." His words rolled over me, through me, *in* me, and I got more tingles.

Then I lifted my hands, arching my back to free his shirt so I could pull it up, and High raised his arms and did an ab curl so I could pull it off.

And with him right there, in my bed, all mine, *again*, I decided to multitask.

I'd get to do the catch-up *I* wanted while we had these final moments of our reunion.

This was such an excellent idea I set about doing it immediately, taking him in, lazy but intent, smelling the smell of Logan I remembered, running my lips along his rough jaw, down his throat, my hands down the bristly hair on his chest.

I followed them down.

I found none of this had changed. The brothers had a workout space and they used it. They might drink and smoke and carouse but they took every opportunity to commune, including while lifting weights.

So the hard swells of Logan's pecs might have been bulkier, but they weren't unfamiliar. The compacted bulges of his biceps might have been bigger, but that only meant better. The furred boxes of his abs were no less defined. The sleek ridges of his ribs no less delineated.

I found a large tat along his side, losing sight of it on his back, but it protruded quite a way across his ribs. It was a set of scales, one tray having the word *Red* on it, blood dripping off the sides, the other having a ghoulish reaper floating up from it with the word *Black*. The base of the scale was the words *Never Forget*.

I took one look at it knowing all the brothers got tats that meant something, told a story, proudly displayed a brand, shared history. Thus the story behind this troubling work of art, I decided, would wait for another day.

So, quickly, I moved my lips across the word *Black* and trailed them down his abs and along the waistband of his jeans.

His hand, already cupping my head, convulsed, the pads of his fingers digging gently into my scalp.

He knew where I was going next. He wanted it.

I wanted it too.

I slid a hand up his hip and in, dragging it over his hard crotch.

His voice was a coaxing growl as he said, "Keep goin', beautiful."

He had nothing to worry about.

I undid the button at his waistband, the next, the next. His fingers tangled in my hair as I went on and undid them all. The minute I was done unbuttoning his fly, I pulled his jeans down an inch, intent on getting to one of my favorite parts of him that I knew I still loved from recent experience, a part I would always *adore*, but I hadn't been together enough to fully take it in.

I was going to do that then.

And I was going to take my time this time.

Intent on that, I yanked his jeans down another inch, Logan lifting his hips to help. I could see the thick root of his hard cock and I couldn't wait.

I yanked again and something caught my attention.

I looked at it, not taking it in at first, except to see it was freaking cool.

The head of a snake, mouth open, fangs bared, inked into the muscles demarcating his hip bone.

Staring at it, all of a sudden my insides froze and my fingers at his right hip yanked down more.

That was when the rest of me froze.

Because the body of the snake trailed down and across his hip, cool as all hell, beautiful really.

But it covered my ink.

It covered what had once been there.

It covered his declaration that he was mine.

All mine.

Only mine.

His ink was still at my back.

My ink was gone.

I stared at his hip, unmoving, for long enough for Logan to call, "Babe."

I didn't even twitch.

He slid his hand to my jaw, putting gentle pressure on to tilt my head so I'd look at him, doing this and saying softly, "Millie, beautiful."

. . . only her.

Gone.

I'd lost that.

I'd lost it.

And I'd never get it back.

Not with our reunion.

Not even if this worked and we had the rest of our days together.

. . . only her.

That was something I'd never get back.

Ever.

Scalded by this knowledge, blistering with the burn, the snake moving before my eyes, fangs bared, ready to strike and lay me to waste, I moved fast, launching myself to the end of the bed.

I started to swing my legs around to get off, to run away, run fast, run for my life in order to get away from that snake.

I didn't even get my legs all the way around before Logan's arm clamped around my belly and he hauled me back into his body.

"Baby," he whispered into my ear.

I pushed against his hold with my body and my hands at his arm. "Let me go."

His arm tightened. "Mill—"

I reared and lost it, shrieking, "*Goddamn it*! If I want *to go*, you need to *let me go*!"

He let me go.

I flew off the bed, into the bathroom, and slammed the door.

Once inside, I stopped dead.

"Okay, God, okay," I chanted, starting to pace, my body controlled by emotions I couldn't fight but I also couldn't let loose or the healing that had begun would be lost and this new wound would open and fester immediately.

I dragged my fingernails over my forehead, along my scalp and fisted them in my hair.

"Okay, shit, okay … *God*," I whispered, remembering.

Remembering how we got those tats together. Me on my stomach on a table beside him lounging back in a chair.

It had been the most romantic moment in my life.

I knew it later, definitely, after losing him.

But I'd felt it even then, my cheek to my arms folded in front of me, watching him, him turning his head to catch my eyes. I knew then that even when we got married, it would be awesome, but it wouldn't be as beautiful as that.

That was everything.

That was us declaring we were *us*.

I dropped my hands, moving to the mirror, yanking off my pajama top and turning my back.

I held the material to my breasts as I twisted to look at the mirror, sliding the hair over my shoulder.

Only him …

No...*only her.*

It was gone.

He got it. Not even twenty-four hours and he got it. He got what I did. He got why.

But I took us away.

He would have understood back then. He would have been there to help me deal with the loss of our dream.

He would have been there to help build a new dream.

He would have *been there*.

And my *Only him*... would have its...*only her.*

Forever.

And I threw it away.

I slid down the cabinets to my ass, locking my arm over my breasts with my thighs as I curled into myself and the tears came.

They were silent.

They were deadly.

"Millie," Logan called through the door.

I pressed my face in my knees, closing my eyes tight.

And seeing snake.

My body bucked with a sob.

"Babe, come out or let me in!" Logan yelled. "You got two seconds!"

I didn't go out or let him in.

I wept into my knees.

I heard the door open. I heard the pained, "*Fuck.*" I felt myself shifted so I was not ass to the floor, face in my knees. I was ass to Logan's lap, face in his neck, his hand pressing it there.

For my part, I didn't touch him. I didn't curl into him. I didn't hold on. I sat in his lap in his arms as the tears fell profusely and soundlessly, all this having discovered yet again how I'd lost it all.

How I'd lost *us*.

Logan stroked my hair and whispered, "I'll tat it back, baby. I'll ink you wherever you wanna be. You pick the spot.

I'll do it tomorrow. Fuck, do it now. We'll get dressed and go out now, Millie. We'll ink you back into me."

"I threw it away," I replied brokenly.

He curled me closer. "We're not goin' back there. We agreed. We're here. Get back here with me."

"You can't get it back," I told him.

"You get dressed with me, doin' that now," he told me.

"You can't get it back," I repeated.

"Baby—"

I pulled my face out of his neck and looked at his misty beauty.

"You can't," I hissed fiercely. "I made it so you can't. I threw us away and it isn't only me anymore, Logan. It'll never be *only me*. I threw that away so I can *never* get it back. You had *a wife*."

"She didn't—"

"I don't care," I kept hissing. "She still had you."

"Millie, you calm down so I can explain, you'll get—"

I spoke over him.

"I have mine. You saw it. I never changed mine because *that never changed*. And honest to God, I don't know what's worse. The pain of knowing I threw that away. I should have told you. I should have never let you go. Or the humiliation at admitting to you mine stayed true. It stayed *completely* true. It was only you. It was always only you, Logan. No boyfriend, no lover, hell, not even that first *fucking date*. Twenty years without you and it was always . . . only . . . *you*."

After my pain-filled, mortifying speech, it took a few moments to get out of my head and back into the room.

A room that was so still, it felt like there was no air to breathe.

Then I saw his face.

And my heart exploded.

It did this right before he surged up, me in his arms, and stalked toward the door.

"Logan...," I began, but trailed off when he didn't even look at me, his jaw set, his face hard.

He stalked to the door, right to the bed, and threw me on it.

I didn't have the chance to bounce because he grabbed my ankles and dragged me his way.

I began panting when he let me go but immediately bent in and latched onto my pajama bottoms. He tore them down my legs, tossed them aside, and I was struggling for breath, my body on fire, as he instantly sunk to his knees at the side of the bed, clasping my ankles again, tossing them over his shoulders.

Then he *bent*; I lost his face and my head dropped back to the bed when I got his mouth as it latched onto me.

He tongued me hard. He sucked my clit harder. He sunk his tongue deep inside me. In no time I was past squirming right to writhing against him, my thighs clamped to either side of his head.

And then it washed over me, my orgasm carrying me away as I cried out in yipping gasps and caught his hair in my grip with both hands.

I lost purchase on him. Hardly having started coming, his mouth left me and his hands were back at my ankles, using them to twist me around to my stomach. I kept gasping for breath against the sensations sweeping me away as I felt him let my ankles go but grasp under my arms and he again dragged me into the bed, coming in with me.

He hauled up my hips and positioned. I felt the nudge of the tip of his cock before he drove inside.

My head flew back at the glory of being filled by him and I automatically started to come up on my hands when I felt his fingers wrap around the back of my neck and push.

"Stay down," he growled, pounding inside me.

Oh God.

This again.

Shivers of pleasure mixed with shivers of fear.

His fingers left my neck but I felt them brush my hair to the side. I felt the trail of his touch across my tat. Then he grasped my hips in both hands.

Oh *God.*

No.

Not this again.

Something else.

Something beautiful.

"Stay down, Millie, and take my cock," he ordered gruffly, still thrusting but now also pulling my hips forward and slamming me back to get more of him, faster, harder, God...

God.

I did as ordered, trying to hold it at bay, trying to concentrate solely on the feel of his cock ramming into me, the feel of his wild, the feel of his control completely gone, the feel of what he was communicating to me.

But I couldn't. All that was making it build again and I dug my forehead into the bed as I moved with his thrusts, whimpering into the sheets.

"You gonna go again?" he grunted his question.

"Yes," I breathed.

I felt his body round me, hand to the mattress, cock powering deep, his other hand slid around and in. He found my clit with his finger and rolled.

God.

God.

"Then go, baby," he whispered.

I went.

Through it, I moaned. Turning my head so I was cheek to the bed, I ground back into him, my back arching as his finger worked my clit, his cock slamming inside me and again I was swept away.

"There you go, Millie," he groaned, then his arm locked around my belly and he held fast as I took his pounding thrusts and listened to his harsh grunts as he came inside me.

I was coasting, no thought, just feeling, languid, peaceful, covered by my man, filled with him, and I stayed that way as he stayed that way.

Until his arm moved from around me, his hand trailing across my stomach, my side.

He flexed his hips into mine and my lips parted with a soft mew.

"My Millie," he murmured.

Oh God.

I stayed still, covered with my man, filled with him, as his hand kept trailing.

To my back.

I started trembling when I felt his finger trace the ink.

"*My* Millie."

I closed my eyes tight as the lazy slid away, the peace started slipping, and the emotion rolled back.

Logan slid out and shifted up. I felt pressure on my hip and at his nonverbal command, fell to my side.

I instantly curled into myself and kept my eyes closed.

I felt Logan's presence leave. I heard the tap go on in the bathroom. Then I felt Logan's presence come back.

I also felt the bed depress when he returned.

"Hitch your leg, beautiful," he murmured.

I hitched my leg.

Gently, like he was so good at being, Logan cleaned between my legs.

When the washcloth was gone, I felt his lips at my hip before he was gone again.

But he came back.

I couldn't keep my eyes closed when he got hold of me again, careful this time. Sweet, tender, he shifted me until we were back in bed, how we started, this time naked, the covers over us, me on top.

"Look at me, Millie," he coaxed, his hand at the back of my neck resting, just his fingertips caressing the skin at the side.

I lifted my head slowly to look down at him and the moment I did, he lifted his other hand to cup my cheek.

"That is not a sacrifice I'm comfortable that you made," he said quietly.

I licked my lips.

"Even sayin' that," he went on. "Knowin' that's the kind of love you have for me, that rocks me. Rocks me in a good way, baby. Knowin' you were in so deep for me you didn't let go even for a hookup, makes me feel like a dick sayin' this, but I'm sensin' you need to hear it, it means a lot."

"I think you kinda communicated that with our, uh... latest session."

His gaze softened with humor but the intensity stayed put.

"I hate that for you," he whispered. "I hate that you had that kind of lonely without me. And I love it at the same time." His head tilted on the pillow. "Do you get that?"

"I think so," I whispered.

"You suffered," he whispered back.

"At my own hand," I reminded him.

"I didn't come back."

I shut my mouth and felt my head twitch.

"Knew you. Knew us," he declared. "Knew what we had. You got shot of me, knew that wasn't right. But I didn't come back. You suffered at my hand, too, Millie. And that fuckin' sucks. I hate that most of all. But I vow to you right now, I'm gonna fix it."

"I..." I shook my head. "Logan, it wasn't your fault."

"It wasn't all yours either and it's not cool you take that on."

"But it was me—"

"And it was me who didn't come back."

I opened my mouth but he spoke.

"I didn't love her."

I shut my mouth again.

"You know that. Now you'll know I never got close. Didn't

even try. What we had wasn't about that and I think that's part of the reason we had it. She's not a woman who wants to be loved. She loves our girls but that's all she wants out of life and she's good with that. She made that plain. She did not suffer through what we had. We existed. And that's all the effort either of us gave it. She gave as good as she got to us. That bein' nothin'. She was down with that and so was I. Lookin' back, that's one of the reasons why I went in with her. Because I didn't have to make the effort. I didn't have to bury what was always at the surface even to pretend. Even in an effort not to hurt a decent woman."

He stopped talking and when he said no more, I replied on a prompt, "Okay."

"In other words, Millie, it's only been you."

I dragged in a ragged breath.

"It'll only be you," he went on.

I stared down at him.

He swept his thumb along the apple of my cheek. "So it's gonna be my throat."

My head twitched again.

"What?" I asked, and it came out breathy.

"You made the choice and even if you said you wanted it on my dick, I'd do that. I'd ink my cock with you. But I want anyone who sees me to know. Anyone who gets a look at my face. Not the back of my neck. No way somewhere hidden. They look at my face, they can see, right across my throat, I'm yours."

A badass biker with his woman's tat emblazoned across his throat?

That was huge.

Mammoth.

Oh shit.

I was going to cry again.

To battle that, I started breathing deep.

And to battle it, I had to concentrate on that and nothing else.

Therefore, I didn't speak.

"That work for you?" he asked.

"I...uh...you..."

I cleared my throat.

Then it overwhelmed me and my body bucked with holding back the sob.

I couldn't look at him, he was too beautiful, what he was saying was too colossal.

So I shoved my face in his neck and started deep breathing again.

Logan slid his hand into my hair and through it. Back to tangle his fingers again, he glided them through. And repeat, all while he muttered, "I'll take that as it workin' for you."

I nodded.

Then I took time to pull myself together.

Logan let me.

Once I accomplished that gargantuan feat, I remarked, "Getting a tat on your throat is gonna hurt, Low."

"So?"

He didn't expect a response and even if he did, I had none. As far as I knew, he'd taken the needle four times. The Chaos insignia that spanned his back. My tat, which was now gone. The tat that covered it. And whatever that was on his ribs (which I wasn't sure I had the strength to understand right then so I avoided even thinking too much about it).

He'd know how much it'd hurt.

I let that go and carefully noted, "Your girls are gonna see."

"Millie, look at me."

He sounded serious.

All that was happening was serious, huge, unbelievable, overwhelming, in good ways and in some bad.

So I didn't want *more* serious.

But I had to get my shit together.

Over the years, I didn't even allow myself to dream that this might happen.

However, now it seemed I was living a dream I hadn't had the courage to have.

Since it was here, though, I had to find the courage to face it. Nourish it.

And unlike the last time, hold on and not let go.

So I lifted my head.

Logan slid his hand to the side of my neck, holding me there with that hand and the one at the back and keeping hold.

"I hesitate with this, beautiful," he started gently, "'cause you're fragile. I get that." He gave me a light squeeze with both hands when he saw what I knew hit my face. "I don't judge it. You're not in my shoes. You don't feel the gift it is that you gave me living the way you did for twenty years, keeping yourself only for me. Honest to Christ, it's not a gift I want but it's precious all the same."

I took in another deep breath.

Logan kept going.

"I know you weren't hibernatin' and I woke you up. I know what I gotta do is like breathin' life back into you. And I hope it's sinkin' in that I'm all in with that. So I'll say careful-like that my girls are my girls. They might not have been raised in a home where their mom and dad loved each other, but they were raised in a home where there was a lotta love. They'll want you for me."

"Okay, Low," I replied shakily, hoping that was true.

"Cleo, she always had her head screwed on straight," he told me. "She's a lot like her old man. Sees the world as it is and takes it as it is. Zadie..." He paused and held my gaze. "My Zadie's a dreamer. It never touched her, the void of what her parents should have had. She made up what she wanted to be there and lived in that place."

Oh man.

Logan continued. "So what I'm sayin', gentle-like, is that I know I got my work cut out for me with you. But you gotta go into this knowin' we both got our work cut out with Zadie. You with me?"

Wonderful.

"Have you . . . I mean, you've been here awhile. Have you spoken to them?" I asked.

"About you?" he asked back, but answered before I could even nod. "No. But while you been asleep, I talked with their mom and I talked with them." His voice dropped. "Talk with them as often as I can so I'll be phonin' them today while I'm with you."

He sounded like that would bother me, but of course he would phone them.

So I just nodded.

"I'm going to do my bit," I told him, likely with more bravado than bravery. "I mean, with you. With us. I won't fall apart on you again."

Something changed in his expression right before he changed our positions, rolling into me so I was on my back and he was pressed into my side, his face close, his hands moving so he had one arm wrapped around me, his other hand still at my neck, thumb stroking my throat.

"Never," he whispered, and my hands resting at his sides curled into his flesh at his tone. "Never, Millie, don't you ever hide or feel ashamed of the emotion you have for me, for us, for what we lost, for all we got back. Don't ever do that. All a' this is gonna be pain right along with pleasure. That is, until we work through the pain and got nothin' but the good left over. And I swear to you, fuckin' *swear*, I'll get us there."

"I've changed," I admitted, a tremor of fear lacing those two words.

"That isn't lost on me," he returned instantly. "There's shit you gotta know about me too. But we didn't walk through fire only to get to the end of that and not get our reward. If we can walk through fire, baby, we can do anything."

I wanted that to sink in.

But there was still fear in my voice when I said, "I'm worried it's too late. I'm worried too much time has passed. We've both changed. Probably a lot. I'm worried—"

He cut me off to ask, "Does this feel like it's too late?"

I took him in, lying on me, touching me, holding me—he was my whole world in a variety of ways and had been since we met. But right then, that feeling was literal.

So it totally didn't feel too late.

Not at all.

"You make it sound so easy," I whispered.

"Doin' anything at your side, no matter how hard it gets, it's still gonna be a fuckuva lot easier than tryin' to do anything without you. So, you're right. It might not be easy. Life is what it is and we're gonna face shit along the way. But I know what it was like, doin' that not havin' you. And I know what it was like doin' that havin' you. And I know which way I like better."

See?

He was *so good* at the flowery, biker goodness.

Too good.

So good I was close to crying again.

And in order not to do that, I got bitchy.

"You're gonna have to stop being so awesome or I'll be bawling like a lunatic all the time," I snapped.

He gave me more of his weight as he dipped his face closer.

"Not sure I can stop bein' awesome, beautiful. It's just me."

I rolled my eyes.

When I rolled them back, I saw his were dancing.

God, I loved that.

I melted and lost the bitchy.

Then I realized I'd melted and lost the bitchy so I regained the bitchy and declared sharply, "You're being awesome again."

He started chuckling.

In order not to let how good that felt, and better, how good that felt having it back reduce me to a blubbering mess, I glared.

While glaring, I announced, "Right, so, this being at each

other's sides business, you should know the obstacles you face include, but are not limited to, me being scared absolutely shitless about meeting your girls and them not liking me. Me not having a good idea about the *other* tat that's new that's inked into your ribs. And last but not least, me warning you I'm no longer anywhere near an old lady. I'm boring. I watch TV, wear designer duds, and work most of the time. And don't get any ideas because my halter top, cutoff shorts days are *way* behind me. And, although I hold no judgment against pot smokers, you still do that shit, you do it outside. I don't want the smell in my furniture."

He'd stopped chuckling but was still smiling when he returned, "Got kids, babe, don't smoke pot except on occasion, only when they're not with me and I'm at the Compound so I can commune with the brothers, then crash."

"That's acceptable," I stated haughtily.

"And I dig your new threads. In fact, you're gonna be wearing that sweater dress thing you had on that day you got up in my face when I was deliverin' the champagne and you're gonna be doin' that soon so I can do the things to you I been thinkin' about doin' since I saw your ass in it."

His words had a variety of effects but I elected to focus on just one.

"I didn't get up in your face. *You* got up in mine," I reminded him.

"I did," he agreed cheerfully. "But then *you* got up in mine."

"Only because you got up in mine," I retorted.

"Whatever." He blew that off and reverted back to the earlier subject. "As for you workin' all the time, you're gonna have to cut that shit out."

Suddenly, we hit rocky ground.

But it all had to be faced and maybe sooner, having it all out there, was better than later.

"I like working," I told him carefully. "And my job is busy."

"Millie, you think I'm gonna settle for you carvin' out time for a quick blowjob every once in a while, you best think again. We gotta lotta time to make up for. While we're doin' that, you're gonna be takin' my dick a lot, doin' it in a variety of ways, and I'm gonna be takin' my time givin' it to you."

These words only had a special subset of effects and I was so busy focusing on them, I had no reply.

"I see that's caught your attention," he muttered, and I hazily focused on him. "So we'll start with that. But fair warnin', your life is gonna be filled, beautiful, with the good shit that makes life worth livin'. So when you get back to work, you gotta think about how that's gonna come about because your days livin' as a ghost plannin' parties for other people to enjoy and not havin' that for yourself are done. Hear?"

I heard.

I liked.

I didn't know how it was going to work out.

I just knew I was going to do what I could to find those ways.

However.

"Are you bossier than before or did I just not notice how bossy you were before?" I asked, and it wasn't testy, it was voiced as I felt it, like I genuinely wanted to know.

Logan grinned. "No fuckin' clue. What I do got a clue about is you best get used to the bossy. You give me stick about any a' this shit, you're gonna see a lot of it."

My gaze drifted to his ear as my lips mumbled, "I'm not sure that's a good thing."

"I am," he replied firmly, and I looked back to him just in time to watch his head angle to the side. "Now, we woke up. We had a surprise family reunion. We had waffles. We had a drama. We had a spectacular fuck. We got some shit straight. In all that, you know what we haven't had?"

"No," I answered.

"A kiss."

My "Oh" was a soft breath.

"So kiss me so we can shower," he demanded. "Then, you're right, we gotta get to a place with my girls before I get you inked to my throat. So the tat is out." He dipped closer. "But I'm thinkin' we'll find ways to spend the day."

I should spend it in my office, sorting through stuff, setting a meeting with Claire to debrief, not to mention unpacking, doing laundry, and getting the stuff Dottie loaned to me ready to return to my sister.

I didn't mention a word of that.

I lifted my head the two inches it took me to press my lips to Logan's.

He slanted his head farther and took my lip press, added tongues, and our lip press turned into a bodies melding, arms clasping, fingers clenching, tongues dueling make-out session.

Logan's phone rang in the middle of it.

He ignored it and carried on.

When he broke the kiss, he did it only to drag me out of bed and into the shower.

It was a good shower.

Excellent.

We used to do that a lot together and I'd missed that too.

I felt the pain.

Then I set it aside to focus on something else. A number of something elses. All of them having to do with Logan, me, warm water, and slithery soap.

And that worked.

Magnificently.

High

His phone beeped with a voicemail after it quit ringing and High looked from it to Millie.

She was sitting cross-legged beside him on the couch. Her

bottom half was under a fluffy afghan even though the house was warm, the fire was going, and one of her legs was resting on his thigh that was stretched out seeing as his feet were on her coffee table (something that brought him a look, which got her a grin).

She was staring at the TV, cheeks wet, sniffling.

When what went down went down on the TV screen and seeing her reaction, High'd been worried. This was because the bitch on the television had bit it after having a baby and when that happened, Millie had mildly lost it.

He was concerned this was about why the woman bit it, dying after childbirth.

Then he realized Millie's blubbering wasn't about the woman losing her life after pushing out a kid. It was just that she was wound up in the show.

So he relaxed.

As the episode went on, she kept blubbering.

Since she was into it, he reached out and grabbed his phone.

He saw the call was from Tack, as was the voicemail.

This was Tack's fifth call that day.

None of them High had returned.

He'd spoken to his girls that afternoon and he did it with Millie around. He didn't lie when he said she was fragile. She'd suffered more than he'd thought she'd suffered. She was happy to have him back but she was piss-poor at hiding the fact that she was also terrified of it.

He got that.

He just had to go gentle.

At the same time she had to find it in her to suck it up.

When he talked to his girls, he noted she found that in her. The conversation wasn't long, it happened while they were putting together a late lunch, and all he got from Millie were some sweet smiles, and after he disconnected, a hug and a murmured, "You're cute with them."

He wasn't cute with them.

He was a father with two daughters.

That was it.

Millie thought it was cute, though, and he'd roll with that.

While talking to them, he made plans to take them to dinner the next night. He'd also talked to Millie about it. She wouldn't be there and she'd agreed that was the way to go. He wasn't going to spring her on his girls. Not like that.

He also wasn't going to delay. Cleo and Zadie would learn about Millie the next night and they'd meet her soon after.

They were going to have to suck it up, too, or at least Zadie was.

There was not much that was shit about being a dad.

But the part where you had to teach your kids that life could throw curveballs and you had to dig deep to find it in you to adjust was a part of that shit.

There was no getting around it.

And his baby girl was about to face a curveball, so it was his job to guide her to learn how to adjust, take the strike but keep her head up, or better, face it and hit it out of the park.

After lunch, life intruded and High experienced more contradictory emotions, hating the fuck out of it at the same time feeling it was good they were facing it.

This being him leaving to hit a store so they had more food (or, Millie actually was stocked up since her cupboards were seriously lacking) and Millie telling him she *had to* hit her desk to get some shit sorted. She also had to unpack.

She had a business and she'd been away. He'd had to let that slide.

So he went to the store, bought everything they could need or want, came back, lugged the shit in, and put it away. She did some time at her desk. Then he did some time hanging in the bathroom with her while she unpacked and started laundry.

After that, they settled in for TV, took a break to make dinner, ate it in front of the TV, and then catastrophe struck her program that he was watching because that's what she wanted but the thing did nothing for him. It was a bunch of uppity folks (even the servants were uppity) wearing old clothes and talking in British accents.

Even when the pretty brunette bought it, it still did nothing for him.

So he went to his voicemail and listened to Tack.

"I get that you're needin' to focus, brother," Tack said in his ear, "but as you know, we got shit to discuss. You're out of it for now, but that don't mean we don't need to go over it with you. So we got a meet at the Compound tomorrow mornin' at nine. Need your ass there, High. Hate to drag you away from what's goin' down, 'specially if you're sortin' things with Millie, but you know it's gotta be done. Especially for Millie. See you there."

High hit the button to turn off his phone, not knowing what the fuck Tack was talking about.

Especially for Millie.

What did that shit mean?

He looked to Millie.

"Babe," he called.

She waved a hand at him, not tearing her eyes from the screen.

"Shh!" she hissed, sniffled, then wailed, *"Oh, Tom!"*

Fuck, she was cute.

And with that cute right there, sitting next to him, weeping for some fictional people who never fucking existed, High decided he'd find out what Tack was talking about at the meeting tomorrow morning.

Right then, he was going to be with his girl.

So he reached out a hand, caught her at her neck, and pulled her to him as he slouched deeper into the corner of her couch.

She adjusted immediately, curling into him as she curled her legs up beside her on the seat.

"You do know we're watchin' somethin' else after this," he told her, to which he felt her body go solid.

She then barked, "Xbox, *pause.*" The show paused and she lifted up and twisted to him.

"We are not."

"Millie, you're bawlin' your eyes out. This program sucks."

"It's brilliant," she declared.

"You're bawlin' your eyes out," he repeated.

"The hallmark of good writing," she returned.

He stared at her, mouth twitching.

He didn't forget. Not any of it. Not any of her.

Including the fact that if she had a choice between a comedy or a drama or something that would send her over the edge and have her sobbing uncontrollably, she'd always pick the last.

Shit, he'd sat through *Steel Magnolias* three times and *Terms of Endearment* four. The bitches in those movies died seven times collectively and Millie blubbered each time like it was the first time she saw it and she didn't see it coming.

And he'd sat through that because she snuggled deep when he did.

"Whatever," he muttered as his cue he was giving in.

"Can I go back to *Downton Abbey* now?" she asked.

"Have at it," he invited.

She grinned at him and he studied her, thinking he had not been wrong with what he threw in her face weeks ago.

His girl was the prettiest crier ever.

However, he liked this best of all, her grinning at him with wet cheeks because she got her way and that was because he gave it to her.

So she turned to the TV and called, "Xbox, play." The action started again and he pulled her deeper into him.

She snuggled even closer.

Then High watched a show he gave not that first shit about.

And he decided he liked it.

Because Millie did.

CHAPTER FOURTEEN

Folded in the Arms of Chaos

Millie

MY ALARM CLOCK went off, and I untangled myself from Logan just enough to reach out a hand to hit snooze as Logan muttered, "Jesus, what the fuck is that?"

I was too sleepy to laugh out loud but I still found that hilarious.

When my man was a recruit for the Club, he had duties that he was assigned, so he was up and at them even before I had to get up to go to school.

After he'd been initiated, when any duties he was assigned happened at night, he hated the alarm clock that I still had to use to get up for school. Told me he hoped there was a time in our lives we could toss it.

I suspected since then and now, he'd tossed it.

I rolled back into him. "Alarm clock, Snooks. I gotta get up and face the day."

I didn't want to. Like yesterday, I wanted to stay tangled up in Logan in as many ways as I could.

But we'd gotten partly back to life yesterday.

At first, it had freaked me out, Logan leaving to get groceries, me facing my desk.

In the end, it was good because it was normal.

But mostly because we did what we had to do separately, then he came back.

Furthermore, this was it. We had to face the new us.

I had to work. Logan had to look after his girls and do... Logan things. We had to sort out life so we could go forward with it, together.

Unfortunately, starting now.

He lifted up, then collapsed back, wrapping me closer and muttering, "It's fuckin' five forty-five."

"I have a lot to catch up on and I work at home, essentially. But I always hit my desk like I'm going to work because it puts you in the right mind-set and you never know what's going to happen. So I have a lot of prep work to do before I go to the office."

He rolled into me, stating, "You can start later."

I slid my hands to his shoulders and held firm there as I replied, "By prep work, I mean breakfast. Shower. Full makeup. The hair shebang. That kinda thing. And that kinda thing takes time."

His lips hit the hinge of my jaw, slid down, where he murmured, "You can start later."

I had felt warm. I had felt snuggly.

Now I felt tingles.

So I decided that I'd take breakfast to my desk. I'd also just blow out the top of my hair and let the rest air dry, then put it up in a ponytail.

That would give me time.

And if it wasn't enough, I'd find other things to cut out.

So I slid my arms around his shoulders and dipped my chin to communicate what I wanted.

Logan gave it to me, lifting his head and taking my mouth with his own.

And it was on.

Eight minutes into it, the alarm sounded.

Logan reached out, grabbed hold of the clock, gave it a vicious yank, ignored my surprised, irritated gasp, and tossed the clock to the floor.

"Logan!" I snapped.

He didn't reply.

He kissed me.

Okay.

Well.

Whatever.

I could plug it in again later (if it still worked).

Right then, I planted a foot in the bed, rolled my man, and went at him.

In the end, it was worth air-dried hair.

Absolutely.

*   *   *

I sat at my desk in a russet tweed pencil skirt, a wheat-colored cashmere turtleneck, and spike-heeled, glossy, dark brown boots, and I turned from my computer to reach out for my mug of coffee.

I did this grinning uncontrollably.

I was grinning not because I had less email to cope with than expected since I'd mostly stayed on top of that in Paris. I was also not doing it because Claire had dealt with any mail that needed immediate attention, so all the rest took little time to finish sorting through. Nor was I doing it because I had very few phone calls to return.

I did it because getting back to life with Logan had perks I wasn't expecting.

These included me putting on makeup and doing my hair, then discovering while I did that that he'd shoveled what was left of the melting snow in the courtyard so I could walk to my office in my fancy boots without ruining them, slipping and falling, or having to delay putting them on so I could tug on my Wellies and shovel it myself.

He also went to my studio, turned up the heat, and started a pot of coffee so it was toasty warm and I had caffeine at the ready when I finally made it to my desk, unlike my old normal when I'd freeze for the first half hour and be delayed in getting to work in order to make coffee.

Sure, the coffee bit only saved me five minutes.

But it saved me five minutes.

More, I got to stand at my back door making out with Logan before I hit my desk and he went to his truck to go off and face his day.

We did this not only kissing but also making plans.

He was going to ask a brother to help him get my car back to me. He was also going to be picking up his girls from school, hanging with them after, taking them to dinner, but he was coming back to me when he was done.

So he'd see me when he brought back my car.

And I'd see him when he came back after dinner.

Then I'd have him. I'd sleep with him again. I'd wake up with him. I'd more than likely make love with him.

Rinse with sleep.

Then repeat.

Hopefully forever.

That did *not* suck.

So I was grinning.

Oh yes, I was grinning.

I took a sip of coffee, put the mug back, and grabbed the phone on my desk to do what was next up on my to-do list.

I had a meeting with Claire that afternoon to debrief on what transpired while I was gone and plan what was happening in the future. I also needed to share with her I wasn't selling out and leaving.

I'd been able to chat a bit with Dottie the day before about the things she'd helped out with while I was away.

Now I needed to phone Justine.

So I did that, put the receiver to my ear, then took it away when she answered with, "*Oh my God! I cannot believe it! Logan's back!*"

My cell might be sitting in my purse in my SUV, hopefully still working after the Denver deep freeze since I'd left it there after my mad dash to Chaos that changed the course of my life.

But Dottie's obviously still was with her and she'd been using it.

I put the receiver back to my ear and replied, "Yeah, babe."

"*I cannot believe it!*" she shrieked again.

I grinned again, this time for different reasons.

Kellie and Justine, like Dottie and my parents, had loved Logan.

Kellie and Justine, unlike Dottie, did not know why I'd done what I'd done. That was for me and the only one I trusted it with, the only one I could handle sharing it with . . . my sister.

So they'd never gotten it.

What they'd done, like any true friend should do, was buried their concern and disagreement with my actions and stood beside me.

"Are you totally, insanely, madly happy?" she asked.

I was terrified.

But I was also totally, insanely, and madly happy.

"Yes," I told her.

"I wanna hear it all, every second, but I'm at the Hubbles, so we're *so totally* getting together for lunch, *soon*. I have Veronica checking her calendar. Dot's in. Kellie's *so* in. I just gotta call Claire."

I wanted to have lunch with them, share the goodness.

No, actually, I wanted to have cocktails with them, have a chance to wear my LBD and share the goodness.

But something she said caught my attention.

Justine had a part-time job so they didn't have to leave their son at a day care for too long and instead he was home with one of his moms. Therefore, with Rafferty in tow, she'd taken care of things for me that Claire or Dot couldn't handle, and things she liked most doing, these being recon on holiday houses and offices for design. I had thirteen emails from her with a variety of pictures for that purpose.

But she knew I was coming back. She knew she was off-duty.

And the Hubbles were my Christmas clients.

"Uh, Jus, what are you doing at the Hubbles?" I asked.

"They had a crisis. The wreaths you want to put on their windows, they likey. Like, a lot. But they don't have an outlet outside to plug them in. No way are they doing battery lights. And they're worried about the cords having to come in through the windows. So there's an electrician here today and they wanted one of us here to help decide where the outside outlets were going to go for the extravaganza you planned for them. Dot told me you were probably going to be out of touch so, since I've been working with them, Claire decided I should be here."

There was a lot to go over with that, so I started with the least surprising considering the Hubbles were Christmas fiends, they'd been my clients for six years, and they'd demanded their décor, inside and out, get more elaborate with each passing year.

"The Hubbles are actually having outlets installed for their decorations?" I asked.

"Totally," she answered. "And I told them the outlet should go between the door and the first window. We can string together the three window wreaths *and* come the other way from the door wreath and use that outlet. The balcony swags and lights are good, there's an outlet up there. But I think another one under the eaves at the back side of the house—"

I interrupted her. "Justine."

"Right here."

"Babe," I started softly. "It means a lot you kicked in. Like I explained, I'm going to pay you and I have this magnificent present for you from Paris. But, girl, I'm back. Things got extreme with Logan but in the end in a good way. That's…I'll explain later…but it's good. Take care of Raff. Get back to your life. You don't have to take my back anymore."

"But I dig this."

I stared at my desk.

"And the Hubbles are a hoot. The Mays are plum loco and totally hilarious. It's not even Thanksgiving and it feels like Christmas, which is *awesome*. And that Barbie woman who we're doing the sweet sixteen party for her daughter is super nice. She loves all my ideas. I don't get to be creative working as a part-time PA for an accountant. Hell, I don't even get to be creative with Raff since he can barely talk; he certainly can't use a crayon."

I heard her words.

But I kept staring at my desk.

I worked a lot because I didn't have a life.

I also worked a lot because I liked my work.

Further, I worked a lot because I wanted to succeed. I'd been a driven person since I was a little kid. I won the spelling bee (three times). I'd been the freshman class secretary, the sophomore class vice president, and class president my junior and senior years.

There was more.

I did it quiet but I did it because it was something I did. It was just who I was.

Last, I worked because I liked to make money. It was only me (before a few days ago) who would enjoy my beautiful home, my beautiful clothes, but they were both things that gave me some of the little happiness I had.

And I had this happiness because I'd worked for it. I'd *earned* it. Me. Only me. *All* me.

Not to mention, in the times that were low, which were a fair few, I had visions (and thus started making plans years ago) of having a retirement where I did all the things I didn't do along the way. Have fabulous parties. Travel. Take art classes or whatever struck my fancy to spend my time relaxing, looking after me, having fun.

But the last few days had happened.

My life had changed.

I had money in the bank. Money in savings. A healthy retirement account. A healthier investment portfolio. And I'd taken a fifteen-year mortgage on my house, which meant it'd be paid off in only four years. This last didn't even take into consideration how much equity I had in the house, not only because of property values increasing but also because of all the work I'd done to it.

And I had a thriving business. At least once a month, but usually more often, I had to refer clients to other planners because Claire and I couldn't take on more work. That year I'd also had to refuse two new Christmas clients because I just didn't have the time. Not with only me and Claire doing the work.

However, if I expanded my human resources, I might be able to take on a few more clients to increase revenue *and* shift some of my work to Claire, who *so* could do it and would *so* love the raise she'd get with it. She then could shift some of her work to a new employee.

Justine worked twenty-five hours a week. She was smart. Loyal. Creative. Full of personality. Over the years she'd kicked in a variety of times just to help or for extra cash when I'd needed her for events. And I would absolutely not mind if Rafferty was with her when she worked, so she could save on day care.

She'd be *perfect*.

"Hell*ooooo*," she called in my ear. "Did I lose you?"

"I need to change my life," I announced.

"No duh," she replied. "You were on the road to recovery but now that Logan's back, you gotta step that up, sistah. He's low maintenance, as dudes go, but I don't see him wiling away the hours in your awesome but *very* girlie pad, watching *Easy Rider* and waiting for you to come home after you make sure the DJ plays all the right songs at some chick's sweet sixteen."

My pad *was* very girlie.

And it was so *not* Logan.

Oh man.

I couldn't think of that.

I had to stay on target.

"Babe, this is personal, but how much do you make at your job?"

"Sixteen an hour," she answered instantly, then went on, "Which is ridiculous, but it's the only place I could find that would do part-time and be cool when I had to take off to see to Raff because Ronnie can't do that at her job."

I did quick calculations in my head, the extra clients I could take on, the raise I'd need to offer Claire with giving her more responsibility.

I should pull up my accounts. Do it correctly. Make absolutely certain I could swing it, for me, for Claire, for Justine.

All I could think of was Logan.

"I'll match your salary," I stated, then went on insanely, "Or better it."

My friend made no reply.

"Justine?" I called.

"Are you serious?" she breathed.

"I need to adjust my life," I told her. "I need to make time for Logan. He has girls. I need to make time for them. I never like turning down jobs and it happens frequently. So yes. I'm serious."

"That'd be *so cool*!" she cried. "Ronnie's company covers our insurance, so no worries there. And, babe, love you, would love to have this opportunity, you know I have fun working with you, but gotta share that I've got three weeks of vacation, two personal days, three sick, and Ronnie has almost the same, so I wouldn't want to lose any of that."

Claire got three weeks of vacation.

Justine couldn't start on the same level with that as Claire.

I'd up her personal days.

"I can do that," I said.

"Holy crap," she whispered.

She could say that again.

I needed to run some numbers.

But in the end, it didn't matter.

Mental calculations told me any hit to my personal income would be minor, if it existed at all.

Money was good to have.

But Logan was better.

"This is...it's...it's awesome, Mill," Justine said.

"I'm glad you think so," I replied. "It meant a lot, you covering me while I had to go off and do my thing. But you're also good at it. And it'd mean a lot to have you on the team."

"I have to talk to Ronnie."

She would. But Veronica wouldn't say no. She loved her woman. She'd want her happy. And they weren't losing anything out of the deal.

"You talk. You tell me. I'll run some numbers to see what I can do to make it worth your while. And then we'll chat."

"It'll be worth my while."

"Let me run some numbers, babe," I said softly.

It took a long moment for her to reply, "Love you, Millie."

I drew in a deep breath.

"I'm happy you're offering this to me," she continued. "But I'm happier with why. I can't wait to hear how it all went down with Logan. But you gotta know, official, I'm happy it went down, now for more reasons than one. The last time you had any joy, it was with him. I'm glad to know you're not dicking around with getting that back."

"Me too," I whispered. "And me too again with the love you thing. You're the best, Justine."

I grinned again when she returned, "I so am." My grin faded and my heart warmed when she finished, "You are too. Just hope Logan reminds you of that because I've told you, Dot has, Kellie has, Ronnie has, and you never got it. Logan gave that to you too. I hope he gives it back."

"Okay, we have to stop this because I have a ton of work and I can't do it crying. I also don't have time to fix my makeup," I warned.

"You're such a freak. Babe, you have no appointments today. You're sitting in a little house behind your big house. Who cares if your makeup is messed up?"

"I do," I retorted.

"Such a freak," she muttered.

"This is better," I declared. "You being annoying. A lot better."

"I give good annoying too."

"Go...take care of the Hubbles," I ordered. "But keep track of the time. I'll find time to run numbers today and I'll call you tonight with a proper offer. Is that okay?"

"Perfect. Later, babe. And, Millie?"

"Yeah?"

"Pleased as punch for you, sister."

I drew in another breath.

She hung up.

I was grinning again when I put the phone back in its cradle.

I checked calling Justine off my to-do list, hit the next up, and was working on the one after that when I heard the growl of a truck in my drive.

I looked up, out the windows, and saw Logan's truck.

I smiled.

He turned into the courtyard and I saw my SUV trailing him.

My smile got bigger.

I had my car back and Logan sorted that for me.

My smile started fading when the growl of the first two vehicles was joined by the roar of a number of bikes.

I stopped looking out my window in order to stare out of it when I saw Tack, Hop, Tabby's dark-headed guy who'd come in with Tyra the day of my scene at Chaos, and Boz, all on bikes, with Big Petey bringing up the rear on his Harley trike.

"What on earth?" I breathed as my door flew open.

Logan was storming in, *storming* in, face full of thunder, eyes to me.

My back snapped straight and I vaguely noticed another young Chaos member with dark hair coming in behind him but the majority of my attention was focused on Logan.

"Follow me," he grunted.

"I..." My eyes darted to the other man as I heard the roar of Harleys die in my courtyard.

"*Follow me!*" Logan barked.

I jumped in my seat and my eyes shot back to him.

When they did, I caught only his back since he was prowling out of my office, apparently feeling he could storm into my place of business, bark at me, order me around, and I'd comply.

"High." I heard it said outside, that one word meant to be both calming and cautionary, the voice saying it was Tack.

"You need to stay the fuck outta this," Logan growled as I sat still in my chair and stared out the door. As I did, I saw Logan turn and clip, "Millie. *Here.*"

He didn't wait for my response to him calling me like I was a dog.

He stalked away.

Something was happening. I didn't know what it was. I did know it was something big.

And I didn't give a fuck.

No man stormed into my office, barked orders at me, then

called me to him like I was his pet, a *naughty* one, and stalked away expecting me to obey his commands without question.

No man.

Hell, no woman.

No way.

No how.

The problem with that was I had Chaos brothers congregating outside my office door, the young one that followed Logan still inside, and I couldn't share that shit did not happen, no way, no how while sitting in my chair while Logan was somewhere else.

So I got up quickly, my chair flying back, and I did my own fucking storming.

I did that passing the young guy, marching through the bevy of brothers hanging outside the door, and I caught sight of Logan at the back door to my house.

I headed right there.

He opened the door and went in.

I hurried my step and followed him in.

He was about to close the door when a hand landed on it and we were both forced back so Chaos could file in.

And they did.

All seven of them.

I didn't have a mind to them.

I had a mind to Logan.

My voice was low and trembling with fury when I declared, "You did not just call me to you like I was a dog."

He slammed the door, lifted a hand, one finger stabbing in the direction of the wall behind the door.

I looked that way and blinked at a security system box lit up there that wasn't there before I left for Paris, and due to all the things that had gone down, I had not noticed when I got back.

"You leave, you arm this," Logan snarled. "Four, nine, one, three, red button." He jabbed at the red button under the keypad.

"You come home, you shut the fuckin' door, lock the fucker, and unarm it, four, nine, one, three, then you fuckin' *rearm* it, *immediately*, four...nine...*one*...*three*."

"How'd that get there?" I whispered.

Logan didn't answer me.

He leaned into me, nabbed my hand, his fingers tight around mine, and started stalking again, through his brothers standing around my kitchen, dragging me with him.

"High," Tack bit out impatiently.

Logan didn't hesitate an instant.

He dragged me to the front door, yanked us to a halt, and thrust a finger at another security panel at the side of the door.

Eyes to me, he stated, "Same thing. Four, nine, one, three. You leave, you arm it. You're home, it's armed. No motion sensors in the house. It's all about the windows and doors. They're breached, a sound goes off raising all holy hell but also a message is sent straight to security dispatch. They contact the police and send a man out immediately. A man will show at the door to ask if everything is fine. You have a code phrase to tell him it's not. You say, 'Everything is fine, sir.' If everything *is* fine, you find different words. If it's not, he'll know and deal. This sinkin' in?"

"How did I get an alarm system?" I asked, then kept questioning. "And *when*?"

"You got it 'cause I had it put in. And you got it while you were in Paris."

"I...what...*why*?"

He tugged on my hand, my arm jerked in the socket and I fell the step toward him that separated us.

Then he bent only his neck to stare down at me from his superior height, doing this still ticked way the hell off and keeping hold of my hand.

And staring into his infuriated eyes, feeling the stretch of the muscles in my arm that lingered after his pull, not painful, but still, I realized I was not astonished I had a security system. I was also not pissed at the way he was treating me.

I was scared.

I was scared because he was scary.

I was scared because Logan was gone. There was no trace of him.

This man was High.

And he was terrifying.

"'Cause I fuckin' *told you* you got windows in your doors and that shit's unsafe," he ground out.

I shifted away from him, pulling at my hand but failing to get free.

"Let me go, Logan," I said carefully.

"High, brother, calm down," Tack ordered from the direction of the hall.

Logan ignored me and Tack.

"I didn't arm the alarm once you got it because you didn't know you had it and I didn't want you or Dot settin' it off. Now you know," he stated. "And now you fuckin' use it, Millie. Anytime you leave, I don't give a shit you're walkin' next door for a cup of sugar. And anytime you're home. Do you *get me*?"

I again tugged at my hand. "You need to let me go."

He moved forward and I scuttled back until I hit wall and Logan held me there with the bulk of his body and the intensity of his rage.

"Brother," a voice I didn't know called, and I felt Chaos moving in all around Logan and me in my foyer.

But I didn't tear my eyes from him and he didn't tear his from me.

"You know that shit doesn't happen to old ladies," Logan snarled.

"Logan, you're scaring me," I whispered.

He dropped his face farther so our noses were nearly brushing. "You *know*, Millie. You fuckin' *know* that shit doesn't happen to old ladies. And if it does, the *first* fuckin' thing you do is *tell your old man*."

His tone was deteriorating to abrasive, scratching at my skin.

"Logan—"

"You had a man in this house that was enemy to Chaos, a fuckin' *gun* pointed at you, and you didn't *tell your old man*."

Oh shit.

How could I forget about my visit from Benito Valenzuela?

I stared into Logan's livid eyes and did it knowing he was right.

That shit didn't happen.

But in the highly unlikely event it did, an old lady, or anyone associated with the Club who had the protection of Chaos, went right to their old man or someone in the Club.

I'd done the latter.

But I was Logan's.

Going to Tack was unacceptable.

It was Logan I should have told.

"I told Tack," I informed him of what he now knew.

"You're not takin' Tack's cock," he growled.

"High, cool off and *back off*." I heard, and that was Big Petey.

I heard it but I didn't process it.

I was busy dealing with Logan's words pinging around in my head.

And as they did, I wasn't afraid of him.

I remembered the many reasons in this scenario I was pissed like fuck at him.

So I retorted sharply, "I wasn't your old lady then."

"You've always been my old lady," he bit back.

This was true.

Whatever.

"You are very aware that it's more complicated than that, Logan Judd," I snapped.

"I am. Very aware, Millie. And I'm very aware that I had

two fuckin' days in this house with you and you didn't say a goddamned word."

This was also true.

Shit!

"Other things, things that were extremely important, I'll note, were taking my attention," I pointed out.

"Yeah. They were. But instead of you bawlin' your eyes out last night 'cause some bitch who doesn't even fuckin' *exist* bit it on TV, you coulda been tellin' me you'd had a *gun pointed at you*."

He was right again!

Shit!

"I told Tack," I repeated.

"And Tack is *not me*," he fired back.

"Logan—"

He moved in even closer and I snapped my mouth shut.

"You did wrong," he whispered menacingly. "And you know it."

I was not going to be menaced.

"You're right," I retorted. "Absolutely, one hundred percent right. I did wrong. I should have told you. I thought about it but other things kept coming up. Then, I don't know how, maybe it was having the love of my life *back* in my life, I forgot about it. But bottom line, I was wrong. That doesn't negate the fact that now *you're* doing wrong by storming in here, barking at me, dragging me around, and attempting to intimidate me."

"Men broke into my woman's house, threatened her, held a gun to her, and she didn't tell me that shit," he returned.

I knew that couldn't stand. I knew with any of these men that was intolerable.

But the fact remained, I was unaware at the time I was his woman.

"You need to dig deep, Logan, and remember where we were when that happened regardless of where we are now, where we've discovered only in the last two days we've always been..." I rolled up on my toes so our noses actually brushed, and finished, "*And cut me some slack.*"

Although a low, sexy growl rolled up his throat, I was able to beat back the tingles at the sexy part because I was just that ticked.

Other than that, he didn't move, didn't reply, just scowled down at me.

I realized with this I'd finally scored my point but I was too pissed to care.

So I didn't move, didn't say another word; I just glared up at him.

This went on for some time.

It only stopped when the guy who came into my office with Logan got close to our sides and, his voice shaking with humor, stated, "Think the biker and biker babe standoff is at a stalemate, brother. Probably a good time to stand down."

Logan turned only his head to the guy. "I'm not feelin' amused, Joker."

"Think the rest of us are amused enough for you, High," he replied.

Logan's eyes narrowed dangerously.

I decided the biker and biker babe standoff *was* at a stalemate.

At least that one.

We had another one to contend with.

I got Logan's attention back when I demanded to know, "How did you manage to put a security system in?"

He didn't move out of my space when he declared, "Shit went down at The Roll. You were gutted. My boys were the ones who gutted you. Kellie laid it out. I jumped on my bike to sort shit out between us once and for all, got here, you didn't answer. I was tweaked because you were fucked way the hell up and when you didn't answer, that tweaked me more. So I broke in like I *told you* anyone could break in, did it easy, in about two seconds, breaking your glass."

I gasped.

Logan kept talking.

"None of your neighbors heard and if they did, none of them called the police. I was in your house long enough to search it, make calls, come back, and board up your door. Then I swiped a key and came back again when the glass guys came to fix your door. And I came back when the security guys installed the system. No one around here fuckin' knows me and not a fuckin' peep from anyone."

I had to admit to some dismay about this information.

However, my attention was caught at something else.

My boys were the ones who gutted you.

I jumped on my bike to sort shit out between us.

I stared up at him, remembering something that hadn't dawned on me in the slightest at the time.

That being, when I'd gone to Chaos and Logan had showed, he wasn't nasty. He wasn't hard. He wasn't cold.

He was watchful and guarded.

And he was gentle.

He also wanted to talk in his room.

I jumped on my bike to sort shit out between us.

I was tweaked.

He'd come after me.

He'd been worried about me.

He'd got to the point he was going to end our insane game a different way.

And when he saw something he felt made me unsafe, he'd paid for a security firm to install a system.

Our reunion had not been triggered with me coming clean about why I broke us apart.

Our reunion had been triggered before that, when his brothers hurt me to the point I lost it and he'd been worried about me.

Now *that* was my Logan.

"How did you know I was in Paris?" I asked quietly.

"Babe, told you," he answered sharply. "I was tweaked. Got a guy I know who's a magician with shit like that to track you. Worried like fuck, was gonna follow you but thought you needed a chance to get your head together. So I waited it out. Was also gonna be here in this house when you got back. But you got back early. Still got an emergency passport partly 'cause I was that worried about you. Now that you're back, I figure it's mostly because I was pissed you went there without me."

Worried like fuck, was gonna follow you.

Got an emergency passport.

Oh yes, that was my Logan.

"I don't know what to say," I whispered.

"I do," he returned. "You're gonna have to put up with those boys comin' back because they're gonna be installin' a system in your office. Don't know why I didn't do that shit the first time around but it's gonna happen as soon as I can set it up. You're also gonna be vigilant about keepin' it active. You're not gonna fall down on that or, swear to Christ, Millie, even if nothin' goes down and I find you did, I'm gonna lose my mind. And you're gonna put up with Chaos protection. My boys got fences to mend with you but you're gonna speed that up because, don't give a fuck you got a system, that motherfucker got to you. Now every old lady, when her old man's not close, has a man on her. First up for you is Joker."

When Logan jerked his head to the side, I turned to the man standing close.

"Uh . . . hi, Joker," I mumbled.

He grinned at me.

He was young.

But he was cute.

"Can you do me the favor of unpinnin' your woman from

the wall so we can have a chat with her?" Tack asked from behind Logan.

At that, Logan moved to my side, hooked me around the neck with his arm, yanked me to him a different way, loving and protective but annoyed (which was acceptable), and looked to Tack.

"Your presence here was unnecessary," he growled.

"You tore outta that meeting; no tellin' where you were goin' and what you'd do," Tack replied patiently. "You hit Millie's, in your mood, what went down, what she didn't share, what you didn't know, you know, any brother got that news, every brother would be on his ass so he didn't fuck things up when he got home."

They'd started out trailing him because they were worried he'd go after Valenzuela.

They'd ended up doing it to make sure what we were rebuilding was protected.

I wasn't sure I had fences to mend. Hop had hurt my feelings with Candlebox but he didn't know what was happening. He was doing what any brother would. Taking his brother's back.

But if there were any fences to mend, the boys there right then would have mended them.

I wasn't certain I intended to share that information at the present juncture.

However, if I was, I didn't get a chance because Logan declared, "That's bullshit, brother, and you know it. Minute a man hit his home, the brothers would ride off 'cause that shit's not their business."

"Right, then I'll amend my statement," Tack returned. "We rode in to keep your shit straight with Millie because you both finally got your heads out of your asses and a fuckin' asshole like Benito Valenzuela shouldn't fuck up anything that important."

Tack had always kind of intimidated me simply because he was so sharp, it was uncanny.

But I'd also always liked him.

I could feel Logan gearing up to reply to Tack but I had work to do and it seemed our latest drama was petering out, so I had to move things along.

I did this by looking at Joker.

"You're in luck," I shared. "Logan did a massive grocery shop, so there's tons of food in the house. And I'm a big TV gal. Anything you want is at your command. That is, if you know how to operate an Xbox. But if you don't," I smiled at him, "I'll teach you."

He smiled back but my enjoyment of the attractiveness of this was abbreviated when I had to turn my attention back to Logan, who was growling at me.

"For fuck's sake, Millie, he's not here to kick back and watch the tube. He's here to watch your ass."

"That doesn't mean he can't be comfortable doing it," I returned.

"Uh...yeah it does," he replied sarcastically. "Hard for him to take in a movie at the same time pay attention to you to make sure you're covered."

I turned in his hold and started glaring.

"Well, excuse me. I've never needed protection before. I don't know the protocol."

That was most assuredly the wrong thing to say considering Logan's face clouded with thunder to the point he looked ready to blow.

"Right, you two can keep squabbling later. Now, Millie, we gotta have words," Tack stated.

I looked to him and took the opportunity he gave to put a line under the current scenario. To do this, I threw out an arm as best I could since Joker was still close.

In fact, all the brothers were still close.

Regardless, I managed it and invited, "Why don't we move this to the living room?"

I watched bikers shuffle out of my foyer, most of them grinning at their boots, some of them grinning at me.

And considering the drama had petered out, belatedly it hit me Chaos was in my home.

That particular hit felt like velvet.

Logan and I were the last to move out but before we did, I grasped onto his thermal at his stomach and stopped him.

He looked down at me.

"I should have told you," I said quietly. "I do feel I have an excuse but I'm still sorry."

Any storm still threatening his expression cleared and he bent his neck to touch his mouth to mine.

When he lifted away, he said not a word as he moved us after his brothers.

But he didn't need to say a word.

I knew my apology was accepted.

"Jesus, this pad is *phat*," Boz declared, and I saw him glancing around when we walked into the living room.

I'd been close to Boz. Losing all the brothers had been a hit. But losing Boz and Black had cut deeper.

I studied him warily, suddenly realizing all I was getting when I got Logan back. Or more accurately, suddenly realizing all I *hoped* I was getting when I got Logan back.

Logan would have been enough. Logan was heaven.

If this was what I hoped it was, it was nirvana.

"Millie—"

That came from our other side and I looked that way to see Hop had his eyes to me.

Attractive gray eyes that held regret.

"Don't," I whispered. He opened his mouth but I shook my head. "Don't. I get it. It's done. I hope we're moving on."

"It was a dick thing to do," he stated.

"It was being loyal to your brother," I returned. "I get it. I've got it." With my arm around Logan's waist, I tugged him closer to me. "Let's move on."

Hop looked at me, at Logan, then at me and he jerked up his chin.

That meant we were moving on.

I gave him a small smile.

"We all got shit to do," Tack declared, and my attention turned to him. "So let's get on with this so we can do ours and leave Millie to do hers."

No one said anything and I didn't look away from Tack, so he kept going.

"I think you get we got an issue with Valenzuela. We're workin' on this with Brock Lucas and Mitch Lawson of the DPD."

I felt my lips part at this shocking news.

Cops?

And Chaos?

Tack ignored my open astonishment and kept talking.

"They'll want a statement from you about the break-in. We've talked and you can press charges for that, and what he did isn't good, but when that asshole goes down, we wanna have enough on him to stay down. We also don't want you any more focus than you've already been with Valenzuela. You press charges for breaking and entering and harassment with criminal intent, it might hold, but it won't hold him long and it leaves his soldiers on the street to do his bidding. So we're askin' you to make a statement so it's on record. But we're also askin' you not to press charges so we can keep doin' what we're doin' to bring him and his crew down."

"I...you..." I shook my head. "You're working with the police?"

"Yeah," Tack replied like that wasn't totally insane. "We're gonna do a sweep, make sure no eyes are on you or anyone who's got our protection. But we still don't want you goin' to the cops or havin' them meet with you here. We'll escort you to a private location so you can share what happened with Slim and Mitch and no one will know. You good with that?"

Hesitantly, I nodded.

"You lived the life, darlin'," he said quietly. "Been a while but you're back and it's not shit you forget. So you know our world. You know what he did earned him more trouble than he already had from us. Old ladies are untouchable." He lifted a hand my way even though I made no move to reply. "We all get where you and High were at but I reckon Valenzuela thought different and he made his approach all the same. We'll be makin' moves to ensure he goes down but I want you to know from what's just happened we're also makin' moves to protect our own. It won't happen again. You're good. We'll keep you that way."

Suddenly, I started trembling.

I had Logan back.

I had his family back.

They had an enemy, that enemy threatened me, and that was not good.

But I had Logan back.

I had his family back.

And they were going to take care of me.

And that was so overwhelming in a good way I could do nothing but stand there and take it all in.

Tack in my living room.

Boz. Hop. Pete.

I was in my home.

But I felt like I'd just come home.

Tack, either allowing me my reaction without noting it or missing it (the latter was doubtful), went on, "High's gonna fill you in on what you need to know. What you need to know from us is what I told you. That shit could happen to you because the circumstances between you two made it so it could happen. And Valenzuela is greedy and insane, but he isn't stupid. He chose well. But if he does get eyes on you, he'll see you're fully in the fold. I don't figure he'll be that stupid again. Won't matter, we'll make sure he isn't."

I managed to nod and then something struck me and I looked to the side of my cuddle chair.

The crate was gone.

Like Valenzuela, in all the time shared with Logan, I hadn't thought of it.

And it being gone freaked me out.

"The crate," I whispered.

"What, babe?" Logan asked.

I tipped my head to look at him. "The crate. He took it from the Dumpster. He brought it back." I pointed to the floor by the chair. "It was by the chair."

High's mouth got tight, his eyes cut to Tack, then back to me.

They came back in time for me to say, my voice rising in hysteria, "It's gone. Do you think he came back and got it?"

"Millie, beautiful, shit was intense with us and I wanted that to play out with no distractions so I moved the crate to the closet in your empty bedroom."

I sagged against him for two reasons.

The crate was home and safe.

And that crazy man hadn't been back.

"Four, nine, one, three," Logan said quietly.

The security code.

He saw my panic.

And he had me covered in a variety of ways.

"Four, nine, one, three," I replied quietly.

He shifted his arm around me so his hand cupped me under my jaw.

Then he bent in for another kiss. No lip brush but also no tongues. However, this one lasted longer than the one in the foyer.

And when he lifted his head, my panic was gone.

He let go of my jaw when a presence moved into our space.

We both looked that way and I saw Pete standing there.

I held my breath at the bright in his eyes as he looked between us.

Those eyes landed on me.

"Fuck, sweetheart, so good to have you back," he whispered.

I made a noise as I choked back the tears and moved out of Logan's hold toward Big Petey.

His arms closed around me tight.

Folded in the arms of Chaos.

Oh yes.

I'd come home.

CHAPTER FIFTEEN

It's Chaos

High

HIGH SAT IN Bonnie Brae Tavern with the remains of a huge-ass pizza on the table between him and his girls in their booth.

Cleo was on her ass, munching.

Zadie was on her knees, leaning into the table, devouring.

It was rare she didn't sit like this, his baby girl. He figured she did it because she always had to be ready to launch herself into any adventure that came her way.

Same with how his Cleo was sitting. Life would be what it would be and she'd face it on her own terms.

As planned, he'd picked them up from school. He'd taken them home. He'd made sure they did their schoolwork and straightened up the breakfast dishes in the kitchen so their mom didn't come home from work to face that shit. Ditto with their rooms.

Then, before Deb got home, he took them out.

He and Deb limited the amount of time they spent in each other's presence. Not that they didn't get along. Just that any of that kind of thing could get Zadie's hopes up.

They didn't make a habit of avoiding each other so the girls wouldn't worry that things between them were deteriorating. They just didn't spend much time together—the occasional dinner and the usual hand-off of visitation being the exceptions—so the girls would know it was cool but wouldn't think anything beyond that.

Now, the occasional dinner would stop. Deb would be okay with that. But any time he had the girls outside his weekends, that time would be spent with Millie.

Since he picked them up, the vast majority of the conversation had been about what they'd done during the dump of snow, even though most of this was hanging in front of the television. Even if it was, Zadie could make wild stories up about anything. She could jabber in the Olympics and win gold, including doing this about lazing around and watching TV.

But the pizza was almost decimated. He needed to get them home so Deb could get them settled before bed. And he needed to get back to Millie.

Even so, these times were now rare, so when he had them, he savored them. That meant High sat back, watching his girls eating, Zadie doing it babbling, and he gave himself a moment to take them in.

And while he did, not for the first time, he noted that, apparently, his genes were dominant.

They had nothing of their mother in them.

Deb was blonde and blue-eyed. When she'd started to go gray, she shocked the shit out of him by caring and turning to a bottle. She did that in their bathroom, stinking up the place, something he didn't like. But he didn't say anything because it wasn't worth it with the result since what she did made her look good.

She was pretty. She was relatively petite.

And she didn't look anything like her girls.

She also didn't look like Millie.

Millie was five-seven, which meant she had length to her, long shapely legs he got off on, but she was short enough she could put on heels and he'd still top her. Millie also had meat on her. A round ass. Full tits. A bit of a belly even back in the day when they were younger, something she hadn't lost in the time in between.

He liked it. All of it. Even before Millie, the shape of Millie was what attracted him to a woman.

Deb was five-four. She was careful with what she ate. She worked out on her lunch hour and went to the gym on the weekends. She had to be at least five pounds underweight.

At her height, it looked good. Her tits grew when she had the girls and she didn't lose them and that looked good too.

But there was not much to hold on to. Not much to dominate in bed. He'd fucking loved hauling Millie's ass around (and still did). Getting her where he wanted her, positioning her how he wanted her.

Deb got off on that, mildly, but there was no challenge to it. Fuck, he could throw her across the room without any effort. Not that he'd do that shit. Still, nothing was worth it that didn't take work.

If Deb wasn't at work and even when she wasn't at the gym, she lived in workout gear. Skintight running pants. Those spaghetti strap camisoles in breathable fabrics. Adding a jacket when it got cold. Running shoes on her feet.

He'd like to see Millie filling out any of that shit.

What he wouldn't like, and didn't, was that being all he got. Neither of their girls leaned toward their mother in any way. Both of them had his hair, very dark brown, lots of body and wave. They had his dark brown eyes too. They also had his frame. Long legs, proportioned torsos. They were tall for their age, so they were going to get his height.

They were already beautiful.

When that beauty ripened, he was going to be fucked.

Worse, they were *girls*. They liked clothes. Hair shit. Boy bands. And Cleo was already asking to use makeup.

So that meant, when they got older, and the lure of boys got keener, he was absolutely going to be fucked, not just because they'd turn their attention to guys, but the way they looked, boys would turn their attention to his babies.

But that was, he hoped to God, a few years away.

Right then, he had other shit to face.

And he needed to get down to it and face it.

"Babies," he called, and Zadie's eyes shot right to him even as she stuffed a piece of pepperoni in her mouth.

He grinned at her and looked to Cleo.

She was watching him soberly and doing it chewing with her mouth shut like her momma taught her.

High leaned forward. "Need to share somethin' with you," he told them gently. "Somethin' important."

Zadie threw her arms straight into the air as she cried, mouth full of pepperoni, "You got a house!" She dropped her arms and leaned into her hands on the table. "Can we go see? This weekend? After school? Do we have a big bedroom?"

He'd found a house.

But more, he'd got back the woman in it.

"It's not a house, Zadie," he replied.

Her face fell like he'd told her the world was coming to an end, but worse, it had run out of ice cream so she couldn't stuff her face with it until the end of days.

"What is it, Daddy?" Cleo asked quietly, and he looked to his big girl.

"Straight up, worried how you both are gonna take this. So straight up, I'll tell you again, it's important. It's important to me. And it's important to me you both get what it means to me."

Cleo's face went guarded.

Zadie's eyes got big.

High took in a breath and shared, "There was once a woman I knew who meant a lot to me. We've reconnected and found that didn't fade with the years. We're back together."

Zadie collapsed back, ass to heels.

Cleo's lips parted.

"She was before your mom," High continued. "Haven't seen her in longer than you been alive. But we're back. She's in my life. And I want you to meet her."

"What about Mom?" Zadie asked, and High focused on her.

"Mom and Daddy are divorced, Zade," Cleo informed her sister matter-of-factly before High could get in there. "And since they are, you need *to deal.*"

"Cleo, baby, be sweet," High said quietly.

"She needs to deal, Daddy," she returned.

"You aren't wrong, Clee-Clee, but you gotta be cool with your sister," he replied.

She looked away, not miffed, embarrassed.

He and his Cleo were tight. They had a bond. Normally, she could do no wrong in her father's eyes and she knew it. Blossomed under it. Fucking loved it.

So whenever he laid it out, she wasn't good at handling it.

"This *sucks*," Zadie snapped, and High looked to her. "You and Mom belong together," she declared.

He opened his mouth but Cleo got there before him again. "Wake *up*, Zade. That's *so* not true."

"Cleo," High said low.

She shut her mouth.

"*You* wake up, Clee-Clee," Zadie, eyes narrowed at her sister, shot back.

"Zadie, darlin', look at your old man," High prompted.

She turned narrowed eyes and pouting mouth his way.

"What your mom and I had is done, baby. She's moved on. I'm movin' on," he explained.

"She hasn't moved on," Zadie returned angrily.

"She has, Zade. She's like, *so totally* cooler now that Daddy's not around," Cleo stated then her eyes darted to her father. "Sorry, Daddy. But it's true."

"I get that," he replied. "And givin' that to your mom and gettin' some of that myself is why we split."

"You're happier with Mommy," Zadie declared, and got her dad's attention back.

"I was happier bein' with you," he shared gently. "And now I'll be happy, you be a good kid, take your dad's back, meet Millie and open your mind because you meet her, you can't help but like her."

"Millie's a stupid name," she spat nastily.

The gentle went out of High and he did what he rarely did.

He stared into his baby girl's eyes, not as her daddy, but as her father.

She fell to her hip in defeat and looked angrily at the edge of the table.

"I'll be glad to meet her, Daddy," Cleo said, and got her father's smile.

"*I'll be glad to meet her, Daddy,*" Zadie mimicked obnoxiously, and got her father's attention.

"Zadie, look at me." She stared at the edge of the table. "Won't say it again," he warned. Slowly, taking her time, she looked to him. "You're upset, be upset at me. You're feelin' a lot and I get that. I know you don't like what's goin' down and I don't like that, but I can't help it. All I can do is help you move along with your sister and me, and yes, your mom, but with your mom it's in a separate way. What you do not do, ever, Zade, is take anything out on your sister. That's not cool and both my girls are cool. Don't prove that different."

He got her with that.

Deb might not have been hip on Chaos but both his girls were brought up in the life. They had their father's blood.

They were raised in his world.

They knew it was a priority to be cool.

He saw her chin wobble before she dropped her head to look at her lap.

"Hand," he ordered.

Slowly, but with hesitation, not attitude, Zadie extended her hand on the table.

High wrapped his fingers around her little ones, and feeling their fragility, their warmth, the knowledge he had a part in creating those fingers, the pulse that beat in her wrist, he relaxed.

He also knew she might not make it easy, but she was her daddy's girl.

She'd get there.

He gave her fingers a squeeze. "I need you to dig deep, Zadie. You got some time to dig deep and get there." He looked to Cleo but kept hold of Zadie and went on, "But I got you this weekend and we're spendin' time with Millie. She'll give us our space but we'll be spendin' a lot of time with her. And you're my girls. I want you to show her how beautiful you are outside and all the way deep down. Will you do that for me?"

"Yes, Daddy," Cleo said instantly.

"Yes, Daddy," Zadie said a lot more slowly, doing that to her lap and tugging her hand from his so he let her go.

He got that. He wasn't going to push for more.

So he let more than Zadie's hand go and asked, "Anyone want dessert or just me?"

"Cherry cream cheese pie," Cleo declared.

He winked at his big girl and looked to his baby, who still had eyes to her lap.

"Zadie?" he prompted.

"Cinnamon bun ice cream," she muttered.

Deb would tell her to look at her mother (or her father) while she was speaking.

High didn't push shit like that. She was feeling a lot, she was a little kid, and she needed space in her head to sort through it.

So he left her to it and flagged down a waitress.

He ordered his girls' dessert.

They ate it.

He paid the bill.

Then he got to the part that sucked, even when Zadie's dreamworld had been crushed and she was in a mood because of it.

He took them home and left, leaving them behind.

* * *

He walked into the back door to Millie's house and saw Joker slouched back in her big chair, Millie stretched out on her couch, and that British program on the TV.

But before he even stepped through the door, he saw Millie's head up and her eyes to him over the arm of couch.

She'd heard his truck.

She was glad he was home.

"You're torturing a brother with that shit program?" he asked.

The gladness leaked out of her face as attitude took its place.

"It's not shit," she returned. "Joker actually likes *Downton Abbey*."

High looked to his brother.

Joker was already looking at him and High could see at a glance that was bullshit.

He was putting up with it because she was Millie.

He'd probably do the same thing with his woman, Carissa.

Many brothers in hard ways, and the older brothers who'd been around awhile in hard ways they learned in the brotherhood, knew what was important.

They all knew a TV show was not that.

"You're off duty," High told Joker, and saw the relief.

He wanted to be home with his woman and her kid, a kid who was not Joker's kid but the man treated him that way.

And he wanted to be free of *Downton Abbey*.

High felt for him having to watch that program but Joker was there because High asked him to be.

The brothers all had assignments on the Valenzuela deal and there was work to do at the shop and store.

High wanted Joker on Millie.

It wasn't that he didn't trust his other brothers. It was that he liked the kid. They were tight. He felt something coming from him. The important kind of something that came from having a shit life, knowing what he was missing, and going all out to find it.

And keep it safe.

Joker found it with Chaos.

Then he found it with his woman and her kid.

And he'd go all out to keep who or what was important to any brother safe.

Truth was, they all would.

But for Joker, he was young, but he'd taken his licks, too many of them, and that ran deeper.

Joker pushed out of his chair, muttering, "Later, Millie."

She called, "Xbox pause," and shoved up, getting to her feet, following Joker to the back door, saying, "It was cool you looking out for me."

"Not a problem," Joker stated, caught High's eyes, and said, "Brother."

"Brother," High replied as Joker moved past him and Millie got close to him.

He took hold of her. He let his brother hit the back door.

"Looking forward to meeting Carissa and Travis," Millie said.

Joker looked back to her, hand on the handle. "She'll be the same. We'll get on that." He jerked up his chin to her, slid his eyes to High, then moved out.

High let Millie go and followed him. He locked the door, went to the alarm panel, armed it, and then looked out her window.

Someone had brought Joker's truck. He was in it and backing out of Millie's driveway.

High turned to Millie.

There she was.

No sexy tight turtleneck, sexier tight skirt, and sexy as all fuck boots.

No sexy jammies either.

Instead, dark gray, loose-legged pants that still clung to her hips and a thin, tight, light pink long-sleeved top that had a deep vee showing cleavage.

Nice.

He moved her way.

"How'd it go with the girls?" she asked.

"Think Cleo's lookin' forward to meetin' the woman in her dad's life 'cause she loves her dad and wants him happy." He got to her, put hands to her hips as she lifted hers and settled them on his chest under his shoulders. Once they had hold, he shuffled her back. "Think Zadie's gonna act like a little snot 'cause she loves her dad and mom and wants to live the dream of her family together. So, my guess with my baby, it's gonna take six point five visits with you to break through with her."

She tipped her head to the side, both fear and amusement warring in her eyes as she asked, "Six point five?"

"Halfway through the seventh, she'll find it," he stated.

She grinned. That had fear and amusement too.

They'd got to the couch, so he let her go to shrug off his cut. He dropped it to the coffee table, where it slid to the floor. Then he put them on the couch, him on bottom, her on him.

"You have your boots on, Logan," she told him.

His reply was, "Xbox turn off." Then when he heard the tone, he said, "Yes."

She looked to the TV that was blanking, then back to him. "I was watching that."

He slid his hands from her waist to her ass. "Now you're talkin' to me."

It didn't take her long to decide what she'd prefer to be doing. It lasted about half a beat.

After she decided, she melted into him, shifting her face closer and sliding a hand up to curl it around the side of his neck.

"You worried about Zadie?" she asked.

"With you?" he asked back. When he got her nod, he answered, "Yeah." He watched worry start to etch into her features and he slid his hands from her ass to wrap his arms around her. "But she'll get there. Still worried but not about her and you. Just worried she lives in her dreamworld and life is far from a dream."

The worry stopped and something else hit her face as she said quietly, "I don't know about that."

He knew what she was saying, and fuck, it felt good.

Even if it did, he replied, "Hard work to get to the good."

"Makes it worth it."

That felt good too.

Even so, he shared, "Babe, you'll see. She figures she's gonna live in a castle with her Prince Charming and when I say that, she's dead set on it in a way it's gonna be a crushing blow if she doesn't get that shit. And she ain't gonna get that shit. It sucks for her and it also sucks knowin' that my baby girl isn't gonna live her dream."

"Castles and Prince Charmings come in a lot of different varieties, Low," she told him. "She'll grow up. She'll learn that as she does."

"Hope you're right," he muttered, his eyes moving to her mole.

"Oh, I'm right."

His eyes cut back.

Fuck.

Now that...

That felt great.

Great enough he did what he should have done the minute he got a hand on her.

He slid his fingers into her hair, brought her down to him, and took her mouth. He also took his time. Only when she'd melted deep into him did he break it off.

"You have a good day?" he asked.

Her eyes were hazy, something he liked, and her words were breathy, something he also liked.

"Yeah. Got a lot done."

He wanted her where she was now. He wanted to do a variety of things to her like she was now.

But they had other shit they had to get out of the way.

It sucked but it wouldn't suck, having it out of the way.

So he set about doing that so they could move on.

"You served up some serious spunk when I showed this mornin'," he noted.

Some of the haze left but she stayed relaxed into his body as she replied, "You served up some serious meanie when you showed up, so spunk was my only resort."

Meanie?

He felt his body shaking as he shook his head on the pillow that was resting on the arm of the couch, doing this grinning.

He felt his grin die and twisted his hand in her hair.

"Wouldn't admit this at the time, but lookin' back, it's good you didn't take my shit."

It was better than good.

She'd been fragile. He knew he had to handle her with care.

But he'd lost his mind when he'd heard Valenzuela had targeted her and done something about it. He'd been blinded by fury at Valenzuela at the same time blinded by fear that psychopath got to his girl.

With no choice other than to fuck the work it was taking way too much time to do to take down Valenzuela, he took it out on Millie.

She shoved it back.

That was the old Millie. She fought her corner. She didn't take shit.

There was once a crew within Chaos who liked their women docile and obedient. That crew ran alongside the crew who wanted women who could roll with the changes, get off on the life, not be beaten down by it and exist through it.

That first crew was gone.

Only the rest remained.

And High had always been a member of that first crew.

Even if he'd allied with the other side.

This thought brought him back to the current subject.

"Tack says Valenzuela said *nudge* to you. He say anything else?"

She nodded. "His visit was short but he said a lot of things."

"What kind of things?"

She studied him.

He didn't like that because it meant she wasn't answering him and more, she was assessing him and what his reaction might be to what she'd say.

"I'm not in that," he told her.

Her head twitched. "Not in what?"

"Too dangerous," he replied. "I'd want that, what you're worried I'd do to Valenzuela. Was a day no way I'd agree to being forced out of dealin' personally with a man who did what he did to you. But we're close to takin' down this guy. Not gonna be me who fucks it up. I think about him fuckin' with you, just that could make me fuck it up. So I got one job. Keep a lid on it and trust my brothers to get the job done. I can do the last. Keepin' a lid on it's not gonna be easy. But I gotta dig deep so I can do that too."

After he was done talking, she broke into a smile.

"Somethin' make you happy?" he asked.

"He said he had to find the hothead," she answered. "The weak link. The *nudge* was about using me to set you off, as he put it, to set things in motion."

As she spoke, High felt his body string tight.

She had to feel it.

But she was still smiling.

"And here you are," she whispered, dipping closer to him. "Looking after me and trusting your brothers. Proving that jackass *wrong*."

"Was that," he grunted.

Again her head jerked.

"Sorry?"

"Was that," he repeated. "The guy who'd use any excuse to set anything off just to ride the edge, see if I'd fall off, not carin' if I took my brothers with me."

Her smile gone, her expression shifted to troubled.

"Logan—"

He cut her off, twisting his hand gently in her hair, doing it automatically to keep her close, hoping his words didn't make her want to pull away. "Lost the woman I loved, didn't give a shit about anything. Fuck, in the beginning, *wanted* to fall off the edge just to end the pain."

Her troubled expression turned pained.

"Logan."

That *Logan* was a breath. A wounded one.

"This ain't gonna work unless we lay it out. So I'm layin' it out," he announced. "You've never been stupid. I know you knew. Chaos was into some shady shit back when we were together. And gotta admit, I got off on it then, mostly 'cause it made a shit ton of money and I wanted to give us a lot of things and to do it, I needed money. But it was more. It was a high and I liked to get high."

He quit talking, letting that sink in.

It sunk in.

"Right," she whispered.

He kept going.

"After I lost you, Chaos descended. Got in deeper everywhere. Lookin' back, this was solely Crank's fuck-you to Tack, who had other ideas about the Club and was puttin' 'em into action, quiet-like. Crank was full-on paranoid that Tack wanted the gavel from the early days and he set about tying us up so tight in shit it was impossible to get loose, knowin' it would tie Tack's hands. Don't think Tack gave a shit about the gavel until Crank started fuckin' with the Club. Then Tack was all about wrestin' that gavel from Crank. Crank underestimated him. Lotsa folks underestimated Tack back then. Tack proved that's a mistake. Only Valenzuela does it now."

"I haven't seen Crank," she said hesitantly.

"That's 'cause Crank's dead," he returned emotionlessly, watching her eyes widen in shock.

"You were close," she noted, still cautious.

"We were. Then we were not."

"Why not?" she asked like she didn't want to know.

And she didn't. He knew it.

But she had to know.

He tightened his arm around her, slid his hand to her jaw, and held her eyes.

He also gentled his voice.

" 'Cause Crank ordered Black to be whacked."

That was when he watched her face pale and it jabbed into his heart as she whispered an agonized, "No."

"Yeah, baby," he confirmed.

"I haven't seen Black."

"Ordered it, Millie, beautiful, and it sucks to tell you this, but that hit was carried out and it was done successfully."

The agony hit her eyes.

Fuck him.

Fuck *him*.

Seeing her deal with it was reliving it.

Fuck.

"He's dead?" she asked, like she wanted him to take that shit back.

He wished he could.

"Tat, babe, on my ribs, to remind us never to forget what's important. Brothers. Blood. Family," he stated. "The name on the other side of the scale is Cherry, Tack calls her Red, you know her as Tyra. Tack pulled the Club loose of the shit Crank tied us up in, turned the brothers around, turned it all around. Me and Arlo were not down with that. Money was less. Club's reputation took a massive hit. We worked our assess off and put a lot on the line to get both only to pull out. And in the early days, because a' that, danger was more for the brothers and our families. We lost Black. Chew renounced the Club. Crank had to be dealt with. All that shit went down ugly. But threads dangling from Tack's cleanup that didn't get snipped 'cause we were squabblin' in the Club caught up Cherry. She was kidnapped. Stuck repeatedly. Nearly bled out in some house no one had ever seen. Tack found her, saved her. She survived. The Club pulled together. Now we'll never forget."

Her eyes were huge. "That happened to Tyra?"

"Yep," he replied.

"Oh my God."

"She's a good woman, Millie. I know you have cause to have issues with her but she saw what I didn't see in you and moved on it. I hold no grudge. You shouldn't either."

"I don't," she told him.

That was his girl.

Fancy house. Designer duds.

But she got the life. You knew when to hold grudges. You knew what earned retribution.

You also knew when to forgive and you didn't fuck around doing it.

High gave her a squeeze.

He figured she didn't feel the squeeze when she said, "I just can't...it's impossible to believe..." She shook her head. "Low, that's two old ladies who got caught up in Chaos business. Mine was nowhere near as bad but—"

"Tyra got caught up in it not just 'cause of the Club but because of what her girl's fiancé was into. Club had history with the man who perpetrated that but it was because of Lanie's dead dickhead of a fiancé she got stuck. Club history just didn't help things."

"Lanie's fiancé?"

"She's Hop's woman now. Her fiancé bit it and she went on to better things."

"I met her," she said.

"Know you did. She's a good woman too. They all meddle. They'll drag you into that shit. It's just the way it is. But it comes from a good place."

She wasn't interested in that.

She was interested in something else and she didn't mess around with telling him what it was.

"What did Crank tie you up in that you found it hard to get loose?"

The rest he gave her was far from easy.

This was going to kill.

But he had to do it. Nothing between them. Nothing held back.

Not this time.

"Whores and security," he replied. "Chew pimped the girls. Arlo and me were in charge of security."

Her eyes were again huge and her face was beyond pale.

"You ran security for Chaos prostitutes?" she asked in disbelief.

"No, babe, I ran security for shipments of drugs and guns through or around Denver."

"Holy God," she breathed, pulling away from him.

Gentle, he pulled her back to him.

And he laid it out just as gentle but he also did it straight.

"You hooked your star to an outlaw, baby. You knew it back then. We didn't discuss it but you can talk 'til you're blue in the face and you won't convince me you didn't know. You loved me. You didn't give a shit. You loved an outlaw and you took me as I was. That didn't change except Crank put me in charge of it rather than me just bein' a soldier. Things started goin' bad for me and Crank when he took on the girls. It never got better."

"Chew pimped women?" she forced out.

"There was an asshole under the decent guy. It was buried deep but it was there. Crank sniffed it out, then pulled it out. Hop was an enforcer for the girls and at Tack's orders outside the table, he used Hop to get them ready to move on when Tack took over and cut all the girls loose. When Hop started that work, one piece of gash talked to Crank. Crank made a decision about what would be the catalyst to unite all factions in a brotherhood that was broken. Takin' a brother out was the only way. He ordered that shit, blamed it on an enemy. Tack's never been stupid, swear to fuck, he didn't sleep until he had it solid the hit came from Crank."

"So who took down Crank?"

He felt his jaw get tight.

Her voice was pitched high when she asked, "You?"

"No clue which bullet did the final deed, seein' as he took one from every brother's gun."

Her body, not relaxed into his, but tense as all fuck, reared like she was trying to flee.

High held on tight.

"Keely goes to Black's grave every week, Millie. Years have passed. Every fuckin' *week*."

She stilled when the tears hit her eyes.

He kept at her in order to get it done.

"They had two boys after you were gone. Both too young to know their dad was solid as a rock. A good man to his core. They can be told that. They've *been* told that. But they'll never *know*."

A tear slid down her cheek.

High kept going.

"Crank picked Black because no matter the split in the Club, Black was the glue. We all felt it. We all knew big shit was coming and the Club might not survive. Only man who held us all together, both sides, even though he'd chosen one, was Black. That was why Crank picked him because he knew we'd all suffer that and bond together for vengeance. He took out a brother, Millie, and that is *not* okay. But he made that decision pickin' the best of us. The most decent of us. The most loyal. And that is *seriously* not okay."

Her "No" was shaky but at least she said it.

"Now it's done," he stated. "We all suffered black marks on our souls doin' it and gettin' it done. I'm not proud to say I got more of those marks than most. Not proud to share that Valenzuela knows part of this shit and that's why he targeted me through you. I was weak. I was hurt and it made me weak. But I'm not gonna hide that because it's done, because it's part of me and because you need it all."

It wasn't shaky, it was tortured, when she stated, "So it was me who did that to you too."

"Fuck no," he clipped, and at the intensity of it, she stared. "Babe, I chose that path. *I* did. I chose the path that led away from you. You made it so I had no choice but to walk away. You did not make it so I couldn't go back. I didn't go back. That was my choice. And it was my choice to do everything I did in between. Every shipment I escorted through town. Every blind eye I turned to Crank's bullshit. That's on me. I live with that. It ain't easy but God's chosen to keep me breathin' so I figure He's got work for me to turn that around and do good. Be a good dad. Get you back and take care a' you this time. Whatever it is, I'm here to do it. I got His message. And I'm grateful."

"I don't know what to do with all this," she admitted carefully.

"Nothin' for you to do with it. You hooked up with an outlaw knowin' you lived the outlaw life and knowin' your outlaw would keep you safe doin' it. Still got outlaw in me, Millie. All the brothers do. We use it to keep our family safe now. We patrol a ten-mile area around Ride, around Chaos, and keep it free of whores and dealers. Valenzuela wants that turf. We're not givin' it to him. We're also not takin' him out. We're working with the cops to take him down. It's a new Chaos era you're back in with, Millie. The future is Joker and Shy and Snapper and Roscoe, and those brothers have been trained by Tack, Hop, Dog, Brick, Pete, and the rehabilitated me. We got one final enemy. We get him gone, we're good."

"And what happens when you get another *final enemy*?" she asked.

"Had years no issues until Valenzuela underestimated Tack," he told her. "Like I said, you don't underestimate Tack. He'll surprise you and not in good ways. And his daughter is married to Shy, his lieutenant. And his son, Rush, is in the Club and Rush wants to clean up the rest of it."

He slid his fingers through her hair and finished it.

"Watched it happen, Millie. God's honest truth, even when we were on opposite sides, marveled at it. Took Tack decades. Longer even than when you and me met. But Tack built Chaos strong and tough in the only way any man should be strong and tough. Brotherhood. Loyalty. Family. Nothin' else matters. It's why a soldier puts his ass on the line for his country. It's why a man walks through his house to make sure it's safe before he goes to bed. It's the measure of a real man. It's Chaos."

"Did you know that was Chaos all along?" she asked.

"What do you think?" he asked back.

"But Tack wasn't the leader then," she pointed out.

"Something drew him to the Club, just like me. Greed infested it. Politics tarnished it. Power plays shook it. But the foundation of the Club stayed strong and it wasn't just Tack who kept it that way."

She said nothing.

So he did.

"Millie, I know this is a surprise but I also know, you dig deep, it also isn't."

"It's a lot to take in," she told him.

"It's history."

Another head jerk as she took the bottom-line truth of that in.

And High felt relief when her body relaxed slightly on top of his.

"I can't believe Black's gone," she whispered.

"Walk into the Compound, look to the bar, think I'll see him sittin' there. To this day. So I can't believe it either. And givin' it all to you, I know it's a lot, I'm still gonna say, like every brother that was there, I hope like fuck it was my bullet who ended Crank."

She stared at him, right into his eyes, hers again bright, and she replied, "I kinda hope that too."

She'd loved Black.

She'd also loved Keely.

And she wore designer threads and lived in a fancy-ass pad.

But Millie Cross was born an old lady.

Fuck, she was born to be *his* old lady.

So she got it.

High loosened his hold on her and started to stroke her back.

"Keely's gonna be glad to have you back," he told her quietly.

"She still hang with the Club?" she asked.

He shook his head. "No, baby. She gets her cut of Club income every month like Black was still alive. Boz's ex, Bev, who he married then divorced after you were gone, was tight with Keely. Bev sticks close. Brothers take turns doin' shit for the boys when they need a man. We stay as close as she lets us. But Black ended and when he did, Keely ended too."

"I know that feeling."

He knew she did.

"Makes the fact we got a second chance one we gotta be sure we don't fuck up," he returned.

She relaxed into him more. "Yeah."

"You had enough?" he asked, and she tensed again.

"There's more?" she asked.

He stopped stroking, slid his fingers out of her hair, and wrapped her up in both his arms.

"No, beautiful," he answered.

"Thank God," she mumbled.

He grinned because that was cute.

But mostly he did it because she took it. She didn't freak out, burst into tears, break down, have a drama.

It was ugly.

She took it all.

She stuck close.

That was done.

The tough part over.

Now their only obstacle was Zadie, and his baby girl would come around.

He drew in a deep breath and let it out.

Millie focused on him and returned her hand to his neck, curling it around.

"That was hard on you," she noted.

"Yeah," he agreed.

"I'm out of practice being an old lady," she told him, and he felt his lips curl up again.

"You'll get it back."

"What I mean is . . ." She looked to the TV and back to him.

"I did hook up with an outlaw. I fell in love immediately with a man who did the same with me, didn't hide it, let it shine, showed he was proud of it, and I had that. It was mine. He gave it to me. And I knew it was precious. So I didn't care. I didn't care what made you. I didn't care what you did when you were away from me. I only cared what you did when I had you and the feeling you left when you weren't with me. And I did it knowingly. Part of that was knowing it might be wrong. But I loved you so much, all of me didn't care if it was."

Oh yeah.

Fuck yeah.

Millie Cross was made to be his old lady.

His voice was gruff when he asked, "That change at all?"

She shot his question of earlier back at him.

"What do you think?"

She was on him, touching him, looking right into his eyes.

It hadn't changed at all.

He turned, rolling her to her back, declaring, "Gonna fuck you now."

She slid her hand back down to his chest and pushed. "Then let's go to bed."

"Gonna fuck you here."

Her brows shot up. "And maybe leave a wet spot on the couch?" she asked in horrified disbelief.

He put his mouth to hers. "Baby, it happens, it'll clean."

"Eww," she replied.

Fuck, back in the day, his girl swallowed.

He was looking forward to finding out if she was still down with that.

But if she takes him down her throat, she could not have an issue with cleaning him off the couch.

He wasn't going to get into that. He was done talking about that shit. It'd take about ten seconds to make her forget about it.

So he went about doing that and took her mouth.

Though, he found out he was wrong.

It only took five seconds.

CHAPTER SIXTEEN

Back at Ya

Millie

MY ALARM WENT off and I started to untangle myself from Logan to hit snooze.

I didn't move fast enough.

Logan leaned into me and yanked the alarm out of the wall, causing the noise of the lamp shaking and the nightstand jolting to be heard. Then I felt my body and the bed shift alarmingly as he forcefully hurled it across the room.

I heard it smash against the wall in a way I knew it was broken and suddenly I was wide awake.

"Logan!" I snapped.

He rolled on top of me, muttering, "Don't live an alarm clock life."

I kept snapping. "Well, I do!"

He kissed me.

And then I didn't.

*   *   *

I walked into the kitchen with the empty mug that had been filled with coffee that Logan had brought to me while I was getting ready. I was in a wool herringbone skirt, a winter white, soft wool boatneck sweater, and black spike-heeled boots.

The minute I walked in, Logan, ass to the counter, mug to his lips, dropped his eyes to my skirt.

Then the boots.

I watched his lips curl up even as he continued to take a sip.

He approved.

That felt nice.

Regardless.

"We need a chat about the alarm clock," I announced. "Primarily you replacing the one you busted."

He sipped and his gaze went from my boots to my eyes.

"Don't make any appointments before ten, you got a human one."

I went to the coffeepot and started pouring more as I explained, "Sometimes I can't make that decision. I have to meet my clients when they can meet as well as when I can."

"Now you can't. Until after ten."

I shoved the pot back into the coffeemaker and looked to him.

"Logan—"

"Millie, not asking a lot."

I stared at him.

Then I shared, "I offered Justine a job yesterday."

His head tipped to the side. "Say again?"

"I'm always booked," I began to explain. "I sometimes turn down clients. I can stop doing that and use the extra income to take on a part-time worker. I can also shift some of Claire's responsibilities to Justine. I can then shift some of mine to Claire. I ran the numbers and it works. I take a minimal hit to my personal income that I'll barely feel. And I'll have more time."

I stopped talking and Logan just stared at me.

So I kept talking.

"I called her last night before you got home and Justine was ecstatic. I could afford to give her a raise in salary to what she's making now, not much but everything counts, and working with me, she'll rarely have to put her son in day care. Same with Claire, who'll take on more responsibility. I talked to her too. She's on board. It's all fixed. Justine is putting in notice today. She'll be on payroll by Thanksgiving, which is my busiest time. Bonus to that, the two Christmas clients I had to turn down I could pick up. I called them yesterday and did that too. They were almost more ecstatic than Justine."

I again stopped talking.

Logan again just stared at me.

So I called, "Logan?"

"My girl," he whispered, and I felt warmth flow through me at his tone.

"Logan," I whispered back.

"She wants somethin', she doesn't fuck around."

He was right. I didn't.

I wanted to graduate early so we could start a family; I did it.

I wanted to contribute, even minimally, to our life financially; I worked my ass off and accomplished that.

I wanted to be a success at my own business, completely renovate a fixer-upper house so it was inch by inch all mine; I did that too.

I wanted to make a statement that Logan was important and I intended to show him that by making time for him; I absolutely did not fuck around.

The only thing I'd wanted that I didn't get was to make babies with my man. And it hit me right then that finding out I couldn't when I knocked myself out to make everything so I could was something I couldn't cope with.

As huge as that was at the time, and how deep it still burned, I realized, in the end, I hadn't done half bad.

"Come here, beautiful, give your man some love so you can get to work."

Voiced tender and sweet, that was an order I would obey. So I set my coffee mug aside and moved into his arms.

I wrapped mine around him, rolled up on my toes, and touched my mouth to his.

When I rolled back, we both kept hold.

"Got the girls this weekend," he told me.

A sliver of cold fear pierced the warmth in me but I ignored it and asked, "Yeah?"

"You got a problem with them stayin' here?"

I went back to staring.

When he said no more, like taking back that crazy question, I asked, "Here? With me? *And* you?"

"Here. With me. And you," he confirmed.

I moved an inch away, still within his arms, and stated, "Low, that's too much too soon for both of them."

I meant that.

I also meant for *all* of us.

Namely me.

"I start the night on the couch, go to you when we know they're out. They sleep for as long as they can on the weekends. We'll be up before them. They won't notice."

"Low, that's too much too soon for both of them," I repeated, then included, "And it isn't just about the sleeping arrangements."

"I live in my RV outside Boz's house," he declared.

My chin jerked sideways at this insane news. "You do?"

"Since the split, been lookin' at houses—seems I looked at hundreds of 'em. Wanna move and do it permanent. So it's gotta be perfect for me and my girls," he explained.

Oh man.

I had a feeling I knew what he was saying, that he intended to move in with me.

I had more than a feeling that it was way too soon too.

I wanted it to happen. I wanted forever with Logan.

But we had a lot of catching up to do, so I wasn't sure about that starting *now*.

"You...I...," I stammered, not certain what to say.

"Now, havin' you back, I'm not layin' down a load of cake on a pad only for us to consolidate. And I'm guessin', the way you are about your house, you're not gonna wanna leave it."

"No," I said hesitantly, because I didn't.

But it was mine. All mine. Inch by inch.

And it was a woman's home.

Inch by inch.

And Logan was very much a man.

"Right," he said. "So it's big enough for all of us for a while. We'll need to add on later. Another bedroom. Dining room 'cause can't have decent Thanksgivings and birthdays sittin' at a bar in a kitchen."

My heart started beating fast and not in a good way at the thought of changing my space after I'd gotten it just how I wanted it.

I mean, I wanted Logan more than anything.

But living in a house under renovation sucked. I knew this all too well.

"Girls share a room," he went on. "But Deb and me promised 'em, when they got to be teenagers, they'd get their own rooms. So we'll need another one because I figure you'll wanna have one for guests."

"I...well, I think we need to discuss this at a time when I don't have to get to work," I evaded.

He nodded. "We can discuss this at a time when you don't have to work and I don't have to get on the road. But you meet the girls Friday. We have dinner together Friday. We go sleep at Boz's Friday night. We spend the day together Saturday and Sunday. They sleep here Saturday and Sunday."

I miraculously kept the panic out of my voice when I noted, "That's like throwing them in a pool to learn how to swim."

"You gonna be in my life?" he asked.

"Of course," I answered.

"Then you're gonna be in theirs. They gotta get used to it."

I moved closer to him and gave him a squeeze. "That's agreed. But I'm gonna be in your life, Logan, and theirs. So we have time."

"Babe—"

I interrupted him. "Friday, dinner. Saturday doing something during the day. Saturday night, if you don't want them to camp out in your RV anymore, I can go stay at Dot's; you guys can stay here. Sunday, lunch or something. When do they go back to their mom?"

"Take them to school on Monday. They go back to her after school."

They went to her after school on Monday?

He must get them back sometime during the week.

"Then Sunday night I'll stay at Dot's again," I offered. "Or Justine's. Or Kellie's or something."

"Not puttin' you out of your own house and, Millie, the point still is they gotta get used to you."

"Sleepover their third visit," I haggled.

"Babe, that weekend will be a month away."

That shocked me.

"A weekend?"

"Deb's got near full custody," he shared. "Girls are still young, but shit's gonna start happenin' soon with them that they'll need their mom. Our deal was, two years of this, then we go half and half and nearly a year of that is done."

"You only have weekends," I stated, but it was a question.

"Every other weekend."

He only had every other weekend?

Did courts decree that kind of thing anymore with dads?

And if they did, why didn't he fight it?

However, it didn't sound like there was a fight.

He said his "deal" with Deb was two years.

Had he *agreed* to this?

"Logan, that's . . . I . . ."

I trailed off speaking because this wasn't my place. They were his kids. It was his deal with his ex. He talked dispassionately about her and it seemed there was no acrimony.

I didn't need to wade in and make any.

"You got somethin' to say," he remarked.

"No. I—"

I stopped talking when his arms gave me a squeeze.

"Millie, you got somethin' to say, say it. Don't hold back."

I studied him.

Then I asked, "Are you . . . *good* with this arrangement?"

"Fuck no," he answered. "But Deb never refuses when I ask for extra time but I still gotta do that shit, ask for extra time because I don't have my girls."

"Did she push this deal? Deb, I mean," I asked.

"My idea," he replied.

His?

"Logan," I began cautiously, "I don't get that, especially if you're missing them and missing out in being with them."

His arms tightened. "Babe, I'm a guy, so I never turned into a woman. Don't know shit about cramps and . . ." his expression changed to one that it took a lot for me not to burst out laughing, ". . . other stuff. Deb obviously does. We get Clee-Clee through that and shit happens when they're with me, she can help her sister through it until they get back to Deb."

"You're telling me you've given near full custody to your ex so you don't have to deal in case your daughters start their periods with you?" I asked incredulously.

The expression came back. I made a noise this time while choking back laughter, the expression left and thunder started clouding his face.

"You got your period, you run to your dad to help you pick tampons?" he growled.

He had a point there.

He was still being funny.

"No," I told him.

"Help get your moods? Which shit you should buy to deal, you get cramps?" he pushed.

"Deb is but a phone call away," I reminded him, deciding not to note just yet that I was right at his side.

"That's precious," he stated in a way that made all amusement flee. "That happenin', it's precious. A girl becomin' a woman. That's a time of life to share with your mom. It's not a memory you should have with your dad not knowin' fuck all about it. How to guide you. How to help you. How to teach you how to experience something that's only gonna have its start once but it's gonna mean changes for years. Important ones. I don't want that for my girls. I want them to have the precious. I want them to remember that happening and it to be a good memory. I don't wanna fuck that up for them. Other shit comes with that. Realizin' boys exist and why. How to deal with that. How to do their makeup. How to find the clothes they like to wear. I don't want any of that shit to happen, Millie. I want them to stay my babies forever. But I got no choice. They're growin' up. And I got no clue how to guide them with any of that. Their mom does. So they need their mom."

"You're the most amazing man I've ever met," I blurted, the feeling behind those words making them husky.

But I found, to my surprise, they were not bittersweet, the loss of all that he could have given a daughter we made.

They were just sweet, knowing he had it to give to his girls.

And I made it so he could.

His arms around me convulsed and then stayed tight.

But I had a feeling he misunderstood the emotion behind my words when he asked, "You okay?"

I snuggled into him. "Yeah. Actually, I think I'm more okay than I've been for a long time."

"How's that?"

"I have you back," I told him. "And you have the babies you have to give what you have to give. It wasn't ours to have. It was yours. And now, not only do you have it, I have you. So it sucked how we got here. But I'm beginning to understand it was worth it."

A scratchy rumble rolled up his throat right before he bent his head and took my mouth.

We made out and there was a lot of feeling to that too.

None of it bittersweet.

All of it just sweet.

He lifted his head and said softly, "Give you this weekend. Friday dinner. Saturday time with you. Sunday time with you. We'll go sleep at the RV. But next time I got 'em, all that time's with you."

I could make that compromise, so I nodded.

"Today, gonna sit down with Deb and explain that."

Oh man.

"Got nothin' to worry about," he assured. "Already told her I was with someone and that someone is important. She doesn't care. Just want her to know how I'm movin' it along with the girls. She won't care about that either. She trusts me to do right by the girls and she isn't wrong in that trust."

That made me feel better, so I nodded again.

"As for me, I'm moving in."

My lips parted.

"I know we're just back but I don't give a fuck. I'm not takin' that slow. Lost too much. Not gonna dick around gettin' it all back. Leave the RV at Boz's until I can get that garage out back torn down. Once that's out, there'll be room to store the RV here and do it not fuckin' up the look of your courtyard."

Before I could say a word, he finished.

"And you can have your alarm clock until Justine gets her teeth into shit and you can sort it so you don't need one."

"You're moving in?" I asked.

"Yep."

"You're tearing down my garage?"

"You use it?"

"No."

"Then yeah."

"You...uh...Low, my house is girlie," I pointed out.

"Furniture's comfortable. Place is tight. Looks nice. Great kitchen. It works," he stated.

"But it's girlie," I repeated.

"What do I care as long as the furniture's comfortable and your ass sleeps beside mine?"

That was very sweet.

But it wasn't the relief I expected it to be.

"I...um...this is a big decision," I noted.

"Not anymore since it's made."

He hadn't been a steamroller before when making decisions.

Then again, he had me then; he never thought he'd lose me, so he didn't need to steamroll anything.

Cautiously, I shared, "We should get to know each other again, Low."

"Came to you yesterday pissed as all shit. I know 'cause I saw you lose it, freaked at how pissed I was. But you lost that and got in my face. Told you all there was to know about the bad of the last twenty years with the Club. You took it in, let me fuck you on your couch and, when I got you to bed, you were out in five seconds tellin' me none of that shit was fuckin' with your brain. Millie, you're an old lady. Doesn't matter what you wear or where you live; it's just in you. That shit happens when you fall for a biker and you got what it takes. You fell for a biker and never dug yourself out to find somethin' else. There's nothin' more I need to know."

"You seem to have an answer for everything," I remarked, and his lips twitched.

"That's 'cause I have an answer for everything."

I frowned and replied, "You're also egotistical."

He started chuckling but asked through it, "Babe, you wanna sleep alone?"

I absolutely did not.

I decided not to answer.

He knew my answer.

"Right," he stated. Then, "You work. I got my thing I do. We eat together. We fuck. We go to bed together. We get up. We fuck. You do your thing. I do mine. And repeat. Why would we do any of that without my clothes in your closet?"

I looked to his throat, muttering, "Apparently he does have an answer for everything."

At that, he didn't speak.

He just laughed.

I found that annoying but only annoying in the way any man who actually had a rational answer for everything would be annoying to a woman.

So I did not laugh.

I asked, "Are we done? Because I have the plans for a sweet-sixteen party to go over and that's not gonna happen in this kitchen."

He was still smiling when he replied, "We're done."

I rolled up on my toes, touched my mouth to his, rolled back, and broke from his arms to move to my coffee mug.

I retrieved it and walked to the back door, murmuring, "Have a good day, Snooks."

"Back at ya," he replied when I had my hand to the handle.

I looked to him.

Very faded jeans. The blue Henley.

He'd retrieved his coffee as well.

He looked comfortable in my kitchen. Not like he belonged,

say, should someone need a model to use to take a photo in order to advertise my fabulous marble countertops.

But like he belonged because those countertops and the entire kitchen were mine.

And he was too.

"Love you, Low," I said quietly.

His face was turned away, mug to his lips, but his eyes were cast to the side and on me when I spoke.

After I said what I said, his expression softened, he dropped the mug, and replied, "Back at ya."

I grinned at him.

Then I opened the door, walked through, and went to work.

* * *

My cell on my desk chimed. I looked from Justine, sitting across from me going over the formal offer I'd typed out, Rafferty crawling around on my office floor, and turned my eyes to my phone.

At what I saw, I snatched it up, slid my finger on the screen, and read the entire text.

"Hang on, babe," I muttered to Justine.

"Sure," she muttered back, then louder, "Raff, baby boy, no on the trash bin."

Rafferty reached out from crawling position, latched onto the side of my trash bin, and pulled it to him.

Wads of paper flew out.

Raff squealed with delight.

Justine moved to deal with the trash I didn't care that Raff was reorganizing.

I hit the buttons to make the call I needed to make and put my phone to my ear, telling Justine, "Don't worry about it. You know I don't care."

"Babe," Logan answered a beat after I said my last word.

It was my turn to squeal with delight.

"The kitties are ready to pick up!"

"Yee ha!" Justine cried.

Rafferty rolled to his diapered tush and clapped his hands, or tried. He missed a lot but it was a good effort.

Logan's voice was filled with humor when he said in my ear, "When?"

"This evening. Any time after six."

"You got the shit?" he asked.

"What shit?" I asked back.

"Litter box. Food. Shit like that."

I didn't have the shit.

I needed the shit.

I glanced at my day's to-do list.

Then I asked, "Uh . . . could you pick up the shit?"

There was a moment of silence before, still with humor but also with some resignation, he gave me the answer old Logan (who was very much like new Logan) would give.

"I'll pick up the shit."

"Thanks, Snooks," I murmured, liking that he was going to pick up *the shit*. Then I ordered, "Kitty chow, not adult food. And that clumping litter, not anything that's cheap. I saw online they have one that attracts kittens for litter training. Find that one. If you can't, find one that might combat odors. And cute kitty bowls. Ones that match the house. Oh! And toys. Ones with feathers and stuff like that."

"Jesus," he muttered.

"Got that?" I asked.

"I'll buy what I buy and it'll work," he replied. "You don't like it, you can go out and get what you want."

"Okay," I said. "If I don't like it, I'll go out this weekend and find something I do like. Maybe the girls will get into that."

"If there's money to be spent on somethin', they will."

That made me smile.

Then I told him, "Justine is here. I need to go."

"Right. Tell her I said hey. Later, beautiful."

"'Bye, Low."

We rang off and I looked to Justine, who was staring at me.

"Geez, it's like twenty years didn't pass. You guys were always like that. Me and Ronnie could fight for three days about who was going to go out and buy a litter box."

This was true.

Justine and Veronica found a lot of things to fight about mostly, from what I could tell, so they'd have a variety of reasons to make up.

"Low says hey," I told her, and watched happy hit her face.

"Say hey back when you see him," she replied right when the door flew open.

I hadn't heard a car come up the drive, so my eyes shot there with surprise and I felt more surprise when I saw Kellie stomping in, Dottie following her.

I didn't pay much mind to Dot because Kellie had her arm raised and she was pointing back and forth between Justine and me.

"You! And you! I just knew it!" she shouted.

"What the heck?" Justine asked.

Dot closed the door as Kellie crossed her arms on her chest, face set right at pissed, that pissed aimed at me.

"I knew you'd tell her first," she accused. "I knew she'd get the lowdown on Logan before we got our LBD on. *I knew it.*"

"Kellie—" I began.

"Admit it!" she snapped. "She's your bestest bestie and I'm second fiddle."

Not this again.

This had been happening since *forever.*

And it wasn't just me she accused of Justine being my bestest bestie, it was also the other way around with Justine.

"You're both my bestest besties," I said on a sigh. "We're *all* bestest besties. You know that."

"The biggest thing that happens to you since you *met* Logan is you gettin' *back* with Logan and she gets the goods first?" She shook her head. "I don't think so."

"I tried to stop her," Dot put in, and I looked to my sister. "We were having lunch. I mentioned Justine was here. She lost it and there was no going back."

I looked back to Kellie and explained, "I've offered Jus a job, babe."

"Ha!" she scoffed. "Likely story. And that bullshi—" Her eyes dropped to Raff, who was staring up at her in wonder, and she finished, "...shtein was what Dot was spouting."

"It isn't bullshtein," Justine stated. "It's true."

"It's bullshtein," Kellie spat.

"I don't know any more than you," Justine returned.

Kellie threw out an arm. "So you're just talkin' about a job and that's it?" She shook her head. "I don't believe it."

"Can I just say," I cut in, "that I've been in Paris for two weeks. I came back to a variety of dramas that changed the course of my life. I'm taking on a new employee. Imminently I face Logan moving in, and by imminently, I mean tonight, but the truth of that is that he's already pretty moved in considering he currently lives in an RV, so I'm guessing there isn't much to move. This weekend I face meeting Logan's two daughters. And tonight we're picking up my new kitties. I don't mean to be mean, Kel, but I don't have time to have a conversation that I've had a thousand times since fifth grade. You have no bestest bestie, Jus or me. Jus has no bestest bestie, you or me. I have no bestest bestie. Because *we're all bestest besties*."

"Logan's moving in?" Justine asked me.

"Like you didn't know that," Kellie retorted.

Justine looked to Kellie. "I didn't," she snapped.

"I didn't either," Dot put in, and grinned at me. "Wow, Mill. The mom in me is freaked. The sister in me is also freaked. The woman in me is ecstatic."

"Roll with the woman one, Dot," I advised, grinning back.

"Why does he live in an RV?" Kellie asked.

"He's been looking for a house since his divorce," I answered. "It's been a while but he wants it to be right for his girls. He hasn't found anything."

"But . . . an RV?" Dot asked.

I did not have good memories of that RV.

I was looking forward to making better ones.

"Well, it's an RV but it's the kind of RV Aerosmith might decide not to buy considering the cost of the upgrades," I explained.

"Ooo," Kellie breathed reverently. "A Rock-Mobile. Radical!"

"Uh . . . Mill, you have an appointment?" Justine asked into this exchange.

I looked to Justine, then followed her eyes out the window where I saw an SUV driving up.

I didn't know that SUV and I couldn't see who was in it, though I could see there was more than one person. A lot more.

"No," I answered Justine.

"Drop in," she said, and looked to me. "More work. I hope it's Christmas. I found these lights online, like big ornaments but with dangly bits at the bottom. They *so totally* have to go into someone's scheme."

"Email me the link, Jus. Wanna have a look," I told her.

"On it," she stated, and then got on it, right there and then, digging in her purse to pull out her phone.

Rafferty crawled around the desk and started teeth/gumming my boot.

I bent down and picked him up to put him in my lap just as the door opened.

I looked that way, distractedly noting Kellie and Dottie were moving aside to let the newcomers in.

I was not distracted in any way noting who the newcomers were.

Tyra, Tack's woman. Lanie, Hop's woman. Elvira, and I didn't know who she belonged to. An exceptionally pretty young woman with lots of curly strawberry blonde hair.

And the amazingly beautiful, all grown-up Tabitha Allen.

I stared at Tabby.

She was looking at me.

"Hey, Millie," she said softly.

She remembered me.

I felt my eyes fill with tears.

"Holy crap, Tab?" Justine asked, straightening from her chair. "Tack's girl?"

Tabby looked to her, not recognizing her at first. Her head tipped to the side and she asked, "Justine, right?"

"Yeah," Justine replied, then moved to her and hugged her. "God, so cool to see you again." She leaned back, still holding on. "All grown up and all grown up so *good*."

"Tabby Allen," Kellie said, moving toward them. "You were a cute kid, girl. Shoulda known you'd turn out to be a raving beauty."

Then Kellie got her own hug.

"Remember me?" Dot asked, also hitting their huddle.

"Dottie," Tabby stated, and looked to Kellie. "Um...Kellie, yeah?"

Kellie nodded.

Dottie gave Tabby a hug.

They moved away from Tab and everyone looked at me just as Rafferty arched up and took purchase on my earring with his mouth.

"Who's that?" Tabby asked.

"Raff..." I cleared my throat. "Rafferty. Justine's boy with her partner Veronica."

Tabby smiled and looked at Justine. "He's cute."

"Damn straight," Justine muttered.

"You gonna hug her too?"

This was asked from the other side of the room and I looked that way to see it was Elvira with her eyebrows up.

I looked back to Tabby.

Then I got up with Rafferty and moved to her, giving her a one-armed hug.

When we were close, she said in my ear, "Weird, you haven't changed a bit."

I pulled away and looked at her. "You have, Tab, and it's all good."

She smiled. "Thanks."

At this point, Rafferty decided he felt like discovering a stranger, so he launched himself at Tabby with a grunt.

Tabby caught him and it was at *that* point I noticed she had more than a small baby bump.

As if to confirm this, Tyra said, "Get used to the feel of that."

Tab looked down at Raff, grinning at him and grabbing his little hand to shake it. "Not thinkin' that's gonna be hard."

"Right, that's done," Elvira declared, and all eyes went to her. "You pissed at us?" she asked me.

I looked at Tyra and Lanie, who both looked anxious. So I smiled at them so they'd stop being that way and looked back to Elvira.

"No," I answered.

"Good, 'cause that woman you sent me to to plan my wedding is *not* gonna work out," she announced. "You got a pretty office. Your office is *da bomb*. She don't have a pretty office. How's she gonna plan the most romantic wedding of the century if she don't even have a pretty office?"

"Well—" I started, but that was as far as I got.

"She's not," Elvira decreed. "And even if her office wasn't god-awful, she wears flats. I don't trust no woman who wears flats. Not at all but *definitely* not to plan my wedding."

"I wear flats," Kellie stated, then finished, "Essentially."

Elvira looked her up and down. "You wear biker chick boots. You get a pass."

Dottie looked to me, prompting an introduction. "Do you know these people?"

"I—" I began again, and again that was as far as I got.

"I'm Elvira. This here's Tyra, Tack's woman, Lanie, Hop's woman, Carissa, Joker's woman. You know Tab. What you don't know is she's Shy's."

I looked at Carissa.

She looked like a grown-up cheerleader.

I didn't know him that well but I still knew somehow that she was perfect for Joker.

"So, Chaos," Dot noted.

"Yes," Tyra finally got a word in.

"Whose woman are you?" Justine asked Elvira a question that I had.

"I don't belong to a biker. I belong to a cop. But I been adopted," Elvira explained.

At the mention of a cop in the same breath as Chaos, in unison, Dot, Justine, and Kellie all looked to me.

"Chaos has changed," I muttered.

"You said it," Elvira chimed in. "Vigilante bikers who ride out now to keep their turf clean of bad folk doin' bad things."

Again, Dot, Justine, and Kellie in unison looked to me.

"It's a long story," I muttered.

"It sho' is," Elvira confirmed. "And it's Chaos and their shit stays tight. Don't mean we won't be sharin' some beverages and wearin' some little black dresses this Saturday night, communin' and building the biker bitch bond at the same time me and Millie here lay down some tentative plans about my wedding of the century." She focused on me. "I'm thinkin' peonies but I could be talked down from that. I want soft and bling and I don't care if those two don't go together. It's your job to make 'em."

I'd heard it all when it came to weddings.

But soft and . . .

Bling?

"Elvira, your mouth," Tabby said. "There's a kid present."

Elvira looked to Rafferty and asked, "You speak English?"

"Gah, goo, dee," Rafferty replied.

She looked to Tabby. "Got more to say?"

Tabby looked to the ceiling.

Lanie started giggling.

Tyra mouthed to me, "I'm so sorry."

"Club," Elvira announced. "Not the biker kind, the Cherry Creek cocktail place kind. Eight thirty. Saturday night. All you all better be there," she ended, circling her hand through the room. She then turned to Tyra. "Now I gotta get back to Hawk. He's got three things goin' down and has his calls forwarded to me. Luckily, no one has called and I wanna keep it that way. Dealin' with Hawk's shit not at my desk is a headache. So I need to get back." She looked to the room. "Awesome to meet you. You." She pointed at Kellie. "Heels, Saturday, girl."

On that, she walked out.

"Elvira's kind of a . . . character," Lanie said when she was gone.

"I like her," Kellie declared.

"Can my wife come?" Justine asked, then added hastily, "We both wear heels."

"Wear what you want," Tabby replied. "Elvira's Elvira but we're Chaos. Anything goes."

"Awesome," Justine said, and put a hand to Rafferty's back. "Did you hear that, Raffy? Your mommies get a night out."

He reached out, smacked her face, and giggled.

Everyone giggled with him.

Tyra moved deeper into the room and my eyes went to her to see she was looking at me.

"This isn't trial by fire, honey," she promised. "This is the welcoming committee."

I knew that. I'd done this before.

I didn't remind her of that. She was queen bee now.

Crank's old lady had minions. I didn't get into that kind of thing because Logan protected me from it, but Crank switched her out before Logan and I had ended anyway.

I had a feeling Tyra was not that kind of Chaos queen but one that was a lot different.

"Thanks," I replied.

"We got off on the wrong foot," Lanie said. "And Hop was—"

"We talked and I'm good with Hop," I told her quickly so she wouldn't worry. "I'm just..." I grinned. "Good."

She grinned back. "Good."

I took her in, liking what I saw. She was beautiful. She was classy. Hop was rough. He was a biker. The same could be said for Tyra and Tack.

Obviously that worked for them.

And I knew it would also work for Logan and me.

No halter tops and cutoffs.

Just me.

"I haven't been a part of a welcoming committee yet," Carissa spoke for the first time. "This'll be awesome."

"Batten down the hatches, Curly," Tabby advised Carissa's way. "And that's not about the Chaos babes hittin' town. That's about us doin' it with Elvira."

I had a feeling she knew what she was talking about.

It had been a long time since I'd had a night on the town, or at least one that ended well.

But looking through the women, three of them my sisters of the blood and the heart, the rest my sisters of Chaos, I was looking forward to it.

High

"Here they are," the woman announced, coming back into the room carrying two balls of fluff.

"Oh my God," Millie breathed, and High turned his attention from the cat breeder to his girl.

When he did, he froze.

She didn't.

Moving with purpose, but not in a way that would spook the kittens, she made it to the breeder and took both cats from her.

"That's the boy." The breeder touched the one in Millie's right hand. "And that's your girl." She moved her hand to the one in Millie's left.

"Look at you," Millie cooed to the one on the right that she'd tucked up high on her chest. "You're my own personal fluff ball, squishy-faced grumpy cat." She turned to the other one, also tucked up high, and continued, "And look at you, my fluff ball, squishy-faced, pretty-pretty princess."

High's girls were going to fall head over heels for those kittens.

But right then, he was watching his Millie, alight with happiness, snuggle two tiny balls of fur and he did it fighting to breathe.

They weren't her own babies.

But they were something to cherish.

There was no doubt she was going to cherish them.

And he was around so he got to watch.

Millie looked to the breeder. "These babies are the best things I ever spent money on."

The breeder smiled.

Millie turned back to the kittens. "Time to go home," she told them, then looked to High.

He forced himself to move. "Crates, babe."

She nodded but asked, "Don't you wanna meet them?"

He didn't.

It wasn't that he disliked cats. It was just that he was a dog man. He'd wanted to get a puppy for the girls for years but Deb didn't like animals.

It was something he intended to do when he got a house. Buy a dog for them and for him.

Now they were all getting cats.

With the way Millie was right then, he didn't mind.

But before he could say no, Millie shoved her right hand to him so he had no choice but to take hold of the boy kitten.

Christ, he was a squishy-faced grumpy cat. He looked kitty ticked.

He also stretched out a paw and clawed High's whiskers with his thin baby claws, his big blue eyes staring at High with an intelligence High'd never noticed from any animal.

"Hey, Chief," he muttered.

"That's it," Millie said, getting close to him. "He's Chief." She looked down to the cat she held. "And this little princess is Poem because only a poem could describe how beautiful she is."

She'd always been good at naming precious things.

The memory made his voice rough when he said, "Let's get them home, baby."

Millie looked to him, searched his face, and smiled a sweet little smile.

"You've fallen in love," she declared.

He had.

Twenty-three years ago.

"He looks pissed off," High replied, and looked to the kitten. "But it's a cute pissed off."

"You've *so* fallen in love," she returned, then stuck the other one out to him. "Here, try this one."

She took Chief and gave him Poem and High looked down at her.

She was pretty, though she looked sad.

"Hope you're smilin' on the inside, darlin'," he murmured to the cat. "'Cause you're goin' to a home where you'll get lotsa love."

The cat yawned.

Millie giggled and pressed her side to his.

High looked to her, then to the breeder. "We'll get outta your hair."

She nodded, looking content, and she would be, seeing as it was clear she found a good home for her brood.

"Keep in touch," she invited. "Send pictures."

High guided Millie to the two cat crates he'd bought as Millie replied, "I will. Tons of them."

"That'd be great," the breeder returned.

They got the cats into the crates and got them out to his truck.

High pulled out of the drive and headed them home, doing all this with Millie twisted in her seat, cooing to the backseat constantly.

"Woman lives fifteen minutes away, Millie. We'll get them home before they're traumatized," he teased.

"I can't take my eyes off them," she said. "They're that perfect."

He reached out and curled his fingers around her thigh.

"Happy?" he asked.

She didn't answer.

So he looked her way and saw her eyes on him.

Before he turned back to the road, soft, sweet Millie finally answered.

"Yes."

He heard it in that word.

He should have known it.

Five days he had her back.

Just five.

And the way she said that word, he knew.

She'd been fixed.

It had nothing to do with High. It had nothing to do with cats. It had everything to do with Millie.

When she wanted something, she didn't fuck around.

She'd been broken.

After putting her together, she'd been fragile.

Then she'd toughened up, sorted her shit, and got on with it.

So yeah.

He should have known it.

That was his girl.

CHAPTER SEVENTEEN

Mom Jeans

High

FUCK.

Fuck.

"Babe," he warned on a growl.

She kept at him with her mouth, body tucked between his legs, having woken him up to get to his dick. All he'd done was cock his knees, stay down, and get blown.

He wouldn't know but evidence was clear, giving spectacular head was like riding a bike.

You didn't forget. Not any of it.

Or at least his girl hadn't forgotten.

"Millie," he grunted. *"Beautiful."*

She kept at him.

Which meant she was going to take him.

And she did when he blew. Through the phenomenal orgasm, he felt her tongue move on his cock when she swallowed and he felt the sucking strokes as she milked it all out of him.

Christ.

Outstanding.

When he came down, she was licking him, sucking him, cradling his balls. It wasn't as good as the blowjob, but it was a close second.

"Bottoms off," he ordered thickly, lifting his head to look down at her.

He felt a throb hit his dick when she kept licking and he saw through the early morning shadows as she lifted only her eyes to him.

Fuck, his girl got off on his cock.

He got up on his elbows.

"Bottoms off, Millie," he repeated.

She wrapped her hand around his dick and lifted up. "Snooks, you don't—"

"Off," he demanded.

"But it's okay for me to give—"

He pushed all the way up to sitting, forcing her to let him go and move up to her knees.

"*Off*," he bit out.

She held his eyes but dropped to her hip in order to yank down her clingy, silky pajama bottoms. Taking her panties with them, she kicked them off.

They barely cleared her feet before High lay back, moving her with him, dragging her up his body and then some in a way she'd not mistake his intent.

So she helped, drawing up her knees to straddle his head.

But it was High that yanked her down, burying his face in her pussy.

She knew better than to protest.

He gave what he got or he gave better.

Nothing less.

So he gave what he got but he gave better, clamping her to him through her first orgasm and keeping at her until she trembled and whimpered through her second.

Only then did he drag her back down and reach for the covers to yank them over their bodies.

She was spent, he could tell with the amount of weight she gave him.

He didn't give a fuck. He just held her to him and drew patterns on the upper swells of her ass.

He gave her time to get sorted before he announced, "That's a fuckuva lot better than an alarm clock."

She giggled.

While he savored a sound that he liked a fuckuva lot, they heard a soft thump at the side of the bed.

High tensed but Millie stretched away, reaching out to turn on the light. Then, bottom half still mostly on him, she collapsed her top half so some of it was on the bed, the rest of it was hanging over the side.

"Hey, babies. Hey, cuties. You trying to get up on the bed with me and Snook'ums?" she cooed.

High rolled, curving into her as well as looming over her.

Poem was sitting by the wall close to the door to the bedroom, staring at them.

Chief was close to the bed, backing away from Millie.

The night before, neither kitten had done much but hide and sleep. Millie got them to the litter box she'd set up in the small laundry room off the kitchen. She'd showed them their food and water. She'd wiggled some toys around them. But they were tuckered out from the drive and wary of their new surroundings, so mostly they hid under furniture and snoozed.

She'd wanted to collect the kittens and take them to bed with them.

High told her they'd survive the wilds of her fancy-ass house on their own.

She'd given in.

Now they were exploring.

She reached out a hand to Chief as the kitten blinked his big, baby blue eyes at her, then looked up and blinked at High.

"It's okay, Chief. It's good, sweetie pie. You're welcome up here," she promised.

Chief backed up, shifted to the side, looked to Millie and High, then backed up more, only to take his shot, run his hilarious kitty run, take a flying leap all too soon and not near high enough. He hit the side of the bed and hung there by his claws before he gave it up and fell to the floor.

He scampered out of the room.

Poem scampered out after him.

"I don't know if that's cute or sad," Millie said, and High looked down at her to see her gazing after the cats.

"Babe, they're eight weeks old. They'll get big and strong enough to make it to the bed."

She twisted her neck to look up at him. "I should get up. Make sure everything's okay. Make sure they have food. Fresh water."

"You should. But before you do that, you should kiss your man." He landed a hand on the small of her back. " 'Preciate the wakeup blowjob, baby. Feel free to do that anytime the spirit moves you. But you leave this bed to start your day, you do it after I get your mouth another way."

She grinned and turned her body under his, pushing up.

Her lips hit his as he wrapped both his arms around her and fell back, she fell on him and she gave him what he wanted.

And as was the only way . . .

High gave it back.

*   *   *

"We appreciate you workin' with us on this, Millie," High listened to Mitch Lawson, Denver detective, say to his girl.

They were at the Chaos cabin in the foothills.

There were men installing an alarm system in Millie's office, so it was a good time for her to get away. Pete had picked her up to bring her to the meet, trailed by Hound and Boz.

High, Hop, and Tack had met them there.

Millie had told her story and it had been recorded. But while she told it, Mitch and his partner, Brock "Slim" Lucas, not only listened, but took notes.

"That's not a problem," Millie replied.

"I know Chaos has you covered," Slim said, and Millie and High looked to him. "You may not have noticed this but we've got cruisers patrolling your area, as well as the homes of other Chaos members who have women and/or kids. Police presence isn't oppressive in order not to alarm neighbors. But if Valenzuela has his eye on anyone, they no doubt will note that presence and back off."

High looked from Slim to Millie to see her nodding.

It was done.

Time to do something else.

"Millie's been outta town and she runs her own business," High said, and looked to Mitch and Slim. "She needs to get back. You get what you need?"

"Got it, High," Mitch muttered. Then to Millie, "Again, thanks."

She pushed back from the table and stood and the men stood with her. These being Slim and Mitch. Tack, High, Boz, Hound, and Pete were where they'd be with any old lady in this situation.

At her back.

She shook hands with both detectives, mumbled, "Nice to meet you," then High moved in and claimed her.

He led her firmly to the door while she called her farewells to the brothers.

He stopped her at the passenger door to Pete's truck.

"I'll ride down, meet you at your house," he stated, and she looked up at him.

Then she looked closely at him.

"Is everything okay?" she asked.

"Absolutely," he answered.

His answer was true but his tone was rough and he knew it. So he also knew it didn't sound like everything was okay.

In other words, it wasn't a surprise when she continued to question him.

"You sure, Snooks?"

Fuck, it was messed up, but he'd missed *Snooks*.

He bent to her, lifting a hand to wrap it around the side of her head, and he took her mouth in a brief but hard kiss.

He lifted away and murmured, "See you at home."

He saw her eyes widen slightly at that and he didn't know if it was her concern at his tone or a reaction to him calling her place home.

He didn't stick around to find out.

He let her go, turned away, walked to his bike, swung a leg over, and fired it up.

He gave her a brief wave before he rode off, seeing Pete heading to his truck as he did.

He was at her house fifteen minutes before Pete dropped her off. Long enough to make certain the cats hadn't destroyed anything. Long enough to witness that they were settling in mostly because they were snoozing and barely blinked their eyes when he found them snuggled in a basket that held extra afghans.

She came in the back door, her eyes to him standing in the space between living room and kitchen with his hands on his hips.

"I think it's safe to say I'm a little freaked out, Low," she told him before she closed the door. "You're acting funny."

He didn't say a word.

He turned around and walked through the living room and down the hall.

"Low," she called.

He knew she followed him because he heard her cooing to the cats and then he heard her boots strike on the wood floors.

He'd stopped inside her room and positioned so he saw her when she entered, rounding into the room, eyes to him, concern now blatant.

"Okay, it's official," she said softly, moving to him. "You're totally freaking me out, Logan."

She got within arm's reach.

Which meant a beat later she found herself pressed face-first to the wall with him using his body to keep her there.

"Low," she whispered, hands to the wall, pushing.

He ground his crotch into her ass.

"Wore my dress," he growled in her ear.

And she did. The sweater dress that clung to every beautiful inch of her body and there were a lot of them.

He heard her breath catch and the way she was pushing back into him changed.

He yanked up her skirt.

"Oh God," she breathed, now grinding into him with her ass.

She wanted what he was going to give and she wanted it bad.

This was not about her not getting any for decades.

This had always been Millie. She'd always been up for it anywhere, any way he wanted to give it to her.

The thought and that proof grinding into him made his dick get even harder.

He looked down, gliding a hand over her hip and thigh. He saw his girl in the dress that had been fucking with him since she walked into the cabin wearing it.

No, since they'd had words when he'd delivered the champagne weeks ago.

He also saw the lace edge of her thigh-high.

Fuck.

"Please, Christ, be turned on," he muttered, sliding his hand up over her ass, into the rim of her panties at the small of her back, down and *in*.

"*Baby*," she whimpered, now he could feel her trembling. Wet.

He toyed with her to get her closer. When she had her head turned, temple pressed to his jaw, and he heard her panting, he yanked her panties down and felt her gasp go right through his dick.

He freed it, wrapped his hand around it, prodding the tip through her wet.

She got up on her toes, tilting her ass to give better access. Fuck yeah.

Anywhere, any way he wanted to give it to her.

He wedged in the head, trailed his hand around her hip and then in.

He found her clit with his finger at the same time he drove his cock home.

Fucking ecstasy.

The back of her head dug into his shoulder as she took him, gasping, moaning, whispering, "God yes," and "So good, Low," and "More, baby."

He gave her more until she got it all and while she was coming he put a hand to her jaw to force her to twist her neck as he bent to her so she was facing him. Then he took her mouth.

So when he shot inside her, he came against her tongue.

When he was done, he freed her mouth but only to tuck her forehead into his throat as they both fought to steady their breath, unmoving and still connected, pressed against the wall.

Eventually, he grunted. "Lost control. Next time you were in this dress, wanted you over my knees so I could hike it up, play with your ass and pussy until you begged me to fuck you."

He felt her lift her head out of his throat and dipped his chin to look down at her.

She was hazy from coming.

She was also turned on.

Anywhere, any way he wanted to give it.

His Millie.

"We'll do that next time," he promised.

Her eyes softened and that look on Millie, High had no choice.

He kissed her again.

This time, he did it easing his cock out.

When he was done with her mouth, he righted her clothes and his, led her by her hand to the bathroom, and cleaned her up.

They walked out together, but with Millie going in front of him, only to stop so he had no choice but to stop with her.

Right away, High saw what stopped her.

Poem was chasing Chief across the floor. She pounced. They rolled, scratched, and mewed. Chief got loose. Poem got to her feet. They went into stare-down.

Then Chief chased Poem out of the room.

There was humor in her voice when she whispered, "Best money I ever spent."

High moved the half a foot that was separating them and wrapped his arms around her from behind.

He kissed the spare inch of skin under her ear exposed by her turtleneck and felt her tremble as she wrapped her arms around his, her hands at his wrists giving them a squeeze.

She turned and twisted as he lifted his head up. She kissed the bottom of his chin.

They'd had moments like this, practically daily, back when they were together. Random moments of tenderness that happened after sex or before it or whenever the spirit moved them.

Fuck, but he'd missed that too.

When she was done with her kiss, he gave her his eyes.

"Need to go check on progress in my office, Snooks," she muttered.

"Right," he muttered back, brushed her mouth with his, and let her go.

He didn't move in order to better enjoy her ass in that dress walking through the room.

She stopped at the door and turned to him.

"I only have one turtleneck dress," she said softly, a look in her eye he liked a fuckuva lot. "But I have three sweater dresses. One's kinda fancy, so my biker best take me out to dinner so he can get his reward."

After delivering that, she walked out.

High still didn't move.

She'd changed a lot since they ended. None of it in good ways.

Except shit like that.

She might not have had a lover but that didn't mean she didn't mature. She didn't come to know herself better. She didn't gain confidence.

She obviously did.

She was a hot piece back in the day. They went at each other all the time. And their sessions could get intense and last a very long time.

But there had not been shit like that coming from Millie.

Not where he'd just fucked her, out of control just because of a dress, and then she'd give him a look and say shit that made him want to drag her back and do it again. Do it until he forced her to lose control. Dominate and get her to the point where she was the one begging for more.

If he'd had her all the time in between, that might not have happened. They would have had what they had, which was great, and kept it. Or that shift would have happened and he wouldn't have noticed it.

But there wouldn't be that nuance of change that hit him right in his cock. There wouldn't be the newness to discover. There wouldn't be fresh things to savor.

It sucked but it seemed there were pieces of the hell that was being apart that were worth walking through to get to what they were building.

The same but different.

Just as good but better.

On that thought, he pulled out his phone, moved his thumb over the screen, found what he wanted, and hit Call.

Then he made a reservation for a fancy steak dinner Monday night at The Broker.

*   *   *

An hour later, after the alarm company had done their final test on the system, it passed, and he'd left Millie, High walked into the Compound.

He moved straight to the brothers who were hanging in a huddle at the bar—Tack, Shy, Hop, Hound, Pete, Joker, and Boz.

"Yo," Hound greeted as he made it to the bar.

High looked to Hound, gave him a chin lift, then looked to Tack.

"Slim and Mitch good?" he asked.

"Yep," Tack answered, and held his gaze. "Valenzuela still had eyes on Millie, brother. Joke noticed them and Snap noticed them when he was sitting on her house yesterday. Speck reports nothin' today."

High did not like this. He didn't like it enough that he was burning to do something about it.

He couldn't. He hated it. But too much was riding on it for all of them.

So he had to bury it.

"Joke told me," he grunted, and returned Tack's steady gaze before he went on. "This shit is takin' a long time. We got no in with Valenzuela's crew. Not even insider gash he sells who gives shit info for a ton of cake. Lucas and Lawson are gettin' more than us but what they're gettin' is mostly dick, too, and we got more pains in the ass patrolling more territory and keepin' an eye on our women."

This wasn't lost on any of them. Months ago, when they

heard that on the street, their reputations had taken a hit and with it, the respect they'd earned, they'd pushed Valenzuela, claiming more turf, growing that from the five-mile radius around Ride that they'd patrolled for years to ten.

They'd also done other shit, like brothers moving out to beat the absolute snot out of the man who shared that he thought Chaos were pussy.

The message had been relayed. No one else had fucked with them.

But looking after more turf took more time. More patrols. More manpower.

Valenzuela landed dealers and whores on their patch regularly, so it wasn't uneventful but it still was a pain in the ass.

"This is why I called you here," Tack said.

"We're all here now. You gonna give us that?" Boz asked.

Tack looked briefly to Shy before he announced, "Got a girl on the inside."

"Who?" High asked.

Tack didn't answer High.

"You need to keep your shit," he warned Shy.

"Oh fuck," Shy muttered. "Natalie?"

Christ, High hoped not.

Natalie was the one who got them stuck in this mess in the first place. A friend of Tab's so deep into Valenzuela for blow, she couldn't pay her debt and Valenzuela got creative. This meant she was going to work a porn set, not doing that manning a camera.

For Tabby, Chaos had intervened before she made that debut. When they did, they bought Valenzuela's displeasure and more of his attention.

It had been a while with both sides butting heads but not much happening.

High didn't like living with that shadow.

One way or another, he wanted it done.

But he didn't trust Natalie. She'd fucked their shit, got

sober for a nanosecond, then fell into the junk again. No one had seen her in months.

If Tack sent her in, he'd be surprised at his brother's play. Tack above all the brothers knew they shouldn't hang anything on a junkie who wouldn't deliver. And Valenzuela liked Natalie less than the brothers did.

"Rosalie," Tack said.

High straightened and moved slightly closer to the huddle as the room went alert.

This was because Rosalie was an ex of Shy's. A sweet girl. Like Millie, born an old lady, though quieter than Millie, less ballsy. Still, Shy introduced her to the life and you could see she took to it, and Shy, right away.

He'd dumped her for Tabby and that might not have been fun for him, but it wasn't ugly. She got burned by him but word was she held no ill will.

Actually, no one held ill will.

And Rosalie was another way High didn't want to see this shit with Valenzuela done.

"What the fuck are you talkin' about?" Shy bit out toward Tack.

"You ended it with her, brother; she got in with a Bounty," Tack explained.

High could see that, seeing as Rosalie was an old lady, and when Shy dumped her, she was this without an old man.

The Bounties were another MC. Chaos had Denver central as well as claiming south Denver, Englewood, Lakewood, and Littleton. The Bounties were East Denver, including Aurora.

The Bounties were outlaws to the bone, like Chaos, and they were a decent club. Good men. But they didn't run a Club business like Ride, so they all had jobs. This meant they dipped their wicks into extraneous shit to make extra cash.

Recently, that extraneous shit became serious.

And part of this was that they'd made an alliance with Valenzuela that earned them Chaos attention and caused friction between two clubs whose members got along, and if they didn't, they gave each other a wide berth.

"As you know, when we pulled out of security, Bounty picked up some of that for players in town," Tack went on. "As you also know, part a' that was them pickin' up some business with Valenzuela. Rosalie didn't know about either. That is, until Snapper caught sight of her with her biker. Snap wasn't around when you were with her. Shot a picture of the biker when she was with him. Showed it to Roscoe. Roscoe knows Rosalie, had the idea. He made the approach. She was not pleased when she heard what was goin' down with the Bounties doin' that shit for Valenzuela and she says she's in to help."

"She's not in to help," Shy shot back.

"We'll keep her covered, Shy," Tack told him. "You know that. Snap is on her, with Roscoe and Speck at his back and hers."

"She's not in to help," Shy repeated, his tone deteriorating.

"Calm, Shy," Hop warned. "You think we'd take her on if Snap didn't have her covered?"

"Snap doesn't have shit," Shy clipped to Hop, then looked to Tack. "She ain't takin' cock to serve Chaos."

"Can't claim pussy that's no longer yours, brother," Tack stated, heat building behind his words, which was understandable since his daughter had Shy's ring on her finger and his kid in her belly and he was throwing in for another woman.

"Rosalie isn't pussy," Shy returned. "She's Rosalie."

"We know that," Tack replied. "But she's tight with her man, thinks she can pull him out of it after shit goes down. And part of this decision includes us knowin' the guy. He's in with the Bounties and like a lot of 'em, he's solid. They're makin' bad allegiances because their president is greedy. Not all of them are down with what's goin' on, including her man. So we think she's not wrong and he can be turned."

"We use her, she's still swinging out there," Shy pointed out.

"Which is why Snap is on her," Tack fired back.

Shy shut his mouth but a muscle jumped in his jaw.

"Won't let anything happen to her, Shy," Pete said quietly. "We know she's Rosalie. She's not Chaos, never really was, but she's a good gal. We wouldn't let her swing."

"I want on her," Shy announced, and the men got more alert.

"No fuckin' way," Tack growled.

"Do not mistake me," Shy whispered. "When it comes to my woman, the family we're makin' she's got inside her, do not ever mistake me, Tack."

Tack held Shy's gaze steady for a beat before he said, "Tabby knows."

"That would be you mistakin' me," Shy returned. "I wouldn't do dick with or for Rosalie without my wife bein' in the know. She's uncomfortable with it, I leave it to Snap, Roscoe, and Speck. She's good, I'm in."

Tack nodded.

When the vibe in the room mellowed, High waded in.

"That's sorted, what's she gonna get for us?" he asked.

Tack looked to him. "Whatever she gets is shit we don't currently have."

"I hear that, brother, but she's covered or not, the fact remains we're puttin' a good woman out there and we should do it knowin' she's takin' a risk that's worth it," High noted.

"Her man works security for Valenzuela's dope transport," Tack replied. "She can get to his cell, see his texts. She hears him on calls. She's already given detail on a shipment and their possible route. We're gonna cover that, see if what she says is gonna go down, goes down. It does, Lawson and Lucas go in on the next one, take it down but do it to turn a Bounty to the cause, informant instead of jail time, this hopefully bein' Rosalie's biker. Rosalie is off the hook without anyone knowin' she was on it and we got someone on the actual inside who can really help bring Valenzuela down."

High turned to Shy. "It's a solid plan, brother."

"It is, we don't give a shit about the woman who's got her neck out," Shy replied. "It isn't we do. And I thought Chaos was not into doin' this kind of shit."

"She's not an old lady, Shy, and never was," Tack remarked.

Shy looked to him. "That matters? She's a woman."

"She's a woman but that don't mean she don't have courage or brains," Tack returned. "She wants her man *out* of that business, brother, and she's willin' to take the risk to get the reward. That's her call. Not yours. And she made it."

"You're good with that, we'll talk again, she's found in an alley with her throat cut," Shy shot back, and before Tack could say anything, he looked around and stated, "This should have been brought to the table."

"Brothers out takin' old ladies' backs, on our kids, we don't have time to sit a table," Tack told him. "Obviously Roscoe, Snap, and Speck are in with this plan. The rest of you are standin' right here."

"Rush isn't here," Shy noted.

"Rush has already voted and I think you get what his vote was," Tack replied.

They all got it. No way in fuck would Rush put Rosalie out there.

Then again, if it was up to him, Rush would retreat off their turf and do nothing but protect Ride, the shop, the garage, the Compound, the parking lot, and the forecourt, leaving the rest to the cops.

This was not a weak decision. A woman Rush cared about was kidnapped and stabbed and he'd watched his father suffer through it right along with the woman who would become his stepmother. All because of shit Chaos waded into.

So it was an informed decision.

Just, to High's way of thinking, the wrong one.

"So I got Rush but if this were to come to a vote, I'd be outvoted," Shy said.

"Seems that way, brother," Boz replied.

"Rosalie isn't gonna get her throat cut," Hound put in.

"You sure about that?" Shy asked.

"Sure I'm sure," Hound returned. "She trusts Chaos. We're your brothers. Not sure why you don't."

That was what got to him. Shy again shut his mouth. Then he shot Tack an unhappy look, turned, and stalked out.

"That went exactly how I expected it," Hop muttered.

"What it did was it went," Tack stated. "Now it's done." He looked Hound and Boz's way. "I want you with Snap, Roscoe, and Speck when that shipment goes. It's on the route Rosalie gave us, tail it, mark the route, stay unnoticed. The next one she gets, Slim and Mitch'll be with you and so will I."

Hound nodded and declared, "I need beer."

He then ambled to a tap, grabbed a random plastic cup that was sitting on the bar that could be clean—it also could be dirty—and he pulled himself a cold one.

"Pull one a' those for me," Boz ordered.

"I gotta go get Nash from Lanie. She's got a meeting comin' up," Hop muttered. "Later."

Then he took off.

"Carrie and me got Travis this week," Joker said. "Goin' home." He took off too.

"You're holdin' your shit a lot better than I expected you would," Pete remarked, and High looked to him. "Thought you'd have Valenzuela hung up by his balls by now."

"Finally got a life not worth fuckin' up," High replied.

"Had that when you got your two girls, High," Pete noted.

"You did, too, lotta folks depended on you for a lotta things when you went off the rails when your girl passed, Pete," High said evenly, not sounding angry, even though Pete had ticked him off with what he'd said. Just making his point.

"Fair enough," Pete muttered, grinned, then looked away and called, "Pull me one, too, Hound," and he peeled off.

Tack got close.

"Shy's on their team, High. Tab won't give a shit about Rosalie. But you know security better than anyone," Tack said. "That dope run is happening this weekend. Know you can't go 'cause you got your girls and they're meetin' Millie. Next run, though, it'd help a lot you were on it."

High nodded.

"In the meantime, be good you keep Snap's shit sharp. Roscoe and Speck got more experience, so they're on the women, only got half a mind to Rosalie and she needs more. It'd help, you helped him cover Rosalie."

High nodded again.

"Millie good?" Tack asked.

High's mind filled with her sweater dress and the lace of her thigh-high.

He felt his lips twitch.

Tack read it.

"Good," Tack muttered, then noted, "Women are goin' out Saturday night."

He knew that. Millie had shared it on the way to go pick up cats the night before.

"Just got her back, hope she survives."

At that, he watched Tack's lips twitch.

"Got shit to do, brother," High told him.

Tack sighed. "We all do."

High slapped his shoulder and Tack returned the gesture. They traded chin lifts.

Then High headed out to find Snap, get a brief, and make sure he was covering Rosalie's shit.

*　　*　　*

"This?" Millie asked.

High was lounging on his side on the bed.

Before he got that way, he'd scooped up the cats and deposited them there. They were wrestling—so damned little, the match was vicious and he didn't feel a thing—and likely fucking up her precious sheets.

She didn't seem to care.

He definitely didn't care.

But she didn't because she was in a fucking tizzy.

She'd just run into the room and was holding up a pair of jeans folded over a hanger at her bottom, a sweater dangling down her front at the top.

He was helping her pick out an outfit to meet his daughters.

This was not what he thought he was going to do when she'd led him into her bedroom after they cleaned up after dinner.

That was bad.

But it got worse when he found out what she was up to.

She started this shit, he'd approved every outfit, and she'd nixed it, tossing crap aside and rushing back to her closet only to come out again with another outfit he'd approve and she'd nix.

This had happened eight times.

He was done on the first one.

"Babe, it's *fine*," he stated.

"I don't know," she mumbled, pulling the sweater away and looking at it. "When it's on, this sweater is kinda tight."

"Then it's *absolutely* fine," High declared, and she turned narrowed eyes on him.

"I'm not gonna wear something suggestive to meet your girls, Low."

"Babe, you got a killer body, you're an unbelievably great lay, and both a' those are mine . . . *again*. You could wear a bag over your head and mom jeans, I knew it was you under all that, I'd still wanna fuck you."

He saw pleasure mingle with irritation in her eyes but she went with the last.

"You shouldn't think those things when you're with your daughters," she announced.

"The only time I don't think those things is when I'm unconscious. But I probably dream about 'em and I'll definitely be doin' that shit after you woke me up takin' my dick down your throat."

She straightened her spine and stated, "I'll never wake you up that way again."

"Fine with me," he returned. "Opens me up to do it to you."

With hanger in one hand, sweater in the other, she planted her hands on her hips and rapped out, "Logan!"

He sighed, pushing up and hauling his ass off her bed. Then he approached and she glared at him as he did, but he ignored it and got in her space, lifting his hands to cup her jaw.

"It's gonna be okay," he said quietly.

He saw her shoulders slump as she replied, "I want Zadie to like me."

"Wear a tiara," he suggested on a tease. "Only way that's gonna step that shit up."

She looked like she was considering that idea and it was cute, so he grinned. But it still disturbed him she'd consider going to those lengths, which indicated the depth of her anxiety.

He dipped closer.

"Baby, listen to me," he coaxed gently. "They're my kids. They're good kids. They love their dad. They're social, good with people. I told you, Zadie will come around. But she won't if you get wound up." He stroked her cheek with his thumb. "Kids are like horses, they can read you're spooked, which will spook them and make 'em act up. You gotta be the adult in this situation, which means you gotta fuckin' *relax*, be patient, and give her the real you, which she's got no choice but to wake up and love due to the fact that there's a fuckuva lot to love."

The clothes she was holding hit the floor as she leaned into him and slid her arms around his waist.

Once she had hold on him, she shared, "You're good at the flowery biker shit."

"Learned early," he replied. "Had a good girl named Millie to win and it was worth pullin' out stupid shit like that in order to do it."

A shadow of regret ran through her eyes at the reminder of what they'd had and lost but she powered through it and returned, "It's not stupid shit."

"Won me you so I guess you're right."

She pressed in until she had her cheek to his chest. As she did this, she held on tighter.

High wrapped his arms around her and returned the tight.

"I'll wear the first outfit. I think it was the best," she decided.

"Great," he muttered. "And so you know, we got plans for dinner at The Broker on Monday night." She tipped her head back and caught his eyes. "Sweater dress," he finished.

She melted deeper into him and grinned.

They heard an angry kitty mew and a soft thump but neither of them let the other go as they twisted in order to see Poem had fallen off the bed and she was kitty run-waddling out of the room.

Their eyes went back to the bed and Millie let out a quiet gasp of alarm when Chief took a flying leap off the side. He didn't land real good but he recovered fast and ran-waddled after his sister.

"I think until they can get up and down themselves without breaking their necks, the bed should be off-limits," Millie declared.

High looked down at her. "They're tougher than you think, beautiful."

"I think until they can get up and down themselves without breaking their necks, the bed should be off-limits," she repeated. He grinned. She kept going. "Unless there's human supervision."

He kept grinning as he asked, "We done with the fashion show?"

She nodded, then started looking around. "I should pick up."

He started walking backward, taking her with him. "You can do that later."

She tipped her head back to look at him. "Low, it won't take a minute."

He hit the bed, went down, she landed on top of him, and he immediately rolled so he had the advantage.

He lifted his head to look down at her but he didn't lift it far, just enough so her brown eyes, her beautiful face, her cute mole were all he could see.

He focused on the mole.

"Think I mentioned I appreciate that you give great head, baby. I also ate you hard and later we fucked fast." He looked to her eyes. "Now we're gonna take all that slow."

She dipped a hand in his shirt so he felt it against the skin of his back.

She was in with his plan.

"I should check the kitties," she said.

Maybe she wasn't in with his plan.

"They weigh less than two pounds each. They couldn't hurt each other or anything else even if they put effort into that shit."

"But—"

"After I eat you."

She melted.

But she started, "Snooks—"

"And you suck me."

She licked her lips but said nothing.

"And we fuck. Then you can check on 'em."

"Okay," she whispered.

"Okay," he whispered back.

Before she could say anything else, he kissed her.

They carried out his plans and took their time doing it.

In the end, she was so out of it after two orgasms, lazy and half asleep, it was him who checked on the cats.

They'd managed to get up on her couch and were asleep on opposite ends of it, one snuggled into an afghan, the other half buried under a toss pillow.

They were good.

So High went back to his girl in order to join her in bed, fall asleep, and dream of Millie's blowjobs.

CHAPTER EIGHTEEN

No Matter How That Happens

Millie

I SUCKED IN a deep breath and pinned a smile on my face, moving toward the back door since I heard Logan's truck pull into the courtyard.

It was Friday night. He was there with his girls to pick me up for dinner.

I was a nervous wreck.

I just hoped I was hiding it.

I was in a nice pair of jeans, a frilly (but not over the top) blouse, and fabulous high-heeled booties. I'd secured my hair in a ponytail at the nape of my neck, had on subtle makeup, subdued perfume, and a touch under my usual amount of jewelry.

In other words, I felt I was ready to face my first meeting with the daughters Logan adored, representing myself as his choice in a positive light.

Or at least I hoped that too.

I unarmed the alarm, opened the door, and stood in it, watching them hopping down from the truck, these activities illuminated by my outside light.

And as I watched, all thoughts of clothes, shoes, and jewelry flew from my head.

I should have asked him to show me pictures.

In all that was happening, I didn't ask him to show me pictures.

Big mistake.

I had no idea what his ex looked like but Logan's daughters looked exactly like him, except young and female, but just as beautiful.

Through all that beauty, the vision of them killed. The hit of it striking so hard it was a wonder I didn't fall to my knees.

I'd never know, not ever, if they were what I'd have given to him. But the idea that such perfect specimens of all that was Logan in girl form might, in some alternate universe, have been what I'd help him to create, what would have been his and *mine*, what we'd watch grow even more beautiful with each passing day, was too much to bear.

I couldn't handle it.

I was stiff as a board and deep breathing as they all moved as one to the door.

I couldn't tear my eyes from the girls.

"Babe," Logan called.

With a great deal of effort, I forced my gaze to him.

He took in the look on my face and I saw the pain of understanding slash through his and that hurt even more.

I realized they'd stopped moving when I heard a relatively snotty, "Is she gonna let us in?"

This took me out of the moment and I looked down to the girls, who were both tall, like their dad.

In fact, taking them in up close, I saw absolutely everything was just like their dad.

God.

I had to get it together.

"Hey," I pushed out. "So sorry." I moved aside. "Come in out of the cold."

The taller, likely older one, Cleo, gave me a careful smile and moved inside.

The shorter, probably younger one, Zadie, gave me a once-over, stopping on my blouse, my boots. Something slid over her face I couldn't read, then she marched in.

After she did, Logan moved in, not to the house, to me.

I felt his hand at my waist, the bristles of his whiskers brush my cheek, and heard him say at my ear, "Fucked up. This was too soon."

I pinned another smile on my face, this one as beaming as it was false, pulled away, and looked at him.

"It's all good," I stated brightly, then moved farther into the kitchen, Logan coming with me and shutting the door, all this happening with me turning my attention back to the girls and declaring, "Welcome! I'm so glad to meet you."

"You too," Cleo replied.

Zadie didn't say anything. She was looking around, though the good part about this was that she was looking around and doing it with her mouth open in what appeared to be wonder.

"Babe, this is Cleo, my oldest," Logan stated, moving in and wrapping his arm around the taller girl, tucking her into his side. "And that's Zadie, my baby."

"Hi, Cleo," I greeted.

She waved and mumbled a shy, "Hey."

I turned to Zadie and opened my mouth but didn't say anything when she looked to her father.

"This house is like a non-fairy tale, fairy-tale castle but in house form," she decreed.

Oh, thank *God*.

Suddenly, all the effort, expense, and hassle of renovations became more worth it than it already had been.

Logan grinned at me. I grinned back.

My eyes shot to Zadie again when she shrieked.

"*Look at that kitty!*"

"What kitty?" Cleo asked, a thread of excitement in her voice. She pulled from her dad and moved toward her sister.

"He has *blue eyes*, he's teeny-tiny, and he's all *fluffy*," Zadie breathed excitedly, now hunched over and walking toward Chief, who was lounged on his side on the edge of the living room rug, studying her warily.

"Oh my *gosh*, they're so *cute*," Cleo whispered reverently. "They're, like, *perfect*. Look, Zade, there's another one on the couch."

She wasn't wrong. Poem was sitting on the arm of the couch, also studying the girls warily.

And suddenly paying through the nose for two purebred cats became more worth it than it already was.

I followed the girls to the space between living room and kitchen and stopped. When I did, I felt Logan move in beside me and he slid his arm around my shoulders.

I wasn't sure about touching in front of the girls but I figured he was their dad, he'd know how to play this, so I had to follow his lead.

Thus I slid my arm around his waist.

Cleo turned to me and didn't even blink when she saw me standing close, holding and being held by her dad.

She was in kitty wonderland.

"Can we touch them? Hold them?" she asked.

"Of course, sweetie," I answered.

She grinned genuinely and it transformed her whole face, making beauty exponentially more beautiful.

Zadie already had a hold of Chief and was cuddling him under her chin.

"He weighs, like, *nothing*," she whispered in awe.

"You have Chief, Zadie," I told her, then looked to Cleo,

who was slowly stalking Poem down the couch. "And that's Poem, Cleo. She's my girl." I looked back to Zadie. "Chief's my boy and your dad named him."

This was the wrong thing to say. I knew it immediately when Zadie's attention cut to me, then to her dad.

She dropped Chief on the back of the couch and declared, "I'm hungry. Can we go?"

My body got tight. I felt Logan's body get tight. And Cleo's eyes shot to her dad.

I could feel he was annoyed but this was a much better beginning than I expected and I didn't want anything, outside of things Zadie might do, to mess that up.

So I said quickly, "Yes. Let's get going. Can't wait for a big plate of spaghetti!"

I moved from Logan's arm and toward the hooks behind the door where my jackets were so we could get on with getting to where we were having dinner. The Old Spaghetti Factory.

I grabbed the suede jacket I'd put there earlier with my pashmina in preparation for that very moment and shrugged it on, wrapping the scarf around my neck and grabbing my bag.

The girls had trooped out and Logan was holding the door.

"Alarm, beautiful," he muttered.

I nodded, hit the digits, and armed it. We got out, Logan closing the door, me locking it.

We moved toward the truck. Logan took my hand and I saw Cleo in the truck, Zadie standing outside of it, her eyes narrowed on our hands.

She lifted her gaze to her father and asked, "Does Millie get to sit in front?"

"What do you think?" Logan asked back.

She huffed like this was an affront beyond the beyond.

Logan stopped us close to her. "Zade, do you ever sit in the front when there's an adult in the truck with us?"

"Whatever," she mumbled, and climbed into the back of the cab.

Logan let me go to shut her door.

I drew in a deep breath and lifted a hand to open the front door but Logan's hand covering mine on the handle stopped further movement.

"Warning," he stated, his voice abrasive and I knew from it precisely how pissed he was at his girl. "She keeps up with this shit, we're outta there. I'll drop you back here and the girls get beans and hot dogs in the RV."

I looked to him. "Don't do that, Low."

"Don't think I won't, Millie," he returned. "That shit is not okay and she can't think it is."

Damn it!

If he did that, she'd dislike me more and maybe Cleo wouldn't like me much either.

Before I could argue (not that I could with the girls in the truck), he pushed my hand aside and opened the door for me.

I climbed in. He slammed the door and moved around the hood. I put my seat belt on as Logan angled in the other side.

He had the truck started and was negotiating a tedious six-point turn to get his big truck around in my courtyard when I asked the girls in the backseat, "Have you guys been to the Old Spaghetti Factory before?"

"Yeah, lots," Cleo answered. "We love it."

"We loved it when Daddy took us when Mom was with us," Zadie mumbled, not quite under her breath.

"Zadie, strike one," Logan growled.

The air in the cab, not exactly free flowing, clogged even further and I knew *strike one* meant to the girls what I suspected it did.

I just wondered how many strikes they got.

I gave it a moment for their father's message to sink in before I instigated conversation, asking about school, friends, favorite subjects, teachers, movies, if they read. Then, finding Cleo liked to read, I asked what her favorite books were.

This lasted us from Cheesman Park where my house was to downtown where the Spaghetti Factory was.

Only Cleo replied. She didn't do it by rote. She was relatively chatty and asked questions back, like what my favorite movies and books were.

Zadie didn't say a word and I didn't have to be a mother or know these girls since birth to feel her pouting.

Halfway through our journey, Logan took my hand and held it. Again, I worried about this display and I worried more when I felt Zadie-induced laser beams burning into our hands from the backseat.

However, I didn't pull away.

We got in the restaurant. We got seated. We took off our jackets and put in our drink orders.

It was there that I noticed that Cleo often looked to her father even when she was speaking to me. And it was then that I realized that she was making an effort for her dad because it meant something to him, he meant something to her, and it wasn't about me.

I'd take that. I could work with that. She'd soon see I loved her dad and that might free her to be open to building a relationship with me.

Regardless, I'd take it simply because it was a good deal better than the petulant silence coming from Zadie.

Logan ignored Zadie's behavior and joined Cleo's and my conversation. He also sat us at our table so he and I were side by side and the girls were across from us. I didn't know if he was making a statement, if he wanted to keep an eye on them, or this was their usual arrangement.

But I was glad he was at my side.

It happened when we fell into a natural silence after we had to send the waitress away because we weren't ready to order; therefore, everyone focused on their menus.

It happened when some sixth sense I had made me look beyond my menu toward Zadie, who was across from me.

Therefore, I saw her overturn her large glass of Sprite, doing it with intent and a little girl evil look on her face. And she did it spilling the drink in my direction.

There was a lot of beverage in that glass and liquid moves fast, so even though I saw her, it saturated the table between us, dripping over my side onto my jeans before I could push back my chair to avoid it.

I threw my napkin down on the spill. Cleo did the same with hers as did Logan. Zadie, moving slowly, did the same with hers. And at the hurried activity and the noise of my chair scraping, patrons around us turned our way.

"Need a towel," Logan growled as I mopped Sprite up with napkins and I saw a busboy rush away. "Jeans are soaked," he went on, this time talking to me.

I looked to my jeans. They were wet. They weren't soaked.

"It's not that bad," I murmured, shoving all the napkins to my place setting.

"Oh no, did we have an accident here?" our waitress asked, moving in with a towel to sweep away the napkins and soak up the spill.

"No, we didn't," Logan answered, and my gaze skittered to him just as he announced, "We need our bill."

Oh no!

"You're leaving?" the waitress asked.

"We're leaving?" Zadie asked.

"Zadie," Cleo snapped in irritation.

No again!

"We're leaving," Logan stated inflexibly, his angry eyes aimed at his daughter, and I felt my heart start to race. "You hear me say strike one?" he asked Zadie.

Apparently, they only got one strike.

"But I just spilled my Sprite," Zadie returned. "It was an accident and it's all cleaned up now, so it isn't that big of a deal."

She did not *just spill her Sprite*. That was a bald-faced lie. She didn't see me catch her doing it but she did it.

I kept that to myself and opened my mouth to get a word in but Logan was pissed and he got there before me.

"Jackets on," Logan ordered in a tone not to be denied, then looked to the waitress. "Bill."

I looked to our waitress too.

"I'm so sorry," I said softly.

She nodded, not looking happy, and took off and we put on our jackets.

"I'll deal with the bill. Zadie stays with me," Logan stated. "Babe, you take Cleo to the truck."

I wanted to question this too. I didn't want him to make a big thing out of what Zadie did mostly because I didn't want to be the reason she got into trouble.

But she'd essentially poured Sprite on me. Not liking me or not liking me with her dad or not liking the fact that her family had fallen apart or all of the above was no reason to do something that naughty. Dot *and* Alan would lose their minds if Katy or Freddie did anything like that at their ages, at Zadie's age, or when they were fifty.

It appeared Logan's daughter wasn't only a dreamer.

It appeared she could be a brat.

So I looked to Cleo and said quietly, "Let's go, sweetie."

She looked to me, her dad, and her sister. She kept her eyes on her sister and I was surprised to see rebuke in them and not just a little of it.

Then she turned back to me and came my way.

We walked through the restaurant but I held her up at the front door so we didn't have to stand outside in the cold for too long.

"Let's stay here where it's warm for a minute while your dad deals with the check," I said.

"He's not dealing with the check; he's dealing with Zadie," she replied, not looking at me, her head turned to look back from where we came.

I decided not to say anything.

Cleo kept her gaze aimed toward the restaurant when she continued, "She's havin' trouble with Mom and Daddy splitting."

"Your father mentioned something about that," I told her cautiously.

She looked up at me. "They split, like, *ages* ago."

I nodded.

"And they were split it seems like *before we were born*."

I was alarmed she held that knowledge and further, I had no clue how to reply.

"She needs to get over it," Cleo told me.

"Something like that is difficult to get over, Cleo. Anything that hurts is difficult to get over. You just have to take the time it takes to lick your wounds and when they finally heal, or when they heal enough you're able to carry on, you do that. You carry on. But things like that shouldn't be rushed or the healing can go wonky. It may take your sister a little time, but she'll get there and the people who love her just need to be patient."

She stared up at me.

Then she said, "But she got Sprite on your jeans."

I smiled at her and replied quietly, "Jeans wash, darling."

She again stared at me but she did it like it was the first time she'd ever seen me and I was a being heretofore undiscovered.

I helped her power through that by tipping my head toward the restaurant and asking, "Do you think we've given them enough time? Should we head to the truck?"

She looked to the restaurant, saying, "I don't know." She turned back to me. "Dad doesn't get mad very often. But when he does..."

She trailed off and I nodded quickly.

"Then let's hang out here a bit," I suggested. "Keep warm.

I'll be on the lookout and we can make a mad dash if I see them coming."

She grinned up at me again without any guard behind it and I was again struck by how her beauty blossomed when she did that.

We chatted until I caught sight of Logan heading our way. I gave her the heads-up and we moved out the door quickly. Once out, I took a chance, grabbed her hand and ran on my high heels, taking her with me.

And I was delighted to find, that as girls were wont to do, for no reason at all, we both found this hilarious, started giggling in the middle of it, and were in the throes of hysterical laughter by the time we made it to the truck.

This might have something to do with the tension casting a pall over the evening and us needing to release it.

But I really didn't care what caused us to do it. We had our moment of bonding and it had come early.

I was batting five hundred and in these stakes, that wasn't as hot as it normally would be.

Even so, I'd take it.

Logan and Zadie showed, Logan still looking angry, Zadie looking chastised and sulky. The sulky part caused her to cast baleful glares at me.

Logan beeped the locks and muttered, "Didn't give you the keys. Two of my girls standin' out in the cold. Sorry, babe."

"Cleo and I found our ways to stay warm," I assured him.

He looked to me. I grinned at him. He studied my grin and I watched as he became visibly relieved.

I turned and got into the car.

Once we were all in, belted up, and rolling away, Logan grabbed my hand again, firmly and demonstrably, held it, and announced, "Not sending my girl home without supper and I don't feel like eatin' franks and beans or makin' Clee-Clee eat it. We're hitting Chipotle."

"Right on," I murmured, and Cleo giggled in the backseat.

I looked over my shoulder and gave her a grin.

She smiled back.

When I caught sight of Logan while turning back around, I saw his profile in the dashboard lights looking vaguely surprised. The squeeze he gave my hand was not-vaguely pleased.

Logan took us to Chipotle. Cleo and I chatted through ordering and food making. Zadie stayed removed and sulking.

During that time, I put on a brave face but I did it realizing that I'd been so anxious about meeting the girls, I hadn't thought of something just as important. That being when dinner was done, it meant Logan and the girls were going to his RV and I wouldn't see him again until the next day. We wouldn't make love. I wouldn't sleep beside him. I wouldn't wake up beside him.

And in realizing this, I decided it was totally *not* too soon for us to move in together.

It was too soon for him to push too much with the girls (*way* too soon for Zadie).

But I didn't want him to be gone and be alone again.

Mostly I just didn't want him to be gone.

Sure, I had Chief and Poem now but they had no clue who I was. Essentially, I was the stranger who put food down for them.

I needed Logan.

And even if it was only three nights, I was going to miss him.

We got our food takeaway, Logan instructing them to put my burrito in a separate bag, and he headed us to my house.

When he got the truck in the courtyard, he turned to the girls.

"Stay here. I'll be back," he ordered.

I turned to them too. "I'm sorry the night didn't go as planned. But however it went, honestly, it was a pleasure to meet you both."

Zadie gave me a glare.

Cleo replied, "You too, Millie. See you later."

I grinned at them, even though Zadie continued glaring

through my grin. I got out and Logan grabbed my burrito bag and got out with me. He also came in with me after I opened the door.

He waited for me to unarm the alarm before he pulled me in front of the cupboards where the girls couldn't see us through any windows and dropped the burrito bag on the counter. Then he tugged me into his arms.

"Shit night," he muttered. "Sorry, baby."

I slid my arms around him. "It wasn't like we didn't know it was gonna be a rough ride."

"Didn't think it'd be *that* rough."

I didn't either but in order to give Zadie a fighting chance, I lied for her.

"You were in the Dad Zone so I didn't want to intervene, but honestly, Snooks, it was probably an accident."

"It wasn't an accident," he returned. "She'd been bitchin' about havin' to go to dinner with you, us goin' someplace we went as a family, since I picked them up from school. I knew she was gearin' up to do somethin' stupid. I didn't know it would be *that* stupid. And we got a rule. They don't do much that ticks me off. But they're doin' something like that, I let 'em know and they know exactly how I let 'em know. If they don't quit doin' it, there are consequences. Just sucks we all gotta eat cold burritos and I gotta leave you a lot sooner than I wanted."

He was going to miss me too.

It felt funny that it would be the case, but that made me feel better.

"Perhaps we shouldn't have picked the Spaghetti Factory," I remarked.

"It's her favorite restaurant, which is why I picked it. Tryin' to get her in a good mood. But, Millie, she can't mark every joint in town we been to with her mom as a sacred place. There's new memories to make and she's gotta get her head outta her ass and make 'em."

"Maybe tomorrow will be better," I suggested, even though I seriously doubted it would.

"Maybe," he muttered. Then, "Gotta go, babe. Gotta feed my kids."

I nodded even if I didn't want to. I wanted to hold on and not let go.

But his girls were in the truck and their food was there too. It was getting late and we all needed to eat.

So I rolled up on my toes, but before I kissed him, I whispered, "Do me a favor and text me when you get back safe and you're settled in."

"Would do that anyway, babe."

I smiled at him.

He gave me an eye-smile back and a squeeze and dipped his head to lay a hard, deep, short kiss on me.

When it was over, he let me go and I walked him to the door.

He was through it when he turned back to me and ordered, "I'm not here, boys are on duty, but arm the alarm anyway. Hear?"

I tried not to give him an annoyed look. "I always do."

"Good," he muttered, leaned in, lifting a hand to curl around the side of my neck and touched his mouth to mine.

He then walked away.

I wanted to give Zadie the relief of seeing the back of me (for the night) but I didn't think that was the right thing to do. Further, I needed both the girls to know how much their father meant to me. I also wanted them to know I wanted *them* to mean something to me.

So I stood in the door and waved as Logan turned around.

I saw him do a chin lift. I saw Cleo (now in the front seat) give me a short return wave.

I also saw Zadie ignore me entirely.

They disappeared and I closed and locked the door and armed the alarm.

Then I turned to my house, my beautiful, perfect, empty house that was glowing charmingly with lamps lit here and there.

It suddenly didn't seem so perfect.

On that thought, Poem came running in, Chief chasing her. They were on a direct trajectory to slamming into the back of the couch and they tried to put the brakes on, skidded and slid until they hit the rug where they rolled and disappeared under the couch.

Slowly I smiled.

Then I burst out laughing, grabbed my burrito, and went to the cupboard with my wineglasses to pour myself some wine.

*   *   *

The next evening, I paid the taxi driver and hurried into Club to meet the girls.

I was late.

I was late due to relaxing far too long in the bath (because I needed to) and dealing with two kittens who had no clue what a bath was but who thought it was something they wanted to try (Chief) or something that was akin to torture and wanted me to stop doing immediately (Poem).

So for ten minutes the bath wasn't relaxing since Chief took repeated but failed flying leaps in order to join me in it and Poem scuttled up and down the side, staring at me with her sad eyes, opening and closing her little kitty mouth in silent, terrified mews.

Now I was here to meet the girls and I wanted to be out all dressed up in an LBD like I wanted someone to drill a hole in my head.

The day had been bad.

No, not bad.

It had been comedy movie bad where you sit comfortably in your seat at the theater and laugh at someone else's string of misfortune, happy that shit never happens in real life *bad*.

I threw open the door to the restaurant, spying the girls who were all dolled up in different but wondrous ways I would normally take a moment to admire. They were in the bar area at two high-top tables pulled together.

I didn't admire them.

I just headed in their direction because that direction meant sisterhood and *booze*.

As I headed their way, I did notice that Claire was not with them. She was at the bar, openly chatting up a hot guy.

Not a surprise.

Fortune smiled on me for the first time that day when I ran into a waitress just as I made it to the table.

"I don't know if this is your table," I told her. "But swear to God, you'll get a huge tip if you bring me a shot of chilled Ketel. No, *three*. And stat."

The waitress nodded as Elvira called out, "And bring her a cosmo!"

I moved to one of two available seats, hiked my ass up on it, shrugged off my coat to hang on the back of my stool, and dumped my clutch on the table.

"Holy hell, you look awesome and awful at the same time," Dot, across the table from me, declared.

I did look awesome. I lost myself in creating big hair and nighttime drama makeup, something I hadn't done in so long, I wasn't sure I'd ever done it.

Another reason I was late.

I looked to her. "Tina Fey may make my day funny if you were to write a movie about it. But in real life, it was *anything* but funny."

"Oh no," Tyra said.

My eyes went to her, noting distractedly that all the women weren't dressed to the nines. They were dressed straight to the twelves. In fact, Elvira looked professionally coiffed. And Kellie, an equal opportunity partier, be it in a bar at a fancy restaurant or a biker hangout that had only one word to describe it—seedy—looked fabulous.

"You were with High's girls today," Tyra finished.

"I was," I confirmed. "For lunch and a movie. This being *the longest* lunch known to man and *the longest* period of time spent with two female tweenies since time began."

"I don't get it," Lanie, sitting beside me, said. "High's girls are sweet."

"Cleo is sweet," I told her. "Zadie wants her mom and dad back together and therefore she's not so sweet."

"Ah," Lanie murmured.

"What happened?" Veronica, sitting next to Dot, asked.

"Hmm...let's see," I began. "There was the moment when they picked me up and Logan had to use the bathroom before we went so he left me alone with the girls. This was when Cleo happily reacquainted herself with my new kittens and Zadie told me right to my face that cats were stupid and people who had them were even *more* stupid, not to mention, cat ladies were *lame*. She said this even though just the night before, before she remembered she was supposed to hate me, she'd fallen in love with the kittens on sight."

"That ain't so bad," Elvira noted.

I looked to her. "Then there was the time when we were walking through the mall to get to the theater and Zadie and I were removed from her dad and sister and she told me that old ladies shouldn't dress like I dressed, my clothes were too young, and I looked like a wannabe. There was also the time when we bought snacks for the movie and she noted her mother would never eat what I chose and that's why her mother has a *killer bod* and I'm fat."

"Yikes," Tabby muttered.

"You aren't fat," Kellie snapped.

"What did High say about all this?" Tyra asked.

"Since she purposefully dumped her Sprite so it would hit

my lap the night before," I started, and all eyes at the table got big, "she learned and waited for times when Logan couldn't hear and she did her best to do it when her sister couldn't either."

"Sticks and stones," Elvira declared. "Girl, you gotta be tougher than that."

I again looked to her. "Zadie sat across from me at lunch and *kicked me* the entire time. She got me in the shins so often, both are black and blue, and that is no joke."

I held my leg out to the side, where Carissa was sitting. I had sheer black thigh-highs on but the bruises still could be seen.

"Holy cow, that *is* no joke," she muttered in horror.

I kept on with my tales of woe.

"I was sitting next to Logan so I couldn't adjust too much or he'd notice so I tucked my calves under the chair. That was when she kicked my knees."

"Oh my God," Kellie fumed. "What a brat!"

Absolutely.

It hurt to say but all evidence was pointing at the fact that it wasn't that Zadie *could be* a brat.

She just *was* one.

"Not to mention," I kept going, "any time she could get away with it, she gave me a look that told me she was plotting my murder. She sneezed into her hand once and immediately touched me, making it look like she was being nice but really rubbing her snot on the sleeve of a blouse. A blouse that's dry clean only. And *twice* she gave me the finger."

"I can't believe this of Zadie," Carissa said. "I've only met her a couple of times and she's super cute."

"And you didn't tell High about any of this?" Tyra asked.

"No," I answered.

"Why not?" Justine asked.

"Because he lost it during the Sprite incident and we left without even ordering food. He took us for takeaway Chipotle but only after giving Zadie a talking-to. It wasn't pretty."

"Good for him," Elvira declared.

Normally, I would agree.

In the circumstances, I didn't.

That day, with Zadie hiding her behavior, Logan had been happy. Straight out, not hiding it, had all his girls together, a biker stomping through the clouds in his motorcycle boots.

So it was also that I didn't have the heart to ruin it for him.

"I'm not sure it was the right thing to do," I said to Elvira. "It's only given her more impetus to try to push my buttons. If he'd left the Sprite thing as being a possible accident and I'd been able to breeze through it, maybe I could have gotten through to her. Now it's like she's on a mission."

"This isn't okay behavior," Tyra stated. "Including purposefully dumping a drink on your dad's girlfriend. It's good High sent that message."

"You're right, it's not okay behavior," I replied. "But it's clear she didn't get the message. And I broke through with Cleo. She isn't texting me to make a date to bake cookies together but it's not like she's just tolerating me either. We have our moments and they don't come often but it's like night and day with Zadie."

"What does Cleo think of what her little sister is doing?" Tabby asked.

"She doesn't like it," I answered. "But I'm not seeing any big sister sway between those two."

The waitress arrived and set my drinks on the table while Lanie shared, "I see that. Zadie lives in her own world. Cleo's a good kid through and through. She'd twist herself in knots for her mom or dad. Zadie's kind of a princess."

"Yeah," Elvira agreed as I lifted a shot and threw it back. "It's like Cleo senses her mom and dad weren't happy, so she bent over backwards to be the good kid who'd make 'em that way. Zadie just thinks everyone exists to make *her* happy. It's cute when you're her age. Not so cute when you get older."

As awful as it was to admit it, from what I'd noticed, this was the truth.

Cleo was alert, responsible, almost adult. She rushed in to help her dad any time there was even the minutest thing to assist with, like carrying our drinks and munchies at the theater or collecting the menus to hand to the waitress.

That in itself was concerning.

I didn't know kids too well, especially girls her age, but she seemed way too young to be that deeply in tune with what was going on around her and that deeply keen to try to smooth out any edges. Most especially her knowledge that her mother and father never really were together and the fallout from that, most notably Zadie.

I knew kids were sharp, they noticed things, those things affected them and they behaved accordingly, in bad ways and good.

But they were still kids.

Cleo should just be a kid. Or if she couldn't just be a kid, there should at least be times when she was a kid. Not a peacemaker or a helper, existing only to smooth out those edges, which was all it seemed she could be.

But when Logan said his youngest lived in her own world, what he meant was that she owned the world and we all lived in it with her.

I could see this as partly his doing.

He poured devotion on Cleo for being all she was, helping her dad out, sticking close, being attentive, smart, thoughtful.

He poured affection on Zadie for being Zadie and gave her her every heart's desire, including her own bucket of popcorn because she didn't like to pass while watching the movie, and *three* different kinds of candy, all of this only hours before we headed out to a late lunch.

"What are you gonna do?" Dot asked, and I looked to her.

"First, I'm calling off tomorrow," I answered. "They're

supposed to come over for breakfast and then we're supposed to spend the day lazing around, watching movies, eating and getting to know each other before we head out for dinner and they head back to the RV. But I'm thinking the girls need a break from me."

Or, at least, Zadie did.

But possibly Cleo did too.

Three days straight having to put up with your dad's new woman was two days too many.

On this thought, I threw back the next shot.

"I'm designated driver and your ass is in our car," Veronica declared.

"You're on," I replied.

"Girl," Elvira called, and I turned to her. "That's givin' Zadie her way," she noted.

"It's giving them some time just to be with their dad so they can be themselves and not have to put up with me, in Zadie's case, or try to take care of their dad by finding reasons to like me, in Cleo's."

"I see the wisdom in this," Dottie remarked. "Logan's taking things too fast."

"I see that," Elvira returned. "*If* Princess Zadie didn't pull that shit. Now a message needs to be sent that she can't act up and get what she wants."

"I hate this for you," Kellie cut into the exchange, and I looked to her. "The big reunion with Low should be all hearts and roses."

This surprised me coming from Kellie. Nothing since we were kids was hearts and roses for my friend. She wasn't a romantic. She loved life and lived it by her rules, but she never expected hearts and roses, not for her, not for anyone.

"She'll come around," I assured her.

"What'll you do if she doesn't?" Justine asked.

I shook my head, lifting my cosmo and taking a sip.

Then I answered, "She will. Eventually. With this start, it might take years but she'll get how much I love her father. And if she doesn't, well..." I shrugged. "I have her father and he and I have learned the hard way that life can suck."

I felt something coming my way from directly across the table, so I looked to my sister.

When I caught her eyes, she didn't try to hide the disappointment edged with pain she felt for me that Logan's girls didn't fall head over heels in love on sight.

They weren't all I was going to get. I had Katy and Freddie that I could love and adore and spoil rotten.

But we both knew just how wonderful it would have been if I also had High's girls to do the same.

"I'm okay," I mouthed.

She nodded but didn't look much like she believed me.

So I gave her a reassuring smile and looked to the table.

"Right," I said. "Enough of that." I turned my attention to Elvira. "Wedding with soft and bling, wrap your head around this..." I paused for dramatic effect, then threw out, "*Velvet.*"

Elvira stared at me a second, then smacked her hand on the table and hooted, "I *knew* you'd deliver!"

"You'll need a late fall or winter wedding," I told her. "But an ivory velvet wedding dress with some strategic diamanté placements would look stunning on you. Nothing off the rack. I know a local designer who makes unique gowns and she's fabulous. Velvet bridesmaids gowns, perhaps in champagne. Bunched swaths of velvet adorning the reception tables or covering the chairs. You'd have to give up on peonies but I see calla lilies with silvered Christmas berries. Or ivory roses bunched with crystals. If you pick winter, we can do a Winter Wonderland theme and incorporate blinged-out pinecones. Glittered twigs. Fur. Marabou or chandelle feathers. Anything, really. Snow glitters. It's also soft. Winter is made to be soft and blinged."

Elvira kept slapping her hand on the table when she cried,

"Oh Lord, Lord, Lord, Lord." She stopped slapping her hand and pointed at me. "I want it all."

All of it?

Feathers *and* fur? Crystal and glittered twigs?

"That's a lot," I pointed out.

"You'll make it work," she declared.

I would because that was me but it would be a design nightmare.

"Good thing she's got more than a year to plan," Lanie murmured, likely taking in the dread on my face.

"And more than a year for Malik to pop the question."

Veronica's eyebrows flew up and she asked Elvira, "You're planning a wedding and your man hasn't proposed yet?"

"I'm thinkin' I don't care," Elvira stated. "I'll just tell him he's gotta put on a suit, get his ass in the car, and drive him to the church. He can stay and do the deed or he can leave and never see me again."

"New reality program. *Extreme Proposals, Denver,*" Kellie whispered through giggles.

"Things are gonna get extreme if that man doesn't put a rock on her finger," Tyra put in.

"As far as I'm concerned, my girl Beyoncé made a call to arms," Elvira said. "And I listened."

"I think the Great One meant that, if you didn't put a ring on it, you would see the back of her. Not that you should go out and buy a handgun," Tabby pointed out.

"Then I shoulda wrote that song," Elvira returned.

"Don't settle for anything less, Elvira," Carissa stated. "But you won't have to. Malik adores you. He'll make you an honest woman."

"Haven't been that in a good long while," Elvira muttered, and everyone smiled. "So it'd be nice to wear an ivory velvet wedding dress during my Winter Wonderland Wedding to wash in the honesty."

"I think I like your new friends," Kellie decreed to me.

I looked to her and smiled.

"I know I do," Justine stated.

Dot raised her cosmo. "Right, girls. To old friends. And to new." Her gaze came to me before it went to Elvira. "And to dreams coming true, no matter how that happens."

"I hear that!" Tabby cried, lifting what looked like sparkling water.

"Hear, hear," Veronica said, lifting her martini.

We all followed suit and clinked.

I looked over my shoulder and caught Claire writing what was undoubtedly her phone number on a cocktail napkin for the smiling hot guy who was watching her do it.

I turned back to the table, suppressing a sigh at the same time I suppressed a giggle.

"Right," Justine turned to Tabby. "When are you due?"

I tuned in to Tab and tuned out my day.

And as it was when the sisterhood gathered—something no relaxing bath, no glass of wine could do better—my crew helped me wash away my shitty day.

᛭   ᛭   ᛭

The next morning, I made the call.

I was in the kitchen in my jammies with my coffee and two kittens with their faces stuffed into a bowl of kitty chow, my phone to my ear.

It rang twice, then I heard, "Babe, we're all up. Gonna be there. Maybe an hour."

"Low, can we talk for a sec?"

There was a hesitation before, "Sure, beautiful."

I drew in breath before I said, "I think we should cancel today."

There was another hesitation, then I heard him say, not to me, "Gonna be outside. Keep on keepin' on." I heard some noises that might be the RV door opening and shutting and then I had Logan back. "Say what?"

"I think we should cancel today," I repeated, then quickly continued. "I think the girls need a break."

"From what?"

"From me," I said carefully.

He said nothing for a moment.

Then he pointed out, "They had fun with you yesterday."

Maybe Cleo had.

Zadie, not at all.

"They need dad time," I told him.

"They had that last night."

I knew this wasn't going to be easy and I'd been right.

"Snooks," I said softly. "They only see you for any period of time every couple of weeks. It'll get to the point where I'm a part of their life, a part of visits with Dad. But right now it's a lot of stress to put on two young girls."

And me.

Though I didn't add that.

"They're fine."

"I really think you should give them a day with just you," I pushed.

I got another moment of hesitation before he asked, "Are you sayin' you don't wanna be with my girls?"

Shit.

"No, absolutely not," I replied firmly. "It's not that at all, Low. I like them. Cleo's sweet and Zadie's coming around." The last was a lie but...whatever. "It's just that I think this is too much too soon."

"They don't see you today, babe, I don't see you."

I'd thought of that. I loved that he wanted to see me and I hated that we wouldn't see each other.

But we, both of us, had to have a mind to his girls.

"Logan—"

"There somethin' you're not tellin' me?"

Shit!

"No," I lied again. "It's just that, if it was thirty years ago and I was in this situation with my dad, this is what I'd want."

"Bullshit," he returned. "You fuckin' love your dad. You'd want him to be happy and you'd wanna be there to see that."

He was right.

"Low—"

"What are you not tellin' me?"

"Nothing," I lied again. "I just think you should give your girls a dad day."

He didn't reply and this wasn't just a moment's hesitation.

This was several moments' hesitation.

Then he asked, "Zadie say shit to you?"

He asked straight out.

Could I lie straight out?

I had no choice. Delaying my answer was my answer.

The honest one.

"She did," he bit out. "What'd she say?"

"It wasn't anything, Snooks," I answered softly. "I just think you need to give her some time to get used to the idea of me before you force her to spend more time with me."

"Burned you," he stated, words that confused me.

"What?" I asked.

"You walked through fire to give me my girls and the first time you looked at 'em, you did it again. Sent you straight to hell, seein' what I had that you didn't. Seein' what I had we couldn't make. You're dealin' with that and Zadie's bein' a snot."

It felt extremely good he noticed and he cared.

But as he spoke, he got angrier with each word and I suspected Zadie would hear about it and that wouldn't make things any better for her and me.

"You need to give her time to get used to the idea of me, Low. She's a little girl. I love that you want this to go well.

I love that you want it to happen fast. But other people are involved and sometimes we can't make what we want happen like we want it to happen."

"Cleo say shit?" he ground out.

"No. We...things are good between Cleo and me," I assured him. "We've had a couple of moments. I think she wants you to be happy but I also think she's getting around to liking me."

"She ain't a little girl, Millie," he stated. "Zadie's ten. She knows better."

"Ten is not twenty-three, Logan," I told him, and hurriedly continued before he could say anything. "And it's not my place, I don't know how to handle your daughters, but I have a feeling that you getting angry at her for having valid emotions is only making her not like me more."

"Shit happens in life and you handle, it, Millie. You don't act out like a five-year-old and pour Sprite on it to make it go away."

He had a point.

"It's not that they need a break," he declared. "It's you who needs one."

"Honestly, Snook'ums," I said carefully, "you're kinda right. But I think it's all of us."

"Right," he clipped irately. "Plans are canceled today, which sucks. For twenty years I have not had a lotta good days that are just fuckin' good. Yesterday, my three girls together, was one of those days. I was lookin' forward to more."

That cut like a knife.

Before I could push past the pain, he kept talking.

"But I don't want you to have to put up with more shit and it won't be good for me, knowin' you are or keepin' a better eye on things and seein' it happen, which is only gonna tick me off."

"We'll plan something, Low," I told him. "Something in between visits. They can have dinner at my house. I'll cook. They can play with the kitties. Maybe we can play a game."

"We'll do that and it'll be more than one dinner," he

decreed. "And I'm tellin' you now, Millie, Zadie ain't gettin' away with this shit."

Damn it!

"Logan, I'm not sure that's the right way to go," I warned.

"I am," he returned. "Was so fuckin' happy to have somethin' good in my life. Two good, pure things that were mine. That I made. Too fuckin' happy. So happy, I fucked up," he said. "Cleo's good 'cause she came out that way. Zadie's a dreamer 'cause I didn't cut that shit off when I should."

Oh no!

This was getting worse.

"Logan, a dreamer isn't a bad thing," I informed him.

"It isn't, you dream of the life you wanna have and you're willin' to work for it. It is when you dream of the way you expect life to be and you manipulate or find ways to make everyone around you miserable until you get it. My girl's spoiled. That's on me. Her mother doesn't let her get away with shit like that. And you're right. She's ten. She's young." He paused ominously. "So she can still learn."

"You do know, Snooks," I said quietly, "that you teaching her that lesson, one that will be hard to learn, when I came into her life means she'll associate that hard knock with me."

"She can't sort her head out and see that her father's happy. Fuckin' unbelievably happy. Straight up, no shit fuckin' with that, for the first time since she's been breathin', know that comes from me havin' her, her sister, and *you*, and she doesn't want that for me and holds a grudge against you, then I failed at teachin' her to learn that lesson right."

I couldn't argue that.

But I wasn't even thinking of arguing that.

I asked, "You're unbelievably happy?"

"Baby, are you back?"

Oh God.

"Yes," I whispered.

"Millie, I was given one good thing in my life, the family I was born into. I found one good thing, my Club. I made two good things, my babies. But in all my life, I only *earned* one good thing. That's you."

Oh *God*.

Feeling so much, I could do nothing but continue to whisper, "Low."

"I'm gonna fix this, beautiful. I promised myself I'd fix you when I got you back and this is part of that. I'm gonna fix it and I'm gonna do it how I gotta do it. But it'll get done."

"I . . . okay, Logan," I agreed shakily.

"Want you touchin' base today. You wanna call, do it. You wanna text, do it. Don't matter I have the girls and they might hear or see. But I wanna hear from you and know you're thinkin' about me."

"Oh, I'll be thinking about you."

He fell silent.

I didn't.

"I love you, Logan Judd. I earned a lot of things in my life, worked hard for them, but the most precious of those is you. And I'll say right now that you come with your girls. So I'll do what I can to help you with Zadie. Do we have a deal?"

I heard the smile in his voice when he replied, "We got a deal, babe."

"Okay, I'll share my exciting day with you sometime today and I'll see you tomorrow."

"Right."

"And, Logan?" I called.

"Right here," he answered.

"Nothing wrong with dreaming. But you got it right. Best way to dream is do it, then earn it, no matter how that happens."

"Damn straight," he muttered, still sounding like he was smiling.

"Okay, have fun with your girls. Love you."

"Back at ya."

"'Bye, baby."

"'Bye, beautiful."

We disconnected and that didn't make me happy.

But we disconnected having a plan. A plan that centered around building a new dream.

Logan had been right. He said if he'd been around when I found out I couldn't give us a family, he would have helped me build a new dream.

It took time.

But now he was doing it.

CHAPTER NINETEEN

Kitties Who're Really Pretty

High

HIGH STOOD LEANING against the kitchen counter in the RV, watching his girls scarf down cereal in preparation for hitting school.

Yesterday, he hadn't gotten in Zadie's face about whatever went down with Millie. He'd just told them their plans with Millie were off.

Cleo looked disappointed but also relieved. She was likely disappointed for him because she'd seen he'd been happy the day before. But she'd been relieved because Millie was right. Even Cleo needed a break.

That sucked and it meant Millie was right about something else.

He was pushing too fast, too soon.

But Zadie had smiled her cat-got-its-cream smile. She tried to hide it but it was clear she thought she'd gotten her way.

His baby girl was not going to get her way.

Though High had no clue how to go about doing it. He just knew he had one shot at giving Millie any kind of family. Maybe not of her blood but something that was still beautiful.

And because of that, he had to pull out all the stops.

"Before you go to school, got somethin' I wanna tell you," he said.

Cleo looked from her cereal bowl to him, attentive as usual.

Zadie looked to him, happily encased in the knowledge things had gone her way.

She grinned and asked, "What, Daddy?"

He stayed where he was and replied, "Worried you're too young to share this with you. Worried you're too young to get it. But it's important enough I gotta give it to you."

Cleo's attentive look went guarded.

His baby's eyes narrowed as the first suspicion she might not have gotten away with being a snot started to hit her.

High ignored that and kept talking, hoping the way he was going to share what he had to share would hit somewhere in Zadie she understood.

"Long time ago, I walked into a party and saw the prettiest girl I'd ever seen. Fell in love with her right then and there. Fell in love the minute I locked eyes on her." He looked between his girls and went on, "Millie did the same."

Zadie's mouth got hard.

Cleo stared at her dad.

"For three years we lived happily," High told them, and looked to Zadie. "But we didn't live happily ever after."

When he said no more, Cleo asked quietly, "What happened, Daddy?"

High turned his eyes to his eldest. "We both wanted a family. We both wanted kids real bad. Knew it before I had it with you two that you were the only things I wanted on this earth. My own babies. Kids I could love and help to grow up strong and good. Millie wanted that too. We talked about it all the time. Had names picked out and everything. Out of the blue, she split with me and it was over."

"That wasn't very nice," Zadie snapped.

"It was," High disagreed. "It was the most generous gift anyone could give seein' as she found out she couldn't have babies and she made it so I could go on in my life and have you."

Zadie blinked.

Cleo's mouth fell open.

"Best Millie can do is have cats," High told his girls. "She wanted more. A lot more. We were gonna have tons of kids. Four. Five. Boys. Girls. We didn't care. Now all she's gonna have is cats."

Cleo's lower lip started trembling so she bit it.

Zadie looked down at the table.

"She makes me happy," he said gently. "I know she's just come into your life but she's been a part of mine for a long time so I'm gonna share with you that I love her and she makes me happy. I wanna make her happy. And it'd mean a lot if you helped me with that."

Zadie's eyes cut to him and declared nastily, "Mom's our mom."

"Not sayin' that she isn't, Zade," he told her, expending the effort not to get pissed that nothing but what she wanted was sinking in. "Your mom will always be your mom. She's not out of the equation. I'm just adding Millie to it. Everyone's got an endless capacity for love. Which means everyone's got the shot at receiving an endless supply of love. Don't matter who you give it to or get it from. Just matters you got a heart big enough to give it and a heart open enough to get it back. I can promise you, Millie's got that kind of love to give." He shrugged. "Up to you whether you open yourself up to receive it." He focused closely on Zadie. "I'll just say, your old man will be disappointed if you decide not to do that."

"I like her," Cleo piped up, and High saw his youngest aim an irritated frown at her sister before he looked to his big girl.

"I'm glad, baby," he said quietly.

Zadie didn't say anything, so Cleo looked to her sister.

"Zade?" she pushed.

Zadie hopped from her knees in the seat and grabbed her bowl, muttering, "We're gonna be late for school."

She didn't give a shit about school.

She wanted this conversation to be over.

She took her bowl to the sink.

"Rinse that and put it in the dishwasher," he ordered.

"Whatever," she mumbled, dumping the milk in the sink.

"Look at me, Zade," High demanded.

She gave him a squinty look that told him she had things to do and he was wasting her time.

"First, wipe that look off your face," he said. She didn't, so he went on, "Now."

She huffed and changed her look to a bored one.

High let that slide.

"Your old man loves you," he told her.

She changed her look to a disbelieving one even though she knew deep down that was not right.

He let that slide too.

"Measure of the love you got for me how you decide to give it back," he said.

"Measure of the love you got *for me* you got rid of Mom and found some other woman," she returned.

He stared straight into her eyes and whispered, "Ouch."

That got her.

She flinched.

But she didn't say anything.

"Honest to God, you okay with layin' that kinda hurt on your old man?"

She stared at him a beat before she turned to the dishwasher, opened it, and shoved her bowl in.

"Now more hurt, you not answerin', which means you obviously are," he noted.

She looked back at him. "Just because I don't like your girlfriend doesn't mean I don't love you, Daddy."

"Hit me, darlin'. Lay it out straight. You won't get into trouble," he told her. "Tell me, what did Millie do to make you not like her?"

Zadie didn't answer.

So Cleo joined the conversation.

"She can't say anything because Millie's nice."

Zadie turned to her sister and hissed, "She's old and *fat*."

"You're so full of it," Cleo snapped back. "She's super pretty."

Right.

This had to end because now his baby girl was pissing him off.

"She's two years younger than your mother," High declared. "And I hope to God you don't think she's fat, Zadie, because you think what Millie is is fat, we got more problems, those bein' about how you think a woman's body should be."

She turned to him while he spoke and opened her mouth when he was done.

He lifted a hand before she could say a word because he saw on her face that what she was going to say he wasn't going to like.

"Enough outta you. There'll come a time when you look back at this weekend and you'll wish for it back. I love you too much to let you make that worse." He dropped his hand and jerked his head to the couch. "Get your books and jacket. We gotta get goin'."

Zadie stomped to the couch as Cleo got up and dealt with her bowl and High poured himself a travel mug of coffee.

Zadie then stomped right out as Cleo helped him shut down the RV to leave.

He'd shrugged on his cut, nabbed his keys and the mug, and was reaching to the door Zadie had slammed when his big girl looked up at him.

"At least she got kitties who're really pretty," she said softly.

Fuck.

His girl.

He put the mug on the counter and reached out to curl his hand around her soft cheek, bending so his face was in hers.

"Comes as a surprise. My girl hides how deep she feels so when she lets that out, comes as a surprise, darlin'. A surprise I love each time I get it. Thank you for that, baby."

She grinned up at him, pleased at his words but more pleased she did her bit to smooth out a bumpy morning for her dad.

He leaned in and kissed her forehead, then straightened away, grabbing his mug and saying, "Now let's get you to school."

*   *   *

After dropping off the girls, High drove straight to Millie's.

He parked the truck in the courtyard, got out, and moved to her office.

He opened the door and heard the alarm beep even as he saw her on the phone behind her desk, hair piled up at the back of her head, another turtleneck, this one beige. He couldn't see the bottom through her desk at his angle, but he could see she had on her brown boots.

She smiled huge at him.

He grinned back, turned to the alarm's control panel, and punched in the code as he heard her say, "I'm so sorry. Someone *just* came in the door and it's unexpected but it's also urgent. I need to call you back. I apologize but I'll call you as soon as I can."

He turned to her to see she was up and rounding the desk, coming his way.

He moved hers.

Tight brown skirt that skimmed her knees and hugged her hips.

Brilliant.

"Right. Of course," she said in her phone, still walking. "Thank you. Talk soon," she finished as she got to him.

She disconnected and instantly threw her arms around his neck.

"Hey, Snooks," she whispered as he slid his hands around her waist.

High didn't return her greeting.

He bent his neck and laid a long one on her. She had the fingers of one of her hands in his hair when he finished it.

"Hey," he replied.

Her smile was hazy but it was bright.

It faded slightly before she said, "Missed you."

He gave her a squeeze. "Then good I'm back."

The smile came back.

"Know you got shit on and I got somethin' I gotta do with Snap, so I gotta go," he told her, and watched her mouth with its cute little mole start pouting. "But I wanted to come by, see you, drop some more shit in the house, connect with Chief and Poem, then I gotta take off."

"More shit?" she asked.

"Don't got much, babe, but I'm movin' in. Packed some things this mornin' while the girls were gettin' ready, put 'em in the truck. Outside of the stuff that stays in the RV, like plates and mugs, with the bag I got in my car, most of my crap is here."

"So you're essentially moved in."

He studied her, thinking they'd gone over this already, and after the shit conversation he'd already had with Zadie that day, not wanting to have another one.

"That a problem?" he asked.

"If you hadn't done it, I would have probably taken off work, found Boz's house, broken into your RV, and done it myself."

He felt a smile hit his face.

Her lips quirked as she said, "Waking up alone sucks."

"Yeah," he muttered. "Goin' to sleep without gettin' off sucks too."

She rolled her eyes to the ceiling and told it, "Men. Sex on the brain."

"You use your toy while I was away?"

Her eyes rolled back and when he got them again, they were bigger and her cheeks were pink.

Fuck.

He'd been teasing.

But she did.

"You made yourself come without me?" he asked.

"Well…" She trailed off. He gave her a squeeze and she kept going. "I was actually doing that *thinking* of you. Does that count?"

"Dinner," he grunted. "Sweater dress. Tonight. And after-dinner plans changed."

Her eyes got big again. "How?"

"You'll see."

She slid her fingers from his hair and wrapped them around the back of his neck. "*How*, Low?"

He bent in and put his mouth to hers. "Trust me, beautiful, it'll be a good surprise."

He felt her tremble in his arms.

"Now gonna let you go 'cause I gotta go. Give me another kiss."

He watched disappointment hit her eyes that he was leaving

before she closed them and pressed her mouth to his, touching her tongue to his lips.

He gave her entry and he gave her time to taste him.

Then he took over before he ended it on some soft, quick kisses, let her go, turned her, and slapped her ass to move her to her chair.

He moved to the door saying, "Later, babe."

"Later, Low."

In the opened door, he looked back at her sitting behind her desk. He reached out a hand and tapped the security panel.

"Rearm, beautiful."

She sighed but nodded and said, "I will. See you later, Snooks."

He lifted his chin, grinned, and closed the door so he could see to hauling the single bag he had that held the rest of his shit and moving into her house.

*   *   *

High leaned against the side of the truck, watching and not liking what he was seeing.

Snap was standing on the sidewalk with Rosalie.

High remembered Rosalie. She was no less pretty now than when she was Shy's.

She was also trouble.

They'd come in his truck. Too easy to be noticed on their bikes in their cuts.

Not that anyone had any reason to have an eye on Rosalie. The dope run had gone down that weekend just like she told them it would. That meant no one had a clue she was feeding information to Chaos.

But neither he nor Snap had their cuts on and before he'd dropped Snapper off, they'd done a drive around the upscale pizza joint where Rosalie was a waitress and they'd spotted nothing.

So the face-to-face meet, which was a face-to-face meet for a reason, a reason that was all Snapper's, could go down.

High watched as Rosalie gave him a number of the reasons why this meeting was face to face. It was winding down and she was smiling up at Snap. She reached out and grabbed his hand, tugged on it playfully a couple of times, then said something to make him smile.

She then took off, aiming her eyes and lifting her hand to wave at High before she aimed another smile to Snapper, turned, and skip-walked, long hair swaying, tits bouncing, to the door of the restaurant.

High watched her go for a beat; then he turned his attention to Snapper and he watched his brother watch her go.

They were watching for two entirely different reasons.

Only when she was out of sight did Snapper move his way.

As his brother moved, High turned to his truck, opened the door, and angled in. He started her up as Snapper hauled his ass in the other side.

High backed out of the parking spot and took them on their way as Snap said, "They're already planning another run."

"You need to stop," High replied.

He did it quiet and careful. But he also did it strong.

"Say what?" Snapper asked.

"Get a burner phone. Give her the number. Talk through that. Face-to-face meets gotta stop, Snap," High advised.

"What the fuck are you talkin' about?"

High slowed for a light, stopped, and looked to his brother. "She's got a man."

He saw the hard hit Snapper's face.

Snap was a good-looking kid. Tall. Built. Blond. He was young but he had that look about him that all that was just gonna get better with age.

What he wasn't was Shy. Shy was lanky. Dark. Before Tab, Shy could charm the panties off a bitch in ten minutes flat and he didn't even have to know her before he did it. He'd been about good times. Getting off. Easy grins. Easier pussy.

High knew Rosalie's current man. He was lanky. He was dark. He'd been a player before Rosalie. He knew what he had in her, old lady through and through who would stick by his side through thick and thin, all that on top of a great ass, long legs, good tits, thick hair, and a pretty face. So he found Rosalie, his player days disappeared, and he held on.

Snap was intense. High knew his story and he never got where that intensity came from. Before Chaos, Snap didn't have it bad. He didn't have it good. He just had a life.

The intensity was always there, though. The brother paid attention, nothing escaped him. It reminded High a lot of Tack back in the day.

He'd shoot the shit. Have a laugh. Unlike Tack, Snapper was serious far more often than he wasn't and didn't talk much. But he did read a lot. In his room at the Compound, door open, him on his bed, eyes to a book.

It wasn't unheard of for a member of Chaos to read. But Snap did it maybe too much.

He might partake of easy pussy if the spirit moved him but he'd had a girl when he'd become a recruit. He'd split with her and got another one where fucking around became something more and it did it fast.

He'd also split with her.

He was now a free agent.

Rosalie was not.

"No reason to put your ass on the line, and more to the point, brother, *hers* by doin' shit face to face. Get a burner. Every time you see her puts her out there."

"No one knows shit about what she's doin' for Chaos," Snapper replied.

"They don't know but people talk. Could be innocent, one of the other waitresses in that joint sees her with you, sees her man, mentions you. It's not smart, Snap, and you need to put a stop to it."

"We'll meet somewhere no one can see us," Snapper returned. "She prefers face to face. Doesn't want to get overheard or have her man see shit on her phone he shouldn't see."

"Then she deletes her texts and calls," High told him.

"I hear you, High, but it's the way she wants it done."

"It's the way you want it done, brother," High returned quietly.

"She's stickin' her neck out for Chaos. We do it like she's comfortable doin' it."

"You're doin' it 'cause she's pretty, she smiles at you, and you're into her."

"It's not that," Snapper bit out.

High saw traffic moving around him, looked back to see the light was green, and moved his foot to the gas pedal, accelerating.

He did this speaking.

"Rule between brothers but that rule extends between bikers and you know it. Pussy's claimed, pussy is *claimed*. You do not go there."

"Told you it's not about that," Snapper replied.

"Got years on you, brother, and I'm not blind. Not sayin' this shit to piss you off. Sayin' it to save you a load of hurt. She's into her man. She's riskin' a lot to get him clean. You're not in that."

"Straight up and no offense, High, but her man is weak," Snap returned.

High's jaw got hard at his words because they spoke to what Snap thought of High because back in the day High had once been like Rosalie's boyfriend, riding that edge, going for the high, doing this with and without his Rosalie.

But fortunately, Snapper wasn't done.

"The no offense part is the fact that the Bounties know Chaos history. They know the shit they're gettin' into is fucked up and they know just how that shit can fuck up a club because it did that to Chaos. And they're gettin' into it. I know a lot of those brothers don't like it but they sit a table just like us.

Gavel doesn't drop until a decision is voted, so they're votin' that shit in. Rosalie doesn't know how her man is voting. But he's doin' that shit and that says a lot."

"Club goes a way, you're a brother, you go that way," High pointed out.

Snapper didn't say anything and High knew why.

Because that was the straight-up truth.

High kept going.

"Tack wanted me in with you to take your back but more, to take Rosalie's. That's my focus. Keepin' her safe while she does Chaos a good turn. You gotta be all in on that and you gotta be that *for her*. It isn't about what she's doin' for the Club or what she makes you feel when you're with her. It's about her. And that's the way of it, brother. She's yours or she's not, she's a woman and you're any kind of man, you look out for her every way you can."

High turned on his signal and slowed to make a turn as Snapper kept silent.

He'd made the turn, they were cruising, and High said no more. His point had been made. Snap didn't take it, for Rosalie, High would have no choice but to inform the brothers and Snapper would be removed from her detail.

"I'll get a burner," Snap muttered.

High drew in a breath and let it out slowly.

Then he just drove.

*   *   *

After High parked at the Compound, Snap didn't waste time jumping from the truck and taking off.

High watched him as he angled out, but he looked toward the back of the store when he heard Hound call his name.

"Man inside lookin' for you," Hound said, raising a hand, thumb extended to indicate over his shoulder and into the store.

High lifted his chin, slammed his door, and hit the locks.

"Know him?" he asked.

"Nope," Hound answered.

Hound headed to the garage.

High headed to the store.

He went in, turned right to head up an aisle to the cash register at the front but stopped two aisles in when he saw Dot's husband, Alan, looking at the fan belts.

He sighed.

Then he moved down that aisle toward Millie's brother-in-law. Alan caught sight of his movement and gave his attention to High, doing this, turning full body to face him.

High stopped a few feet away.

"Alan," he greeted.

He didn't get a greeting back.

"Dot says you're movin' into Millie's," he stated.

"Not doin' it," High told him. "Did it. I'm in."

He watched Alan's mouth get tight before he noted, "Movin' real fuckin' fast, man."

"May seem that way to you. Me, waitin' twenty years to have her back seems real fuckin' slow," High replied.

High watched as something changed about Alan and he watched it knowing he wasn't going to like the change.

Then the man opened his mouth and proved High right.

"Pretty lucky for you, you walk away from your family, find yourself livin' in an RV, you also find an ex who's still hung up on you. An ex with a sweet crib. And you got her back a coupla days and your clothes are in her closet."

High stood there, motionless except to take in a deep breath.

Then, quietly, he returned, "Could buy my girls a house, that bein' *all* my girls, my two babies and Millie, layin' cash down on somethin' that'd make Millie's pad look ghetto. Could do that, upgrade my truck, buy another bike, and, bud, I already got three, and do that in cash too. Do all that and take Millie on a five-star trip back to Paris, give her the luxury. Do all that and not even touch my girls' college funds. You didn't know any a' that shit. I get that. Now you do."

"You could buy your girls a pad, why're you livin' in an RV?" Alan shot back.

"You got kids," High said. "Hope like fuck you and Dot stay strong. Shit happens and you don't and you gotta put your kids through a split, you don't just rent any place where they gotta lay their heads. You give 'em a home. You find the right one. I looked. Didn't find it. While doin' that, found Millie. Her place is nice. Not my scene but it's hers, she loves it. So that's where we are. And when I have my other two girls, that's where we'll all be."

"Got all the answers," Alan clipped irritably.

"Got 'em because there are answers," High replied.

The man crossed his arms on his chest. "Right. That's good. 'Cause, see, I need more answers. You got a history, man. In that history, it's clear you got no problem walkin' away from things that matter. Walked away from Millie. Walked away from your family. History like that repeats itself and you're livin' proof of that shit."

High again stood silent and motionless to give himself time to talk himself out of laying the hurt on Dot's old man.

When he found control, he spoke.

"You look at me, you know the man I am 'cause I reckon you see yourself in me. So you know I'm not a big fan of explainin' myself to anyone and sure as fuck not a man who's comin' at me like you're doin'. But you mean somethin' to Millie and you're gonna be in my life for a long time so I'm givin' you this respect. Once. Just once, Alan. Not fuckin' with you. You keep comin' at me like this, it's not gonna be good."

Alan's eyebrows went up. "So now you're threatening me?"

High shook his head. "Bud, you walked into my store on my turf and came at me with this shit. I pulled up the patience and shared where I was at. I get this is new for you. I get you're lookin' after Millie, which is another reason why I'm eatin' your shit. What you gotta get is that your wife and Millie's girls are all down with me bein' back. You give me a shot, I'll show you it's good for you to be down with that too. But advice. Look around at how the people who matter to Millie, who know the *real* history, are behaving. And do it bein' careful. 'Cause not only am I not gonna take more of your shit, I got a job of it bringin' Millie back to happy and I'm not lettin' anyone fuck with that. Not even you."

"Can't say you're impressin' me," Alan fired back. "Me askin' pertinent questions and you makin' threats."

High took a step toward him and it said a lot the man didn't move a muscle.

"You've got no fuckin' clue," he stated low.

"I got a clue, Logan," the man returned. "I heard everything Millie said about what you did to her when you two got back into each other's lives. No decent man treats a woman like that."

"You got no fuckin' clue," High repeated.

"Know we nearly lost her to your shit." He lifted up his brows again. "She does somethin' where you feel she needs taught another lesson, what's she gonna get?"

"You know, you turn the tables, you *know* this shit isn't any of your business."

"You're wrong," he spat, losing it. "Millie's absolutely my business. Been in my life for twelve years, Logan. Longer than you had her. Through that time, I watched her exist. Saw the mess you and *your brothers* made of her before she went to Paris. *You* turn the tables, man, and tell me again it isn't my business."

It sucked, but the man had a point.

"She kept comin' back for more," High told him through gritted teeth.

"Way I heard it, *you* kept comin' back to give her more."

"And she took it. Took it. Held on tight. And didn't let go."

Alan shut his mouth.

And there was High's point.

"It would suck, what you got with Dot isn't what I feel for Millie. What Millie gives back to me," High said. "I'd want that for Dottie, to have something like that. She's a damn fine woman. She deserves that beauty. I'll tell it to you straight, when I saw Millie again, I had no idea the heartbreak my girl's been dealin' with for twenty years. What she sacrificed to give me all I got. But even if that shit wasn't there, I wouldn't care. The dance we danced when we hooked up again was fucked right the hell up. But it was a dance we had to dance. A dance that led us outta hell and back to beauty. Lotta folks work the hurt out a lotta ways. Even if Millie didn't have the best reason in the world to get shot of me twenty years ago, I'd be back in her bed 'cause that's what we got. That's what we've always had. That's what we been missin'. And older now, a fuckuva lot smarter, we know not to let it go."

High stopped talking and Alan didn't start.

So High kept going.

"Straight up, you got this kinda love for my girl, I dig that. But she's walked through fire, man. That's done for her. You don't like my threats, don't be a threat to what I gotta build for my woman."

Alan held his gaze steady.

Then he looked to the fan belts.

High leveled his tone when he spoke again.

"Millie's the kinda woman who deserves everything in life but life chose to fuck her and not give her the one thing she wanted most. Only way she can get even a little of that is through your kids and through mine."

Alan looked back to him.

High went on, "I know you don't like this now but we're a team. We got a goal we gotta see to the rest of our lives. We both love Millie and we both got the job to find a way to give her what she deserves. You're not with me on that, bud, that's your problem. But I'm not gonna let you make it Millie's. You don't like me. *Pretend*. But I got a big job ahead of me. I'm not expendin' a lot of effort on you."

When Alan didn't say anything, High decided he was done. So he made his way around the man and moved toward the front of the store.

He was five feet beyond him when Alan called, "Logan."

High turned around.

"Millie calls me that. Dottie calls me that," High stated. "I'm High to you. You don't get that, man, I don't give a fuck. Logan is theirs. It ain't yours."

Alan looked confused for a beat before he powered past it and focused, muttering, "Whatever." Then, louder, like a command, "Be real."

"I'm real," High returned.

Alan again held his gaze steady and High could barely hear him when he repeated, "For Millie, for God's sake, be real."

He said nothing else and didn't give High a chance to reply before he turned and walked away.

* * *

At five oh five that night, High found himself leaning against his truck again.

He was this way outside Deb's work.

He'd called her and asked her for fifteen minutes after work to have a chat about Zadie.

When he'd done that, she'd replied, "Yeah. Figured Zade didn't take this weekend too great."

She said no more and agreed to meet.

High did not want to be there. It was the last place he wanted to be. The first place he wanted to be was at Millie's waiting for her to come out in her sweater dress.

But their reservation wasn't until seven.

He had time to do this and he had to do this.

So he was there, doing it.

He watched as Deb walked out, plastic lunch bag in her hand that she undoubtedly packed with carrot sticks, apple slices, and other shit that was good for you. Purse on her shoulder that he knew cost over five hundred dollars because he saw it on the credit card statement—handbags, dyeing her hair, and buying expensive makeup at department stores the only girl weaknesses she had.

Other than that, she was in jeans, a maroon button-down that had her company's insignia over the breast pocket, her hair in a ponytail, her face made up like she did it for work: mascara, foundation, some blush, and done.

It'd help if she found a man. Zadie would begin to catch on if his ex also moved on.

He suspected she might go to a bar and hook up.

Other than that, she'd never bother.

"Hey," she greeted as she got to him at his truck that was parked next to her car.

"Hey," he replied. "Thanks for the time."

She nodded.

"Won't take a lot of it," he told her. "But gotta share with you that Zadie was not good with meetin' Millie."

"I figured that," she said. "She bitched about it a lot since you took them to pizza at Bonnie Brae." She threw out a hand. "Sorry. I probably should have warned you about that."

"She warned me at the time seein' as she wasn't pleased about it then and she's Zadie. She had no problem communicatin' that. I warned Millie but I didn't know where she'd take what she was feelin'. Where it took her was pretty much dumpin' her full Sprite in Millie's lap even though we hadn't even ordered dinner at the Spaghetti Factory."

He watched Deb's eyes get big and ticked.

"You're kidding me," she snapped.

"Wish I was," he told her. "Consequences of that were we

left without dinner. She hid the shit she did the next day and Millie didn't share what it was. But got it outta her that Zadie said some things to her. Millie canceled plans because she thought the girls could use a break. She was right. I was pushin' too fast, too soon. But I had a chat with them this mornin', laid some things out about Millie and my history, and nothin' sunk in with Zadie. She was a snot to Millie and she was a snot to me."

Deb tipped her head to the side and asked with mild curiosity, "What's your history with Millie?"

It struck him then he'd never given her that.

And it struck him then, since he hadn't, even in the little he knew they had, how little they'd actually had. He didn't dig deep with her. She didn't dig deep with him.

He and Millie had talked all the time. It wasn't just good times and good fucking. She knew everything about his life. His thoughts about it. His feelings about it. And she'd given the same.

He gave none of that to Deb.

And he got none of it back.

"We were together, my early twenties, and we were together awhile," he explained. "We both wanted a family and were gonna start when she finished school. We started. Or we tried to start. She found out she couldn't have kids. Instead of tellin' me that, she dumped me so I could have them."

Deb straightened her head and he saw understanding wash through her features.

She knew how much he loved his girls. She knew how tight he was with all the family he had. Fuck, it was him who opened the negotiations that led to them having Zadie.

And he reckoned the only things in her life she truly wanted, truly loved, were their girls.

"Oh, High," she whispered.

Yeah, she understood.

"It sucked. We reconnected, wasn't pretty 'cause I was in deep with her and didn't take it real good when she cut me out.

Eventually found out why she got shot of me. We worked it out. But she made a sacrifice for me that I get 'cause if I was in her shoes back then, I'd make the same one. That's over now and we're movin' on. I just need the girls to move on with me."

"I'm not trying to be a bitch, really I'm not, when I say that the way Zadie's being has a good deal to do with you. You're too soft on her, High."

"That's why we're talkin'," he stated. "'Cause I got that right in my face this weekend. Millie got more of it. And I gotta put a stop to it. Zadie's gonna react, you're gonna hear it, likely see it and have to put up with it. I realize it's totally uncool, me standin' here askin' you this shit, but I got three girls in my life who I want to get along, so gotta do it. And that's me askin' you to take my back with this."

Her brows snapped together and she said, "Of course, High. God, you don't even have to ask. It's not like I don't want you to be happy."

He had no fucking clue what Deb wanted second to second, day to day or for her life.

But he was shocked as shit she wanted him to be happy.

It wasn't that she'd want him to suffer.

It was just that he didn't think she gave much of a shit.

"Means a lot, Deb," he muttered.

"You want me to talk to her?" she asked.

"Think she should sit on what she's done and what she knows. Cleo is Cleo. She's on board. Maybe she'll have a word."

Deb made a face that said it all.

No one had much effect on Zadie when she wanted something, not even her big sister.

He grinned. "Worth it to hope."

He watched Deb's lips curl up slightly.

He continued, "Just want you to be aware so you aren't blindsided by any of her shit. And if she starts bitchin'..." He shook his head. "Whatever you could do would be appreciated."

"I'll keep an eye and we'll have a chat if she gets bad," Deb offered.

"Like I said, whatever would be appreciated."

She nodded.

Great.

That was done.

"Leave you alone to get back to our girls," he muttered, pushing away from the truck.

"Right. Talk to you later, High," she said, starting to move to round the hood of her car to get to the driver's side door.

"Deb," he called.

She stopped and looked back at him.

"Hope you know, want you to be happy too," he told her.

"I know that," she replied.

He was mildly curious when he asked, "Got any clue what'd do that?"

"Got it," she told him. "Good job that pays well and is only a headache on occasion. Two good girls, though one can be a pain in the ass, but that's usually only on occasion too. Really all I need, you know?"

He didn't know.

Getting woken up with a phenomenal blowjob.

Bickering about alarm clocks.

Kittens underfoot.

Watching TV you don't give a shit about just to make someone you love happy.

Looking forward to what that someone you love was going to wear that day because you know it'll turn you on.

Knowing if you showed at her office, no matter who she was talking to on the phone, she'd get off it so she could get her arms around you and you could put your mouth on hers.

Working for a smile.

Then earning it.

No, he didn't fucking know.

Not at all.

"Would want more for you, Deb," he said gently, and had to stop his chin jerking back when he watched her face get soft.

"Some people aren't built like others, High. It's sweet that you'd want that for me. You're a good man. I think that's why we worked for as long as we did. But I'm just not built like that." She held his eyes and her lips curved up slightly again. "Though, I'm glad, since you are, you finally got what you needed."

"You're a good woman, too, Deb," he told her because she was.

And she was right.

That was why they'd worked for as long as they did.

And that was why they'd had to end it before they stopped working.

"I'd like to meet Millie one day," she replied.

"We'll get on that as soon as Zadie gets her shit together."

She nodded. "That'd be good."

"It would," he agreed, turning to his truck. "Now be safe gettin' home."

"Always am."

Without another word to her, High got in his truck, started her up, but idled until Deb was in, buckled up, and on her way.

Then he pulled out of his spot and followed her to the exit of the parking lot.

She turned left.

High turned right.

*   *   *

"Low," she whispered, riding him hard.

He had her on her knees, torso up. He was behind her, his dick was buried inside her, his hand curved around her tit, finger and thumb pinching and pulling, and he had her toy to her clit.

She was *gone*.

Part of this was because she'd tortured him through a fat

shrimp appetizer, a big steak dinner, and a fucking dessert, all of this wearing a clingy sweater dress that had the added temptation of having a wide collar that fell off one, the other, or both her shoulders.

So when he got her home, he'd wasted no time getting her hot, then making her hotter as he turned her over his thighs at the side of her bed, yanked up her skirt, and dove in.

He toyed with her watching her ass move, feeling her squirm, listening to her whimper then beg, and doing this with her laid out for him, another pair of thigh-highs and her brown high-heeled boots a bonus to the goodness.

Only when she'd begged had he torn off her clothes, bumping up against her repeatedly as she tore off his. He grabbed her toy and positioned her to get the rest.

And there they were and if she didn't get *there*, things would get messy.

Lips to her neck watching her tits bounce as she drove herself down on his dick, he murmured, "Get yourself there, baby."

"Low," she whimpered, her hands moving high and low to wrap around his wrists tight.

"Take it and get yourself there," he growled, needing her to do that in about two seconds or he'd be spent and need to use just her toy to take her there.

She bucked harder, moaning, "*Oh my God.*"

Fuck.

She was killing him.

"Millie—"

"*Oh my God,*" she breathed, letting go of his wrist at her tit and reaching back to clamp her hand in his hair as she drove down hard and started grinding.

Finally, she was coming.

Thank Christ.

He cupped her tit, tossed the toy, wrapped his arm around

her belly, and held her steady to power up into her until he found it, grunting his orgasm into her neck.

He felt her breath even as his own grew steady.

Then he growled, "New rule. No fuckin' toy when I'm away from you."

She released his hair. "What?"

He pulled his face out of her neck and looked at her profile. "You made yourself come. Meant you could take more and take it longer. Thought my dick was gonna explode waitin' for you to come."

She twisted to look at him.

"Is that a problem?" she asked.

"You finish before me, Millie," he answered with information she fucking well knew.

She grinned. "It isn't a cardinal rule."

He raised his brows. "It's not?"

She looked to his brows, then back to his eyes, hers were dancing. "It's not my fault you're so hot, generally, but also being that in bed so I have to take care of business at the very thought of you if you're away."

"Abstain."

She giggled.

He did not.

She lifted a hand to stroke his cheek, whispering playfully, "You can handle it."

She gasped as he pulled her off his cock, turned her, put her in bed on her back, and followed her down, giving her a good amount of his weight.

"How playful you feelin', beautiful?" he asked quietly.

"I may," she kept whispering, "need a nap before I get more playful."

He slid a hand down her side, in, and used his fingertips to stroke the skin of where her panty line at her front would be if she was wearing panties.

"Sure about that?"

Her whisper was breathy when she replied, "I might be coaxed into continuing to be playful."

He hid his grin by kissing her.

After he finished kissing her, he started doing other things to her.

He didn't stop even when, after he'd just started, she turned her head and said in his ear, "So glad you're home, Snooks."

That earned her another kiss.

As well as other things.

Which meant he was glad he was home too.

But he'd already felt that earlier when he walked in her back door and Chief had come sailing across the floor and hit his boot.

And then she'd walked out in her phenomenal dress.

But mostly it was after she did that.

Which was when she'd smiled.

CHAPTER TWENTY

Anything We Could

Millie

THE DOORBELL RANG and I opened my eyes.

"Fuck," Logan said from behind me right before he rolled away and I felt him continue to roll as he rolled out of bed.

I twisted his way and peered at him through the predawn dark.

"Someone's at the door," I informed him of something he obviously knew, considering he was at the side of the bed pulling on his boxer briefs.

"Yeah," he muttered.

I looked to the (new) alarm clock, then back to him. "At six in the morning."

Due to Logan's extreme dislike of alarm clocks, and his contribution to my morning (and household) routine, I'd adjusted the alarm so it didn't wake us up before six but at six thirty.

With Logan making coffee, bringing me coffee, bringing me cereal or toasted, schmeared bagels, feeding and watering the cats and going out to jack up the thermostat in my studio and making coffee there, I had more time in the morning.

Not to mention doing other things that just gave me more time in my day. Like taking out the trash, getting in the groceries (he had no aversion to the grocery store and my groaning fridge and cupboards laid testimony to this fact), loading and emptying the dishwasher, nabbing my mail (both personal and office), and dropping it at a post box (even going to the post office if something needed special treatment).

It was now the Thursday after Logan's weekend with his girls. He and I were getting into a rhythm. And this was part of our rhythm.

A happy part.

But there was more.

Like Logan noticing the light switch that turned on the lights to the kitchen by the living room didn't quite catch unless you had the patience to flip it half a dozen times. So he'd gone to his RV, collected his box of tools, brought it back, opened the plate, and fixed the switch (then left his tools in my laundry room).

Like Logan noticing the spray function on my kitchen faucet didn't work right. So he'd fiddled with it for a while, couldn't fix it, then went out and bought a new faucet (that was not the same as the old one but it was even more awesome).

When he got back with the faucet, he didn't screw around. Right then, he installed it.

These were things I'd lived with. Things I'd repeatedly told myself I was going to mention to Alan and ask him to fix or find a handyman to fix them. Things I always forgot to bother with then kicked myself when they came to my attention and annoyed me because I hadn't bothered with them.

Things Logan noted weren't working and he immediately fixed them.

In ways that I hadn't noticed, life was kind of a bummer, having to do these things myself, I didn't miss how the additional ways having Logan back made life *not* a bummer.

And it was strange, since back when we were together he didn't do any of this stuff. He might take out the trash (if I asked). He might help me unload the dishwasher or do the dishes (if I asked). But mostly, I took care of him.

He took care of me, but not in those ways.

Now he was taking care of me in those ways.

There was something about this that made weird mix in with the wonderful because I knew that he was probably like this because when we used to be together, we were young and neither of us knew any better. We'd found our way, a way that worked, but maybe, looking back, it wasn't the right way.

He'd learned to be that way through Deb and having a family.

You grew up, you grew smart, you had a partner, you made babies, you pitched in.

I couldn't help but wonder if I'd had him all that time, since we couldn't have a family of our own, if he'd have learned all this or if he'd have just gone on letting me take care of him (which might end up being a pain in the ass).

In other words, I wondered if I had Deb (and the girls) to thank.

In the end, what I came up with was the fact that life as a

whole mixed weird with wonderful because I'd never know the answers to my questions. I just knew I had that new part of Logan now, no matter how he learned it, no matter that I likely did have Deb (and the girls) to thank. It just was.

And it was mine.

"Demolition crew."

When Logan spoke, I jerked out of my thoughts and looked to him to see he had his jeans up and was bent to nab his thermal off the floor.

"Demolition crew?" I asked.

He was pulling on his shirt while walking swiftly around the bed. "Take down your garage."

Oh.

Right.

He'd mentioned that but I'd forgotten it was today.

I'd forgotten because the girls were coming that night for dinner. I was making beef Stroganoff. And I was again a little nervous.

Just in time, I turned my head so when Logan bent in to give me a peck, I got it on my lips before the doorbell rang again and he was off to go answer it.

I reached out, turned on a light, and swung my legs off the side of the bed.

I was brushing, wondering how my neighbors were going to feel about a demolition crew starting work at six in the morning, when Logan walked into the bathroom.

"Coffee started. Cats fed. They're movin' their shit out back. Goin' back there to make sure they know what they're doin'," he informed me.

I nodded.

He looked me top to toe to eyes, taking in my jammies, my bedhead, and the sonic toothbrush in my mouth.

"Only bitch on the planet who can brush her teeth and make me wanna fuck her while she's doin' it," he remarked.

I narrowed my eyes, pulled my toothbrush out of my mouth—the movement of the head splattering spit, paste, and foam everywhere—and snapped a frothy, "Don't call me a bitch."

He grinned like I was highly amusing and disappeared.

I shoved my brush back into my mouth, looked back into the mirror, stopped scowling, and kept brushing but did it grinning.

* * *

The door to my studio opened and the alarm didn't sound.

It didn't sound because Logan was on the premises, making sure the demolition crew did what he was paying them to do but also keeping his eye on me.

So the only sound I got when Logan opened the door and stuck his head in was, "Babe."

"Yeah?" I asked.

"Got a second?"

I didn't. I had to leave in fifteen minutes to meet a corporate client, a law firm that did three to four parties a year, all with me, and they were gearing up for their annual holiday party.

"Sure," I said, rolling my chair back and getting up.

As I walked his way, Logan treated me to another appreciative top to toe glance, cementing what was already firm in my mind.

He didn't need halter tops and cutoff shorts.

He just needed me.

I was already feeling warm and happy inside when I got close and he reached out, took my hand, and pulled me out into the chill, something that incongruously made me feel warmer.

"You gonna be okay without a jacket?" he asked as he shut the door.

No way I could get a chill hand in hand with Logan.

And anyway, I had on a sweater. I'd be okay.

I nodded.

Logan kept hold of my hand as he walked me through my courtyard to the gate to the backyard.

The minute we were through the gate and moving across the bricked patio toward the steps that led us down the terraced backyard to the lower bricked patio, I saw over the fence at the end of the yard that the garage was gone.

As I saw it, I also marveled at the change it made.

It had been an eyesore. I'd always planned to knock it down and put a decent garage there so I didn't have to scrape my windshield in the winter.

Currently I parked in the courtyard even though, beside the garage, I had a parking space in the back and parking in the courtyard messed with the vision of the courtyard, one that included (eventually) getting a fountain. But parking way out back just never seemed safe, walking through my dark backyard to get to my house. Not to mention, lugging groceries would be a pain.

Nevertheless, scraping windshields in the Colorado cold was more of a pain, so I'd wanted a garage. It was the last big project and I hadn't done it because any project I did I did paying cash and I hadn't saved enough to put in the garage.

Seeing the dilapidated old garage gone, I realized I should have used what I'd already saved just to demolish it. The absence of the garage made the entire yard look better.

Logan led me out the back gate to the large, cleared, and tidied space at the edge of my property and I couldn't help but to smile.

They'd showed at six. They'd set up. They'd demolished. They'd carted off the remains. And it wasn't even eleven o'clock.

"They're fast," I noted, looking up at Logan, who was still holding my hand warm in his.

"Yeah," he murmured, glancing around. His gaze came to me. "Now, Millie, you're cool with it, gonna grade this, gravel it, then build a fence around the perimeter."

He lifted the hand not holding mine to indicate the entire area. An area that to one side my neighbors had a relatively new fence leading to the very edge of their property line, and on the other side, my neighbors had a shabby fence also leading to their property line.

"Big doors to the alley," Logan continued. He turned us to the back fence to my property. "Build a new fence there, coupla feet higher. Swing my RV in here. Fence higher at the back, won't see the RV from the yard. Fence around the RV, keeps it safer. Motion sensor lights out here, makes it even safer. Put smaller gates in at the side." He pointed. "Easy access to the alley and the Dumpsters."

Although he clearly had it all thought out, and his vision was a good vision, one could say I didn't like this.

Logan's RV was huge. It'd take up the entire space.

Which meant I wouldn't get my garage, and more importantly, I wouldn't eventually be able to avoid scraping my windshields.

"You're not down with that?" he asked.

I looked up to him. "No. It's cool."

His hand gave mine a squeeze. "You're not down with that," he stated.

I smiled at him. "No, really, I'm cool."

"Babe," he said.

"What?" I asked when he didn't continue.

"You're not down with that," he repeated.

I shook my head and replied, "It's not that. It's just that I wanted to put a garage out here, a new one. A nice one. One with an opener and one that would mean ice scraping would be history. But you need a safe place for your RV. I'm used to parking in the courtyard. And a new garage would mean putting in motion sensor lights everywhere so I didn't kill myself in the dark getting up to the house. That's a big project and a lot of money. So," I shrugged, "whatever. I like your vision. It's all good."

He studied me a second, then tugged on my hand, leading me back through the gate but stopping us on the lower patio.

He looked around. He did it holding my hand but he did it for a long time.

I didn't know what was on his mind. I wanted to know what was on his mind but I also had a meeting.

So I needed to step this up.

"Low," I called his attention to me.

When I got it, he declared, "We got a problem."

I was confused.

"What? How?"

He turned us to the back fence. "'Cause if we move that fence in to give you room for your garage and me room to pull in the RV nose-first at the side, you lose at least half this patio, probably more." He pointed to the brick beneath our feet. Then he turned us to the house. "And we gotta look at building on two rooms. We do that, not only gonna eat up some of your courtyard, also gonna eat up some of that top patio."

This also didn't fill me with glee.

To give his daughters their own rooms and the house a dining room meant I'd lose even more of the vision I had for my house that I'd nurtured and fed for eleven years.

That would suck.

Not allowing Logan to have what he needed for himself and his daughters would suck more.

"So grade the back and put the RV in as you planned," I decided.

He looked down at me. "Means you don't get your garage."

"I've lived without it since I've lived here," I told him. "I can continue to live without it."

His hand tightened in mine. "Millie—"

I cut him off. "Alternate scenarios are to extend the pergola over the courtyard or fully roof it so we can park under that. We'd avoid snow on our vehicles even if we didn't avoid ice."

This I didn't like either unless carefully designed. Not carefully designed, it'd look ugly. And that was not only my view out the kitchen window but out the studio windows as well.

"Or," I went on, "we can make the courtyard into the backyard space. Put in a fountain. Some furniture. Clients can park out front or in the drive. And we can eat up this patio for the garage and your RV space because we'd still have our outside area and it'd be closer to the house."

"May need part of the courtyard for the dining room and bedroom, beautiful," Logan reminded me.

I lifted my shoulders and gave it all.

"So, we grade the back, put your RV there, and when it gets to the point where you have the girls more often, we move to a new house."

Logan's hand tightened in mine again, doing this firm, and it felt like it was automatic.

This reaction confused me too.

I used his name to ask my question. "Logan?"

"You made this yours. You dig it. Not gonna make you move," he said.

He was right. I liked that he cared about that for me because I cared about it too.

However.

"It's just a house."

"You made it yours, Millie."

"So I'll make another house mine, actually *ours*. And that's probably good. My house is girlie. I think Cleo and Zadie dig it, even though Zadie wouldn't admit that now. But that doesn't negate the fact that a man will be living with us and we have to have a mind to that. Though," I carried on quickly, "I will say now, no more fixer-uppers. Even if it takes us two years, we find something right for all of us and that right will be an as-is right. Not a do-a-load-of-work-on-it-for-years right. I've been there done that got the T-shirt with the renovation thing and I use the T-shirt as a dust cloth because the results were spectacular but the road to that was a pain in my ass. Not to mention super-freaking-expensive."

He stared down at me a beat, the look in his eyes one I couldn't read.

Right before I was going to ask what was up with him, I found my mouth engaged in doing something else. Namely him plundering it with his tongue.

I held on tight, my arms around his shoulders, my body pressed to his, his arms snug around me, and felt the gratitude (and other things) he communicated through his kiss.

Upcoming meeting I was soon to be late for or not, I was disappointed when it ended.

But it ended and it ended on an extremely high note when he said immediately after, "Love you, Millie."

"Love you too, Snooks," I breathed.

He rested his forehead on mine a second before he lifted a bit away. "Grade the back for now, build the fence. Cost won't be too high, we figure somethin' out about stayin' at your pad and change our minds and hafta tear the fence down to build a garage. Yeah?"

I nodded.

"No answer now," he said. "But want you thinkin' on it. When you got an answer, you give it to me straight up, no worries about my reaction. But you built somethin' beautiful here, babe." He jerked his head toward my house. "If you're gonna have a problem lettin' that go—"

"Logan," I interrupted him. "The only problem I'll have is if I don't have you wherever it is I am." I pressed closer and dipped my voice quieter. "Like I said. It's just a house. Do I love it?" I asked, then answered myself. "Yes. But it's an *it*. You're *you*. You're back so that means my home is where you are. It's that simple and that's your answer. I don't have to think about it for even a second."

I got done with my speech and got another kiss. This was longer, hotter, harder and it spoke of gratitude and a lot of other things, *lots* of them, and they were all good.

Unfortunately, when he broke it that time, I had to share, "I've got a meeting, Snook'ums."

"Right," he muttered, staring at my mole.

"Low," I called.

He looked to my eyes.

"Sort out the back. Get your RV here. All that's you. *Really* come home," I ordered.

"Fuck," he growled. "You don't quit the sweet, you ain't gonna be late for your meeting. You're not gonna make it."

I grinned. "Okay, then let me go so I don't lose a client and perhaps my ability to pay for more staff so I can have more time for you."

"I let you go, gotta watch your ass in that skirt walkin' up to your studio," he returned.

I grinned again but on the inside.

"You really do have sex on the brain," I noted.

"Think you missed it, Millie, but haven't fucked you yet today."

I hadn't missed it.

"I think that means tonight's gonna be fun," I replied.

He shook his head but did it with lips curled up.

"Are you gonna let me go?" I asked.

"No," he answered, even as he did what he said he wasn't going to do. "Never. Not ever, babe." His eyes warmed. "But I'll let you go to your meeting."

Now *he* was being sweet.

"No fair. Now *I* wanna jump *you*."

His eyes stayed warm but his smile was cocky.

This could go on all day. And in order to be able to jump him whenever I felt like it (eventually), I needed Justine on board.

Which meant I needed my client.

So I reached to his thermal, grabbed a fistful, and pulled him to me. I got up on toes to press my lips hard to his and then shifted away.

"Later, Snooks," I whispered.

"Later, baby," he whispered back.

I grinned at him and let him go.

Then I walked away. Even in a hurry, I did it slow so I could give him a show because I knew my man was watching and I was his old lady.

We gave like that.

We gave anything we could.

*   *   *

It was that evening and I was walking on clouds because it was going *great*.

Logan had picked the girls up from dance practice on Tuesday and taken them out to dinner, just him and them. Other than that, it had been only phone calls.

But having them there now, I noticed that since our weekend, something had changed.

They'd arrived at my house that night, Logan picking them up from their mother's, and although Zadie was a bit moody and uncommunicative, Cleo was not.

There had been barriers before between Cleo and me. She'd been the way she was with me solely to get the approval of her father.

I knew this now because those barriers were eroding.

Through chitchat while cooking, horsing about, and eating beef Stroganoff at my bar, Cleo introduced me to the real Cleo.

And she was a love.

Sure, she adored her father and wanted his approval.

But when it wasn't something she was working at, when it

was just a natural part of her, coupling that with Logan's reaction to it, it was sweet to the point it was downright cute.

So cute it gave a happy glow that I was beside myself with glee I got to bask in it.

Though it was more.

She was unreservedly delighted when I let her give fresh food to the cats. When I asked about dance, she'd timidly (then with my encouragement and compliments, not so timidly) showed me some of the moves they were rehearsing for their routine, so damned adorable doing this in my kitchen, I felt even more glow warming me to my bones.

And she didn't hide how much she liked my house and the studio when I took them on a guided tour of both after the dinner dishes were done, saying to me shyly while standing in the guestroom, "It'll be fun when we get to sleep over, Millie."

More glow.

Further adding to this goodness, it seemed that as all this went on, Zadie was studying it, watching Cleo come out of her shell and my reaction to it. And I hoped, in watching, that she'd find she'd want to start building something like that with me too.

Now things were winding down. We were going to hang in front of the TV with a batch of cupcakes from Tessa's Bakery that I'd picked up on the way back from my meeting. We were going to do something normal that a family would do at the end of the day before Logan had to take them back to their mom's.

The girls were selecting seats (Zadie, not surprisingly, pulling a princess and getting the cuddle chair, Cleo, not suffering in getting the love seat) and Logan had claimed his, the corner of the couch.

He also claimed me. His hand catching mine, he was pulling me down beside him when I watched Poem struggle up into the love seat with Cleo, unable to jump that height, so she used her claws.

Seeing that, I put tension in my arm to resist Logan's pull and looked around, asking, "Anyone seen Chief?"

I asked this because I hadn't. Not since Cleo gave them fresh food before we sat down for dinner.

Chief and Poem had settled into their new abode, putting up with me loving on them, enjoying me playing with them, and were currently in the throes of figuring out who ruled the roost.

This meant a lot of kitty wrestling.

However, I'd noticed that Chief was winning. Poem was starting to hang back and wait to see where Chief would claim before she decided to challenge his claim or allow it.

It was rare when they weren't both around, jockeying for position.

Rare as in, it never happened.

But Chief was nowhere to be seen.

"Haven't seen him, babe," Logan muttered.

I looked to Cleo, who had a hand stretched to a skittish Poem but her eyes to me. "I haven't either."

"Think he went outside when we went to your office," Zadie stated, and my eyes shot to her, my blood freezing in my veins.

"What?" I whispered.

She stared at me and I was way too freaked to see anything but confusion in her face. "Not sure but I think I saw him wander outside when we went out—"

I tore my hand from Logan's and raced to the back door, throwing it open and sprinting outside.

It was cold. It was dark.

And my Chief was tiny.

They were not going to be outside cats and not because they cost a fortune and had bushy coats that were hard enough to keep tamed as indoor cats and this would be impossible if they went outdoors.

But because I'd read that indoor cats lived longer than outdoor cats. *Way* longer. Like ... *years.*

Further, they'd showed not the first sign of being interested in the outdoors or being bored with the playroom of a house they'd already been given.

So they were good indoors, which was where they were going to stay.

But now Chief had gotten out. A baby, tiny, anything could happen to him. He could get lost. He could be attacked and stand no chance. Not even if a bird swooped down.

Oh God.

God.

How had I not noticed him getting out?

"Chief," I called, my eyes darting around as I quickly roamed the courtyard. "Come on, baby. You out here? Chief?"

"Chief." I heard Cleo call. "Here kitty-kitty. Here Chiefy-Chiefy."

I then heard the gate to the backyard open and looked that way to see Logan prowl through it with a flashlight.

"Chief!" I cried, moving toward the studio. "Come here, kitty. Come to Momma, baby."

Cleo called. I called. I felt and saw her searching with me. I skirted the entirety of the outside of the studio. Cleo and I then moved down the drive and searched the front of the house. Cleo was edging toward my neighbor's yard when I headed the opposite way and saw Logan stalking down the drive.

I raced to him.

"Nothing?" I asked, my voice pitched high with panic.

He looked toward his daughter. "Clee-Clee. Come back with me."

I grabbed onto his thermal for the second time that day but in an entirely different way.

When I got his attention, I cried frantically, "Did you find something?"

"Open space up here, baby," he said gently. "More hiding places back there. Need two sets of eyes. You keep lookin' up here." He glanced around. "Where's Zadie? She not helpin' you up here?"

I didn't know where Zadie was and the only thing on my mind in that moment was where Chief was.

"I don't know."

"I'll go back with you, Daddy," Cleo said, already rushing up the drive.

"Keep lookin'," Logan urged to me as I stood frozen and stared after Cleo.

I aimed my eyes to him. "He's so tiny."

He lifted a hand to curl it around the side of my neck. "Keep lookin', baby."

"He's so tiny, Low. Just a baby. What if a dog—?"

He gave my neck a squeeze. "Keep *lookin'*. Hear?"

It was the *hear?* that got me.

I pulled my shit together, nodded, moved away, and hurried toward my neighbor's yard. I sensed Logan going back up the drive.

I barely got into the yard, calling out to Chief and heading to my neighbor's door to knock on it and ask if they'd seen my cat, then beg them to help us look when I heard Logan bellow, *"Millie!"*

I sprinted toward his voice, which meant up the drive and into my courtyard.

When I arrived, I saw Cleo was standing at the back gate. Logan was standing several feet away from the back door to my house.

Zadie was standing in the opened door, holding Chief tight to her throat.

"I found him—" she started.

She didn't get it all out. I flew to her and tried (but failed) to keep my shit together as I pulled Chief out of her hold and into mine.

I cuddled him close, whispering, "Oh, God. Oh, baby. I'm so glad you're safe."

"Where'd you find him?"

My relief was pierced when this was barked by Logan.

"In-inside," Zadie stammered her reply.

At her tone, I took a step back so I could look at her.

She was looking at her father and doing it looking terrified. And guilty.

Then I looked to Logan, who simply looked infuriated.

He'd read his daughter's look.

"M-m-maybe I was wrong," she went on. "Maybe I-I-I didn't see him run out." Her eyes glanced off me before looking beyond me. "F-f-found him curled up on that long chair in your bedroom."

"Everyone inside," Logan snarled, and I held Chief closer as Logan waited for Cleo to dash inside before he strode purposefully toward the door.

I darted a hand out when he got close to me, wrapping it around his forearm to waylay him.

He looked down at me and he was my man, I knew him. I knew the old him and the new him. And I knew, even with the fury burning into me from his gaze, he'd handle this and not lose it (too much).

But still, at the look on his face, I had to fight back quailing.

"Take a second," I whispered, still holding a now squirming Chief close. "Take a breath."

He didn't take a second and he didn't take a breath. He twisted his arm from my hold but in turn took hold of my hand and dragged me (and Chief) into the house.

He slammed the door and Chief jumped in my arms, starting to claw when he heard the loud noise.

Then Logan dragged us into the living room where Zadie

was now standing, looking more terrified and still guilty. Her sister was standing several feet to her side, looking at her like she wanted to shake some sense into her.

Logan let my hand go, and before he let loose the wrath I felt sweltering from him, I hurriedly spoke.

"Okay, everyone," I started. "It's all good." I kept talking as I bent to release Chief on the floor. He scampered away and I straightened. "Chief's here. He's safe. Let's all take a quick moment to collect ourselves—"

Logan cut me off.

"Right now. The truth," he demanded of his youngest. "You see that cat run out the door?"

"I thought—" she began.

He bent forward and thundered, "*The truth!*"

Her chin quivered and it took her some time to get up the nerve, the time she took building more heat in her father, so it was fortunate she found the courage before he exploded (again).

"N-no," she whispered.

"So you're standin' there tellin' me you scared the shit outta Millie just to be a snot," Logan declared.

I put a hand to his biceps and held tight.

"Low, you need to take a moment," I advised.

He didn't even look at me.

He kept his gaze pinned to his girl.

"Answer me," he demanded.

"I..." she started, trailed off, looked to me, and burst into tears as she burst into a flurry of words. "I'm sorry! It was mean! I didn't think you'd get so scared! I thought you'd look inside first and find him!" Her watery eyes went to her father. "I'm sorry, Daddy. I didn't mean to scare her that bad."

Logan was immune to her tears. "But you meant to scare her."

She pulled in a painful, hiccoughing breath, still bawling, nodded, and looked at me. "Not that bad, though. Swear. *Swear*! Not that bad!"

"It's okay, sweetie," I said gently.

"It fuckin' is not," Logan bit out.

I looked to him. "Low," I said, this time quietly. "Careful. Language."

Again, he didn't even look at me.

But he did gesture to me, jerking his head my way.

"Love her," he growled. "Bottom of my soul, straight to my gut, I love this woman. Told you that so you already know she's got that from me. But she decided she didn't give a shit about my girls and did nasty things to you that made you hurt or made you scared, she'd be gone. She'd never see my face again. She'd be history. Now, love her and love you, Zade. So you do that shit to her, what am I supposed to do with you?"

Zadie's hiccoughing sob tore at my heart but still, I had it in me to move swiftly to Zadie, pull her into my side, wrapping both arms around her, while snapping irately, "Logan! Calm down!"

Finally, he looked to me. "It's not okay what she's done."

"You're right and the lesson is obviously a hard one but I think she's learning it," I returned.

"I agree but I gotta make sure she learns it in a way she won't forget," he shot back.

"I'm thinking that's working," I retorted.

He looked to his girl. "It working?"

She nodded her head desperately.

Poor thing.

I lifted a hand and swept her beautiful, thick, soft dark hair from her face, then bent to her and used my thumb to wipe her cheeks.

"Okay, darling, it's over now," I said gently. "All done. All good. Okay?"

She turned wet eyes to me and didn't get a chance to answer because Logan ordered, "Get your shit. I'm takin' you back to your mother's."

That was not a good idea. We needed to calm this here and now and move on.

I straightened and glared at him.

Zadie pulled away from me.

I didn't get a shot to try to get Logan to step into another room with me so we could chat about what was going on. He turned and strode to his cut that was hanging on the hook by the back door. He shrugged it on and handed his girls' jackets to each in turn as they hesitantly moved to him. He then swiped his car keys off the counter and came to me.

Hooking me at the neck, he gave me a quick, hard kiss and muttered, "I'll be back."

After that, he let me go, walked through his girls and right out the door.

"Uh...see you later, Millie," Cleo said shakily.

All I was able to do was nod before she followed her father.

Zadie began to move after her sister but I quickly moved, too, grabbing her hand so she was forced to walk with me.

Logan was behind the wheel, Cleo closing her door at the front passenger side so I moved Zadie to the passenger side back.

I stopped her before she could reach high to open the door, and with a tug at her hand, turned her to me.

"He loves you, sweetie," I told her a truth I hope she knew in her heart. "He'll cool down and it'll be okay."

I spoke these words and then watched her face twist in a way so ugly, I dropped her hand.

"He hates me," she spat. "Because of you. Which means I hate *you*."

Right.

So maybe she didn't learn her lesson.

I had a split second to make a choice.

I made it when she turned away from me and reached to the door.

I reached beyond it, crowding her and pressing my hand into the door so she couldn't open it and was forced to turn back.

The instant she did, I bent to her and declared, "I love him. Bottom of my heart, straight through my soul, I love your dad. And when you love someone like that, your only reason for breathing is to make him happy. I want that more than anything, to make him happy. And I can make him happy in a lot of ways, Zadie, but the only thing that would make him truly happy through and through is if all his girls got along. I know this is hard on you. I'm very sorry it's hard. You might not believe that but my heart breaks for you, what you want you can't have and learning that so young. It's tough, the toughest lesson you can learn in life. So tough, people a lot older than you don't learn it until it's too late. But sometimes we gotta let go of what we want when it isn't to be had, find a new dream and work for that. I want that dream for your dad. And I hope you'll find some way to want that with me so we can work together and give it to him."

I delivered that speech, straightened away from her and the door, and took a step back.

She glared up at me a moment before she turned away, reached high, tugged open the door, and hauled her little girl body inside.

She slammed it.

I sighed and backed away from the truck.

Logan gave me a chin lift and Cleo gave me a wave that was back to hesitant before he instigated his multipoint turn to drive away.

As he did this, I moved to the door and stood in it until I couldn't see them anymore.

Only then did I go inside.

*   *   *

I heard the truck on his return.

Therefore, I was sitting on the arm of the couch, facing the back door, when Logan got back.

He came in, eyes to me before he turned away, closed the door, unarmed and rearmed the alarm, and locked the door.

He then walked to me.

I spread my jeans-clad legs so he could get close but kept my seat.

He got close, walking to stand between my legs.

He then lifted a hand to cup my cheek. "You okay?"

I put my hands to his flat stomach. "You were hard on her."

"Didn't ask your opinion 'bout how I dealt with my kid," he replied—not mean, he just had other things on his mind that took precedence. "You okay?"

"Chief's all right and was never in any danger so, yes. I'm fine about that." I shook my head but did it while he held his touch. "Not sure I'm fine with how you dealt with it."

"Nasty's escalating. No tellin' where she'll take it if I don't nip it in the bud."

"She told me outside your truck she hated me because now you hate her."

His jaw got hard before he asked, "And what'd you say to that shit?"

"I told her I loved you and it was my job to make you happy and I hoped she'd help me do that."

"Good cop, bad cop."

I stared.

Then I asked, "What?"

"Babe, I lost it and I get that you think it was over the top but it wasn't. That shit was not right and no way she should even have a *hint* of thinkin' that was okay. Not to get what she wants from me. Not to get what she wants from a teacher. Or kids at school. Not ever. Through that, you didn't pile shit on her with me. You were calm. You were nice. You were forgiving. She got it rough from me so what you were givin' her didn't sink in. My girl's bein' a snot but she's not stupid. She'll think on it and clue in."

"So you were that hard on her because you wanted to make me the good guy?" I asked in disbelief.

He bent slightly to me to get his face closer to mine. "I was that hard on her because she deserved it." When I opened my mouth, he stated, "Bottom line. Burns in me my baby girl's even got it in her to do somethin' that fucked up. So, Millie, she deserved it."

I had to admit, I saw his point there.

"Deb's gonna hear about this," he continued. "And she's not gonna be happy. She doesn't put up with crap like that. She offered to wade in. I'm gonna call her and tell her she's up."

That was a surprise.

"She offered to wade in?"

He dropped his hand from my face and straightened to look down at me from his full height.

"Talked to her after last weekend so she'd know I got this battle on my hands with Zadie and I intend to win it. She said she's on board however I need her to help. She also said she wants to meet you and I'm thinkin' that's a good idea."

That was also a surprise and a scary one.

Not the part that he'd talked to his ex.

One thing I knew for certain about men like Logan was, you trusted them. You didn't invade their phones. You didn't search their cars. You didn't listen in on calls. You didn't ask them to account for every second of their days. You trusted them to do right, if not all the time, at least by you.

He and Deb shared kids, so he was going to talk to her and I wasn't going to be the woman in his life that demanded he detail every conversation they had.

No.

The scary surprise wasn't that.

It was that she wanted to meet me.

I barely controlled my voice pitching high when I asked, "What?"

"You meet her. You two connect. Not sayin' you guys are gonna be best buds. What I'm sayin' is, you meet her, you connect, we do somethin', the three of us with the girls. Maybe not dinner but maybe she drops 'em off here, comes in, you make her welcome. She has a drink and a chat, takes off before we take the girls out to do somethin'. They see you and Deb gettin' on and Deb supportin' what we got, they'll move toward doin' the same thing."

This was actually somewhat ingenious.

"That's not a bad idea, Low."

His brows shot up in manly affront. "I know it's not."

"Are you...is she...?" I shook my head and started again. "Are you sure she's cool with meeting me?"

"She wants me happy."

I stared at him again.

Then I muttered, "I seriously don't get what you had with her."

"Two kids. That's it," he replied, even though I didn't expect a response. "It's totally fucked. Lived the whole time with her knowin' that. It's just the way it is with her. She's not a woman you love. She's not even a woman you try to make happy 'cause you'll fail. She's just a woman. And she's good with that. She says she's happy. Cleo says she's happier without me there. She's got what she wants, two daughters she can give what she's got to give without tryin' to pretend she has somethin' with her man. But she's also a decent woman and she says she wants me happy. I believe that because she's a decent woman. Now we both got what we want so it ain't fucked anymore. It just is."

"I have to admit, you having a non-psycho, pining, or pissed-off ex is definitely a plus to our ongoing situation," I blurted.

Logan grinned.

"Yeah. Deb gave me two beautiful girls and not much else. But she's givin' us that. Outside my girls, best thing she can give."

As insane as that was, it was also true.

I stood, and since he didn't move an inch when I did, this put us deep in each other's space.

When I got there, I pushed my hands in his cut so I could curl them in the sides of his shirt.

Only then did I carefully advise, "You need to have more patience with Zadie."

Logan lifted his hands and rested them lightly where my neck met my shoulders. "She's had ten years of patience from her old man, baby. This is a monster I created. It's tough work, I didn't like doin' that to her, but I gotta do the work to beat back the monster and bring out my little girl. I know she hasn't givin' you any of it, babe, but when she's not bein' like that, which she's never been as bad as that, but she still can be a princess, she's sweet as can be. God's honest truth. She's funny and full a' love. And I want her to give you that."

"I understand that," I replied. "But you need to have more patience, Logan."

He looked into my eyes before he agreed by nodding.

I let go of his shirt, pushed closer, and wrapped my arms around him, tipping my head way back as I erased any space between us while watching him tip his head way down to keep my eyes.

"You only had half of what you wanted for a long time. I understand tasting the promise of getting it all and wanting that to happen now," I said quietly.

"Yeah," he murmured, stroking my throat with one of his thumbs.

"What you have to get, Snooks, is that we're all here, all you wanted you now have, and things might not be great right now, but we're not going anywhere."

He dipped his head even closer so all I could see was his eyes and I could feel the whisper of his nose.

"Yeah," he repeated, sweeping his thumb along my jaw.

"Now, are *you* okay?" I asked, and watched his eyes smile.

"Yeah," he said again.

"Good," I whispered.

"Be a whole lot better, you dropped to your knees and got down to business."

I felt my eyes widen then narrow before I rolled them to the ceiling.

"Sex on the brain," I said to the ceiling.

"Babe, you haven't blown me in three days."

I rolled my eyes back to him. "You're counting?"

"Do I have a dick to be blown?" he asked.

"Yes," I snapped.

"Then fuck yeah I'm counting."

I unwound my arms from him so I could plant my hands on my hips, suggesting, "How about we make that *thirteen* days?"

"You can keep your mouth from my cock that long, have at it."

"Like you're down with that," I scoffed.

"Nope," he said. "But done with this conversation seein' as I'm about to be down on something else."

"Logan!" I snapped.

He moved a hand to my chest, pushing me so I fell over the arm of the couch.

I landed and had no chance to get my body under my control before his hands clamped on my hips and yanked them to the arm so my ass was resting there.

Then they went to my zipper.

"Logan," I whispered.

In the end, it was Logan who dropped to his knees.

He didn't mind.

I didn't either.

I *so* didn't.

Not even a little bit.

CHAPTER TWENTY-ONE

Stop It

Millie

LOGAN CAME.

I swallowed.

Then I suckled, licked, stroked, and finally left his cock to kiss my way up his chest until I could rest my weight on him and work my mouth under his ear.

He wrapped his arms around me.

"That's what I'm talkin' about," he muttered, sounded satisfied, languid, and happy.

Suffice it to say, I hadn't been able to hold out thirteen days.

Just five.

But I made it that five.

He rolled to take us to our sides, one of his hands sliding down my spine to my ass.

His mouth was under my ear when he murmured, "Your turn."

As it always was with Logan.

You give.

You get.

I grinned.

Then I got my turn.

* * *

"Okay, straight up, that shit is cray-cray."

I was sitting in my office, Kellie across from me, and I'd

just told her that part of that day's agenda was meeting Logan and his ex-wife for lunch.

Kellie was at my studio because Kellie was currently taking a sabbatical from work, that being, she quit her job so the sabbatical was actually from employment.

She did this with relative frequency. I didn't know how she did it. I just knew she did.

She'd had a variety of jobs, everything from waitress to bartender to data entry to office manager of a thriving medical practice (her last job). She was a certified nurse's assistant and she could type faster than anyone I'd ever seen.

She also had a one-room condo she bought ages ago, fixed it up rock 'n' roll (like she liked it), and left it at that. She didn't move on up. She did trade out cars like some women traded out handbags but she did this in ways I didn't ask about either since they were all used cars, but nice cars; she got them on the cheap and not from a lot.

Further, she would often get a man. She'd keep that man. She'd then dump that man. After dumping, she'd have fun. Then, when she got sick of waking up alone or doing it facing some hookup she barely knew, she'd find a man and keep him awhile only to eventually dump him.

In other words, Kellie did what Kellie wanted to do.

And part of what Kellie wanted to do was live life and to get that, she worked to live, not the other way around.

I'd always worried about her living her life this way. In fact, Dottie, Justine and Veronica, and I had had a variety of conversations over the years because we'd all worried about her.

But looking at her now, off work, fresh manicure, fresh highlights in her ash blonde hair, relaxed and kicking back with her girl, I wondered if I shouldn't have paid more attention, quit worrying, and seen that Kellie was actually living the life I'd once had.

Instead of living to work, working to live and then living it up.

"Logan and Deb don't have an acrimonious relationship," I told her.

"Shit like that happens, it's rare, but it does. Lunch with the ex is *still* cray-cray," she replied.

"Logan feels that if Deb and I get along, and the girls see that, we'll move forward with solving our problems with Zadie," I shared, and Kellie knew all about Zadie. I kept all the girls up-to-date, including my new Chaos sisters.

"And that's not a bad idea," she returned. "So meet, shake hands, commit to the cause, and *adios*. Not sittin' down for a full lunch with the woman. One word: *awkward*."

"She only gets an hour for lunch and part of that will be taken up with getting to the restaurant," I informed her. "It won't last that long."

She just shook her head.

"It's gonna be okay," I assured.

"I hope you're right," she replied. "But this is what I know. You're hot. You've always been hot. You're sweet too. And Low is seriously hot for all that's you. He's into you and he doesn't hide that. None of it. Never did. Haven't seen him with you since he's been back but I'm seein' you right now and what I'm seein' is my girl's recently been laid so I'm thinkin' that shit hasn't changed."

She was right.

I didn't get the chance to confirm. She kept talking.

"They might have split because it was just time and now it's all good. But no woman, no matter what went on with her man, would be thrilled to sit down to lunch across from him and the woman that lights up his life. It's just not gonna happen. So brace, sister, and be cool with her on that. Logan's a dude so he's not gonna have any clue about this if he thinks they've both moved on. So that shit's gonna be up to you."

I thought this was good advice, so I nodded.

"Now, is his girl still being a brat?" she asked.

I shook my head. "I don't know. I've only seen them once since the kitty incident. Deb let Low have them on Saturday and I met them at the Compound for lunch. It was fast food. We ate it fast; then I got outta there so he could have time with his girls. He picked them up from dance last night and took them out to dinner before he took them home. He did that last week, too, and neither time I was involved. I've convinced him to slow things down. Give them time with their dad. Only inject me into the scene on occasion so they can take their time to get used to me."

"Welp, that shit's out the window come Friday," she declared. She was right.

It was Wednesday, almost a full week after the kitty incident. Logan had set up lunch the first day Deb could get away, so that day, we were having lunch.

And the coming weekend, even though I still felt it was too soon, the girls were coming to stay.

According to Logan, Deb was all in to help and once she'd learned what Zadie had done (which was the very next day when Logan called her), scaring me about Chief, she'd laid into her daughter.

I'd worried this would make Zadie hate me even more.

But lunch at the Compound was another ingenious Logan move.

He'd told me Deb had never been one with the biker life. She rarely came on Chaos or participated in any of the things they did with old ladies and families.

But she didn't stop the girls from doing it and Logan also told me they loved their Chaos family, enjoyed hanging at the Compound with their dad, his brothers, their women and kids.

Even though our time having lunch there was short, Logan's message to his daughters being that I was still around and not going anywhere, for the girls, it was also a revelation.

I didn't know how the Chaos brothers and their families had treated Deb, but after our lunch, I had a clue.

This was because there were a lot of wide eyes from Cleo and Zadie about how they treated me. Along with the Chaos family giving that to the girls (and obviously Logan), to me they were welcoming, affectionate, loving, teasing. Even the new brothers, Shy, Snapper, Roscoe, and Speck were all over meeting me and getting to know me in a way it was obvious they were opening their arms along with the rest of Chaos.

And then Rush, Tack's son, had come in.

He was older than Tabby and maybe that was why he remembered me better.

But remember me he did.

And when he walked in and looked at me, and while I was staring at his adult handsomeness that was on par with his father's back in the day (and now), he folded me in his arms and said loud enough for the girls to hear, "Heard you were back. Since I heard, been lookin' forward to seein' you and givin' you a hug. Good you're finally home again, Millie."

It was sweet as Rush could always be. He'd been a little boy on the go, something to do or see or experience and he didn't want to waste any time doing it, seeing it, or experiencing it (thus his nickname was Rush).

But in all that, he was always sweet, a good kid, a loving son to his dad (and his mom, even though I knew that was more difficult for him because he was also a loving brother and Naomi never treated Tabby right).

So, for me, it had been a lovely reunion.

For the girls, it was an eye-opening one.

I'd worried in the dramatics of the kitty incident that I would lose headway with Cleo along with Zadie digging in against me.

Luckily, that didn't happen. Cleo greeted me with a big smile the minute I'd walked in and with the way Chaos was with me, it just got better from there.

On the other hand, Zadie hadn't been bratty, but she'd been back to sulky and mostly silent.

The good part about that was that she had plenty of attention to give what was happening at the Compound with Logan and Chaos.

And Logan was a part of that because he'd also changed his strategy.

Apparently, he *had* been withholding some of his displays of affection for me.

I knew this because at the Compound he'd let it loose. There was more touching, hand holding, arm around shoulders or waist, and a lingering (though not wet) kiss when I first arrived to meet them.

Not only in deed but in word and in look, he gave it to me.

He also gave it to his girls, lavishing the same on them at every opportunity in a way that was so natural, I knew it was just how it was with them.

It was cute.

No, not cute.

Beautiful.

Cleo obviously blossomed under it.

But Zadie did too.

I figured she just loved her dad. Though I figured it was more, his behavior with her when I was around being indication he was not angry with her and was moving on.

I just hoped she'd sort herself out and move on, too, the right way.

I would find out that weekend when Deb dropped the girls off at my house for them to stay the weekend.

"Mmm," I mumbled to Kellie's comment about the girls spending the weekend, my mind consumed with that, my eyes wandering to my computer monitor.

"Why'd you end it with him?"

Her question, voiced gently, but still a sneak attack, made my gaze fly back to her.

I'd never told them, not her or Justine. Only Dottie.

And I'd still not told them.

It was now time to tell them but both my bestest besties weren't there and, after all these years, giving that only to Kellie wouldn't be fair.

"I think that I should share that with you when Jus is around, babe," I replied in the same tone she'd given me.

"You can't have kids," she declared.

I felt my lips part.

She shook her head, her face softening in a way that made my heart fill with such love, it became so heavy it hurt, and she leaned toward me at my desk.

"Me and Jus, we guessed a long time ago. Figured it out when you were all about trying to surprise him with getting knocked up and goin' at each other like bunnies. Then, *poof*," the word was a soft explosion, "he's gone."

I watched her eyes get bright and fought the same happening with me as she continued speaking.

"Then the way you were when Dot had Katy, then Freddie, all happy at the same time so fucking sad. Same when Jus and Ronnie had Raff. Killed watching that, babe."

"I'm sorry," I whispered, my voice husky.

She shook her head again. "Nothing to be sorry for. A girl's no girl at all for her sisters if she doesn't get that sometimes a sister has to share the hurt, sometimes hold it close. That happens, a girl's gotta stand by her sister the way she needs her, not the way that girl needs to do it."

God, I loved Kellie so...fucking...much.

"Thank you for doing that for me," I said.

"Not a hardship. You give back, Mill. The sisterhood works that way."

That was true, and I was getting choked up, so the only thing I could do was nod.

I pulled it together before I shared, "I messed up. He understood when it all came out but I lost—"

She leaned back and her tone was now firm when she ordered, "Stop it."

It was me shaking my head when I told her, "It keeps coming to me. I'm happy he's back. We're working. We slid right into what we had before and it's good. It's good like it was, which means it's great. But it's actually better because we're older and we know more about life and what's important. But there are things that hit me. Like he's a partner now, Kell. Not in the way he was before where he'd make me coffee when I had to study or tell me how beautiful I was anytime he looked at me. He's a *partner*. Like he takes out the trash. And I didn't teach him that. Deb did."

"See you'll be having some things fuckin' with your head when you sit down to lunch with her too," she muttered.

"I envy her, no doubt about it," I confessed. "She had him for thirteen years. They weren't a love match and that never grew between them. She still had him. And she gave him—"

"Stop that too," Kellie cut me off.

"Kell, you have to know that cuts deep," I told her.

"Of course it does," she replied.

"He has his two girls. He dotes on them. I cannot express how happy I am that he has them but that doesn't mean I don't think. Even though he isn't holding any anger about what I did, he still told me that what I did meant he couldn't be around to help us build a new dream. He's a biker and there was a good deal of shady going on in the Club back then but maybe we could have adopted. Maybe—"

"Girl, *stop it*."

I shut my mouth.

She went on.

"Sister, you came this far. You went through hell. You gave it all up and then you got it back. Your story is impossible. Shit like that doesn't happen. Seeing your guy at Chipotle and ending up with him back in your life, just as into you as he ever was, committed to building a future. Now there are so many ways to fuck that up, it boggles the mind."

She leaned into me again and, as was sometimes her way, got bossy.

"Beat that back, Mill. You get stuck in your head about all that you lost. All that's passed that you can never get back. All you couldn't give to him. All he couldn't give to you. Mistakes that may or may not be just that. You get stuck in that, you're gonna lose hold of the one thing in your life you ever *truly* wanted, Millie. And you can't do that."

She held my gaze, reached out, put her hand on my desk, and gave me the rest.

"I know you wanted kids. I know you wanted a family. What you gotta get is that maybe you didn't. Maybe you wanted that because you wanted it all from Logan and *with* Logan and you wanted to give it all *to* Logan. Because, babe, seriously, you have family. Lots of it. You have love around you. Lots of it. From the moment I met you, anything you wanted, you got because you worked at getting it. But the only thing I ever saw you really, *really* want, the only time you were really, *really* happy, was when you had him. Now you have him. Do not get mired in what could have been. Rejoice in what is now."

She was *soooooo* right.

"For a crazy bitch, you're also super smart," I blurted in order not to get emotional and burst into tears.

"Van Gogh was crazy. The guy was also a master," she returned, taking her hand from my desk and sitting back in her seat, grinning.

"I think I read somewhere he might have had a neurological condition," I told her.

"Yeah. His neurological condition being that he was crazy and crazy talented," she replied.

"Are you taking up painting?" I asked.

"Nope. And not gonna win the Nobel Prize like that dude

from *A Beautiful Mind*. But that guy was a genius and he was bonkers too."

"He wasn't bonkers, Kell. He was ill. He had schizophrenia," I informed her.

She smiled. "We genius folk who are bonkers can call each other bonkers. It's in the handbook."

I started giggling.

She joined me.

I stopped giggling abruptly and said, "Thanks for understanding about..." I paused before finishing lamely, "everything."

She shook her head again, no longer giggling but her lips were curled up.

"Sister, I got a ton a' friends but only four real ones. That's because the others like having fun with me but they don't get me. You don't have to thank me for shit. You give that understanding back and that's just the way it is."

"I think I feel the need to hug you now," I told her.

"Beat that back too," she returned. "The only time I feel physically affectionate is while riding the rush after crowd surfing and there's no concert on my imminent schedule, which is bumming me out."

I raised my brows. "That's it? There's no one you feel physically affectionate for at the present moment?"

"If you're asking if I'm getting it regular, no. Which is also bumming me out."

"Time to go on the prowl," I remarked.

"There was a time when I'd try to drag you with me but I'm thinking Low would frown on that."

I was thinking she was correct because he always had. He hadn't said much when Justine, Kellie, and I hit the town or a party without him. But back then we were all young, fun-loving, and attractive, so he also didn't hide he didn't like it much either.

We might not be able to claim the adjective young anymore, but we were still fun-loving and attractive, and at this early juncture, I didn't think it would be good to test Logan on that unless he was at my side.

Hard for Kellie to be on the prowl with a hot biker hanging around.

"Perhaps you should take Justine with you," I suggested.

Veronica didn't mind that Justine went, mostly because both of them had been through the romantic wringer before finding each other. Neither would stray and both knew it.

Logan knew I'd never stray either but he was a badass biker. They got aggressive about that kind of thing.

"Gonna set that shit up," Kellie declared.

"And Claire. She's probably due to get dumped by one of her six boyfriends soon. She'll need to fill that slot."

Kellie grinned.

I grinned back.

And I did it thinking again life was as weird as it was wonderful.

Because we'd discussed something that lay buried between us for years. Something she and Justine had guessed, but I'd never dug it up for them.

Now it was out in the open.

And we were as we always were.

She was right.

I had a lot of family around me.

I also had a lot of love.

*   *   *

I caught Logan in my rearview on the way to the place we were meeting Deb for lunch and I almost got in a wreck due to experiencing a mini-orgasm on first sight.

It was cold, but sunny, no chance of snow.

So he was on his bike.

But to keep warm, he not only was wearing his cut.

He was also wearing a black bandana around the bottom

half of his face, shades over his eyes, and his unruly, thick, dark, overlong hair was untethered.

He looked like exactly what he was.

A modern-day outlaw.

It was *hot*.

I found a parking spot that had a free one next to it. I parked and, as I expected, Logan backed in beside me.

I jumped down in my high-heeled pumps, slammed my door, and turned, seeing him off his bike, lifting a leather-gloved hand to yank down the bandana.

"I will seriously make it worth your while if you consider doing me wearing that bandana," I announced before I even said hey.

I couldn't see his eyes behind his sunglasses but I saw all his white, even teeth because he smiled huge.

Then he stated, "Gag you with it, blindfold you with it, but, babe, nothin' hinders my mouth when I'm doin' you."

"Those alternate scenarios are acceptable," I declared immediately.

He burst out laughing, doing it with his arms shooting out to take hold of me so I slammed into him when he yanked me to his body.

I rested my hands on his chest below his shoulders, head tipped back, smiling up at him, watching him laugh.

I hadn't seen him laugh that freely or for that long since I got him back.

I'd have to see to that.

Immediately.

His laughter quieted down to chuckles, through which he said, "See we got our plans for tonight."

"Stop it," I retorted. "I nearly crashed having a mini-orgasm seeing all that's you in my rearview, that bandana over your face. I don't need another one or it'll take you forever to get me where you want me to be so you can get what you wanna get."

He pulled me closer, dipping his chin to bring his face near mine.

"You had a mini-orgasm?" he asked.

"Yep," I answered.

"What's a mini-orgasm?"

"It's yet another boon to being a woman you men won't ever understand since it's something you men don't get but we can have them willy-nilly. Say, while watching the TV show *Vikings* or driving our cars to salad bars with a hot biker trailing us."

He was still smiling big when he continued questioning. "What are the other boons to being a woman?"

"High heels. Handbags. Facials. We get to look at and touch our knockers anytime we want, even if festivities are occurring alone. And we get to take cock in a variety of orifices."

His eyebrows over his shades flew up. "You seriously talkin' dirty to me before I gotta force down a fuckin' salad?"

"Yes," I replied.

His eyebrows disappeared as he muttered, "One of the reasons I love you," right before he dipped deeper and gave me a lip touch.

Our enjoyable chat was clearly over, for when he lifted his head, he released me but slid an arm along my shoulders and started guiding us to the restaurant.

We'd taken three steps when he noted quietly, "You seem okay."

"Not sure this is gonna be easy on Deb or me. So we're on common ground."

His hand at my shoulder gave it a squeeze. "She's cool, Millie," he assured.

"And I'll be cool too," I promised.

"Already know that," he said, eyes to the restaurant.

But it wasn't exactly a restaurant, as such. I didn't know what you called it outside calling it a salad bar.

It was Deb's choice. This was because it was her favorite place close to work. This was also because, Logan told me, she was very healthy, worked out a lot, and ate food that was good for her.

Learning this, I was beginning to lose my surprise at all things that didn't jibe about Logan and Deb.

Logan worked out, definitely. But he ate and drank whatever he wanted, back in the day and, I'd noticed, now.

I did the same, for the most part, not counting the seventeen thousand, two hundred, and eleven diets I'd been on since losing him, all of these lasting from one day to three weeks, and, of course, the one Pilates session I'd attended.

Normally, if told I was going to a salad bar for lunch, I would balk.

But I knew this one and they had squares of pound cake and really good vanilla pudding at the end so I was looking forward to it.

I was thinking this as I got another squeeze of my shoulder. I looked up to Logan to see his profile had changed. It was no longer relaxed and natural. It wasn't hard either.

It was alert.

I turned my attention back to the restaurant and saw a pretty, petite blonde woman in a maroon button-down shirt with a fleece jacket over it standing at the doors, looking at us.

No, *watching* us.

I knew this because I'd vaguely noticed her when I'd pulled in.

And she was still there.

Oh God, that was Deb.

Oh God, Deb had watched Logan and me greet, me make him smile and laugh, hand him some dirty talk, him kiss me and guide me her way holding me close.

Shit.

"Yo," Logan called when we were at the bumpers of the cars parked in front of the salad bar.

"Hey," Deb called back.

I lifted a hand and waved.

"Hey," I repeated.

Deb looked at me and I saw as we came close she didn't wear a lot of makeup and her hair was pulled back in a pony-tail, but the blonde was pretty, the color suited her, she had a killer bod even if her work outfit wasn't the greatest, and she was a lot more attractive up close.

"Hey, Millie," she said to me, and when we stepped up to the walk in front of the salad bar, she extended her hand. "Nice to meet you."

I took my arm from around Logan's waist (he did not recip-rocate the gesture when I did) and took her hand.

"Nice to meet you too."

She smiled at me and I smiled back but did it studying her hard.

I did this but I could find nothing there. Even though she looked nothing like either of her girls, her smile was like Cleo's when she wasn't forcing it.

Natural. Genuine. Friendly.

And it made her even prettier.

"Let's go in," Logan prompted. "I wanna eat lettuce like I want someone to drill a bullet in my gut but at least these fuck-ers always have a vat of chili at the end."

Deb shook her head at him but did it grinning before she looked to me even as she turned to the doors of the restaurant.

"Getting him to eat anything healthy was like pulling teeth," she told me like she was sharing just any tidbit of infor-mation with anyone from friend to stranger. "I gave up about six days into our marriage."

"Thank fuck," Logan muttered.

Okay.

Hmm.

I didn't know what to think about that.

What I did know was that I wasn't sure I was up for a trip down the memory lane of their marriage even if that marriage wasn't full of joy, love, and laughter.

I said nothing, just aimed a noncommittal grin to Deb as we moved to the cash register.

There, Logan made it clear he was paying for all of us. Deb made it clear she didn't think that was necessary and offered to pay. They had a mild fight.

And I didn't know what to think about that either.

To end it, I said to Deb, "Sorry, but I'm a little hungry and I know you have to get back to work, so do I, so why don't we let Logan pay and if we do this again, we can take turns."

"Good idea," she replied on another natural smile and headed to the salad bar.

We got our food. We took our seats, me pinned in our side of the booth by Logan.

And after taking them in, I didn't know what to think about the state of our trays.

After getting his tray, Logan didn't even bother walking the salad bar. He went straight to the hot stuff at the end. Therefore, he had a bowl of chili, a plate full of nachos, two pieces of corn bread, three garlic sticks, and four cups—one filled with pound cake, one filled with whipped cream, and two filled with vanilla pudding.

Halfway through the salad bar, I'd given up on the plate idea since I was piling it on so my salad dripped off the sides. I also had two garlic sticks and two cups, one filled with pound cake, one filled with pudding topped with whipped cream.

Deb's salad was an eighth the size of mine; she apparently was using cottage cheese as dressing (about a tablespoon of it) and she also had two dessert cups. One filled with pineapple, one filled with strawberries.

I'd never had an issue about my body or the food I ate. This was because my parents didn't have an issue with either. They gave us healthy food. We were also free to eat whatever treats we wanted. And they complimented us frequently on a variety of things, including telling me and Dot we were beautiful.

Further, I'd garnered male attention from early on. Not any of those males seemed to have a problem with my curves.

Primary to this was hooking up with Logan at an early age.

He'd not only not had a problem with my curves, he showered attention on them. Never had he given me any idea that he wasn't fiercely attracted to *all* that was me.

Not even a hint.

But he had two children with Deb, which meant something drew him to her in the first place.

And she was not one thing like me.

"Shit," he muttered. "They didn't have taco shells when I went through and just put 'em out. Gonna get some tacos." He looked to me. "Want some, babe?"

I pressed my lips together and shook my head.

He took off, not bothering to ask Deb because it was clear he knew her answer would be no.

I watched him go, then picked up my fork and started stabbing at my salad, feeling strange.

"You're not what I expected."

Deb's words made me look at her and brace.

"No?" I prompted, even though I didn't want to and even though I felt the same thing about her but had no intention of sharing that.

She dipped her head my way. "He said you had history, met when you guys were young. I expected total biker babe. Leathers. Harley tees. Stuff like that. Not a class act."

Well, that was nice.

However.

"Years have gone by, Deb. I've changed," I told her. "I never wore leathers but I used to be top to toe old lady. My cutoffs and halter top days are over but I gotta admit, I kinda miss them."

She shrugged through a grin. "Life surprises us. Stuff happens, we change. Not that I'm saying if you showed all biker babe, I'd think anything bad," she assured me quickly. When

I nodded, she continued, "No matter what, seeing what I saw, it'd be good because that was cool."

"Sorry?" I asked, not knowing what she meant.

"You. High. Seeing him laugh like that. I swear, Millie, never saw that." She smiled. "He said you made him happy. He didn't lie."

Suddenly, the depth and breadth of my salad didn't enter my mind.

"Never?" I asked.

She shook her head. "Nope. No wonder Cleo likes you. She and High are close. Two peas in a pod. You make him laugh like that, she'll love you to the end of time."

That felt good.

But.

"Things haven't been..." I hesitated and decided to say, "*such* that I've had many chances to make Logan laugh like that around the girls."

Or at all.

She nodded and speared a spinach leaf. "I hear that. Princess Zadie." It was then she shook her head. "Love that girl but so does High. If he could build her a princess castle that had turrets that reached to the clouds, he would. He'd do the same for Cleo but she's got her feet on the ground and she thinks of other people as well as herself. She knows not even to ask because doing it might break her dad's back. Zadie's thought process doesn't go that far."

I decided not to respond to that.

"She gets there, though," Deb assured me, finishing with, "Eventually."

"It's really kind of you to wade into all this," I told her.

She'd shoved the spinach leaf into her mouth while I was talking so she flicked her fork out to the side when I was done.

Once she swallowed, she said, "This kind of thing is the way it is now. Families aren't like they used to be. Don't know, didn't live back in the fifties where women had zero choice, even if they were stuck in a marriage that wasn't working. But my guess is, this way is better. People adjust and if they don't know how to do that, they should learn. We're adjusting." She shrugged. "Making a new family for the girls."

I tried not to look like I was staring at her.

But.

Could she honestly be this cool?

Before I could blurt that question out, Logan slid in beside me with a plate holding four loaded tacos.

He grasped hold of one and dropped grated cheese, lettuce, and meat on a trail to my tray as he plopped it beside my salad.

I looked to him. "I said I didn't want one, Low."

He looked to me. "You lied, Millie."

He was correct.

I gave him a glare.

He gave me a grin, then turned to his tray.

"So, High, thinking on this, this is gonna make things a lot easier," Deb remarked, spearing more unadulterated vitamins, fiber, and protein and shoving it into her mouth.

"What?" he asked, speaking through a mouthful of taco.

Deb circled her fork around. "Us three. I mean, we sort this out, we can do Thanksgivings together. I have the girls Christmas morning, you guys can come to dinner Christmas night and vice versa. Birthdays will be awesome. Lots of family around. Girls get to feel super special." She stabbed her salad again. "It'll all be good."

I couldn't help it that time.

I stared at her.

God, she honestly *was* this cool.

"Yeah," Logan agreed. "And Thanksgivin' is comin' up and we agreed I got the girls this year 'cause you get 'em most of the time but Millie's kickass pad doesn't have a dining room. So now, we can all come to your place."

"Done," Deb decreed. "Mom'll love it. She told me to say hi, by the way."

"Hi back," Logan muttered, tipping his head to the side and taking another massive bite out of taco. As he did this, he must have caught sight of my tray and my lack of interest in it because his eyes came to me, and through a mouthful of taco, he asked, "Babe, why aren't you eating?"

"I will when I quit freaking out," I answered.

He straightened his head, swallowed, and drew his brows together. "Freakin' out about what?"

"I . . . you . . ." I looked to Deb and announced, "You're very cool."

She smiled but didn't say anything because Logan did.

"Told you she was."

I looked to him. "I know you did but you didn't say she was *cool*."

"Not sure how I can say she's *cool* when I'm sayin' she's *cool*, which means Deb's *cool*," Logan returned.

"Cool is not *cool*," I replied.

"Beautiful, also told you she was a decent woman who wants me happy. So how you can't get that her cool is *cool* I have no clue."

I quickly looked to Deb and stated, "No offense," before looking back to Logan and stating, "Women don't work that way. Rarely are we *that* cool."

"Jesus, that's fuckin' ridiculous," Logan returned.

I opened my mouth to retort, not knowing what I intended to say, just knowing it would likely be heated, but I didn't say it because I heard Deb snort prior to busting into laughter.

Logan and I looked her way.

"I get you," she said to me through her amusement. "And I get you," she said to Logan, tamped down the mirth, and went on, "And I just realized something. You asked what would make me happy, High, and I'm good. I'm happy. But when I answered you, I didn't know I'd get more of that happy knowing you'd finally got yours."

"And there it is!" I declared, pointing my still loaded with unhealthy salad fork at her. "More cool."

She burst into laughter again but this time did it while Logan chuckled.

I belatedly stuck my salad in my mouth and chewed.

When I was done chewing, I also had pulled myself together.

"I don't know if Low's told you this, but I'm a party planner so whatever you need for birthdays and such, I'm your go-to girl. Family discount. Meaning free," I said to Deb.

"Perfect," she replied.

"And just to say, I'm attempting a new recipe on Friday night. I haven't decided what yet but whatever it is, it's gonna be awesome. When you drop off the girls, you should consider staying."

"Got no plans," she replied. "I'd love to."

I grinned, then noted, "Your handbag is the bomb."

"Stella McCartney," she told me.

I stabbed salad, smiling at her. "I pegged that. Saks?"

"Neiman's."

"This season?" I asked.

"Yep," she answered.

I turned my attention to my salad, murmuring, "Quick trip to the mall before going back to work."

"If you do, there was an Alexander McQueen clutch, black, skull clasp, rhinestones for eyes. I have absolutely no reason to own it since I saw it I can't get it off my mind. I'll give you my number. If it's still there, text me. I'll swing by this weekend."

"I'll text," I told her, then asked, "You want me to put it on hold?"

"That'd be great."

"Now, I *want* someone to drill a bullet in my gut," Logan groused.

Both Deb and I looked to Logan. He looked mildly

annoyed at our lapsing into girl talk and less mildly bored as he shoved an entire piece of buttered corn bread in his mouth.

At that, it was my turn to burst out laughing.

And I was tickled pink when Deb laughed with me.

*   *   *

"*Babe!*" Logan bellowed.

I moved to the door of the laundry room, which was perhaps five feet from where I'd been while *in* the laundry room, and when I stopped I was perhaps three feet from where Logan stood at the back door, *bellowing*.

"I'm right here," I told him.

He turned to me. "You hear my bike in the drive?"

"Yes," I replied. "But I was separating colors."

"You greet me," he declared.

"I . . ." I shook my head. "Sorry?"

"I come home, you greet me. Since we been back, I come home, you're waitin'," he stated.

This was true. If I heard his bike or truck, I was often waiting in the kitchen, close to the back door. But if not, I was in eyesight and my attention was on him coming in said back door and as soon as I could, I made my way there.

"I'd never been separating laundry when you got home," I explained.

"Millie, I come home, you greet me."

These words were firm.

These words were a demand.

"You're being bossy."

My words were a warning.

"I come home, you greet me," he repeated.

"The annoying kind," I went on.

"I get home, babe, *you greet me*."

I stiffened.

Because I got it.

Then I walked the three feet separating us as I said quietly, "I'm right here, Snooks. In the laundry room, doing our laundry."

He reached to me, one arm around me pulling me closer, one hand sifting his fingers into the side of my hair.

In return, I slid my arms around his middle.

We held each other for a few beats before he spoke.

"Maybe never get used to havin' you back," he said. "Maybe never get used to comin' home to you again. Like it when your eyes are to the door, tellin' me you're glad I'm home. Maybe won't need that forever. Just sayin', I need it now."

And I needed to hang on. Hang on to the words Kellie told me. Hang on to rejoicing in the now. Doing that and not sliding into getting stuck on remembering all we'd lost and how that affected both of us.

"Then I'll give it to you," I told him.

"Thanks, beautiful," he replied, bending his neck to give me a swift kiss before he let me go to shrug off his cut.

"You want a beer?" I asked.

"Yup," he answered.

I went to the fridge.

When I'd popped his beer, I saw him at the kitchen island.

"Got your purse," he said, his eyes coming to me.

The purse, the same one Deb had at lunch but mine electric blue, was on the island.

I grinned at him and brought his beer to him.

"Yup," I answered.

He took the beer, then tapped the other things on the island.

"What's this shit?" he asked.

I looked down at the plethora of gift cards I'd also bought at the mall. It wasn't the plastic version of a shopping spree to end all shopping sprees, but it did herald fun.

"Gift cards," I told him.

"Know that," he said, dropping his beer after taking a pull. "For who? You got someone's birthday comin' up?"

"No. I have two tweenie girls coming to spend the weekend at my house so I have two attempts at bribery, this in hopes of using it to pave the way to loving me, even if it's for a moment and all based on materialism."

His head jerked to the side. "You're givin' that shit to my girls?"

"I would have asked before I got them but they're gift cards. They don't expire. If you think it's a bad idea, I can put them in their Christmas stockings or something."

He looked down to the cards.

As he did, I tried to decide if I wanted a beer or a glass of wine.

He looked to me.

Then he smiled.

"Zadie's gonna love that shit," he said.

I smiled back.

"Cleo's gonna like it too," he continued.

I decided against beer and wine and instead getting a dose of Logan.

So I leaned into him, giving him a lot of my weight.

He rounded me with the arm that didn't have a hand holding a beer.

"They're gonna love you," he told me.

I wanted that. I wanted that for me.

But more, I wanted it for him.

"Yeah," I replied.

His arm gave me a squeeze. "Can't help but happen, baby."

I gave him more of my weight.

"Love you, Snooks," I whispered.

"Back at ya," he replied. Then he lifted his beer, took another tug, and looked down at me. "Now, what you gonna feed your man?"

"Hamburgers," I told him, pulling away. "But I need to get a load of laundry in. I don't wanna be doing it while the girls are here."

"I'll pull out your fryer," he said, putting the beer on the island and moving to the cupboard that held many of my countertop appliances.

"The Foreman, Low. We're not gonna fry hamburgers. Yeesh," I said, moving to the laundry room.

"But we are gonna fry tots," he returned.

"We can bake those," I told the laundry room as I entered it.

"We could. And they'll suck. So we'll fry," he called to me.

"I don't know if we have canola oil," I semi-yelled, bending over the hampers.

"Woman, who goes to the store?" he semi-yelled back.

"Oh, right," I kept semi-yelling.

I heard him chuckle.

Then I heard a cupboard door close.

I knew my lips were turned up when I shoved a load of lights into the washer.

And this was not because fried tater tots rocked.

Not at all.

CHAPTER TWENTY-TWO

Worth It

Millie

THAT FRIDAY EVENING, Logan opened the door for Deb and the girls while I continued my efforts at preparing our dinner.

I still watched as Cleo came in, carrying a small pink overnight bag, smiling and saying, "Daddy," before she gave him a big hug.

Zadie came in next, rolling her own small purple overnight bag (with big daisies on it), and Logan got his smile and hug from her as Cleo came my way.

"Hey, Millie," she greeted.

"Hey, sweetie," I replied, giving her my own smile.

Then she got even closer and I was uncertain for a moment as she did.

I lost my uncertainty when she wrapped her arms around my waist for a quick, timid hug before she jumped back and ducked her head.

It went so fast, I didn't have the chance to touch her.

But I wasn't going to let that moment slide.

"Good to see you again, beautiful girl," I said softly.

She looked up at me from under her lashes and even with her lips pressed together, they were still curled up.

I winked at her.

"Oh my God, you got it!" Deb cried.

I turned my attention her way and saw her walking in, going straight to the countertop where my electric blue Stella bag was.

"Totally," I told her, and went on, "I just hired a new member of staff. I need to be buying Stella bags like I need a hole in the head. But I couldn't resist."

Deb grinned at me. "I'm jealous. You went electric blue. I'm not adventurous like that. But I wish I was because it's phenomenal."

I grinned back and commented on the color she chose. "Black is nothing to sneeze at, sister."

"Too true," she replied, then glanced around before casting her eyes back to me. "You have a gorgeous home, Millie."

I was still grinning when I returned, "Thanks, babe."

"What's that smell?"

This came from Zadie and it wasn't snotty. It also wasn't simply curious either.

What it was was indication that she still wasn't there with me.

However, she did seem to be alert and this alertness centered around her mother and me.

"And hello, Millie, how have you been?" Deb replied as a rebuke.

Zadie gave her mother a look that also wasn't snotty but it wasn't sweet. She then gave me the same look.

"Hello, Millie," she said by rote.

"Hey there, Zadie," I replied warmly, giving her a big smile.

"Lettuce wraps," Logan declared, and everyone looked to him. He had the girls' bags in his hands and was on the move toward the living room. "I'm thinkin' of ordering a pizza," he went on.

"I like pizza," Zadie declared.

"You're eating lettuce wraps," Deb returned.

"Yeah, you are," Logan confirmed. "But before you do that, want my two girls followin' me. Gonna show you where you're sleepin'."

"When I get back, Millie, I'll help," Cleo called as she followed her dad.

Of course she would.

"I'd love that, Cleo," I replied.

"And, Mom!" Cleo cried, still walking. "Wait 'til you meet Millie's cats!"

Zadie followed her sister, glaring daggers into her back.

Nope, she totally wasn't there with me or any of this.

Deb got close and said low, "Just so you know, the mini-attitude Zadie is throwing isn't all about you. I gave it to her in the car about how she's going to handle this weekend. She isn't a big fan of being told what to do. So she's not super happy with me."

"I'm sorry," I muttered, turning my attention back to carefully separating leaves of lettuce without tearing them. "Seems I'm a pain in the ass for Zadie on a variety of fronts."

Deb got even closer and I turned my attention from the lettuce to her. "Don't think this is you, Millie. It's not. I actually think this is good. It's a life lesson she needs to learn. And it's something High needs to get too. It's not gonna be easy on any of us. But it's been needing to happen a long time. You're just the catalyst for it."

"Not doing cartwheels about that," I shared. "But I understand what you're saying and hope it works out for everyone in the end. Though, I have to tell you, I bought them both a few gift cards. We're gonna go shopping this weekend." Her expression didn't change, in other words, I couldn't read it, so I went on to admit, "It's transparent bribery. But I'm not above doing anything to get past this hitch in the road. Unless, of course, you don't like that idea. Then they'll be stocking stuffers. Logan's okay with it but you need to be too."

"I don't mind," she replied. "Unless you do it every time you get them." Her eyes danced. "If you do, they'll never wanna come back to me."

My voice was filled with humor when I said, "I doubt that."

She looked down to the lettuce, then back to me and again her voice was low when she said, "You're pretty cool, too, you know?"

I'd been cool, once, back in the day, in my cutoffs and halter tops.

I didn't think I was cool now, especially since I just admitted to my plans to attempt to bribe her daughters for their love (or at least like).

"I am?" I asked.

"What are you putting in those?" She tipped her head to the lettuce.

"Well, I have this chili peanut chicken thing happening,"

I answered. "And then I'm searing some ahi tuna with some sesame seeds, serving it with julienne cucumbers, and a crème fraîche tartar sauce. Low was not pleased with the grocery list, seeing as he had to go to three stores, including LeLane's, which isn't his scene, and what was on the list he wasn't real fired up about. But he got us covered."

"You eat lettuce wraps often?" she asked.

"No," I told her. "Never. Not even at P.F. Chang's. In fact, it's a crapshoot this stuff is gonna taste good at all."

"And that's what's cool," she returned. "Because I know you're doing that for me and I appreciate it. The girls will notice and they'll appreciate it, even Zadie. I haven't had pizza in seven years so I'm not even sure my body can *process* pizza. Ahi tuna…" she smiled, "definitely."

"I wish I could say that I was sacrificing for my coolness," I replied. "But I totally love ahi and if that peanut chicken is even a little close to as good as it looks in its picture on the Internet, even Logan won't complain."

"Clee-Clee loves ahi and Zade gets chicken satay with peanut sauce anytime she's got her shot, so if you can please High, you've got us all covered."

"Really?" I asked, shocked I'd hit the nail so firmly on the head…and did it with *lettuce wraps*.

"Really," she answered.

"Mom! Look!" Cleo cried, walking in, snuggling Poem. "This is Millie's girl. Poem. Chief ran under the couch but I'll get him so you can meet him next."

"Wow!" Deb cried back, moving to her daughter. "She's so cute."

"I hope they sleep with us," Cleo murmured.

They might. If they could make it up on the bed, something they had yet to master.

I didn't share that with Cleo. I turned to Zadie.

"You want a drink, Zadie?"

She shrugged, not meeting my eyes. "Whatev—" she started, but must have felt her mother's and father's attention go to her because she quickly finished, "Sure."

"I'll get it," Logan stated, and looked to his ex. "Deb? Wine?"

"I'll have a glass with dinner," she answered, then came back to me. "Now, Millie, what can the girls and I do to help?"

"First you can tell me if you're picking up that McQueen tomorrow," I replied. "Then you can julienne cucumbers and the girls can set the bar."

"McQueen, affirmative," she told me.

"Right on!" I declared on an excited sister's-gonna-get-a-fab-bag smile.

Deb, the sister who was going to get a fab bag, smiled back and hers was bigger for obvious reasons. "Now, do you have something to julienne, or am I gonna need to perform miracles with a knife?"

"Gadget drawer to your left," I told her, delighted the thingamabob I'd bought probably six years ago to do fantastic things with vegetables was going to get its first use.

"Gotcha," she muttered, and moved to the drawer.

Before I turned back to my lettuce, I looked to Zadie. She had a can of pop in her hand and was standing by her father, who had his head in the fridge. She was also watching her mom.

When she felt my eyes, she looked to me.

I tipped my head to the side and curved my lips up.

She looked away and took a sip of pop.

I sighed.

"Do you have placemats?" Cleo asked.

"Drawer across the way, sweetie," I answered.

"On it!" she cried, and skipped across the kitchen.

I watched her doing this thinking she was totally freaking cute.

I also watched her doing this thinking that I liked how she seemed to be getting comfortable in my space.

So I watched her doing this, feeling happy.

Cleo, good.

Deb, good.

Logan, always good.

Zadie, no change.

Not brilliant.

But I'd take it, work on it...

And hope.

*   *   *

Lying in bed, tangled up with Logan that night after the girls settled in the guestroom and we gave them time to drift off before we went to bed, I murmured, "I think that went okay."

He gave me a squeeze. "Know it did. Do not know how you pulled off good-tastin' lettuce wraps, but you nailed it."

Being a man, he was talking about food.

I was talking about our modern-day family dinner.

I decided not to point that out.

I should have known better. Logan knew exactly what I was talking about.

He shared this when I heard his head move on the pillow so he could say into the top of my hair, "Tomorrow, you give 'em their cards and we'll take 'em shoppin'. They're both gonna like that and even Zadie's gonna have to melt a little 'cause I know she's *really* gonna like that. And I'll endure the mall 'cause I'll have three happy girls on my hands." He gave me another squeeze. "So it's all gonna be good, beautiful."

I tipped my head back to catch his eyes in the dark. "If the mall doesn't work, I'm gonna need more ammunition. Her favorite foods. Her favorite desserts. Television shows. Movies. Boy bands." I looked to his shadowy chin. "Actually, I need that intel on both girls just because."

"Babe," Logan called my attention back to him. When he got it, he carried on, "This is not an exercise in spoilin' Zadie more than she already is. This is an exercise in breakin' her of that shit."

"I know, but—"

"I hear you. I get you. You do need to know that about them. So ask 'em. But I'm lettin' this bribery scheme of yours go because you wanna do that for them and I want them to see you are how you are. Generous and a woman with a big heart. But from here on in, special occasions only. They gotta get that with me and me bein' with you, life is just life. Hear?"

I nodded.

He bent in and touched his mouth to mine.

When he pulled away, he grumbled, "Gonna be a long fuckin' weekend, girls here, which means not bein' able to do you."

He was right.

I snuggled into him, rubbing my face in his throat, mumbling, "Mmm."

"Drop the girls at school, come back, end that shit," he went on. "Be prepared to hit your office late on Monday, Millie."

Something to look forward to.

Therefore my repeated, "Mmm," had a different tone.

Tangled up in me, Logan slid his hand up my spine to entwine his fingers in my hair.

"Love you, baby," he whispered into the dark.

I lay in his arms, feeling his solid warmth, his strength, the truth of those words wrapped all around me and I wondered how I could be so lucky.

I'd had it all, let it go, and got it all back...and more.

That shit was impossible.

But there it was, in my arms, in my bed, in my house.

Oh yes.

I knew Kellie had been right when she'd laid it out.

But hearing those words, *feeling* them, I knew Kellie was *right*.

I'd gone through a rough patch. It was my doing. It lasted a long time.

But now it was over.

"Back at ya," I whispered.

Logan kissed the top of my head and settled in.

I felt him do it and I fought sleep after he did it, wanting to remain awake and feel all he was giving me even after his breath evened out and his body got heavy around mine.

I couldn't fight sleep for long because I was right where I was supposed to be.

But I fell asleep on two thoughts.

Our lives might not be perfect.

But that didn't mean I wasn't perfectly happy.

*   *   *

"Babe, just got a call," Logan announced the next morning as he walked into the living room.

I was in the kitchen preparing brioche French toast. I had two sleepy girls sitting at my bar, Cleo cuddling Chief, who wasn't certain he wanted to be cuddled, Zadie noticeably, and lamentably, steering clear of both cats even though I could tell she didn't want to.

I'd have to figure out a way to do something about that.

But in that moment, I was just pleased that neither seemed traumatized after having to spend a night under my roof with me.

It was now their father's roof too.

Still.

"Yeah?" I asked Logan.

"Boys can do the grading and graveling tomorrow," he told me, going to his girls and wrapping his arms around both, pulling them together and bending in to kiss the tops of their heads.

Cleo sleepily and happily cuddled into her dad.

To my surprise and delight, Zadie did the same.

I allowed myself to take in that awesomeness before I focused on Logan.

"On a Sunday?" I asked.

"Yep," he answered, letting his girls go and moving around the bar toward me. "They get it done in the morning, we'll go to the RV, pick it up, bring it back."

"Works for me," I muttered, dropping a slice of brioche into the egg mixture and turning it.

And it did work for me, Logan all moved in and settled. That totally worked for me.

"Today, Millie's got a surprise for you."

I knew this particular announcement from Logan was for the girls.

"Yeah?" Cleo asked as Logan got in my space.

"I'll get on this. You give my babies the goodness," he bossed me.

That was a boss I'd accept, so I didn't object. Instead, I moved to the bar and opened the drawer where I'd stashed the gift cards.

I took them out and lined them up in front of the girls, all ten of them, five for each, side by side, saying, "Mini-shopping spree. Your dad has relented to taking us to the mall. We'll have lunch there first and after we lay waste to the stores, maybe we'll go to that place where you can buy frozen yogurt by the pound."

I watched closely as Zadie stared in disbelief at the cards.

Cleo didn't stare in disbelief.

She aimed shining eyes at me and exclaimed, "Seriously?"

I smiled at her. "Seriously."

"But...Forever 21. And Claire's. And Buckle. *And* H&M. And *Urban Outfitters*!" she exclaimed with glee.

Apparently, I'd picked the right ones.

I felt extreme relief but only lifted a shoulder. "It's kind of a welcome to my house for your first sleepover type thing. A little celebration for an occasion that's special to me. It's also special to your dad. Just my way of saying I'm happy to have you here."

"That's so cool!" Cleo cried.

Zadie didn't say anything.

So I found my mouth babbling, "And maybe, when we get home, we'll do girlie stuff. You know. Give each other manicures and pedicures. We can stop by Target on the way back from the mall and pick up some fun colors."

"I didn't relent to that," Logan muttered from his place at the stove.

"Oh my gosh! That's so awesome!" Cleo yelled.

"It is," Zadie said, and I looked to her. She wasn't looking at me. She was nudging a Claire's gift card with her finger.

"I'm glad you think so, darling," I said carefully.

Her eyes came to me for the barest of moments before she looked back to the cards.

I was so focused on Zadie, I jumped when Logan got close, tossing an arm around my shoulders.

"My girls do girl crap all day, I pick the movie tonight," he declared.

"Okay, Daddy," Cleo immediately agreed.

Zadie's head came up, her eyes going to her dad.

"Just as long as it's not scary," she stated, just like she was a part of the conversation, not pouty or demanding.

I pressed my lips together to hold back my cautious excitement because maybe I was getting somewhere.

"Would I scare my baby?" Logan asked.

"No," Zadie answered.

"I like scary," Cleo announced.

"That's what I'm sayin'. You wouldn't, but Clee-Clee would," Zadie explained.

"You and me can have our scary nights when I get another TV in this joint," Logan told his oldest. "That way, we do that, Zade and Millie can go watch somethin' else in the bedroom."

I was *not* putting a TV in the bedroom. It would be ugly, ruining the aesthetics. I knew this because I'd considered it and even looked for a media center with doors that closed the TV away in order to have a TV in my bedroom. Years of looking, I'd found nothing that would work.

So that was not going to happen.

However, Logan and I would have that conversation at a later date.

Right then, I looked up at Logan. "I actually DVR'ed *Pitch Perfect* and *Easy A* a while ago and I've been wanting to watch both of them for ages."

"I love *Pitch Perfect*!" Cleo squealed.

"Jesus," Logan muttered, frowning down at me.

"Of course," I said hurriedly, "we can watch them another weekend."

"Oh, Daddy, we *so* have to watch *Pitch Perfect*," Zadie stated excitedly.

So excitedly, my eyes flew to her.

She was looking up at her dad, her eyes now shining, something I'd never seen.

Like her sister, the transformation was amazing.

She was a cute kid, a budding beauty, both impossible to miss.

But now, both the cuteness and the beauty shone from her like a beacon that was blinding.

Seeing it for the first time, I got why her father spoiled her. I, too, would do anything in my power to get that aimed at me on a regular basis.

It might not be good parenting.

But staring into that beam, I knew it would be near impossible to beat back the urge.

"It's funny and so good," she went on, "even *you'll* like it."

I hadn't seen the movie yet.

Still, I knew a movie based on a capella groups dueling each other in college was not something Logan would *ever* like.

"That movie too old for you?" Logan asked.

"No," Cleo answered.

"Totally no," Zadie put in.

"Zade's right, Daddy. You're *so* gonna laugh. It's really funny," Cleo stated.

Logan let me go to move back to the stove, muttering, "So I gotta put up with the mall, nail polish smell, and I don't even get to pick the movie."

"Millie, Cleo, and me'll make chicken, bacon mac 'n' cheese," Zadie bartered.

When she did, I went still.

She'd included *me* in that.

Me!

I didn't know what chicken, bacon mac 'n' cheese was. But I was *so totally* making it.

I fought back giggling like a lunatic and twirling in delight.

"Chicken, bacon mac's the only thing worth watchin' an asinine high school movie," Logan murmured to the skillet.

"They're in college, Daddy," Cleo informed him.

"Chicken, bacon mac's the only thing worth watchin' an asinine college movie," Logan murmured to the skillet.

Cleo giggled.

Zadie did too.

My heart got so light, it lightened everything about me to the point it was a wonder I wasn't floating on air when I went to the pantry to get the syrup.

I had that out, plus the butter and plates, forks, and napkins on placemats before I went back to the stove to relieve Logan of his duties.

"Heat up your coffee, Snooks," I said softly, pushing in to take the spatula from him. "And grab a stool. I'll finish here."

"Babe," he replied.

I looked up at him.

It was then my heart stopped.

Because now, *his* eyes were shining. Shining and happy and relieved.

And I saw his girls got that from him, too, that look transforming his beauty into something breathtaking.

As I gazed up at him in wonder, he bent and touched his mouth to mine. It was a swift kiss. Light. There and gone.

But it was happy too.

He relinquished the spatula, grabbed my mug as well as his, and heated up both our coffees before he took a stool.

I served French toast. It was good French toast. But it was just French toast.

Still, I was going to remember that French toast for the rest of my life.

Because I ate it listening to Cleo babbling, Zadie joining her, and watching my man eat his surrounded by all his girls, looking straight down to his bones *happy*.

*   *   *

"Okay, so that went good," I said to Logan, who was moving around me in the kitchen.

It was late evening. He was finishing up his last beer. I was cleaning my wineglass.

We were headed to bed.

The girls were already down.

Bribery apparently worked.

It worked so well that even when *Pitch Perfect* proved to be a tad bit too adult for Logan's girls (as decreed by Logan, even though they'd both already seen it so he couldn't put the kibosh on it) and he'd shared that unhappily, nothing came of this since we were still riding the wave of mall, yogurt by the pound, and girlie treat in-house mani-pedis.

Zadie may not have been about hugs and shouting endorsements of me from the top of her lungs, but she hadn't done a single bratty thing all day. She'd even shyly, almost like it was against her will but she couldn't stop it, asked my opinions on things she'd purchased.

And she'd listened to my answers.

As for Cleo, any barriers that may have remained between her and me had crumbled down. She saw her mom with me. She saw her father not happy to be at the mall shopping but definitely happy to be with his girls. And she appreciated all my efforts, and not just the gift cards.

The people she loved were settled and content and that was all Cleo Judd needed.

Therefore, she was open and talkative, friendly and familiar, and riding a near-teen-girl wave of joy at having a new top, earrings, bangles, hair stuff, and girl gizmos.

She was just a phenomenal kid. It was remarkable watching her be carefree after seeing her so often be careful about all around her.

I watched this falling in love with Cleo.

I knew Logan agreed with my assessment on the day when I felt his arms round me from behind.

He gave me his verbal agreement when he shoved his face in my neck and muttered, "Yeah."

"You were wrong," I told him, placing my glass on a spread kitchen towel by the sink.

He took his face out of my neck and turned me in his arms.

When he got me face to face, I wrapped mine around him.

"Yeah?"

"You said six point five visits for Zadie." I grinned up at him. "It only took four."

"Five," he returned.

He was counting too.

But he was wrong.

"Four," I returned.

"Five, babe. She was still holdin' back over dinner with Deb."

This was true.

Which meant he was right.

Therefore, I muttered, "Whatever."

He gave me a squeeze not to give me a squeeze, because he'd begun laughing.

It wasn't unadulterated mirth. He was being quiet because we had two sleeping girls in the house.

But it was still open, genuine, and amazing.

And further, we had two sleeping girls in our house.

I stood in his arms, in the kitchen, watching my man laugh quietly.

The road to that moment sucked big-time.

Having that moment, just that one, Logan and me holding each other in our kitchen, him laughing and happy, two girls who'd had a good day with their dad and his woman sleeping in our house, that road was worth it.

So I gave him a squeeze and I did it to give him a *squeeze*.

He focused on me, still chuckling.

I was not chuckling.

I wasn't even smiling.

And when Logan caught that, his amusement died.

"Baby?" he whispered.

"Sometimes I felt consumed, like I didn't exist, gone," I whispered back. "Every day it was just going through the motions."

He dipped his face close to mine and his repeated, "Baby?" was rougher.

It was also confused.

I didn't explain outright, even as I did.

"But it was worth it. Every step was worth it. Even if all I ever get from it was this one moment with you."

"Millie."

That was abrasive.

He got me.

I gave him the rest anyway.

"I'd do it again for another moment like this. And again for a moment like I had over French toast with you and your babies. And again and again and again, for each night I get to sleep with you. No joke, Snook'ums. No lie. I'd do it every day it was so worth it to walk through fire for you."

He didn't call me baby. He didn't call my name.

He kissed me.

Not a touch. Not a peck. Not light.

Hot and hard and so, so wet.

I ended it, breaking the connection to slide my lips to his ear because I wasn't done.

"I love you, Logan Judd," I whispered there. "I never stopped loving you. Thank you for making it worth it."

He groaned, grasped onto my hair, and turned my head so he could kiss me again.

It was as good as the one before and then some.

Yes.

Absolutely yes.

Consumed by the flames for twenty years, every second was totally *worth it*.

*   *   *

"Zadie?" I called, then stutter-stepped on my way down the hall because Chief, chased by Poem, ran under my feet.

There was no answer.

I looked into the living room and saw nothing, which I wouldn't, since I'd left her on the couch.

Perhaps she'd gone out back with her dad and sister.

It was the next morning. The workmen hadn't come early. By the time they arrived, we were all up but Logan had gotten up before everyone and he'd gone out to get LaMar's donuts.

So we were all sugared up too.

When the men arrived, Logan went out back to go over the project with them and oversee the work.

Cleo, daddy's girl, had gone with him.

Zadie, possibly sugar crashing on the couch in front of some program, probably not wanting to move because Poem had fallen asleep curled into the curve of her little body, had elected to stay in the house with me.

I didn't suspect she wanted to be with me but instead with Poem as her giving me a shot meant her not avoiding the kittens anymore.

I also suspected that even though this weekend was going great, she didn't need me up in her face all the time, continuing to try to win her.

She needed to get to a normal with me, her dad, her sister in our house.

So I'd decided to give her some alone time and left her and Poem to hit the shower and get ready to face the day.

It was totally a half-hair-air-dried day. We didn't have the girls much longer so even if I needed to give them normal, I also wasn't real fired up they'd be gone the next day. It was awesome to have them around because they were awesome (even Zadie), they filled up the house, and made it feel homey and Logan loved having his girls with him. So I wanted more of all that before it went away, which meant I wasn't wasting time spending eons on my hair.

I still had to roll out the top.

However, between blasts of the hair dryer to the roller brush, I'd heard the doorbell ring. So I'd quit my preparations to find out who was at the door (with Chaos back in my life, it could be anyone—I was still thinking it was Dot, Alan, and the kids, just so they could check up on me knowing the girls were there for their first weekend).

When I'd walked by the front door, no one was in the window.

And now Zadie wasn't answering.

I hit the living room, going to the back of the couch and looking over it.

Poem, obviously, had woken up and decided to play with her brother.

Zadie also had clearly decided to do something else because she wasn't on the couch.

"Zadie?" I called again, looking toward the kitchen to look out the window of the back door even though I couldn't see all the way to the end of my property from there.

She didn't answer.

She must have gone out to check on progress with her dad and sister.

My body moved that way but, for some reason, my head turned the other.

When it did and I saw what I saw through the sheers, I froze, as did all the blood in my veins.

Then, my feet bare, I ran, right through the living room to the hall, the foyer, and out the front door.

Once out the door, I kept running, straight to the two good-looking, well-dressed Hispanic men who were talking to Zadie on the sidewalk.

Benito Valenzuela's henchmen. The one that held a gun to me and one of the men who stood behind him when he sat in my cuddle chair.

"Zadie!" I snapped.

She turned to me as the men's eyes came to me.

"Daddy's friends are here," she informed me. "I told them he was out back."

"Get in the house," I ordered, making it to her and pushing in with my body, at the same time pushing her back and putting myself between her and the men.

"Lookin' for you," one of the men said. "Thought we found better. Now we got both."

Oh God.

I took a step back, feeling Zadie's body forced to move back with me.

I kept my eyes to the men as I demanded, "Go, Zadie. Run and get your father."

One of the men made a move toward me. "Now, hang on—"

I pushed back farther even as I whirled and bent to Logan's girl. "Go! Now! Run and get your father!"

"They're Daddy's friends," she retorted, not bratty, looking confused. "They told me—"

I got in her face.

"*Run!*" I shrieked.

When I did, her body jerked perhaps due to my tone but also because one man wrapped his fingers around my elbow and yanked me away from her as the other one made his move...toward Zadie.

"*Go!*" I screeched, swinging my body still in the other's hold toward the guy who was moving to Zadie.

She turned and ran.

The other man started to run after her.

I wrenched free and threw myself at him. I managed to take him off trajectory of Zadie, scuttling him to the side.

He wrapped his arms around me and tossed me at the other guy with such force, I flew at him, unable to stop myself.

Far away, I could hear the noises of the trucks working out back.

Still struggling against my captor, I screamed, "*Logan!*"

"We'll take her," the man holding me stated.

The guy I feared would go after Zadie turned to him. "Benito said—"

"We got her. We'll take her," the guy I was fighting declared.

"*Logan!*" I shrieked.

"Shut her the fuck up," the one coming back our way ordered.

A hand came over my mouth.

I tried to bite it but he felt my intention and moved it away and then right back even as he pulled me toward the curb.

"Let me go!" I demanded, the words muffled. I was swinging my body viciously this way and that, hoping for the desired result.

"Benito told us—"

"To force it," the guy with me finished for him. "We're forcin' it."

The other guy looked at us a beat before he said, "'Spose she'll work."

Really?

Broad daylight?

Even if Logan couldn't hear me over the trucks out back, *where were my neighbors?*

"Move your hand, *muchacho*," the guy advancing ordered.

The hand was moved.

I sucked in air in order to scream.

I didn't get it out when his arm shot back and slammed forward, connecting with my temple, and I was out cold.

CHAPTER TWENTY-THREE

Like Any Good Old Lady Should

High

"DADDY, THEY SAID you were friends."

"Quiet, Zadie."

"But they said they knew you."

"*Quiet!*"

His word was a roar and he saw his baby jump in fear.

He fucking hated that.

But he and his girls had just gotten back inside from going out front, where Zadie told him two men had Millie.

When he finally sprinted to her front drive, a neighbor was standing in their yard looking down the road. Catching sight of High and his girls, that neighbor yelled that he'd seen someone shove Millie, who appeared unconscious, into an SUV.

Then he'd asked, "You want me to call the police?"

It was the stupidest fucking question High had ever heard in his life. The man had watched his unconscious neighbor shoved into an SUV. Of course he should call the fucking cops.

High didn't answer. He couldn't. He had zero control.

He'd just stalked into the house, his girls following, and pulled out his phone.

Commence him scaring the shit out of his baby.

But he couldn't think about that because he heard, "Yo," in his ear.

"Valenzuela sent some guys," he told Tack, his voice low, rough, and tight. "I was out back with Cleo. They got Zadie out of the house at the front. Millie saw it, went out to protect her. Zadie ran and the neighbors just informed me they saw Millie, unconscious, hauled away in an SUV."

"On it," Tack stated urgently.

High turned his back to the girls and started to prowl down the hall, saying quietly, "Oh no. Fuck no. You get Tyra here or some fuckin' old lady, I don't care who, to look after my girls. They got Millie. *I'm* on this."

"That's what they want, High," Tack told him.

"Yeah. And that's what they're gettin'," High returned.

"Brother—"

"Get . . . an . . . old . . . lady . . . *here*."

"You ride out with us," Tack declared.

"I ride out in five minutes. You don't get an old lady here, I'm droppin' the girls at Deb's and I'm *on it*."

"Copy that, High."

High disconnected and stalked back into the living room.

He did this with his brain not functioning.

I'd do it every day it was so worth it to walk through fire for you.

He knew what she meant and it wasn't having him back in her home, in her bed, in her arms.

It was having him back, having his daughters asleep in her guestroom, giving him a day like he had that day. Giving him everything he'd ever wanted.

He stopped in the living room, not able to look at the two beautiful daughters his woman sacrificed years to give to him. Instead, he dropped his head and lifted his hand to curl it around the back of his neck, shutting his eyes tight at pleasure that could now turn to pain if anything happened to her at hearing her words rattling his brain.

Valenzuela was a lunatic. Valenzuela was getting impatient.

And Valenzuela was not stupid.

High was the weak link. Pushed, High was probably the last brother of Chaos who would lose it, fuck everything and do anything, *anything*, to rescue his woman.

And when that was done, get his vengeance.

But it was more.

The motherfucker had lured his baby girl out of the house.

Fuck yeah.

High was the weak link.

Rescue.

Then vengeance.

"She didn't mean anything."

Cleo's trembling words had High righting his head and dropping his hand to focus on his girls in Millie's armchair, holding on to each other, Zadie with her face pressed into her sister's chest, her body shaking with silent tears.

"She didn't, Daddy," Cleo kept on. "She told me last night when we were in bed that she thought Millie was cool. She wasn't being bad. She was just being…" Her face and her voice said she knew the rest was lame. "Maybe not too smart."

A stifled sob came from Zadie, which meant High's legs moved him to their chair.

Cleo watched him do it, holding on to her sister. Zadie sensed him doing it and burrowed deeper into Cleo.

She was scared of her old man.

He hated that too.

Oh yeah.

Vengeance.

He crouched down in front of them.

"Look at me, Zade."

It took her a beat but she did, doing it just twisting her neck a little so she could peek at him still pressed to her sister's chest.

"We'll talk 'bout you talkin' to men you don't know later, baby. Though that's a lesson I think you already learned today and I know you didn't mean to do anything bad. This isn't on you, Zadie. What happened isn't your fault. But right now what's important is that I need you to tell me about the men who took Millie."

She drew in a broken breath and High fought clenching his teeth because it felt like it took her a week to draw it in.

Then she stuttered, "I was . . . I was m-mean to her."

Fuck.

"You got over that, Zade," he reminded her. "This isn't about that. That's done. Now you gotta tell me about those men."

"I didn't know, they . . . they were b-bad men. Never, Daddy, *never* would I be that mean, going out so Millie would come out after me. She's . . . Millie, she's . . . I did. I did tell Clee-Clee she was cool. And I've been mean to her. I did bad things. I scared her about Chief. But now I *like* her. She's nice. She has a super nice house. She has cute kitties she lets us play with. But even if I didn't like her, I'd never be *that* mean."

"Zade," he said, forcing his voice to soft and lifting a hand to lay it on her back. "I know you didn't mean anything. You're not in trouble. But I gotta know about those men."

"Y-you yelled at me," she whispered.

His voice was firm, and with his patience slipping he couldn't smooth the edge when he stated, "Zadie, this is not about you. There are gonna be times in your life, a lot of them, when it's not about you. You gotta get used to that and do it now, darlin', 'cause this is one of those times. A big one. Now you dig deep like I know you can and *tell me about those men.*"

"They...they were Mexican," she said.

He was right.

Valenzuela.

"Older? Younger?" he asked.

"Younger than you," she answered.

Valenzuela was close to his age.

That meant soldiers.

"Dressed nice?" he went on.

She nodded.

"The color of their SUV, you remember?" he pushed.

"B-black," she said.

"Did you see the kind of SUV they were in?"

She shook her head.

"What'd they say to you?" he kept at his girl.

"Just that...that..." She pressed her lips together and when High was near to losing complete hold on his patience, she continued talking. "They were friends of yours and they had something in their car for you. A present. A surprise. Something special. They asked me to come get it and bring it to you. I know it was stupid," she whispered the last, sounding beaten. "But I...I..." She shoved into her sister. "This is a nice neighborhood. Millie has a really pretty house. They seemed nice." She took another broken breath. "I didn't think they were bad."

She just didn't think. She knew better. Even High had drilled the don't talk to strangers shit into her head since she could cogitate.

Then again, a ten-year-old shouldn't have to know what kind of bad could knock on the door in any neighborhood.

"Is Millie...?" Cleo started, and got her old man's attention, paused, then pushed on. "Did Millie do something bad?"

Only the kind he gave her.

But this shit should never touch his girls. Any of them. He should never be in the position to field questions that would lead to the kind of answers he'd have to give.

That was on Valenzuela too.

"No," he told his big girl. "Millie's good to the core."

"So why—?" Cleo began.

"That's not for now, Cleo," High stated, straightening.

"Is she...?" That was Zadie and he looked to his baby who was pulling away from her sister, looking up at her dad. "Do you think she's gonna be okay?"

He knew she'd better be.

"She's gonna be fine," he told her.

Her lip trembled.

His phone rang.

He stepped away from them, looking at it. When he saw the caller, he took the call.

"Where are we?" he asked as greeting.

"Keely's headed over," Tack told him. "Brothers are rendezvousing at the Compound. Mitch and Slim have been informed."

High stopped at the side of Millie's couch. "Keely?"

"She's closest to you," Tack explained. "She should be there in a few."

The girls had met Keely only a couple of times. They barely knew her. More, after she lost Black, pulling her into Chaos mess was not cool.

He'd prefer Tyra, Lanie, Tab, Elvira.

He'd have to take Keely because he had to get out of there. He was holding it together but only because his girls were watching. Inside, it felt like he was about to come out of his skin.

"He's not gonna do shit to her, brother," Tack assured him.

High wanted that to be true.

But Valenzuela was ready to roll. He was bringing it. He was forcing it so Chaos would shove it back.

Which meant anything could happen.

Millie

I sat curled into myself on the bed in a motel room that wasn't all that nice but it wasn't shabby either.

I did this and I didn't take my eyes off Benito Valenzuela, who was standing at the door with his henchmen.

Another man who was even scarier than Valenzuela was standing in the corner, surveying the entirety of the scene (in other words, keeping his eye on me as well as the action at the door) even as a woman walked my way.

She got my attention when she sat on the edge of the bed.

She was a hooker.

It wasn't like she was wearing Julia Roberts's stretchy outfit and thigh-high boots from *Pretty Woman* but still, she was seriously made up and her clothes were revealing and it wasn't even noon on a Sunday, so I didn't think it was jumping to conclusions to guess her occupation.

"Got some ice from the machine outside," she said quietly, offering me a wet, bulky towel. "You should put that on your eye, shug."

She was right.

I took the ice and put it to my eye.

Then I turned the one eye I could still see out of toward Valenzuela just as I heard him whisper, "...do with you after this *colossal fuckup*."

"You said force it, *jefe*," the one who grabbed me replied.

"I meant scare her, not fucking kidnap her," Valenzuela bit back.

"Still, think this'll force it, Benito," the one who hit me said. "Chaos ain't gonna let this stand."

I felt something and tore my eyes from the conversation at the door to look at the woman seated on the bed in a not-too-shabby motel with me.

"They aren't, are they?" she whispered, and she didn't sound happy.

In fact, she sounded absolutely, one hundred percent *freaked out.*

Considering I was that, and more, I didn't need her freaking out with me.

"I'm right," she said when I didn't respond, and she was still whispering. "You're an old lady. They're gonna ride."

They were gonna ride.

And I needed them to ride. I needed Logan to come and get me, and to do that safely, for him and me, he needed his brothers.

I still was terrified of what Chaos riding meant.

I didn't answer her, partially because I didn't want to think about it but mostly because I sensed movement so I looked toward the door.

Apparently, even whispering, our conversation had gotten the attention of Valenzuela.

Great.

He came my way, stopped by the bed, cast a split-second glance at the hooker, and she vacated her place, scurrying on her platform heels straight to the door.

I didn't take that as a good sign.

Even so, I kept my eye to Valenzuela, my position on the bed and the ice to my swelling face.

"Which one decided to take you?" he asked after the door closed on my unusual Florence Nightingale.

I pressed my lips together.

Then I pressed into the headboard when he snapped right

before my eyes, leaned toward me, his face twisted with rage, his eyes burning with it, and he thundered, *"Which one took you?"*

Oh my God.

He was totally crazy.

"Th-that one," I answered, lifting my hand to point at the one who'd held me.

Valenzuela leaned back. "He hit you too?"

I shook my head.

"So Pedro took you, Carlos hit you," he stated, all evidence of his fury gone, this was uttered matter-of-factly.

God, he'd been freaking me out but that about-face scared the absolute *crap* out of me.

Thus, even if it seemed he didn't intend to hurt me further—in fact, he was pissed way the hell off I'd been taken and hurt at all—I felt it prudent not to relax quite yet because this guy was clearly fucking *loco*.

I would have no idea how right I was.

I would also have no idea that I shouldn't confirm his statement even if I didn't know which was which, Carlos and Pedro.

I shouldn't have even spoken.

But I did both.

"Yes," I said.

And right then, right there, he twisted his torso, doing this nodding to the other man in the room.

I looked that way just as the guy reached into his suit jacket and came out with a gun.

Before I could even brace or open my mouth to scream, he lifted it. I heard two strange, loud zings followed instantly by far less welcome sounds at the same time my eyes jerked toward the door. I saw blood and brains spatter against walls and Pedro and Carlos sink to the carpet.

I dropped the ice and shuffled frantically back on the bed, shocked I could move because it felt like my body had frozen right to the bone, terrified at the same time that, because of this, it felt my limbs would crack right off. My brain saturated with images of carnage, I couldn't gauge where I was going and fell off the side of the bed.

I scrambled to my feet as Valenzuela turned back to me. Mind in turmoil, my only thoughts were escape and the chilling knowledge that there wasn't one.

"Stop moving. I won't hurt you," he ordered.

I kept moving, making preparations in order to take flight.

He reached into his suit jacket, pulled out his own gun, and lifted it my way.

"Stop...fucking...moving."

Automatically, I stopped moving.

He turned his head and dipped his chin at the only other live person in the room.

I stared, shock beginning to overcome me, my body starting to tremble as the guy coolly dipped his chin as well and sauntered to and out the door, closing it behind him.

"You're at the Mile Hi Motel in room two sixteen," Valenzuela stated, and my eyes darted back to him. "You call your biker, you tell them where to find you, you tell them that's for them." He swung his gun toward the two dead bodies on the floor, then back to me. "You tell them I did not order what happened today. You tell them Carlos and Pedro acted alone. You tell them I was not happy about this and saw to their punishment."

Punishment?

That was his brand of *punishment*?

I stared at him, suddenly realizing that I was not only trembling from hair to toenails, my chest was rising and falling with shallow breaths and my fingers felt like they'd been asleep but were coming awake, tingling in a way that skimmed the edge of pain.

But what I saw as I stared at his face was not fear.

He wasn't scared of Chaos's retribution for the mistake

made by his men that day and taking care of it so they wouldn't
lose their minds.

It was something else.

And right then, I went from scared out of my brain to terrified down to my bones.

"You should leave town," I blurted.

He dropped the gun, which was a relief, but he also smiled
a creepy smile, which wasn't.

"Thank you for the advice, but I think I'll stay," he replied.

Regardless of the fact that he didn't want my very good
advice to penetrate—seeing as I was witness to his minion's
double homicide and an old lady to a member of a band of
brothers who took family and the protection of it really fucking
seriously, so I knew what I was talking about—I kept going.

"You don't touch old ladies."

"I didn't."

That was the truth.

"Your men lured Lo...I mean, High's daughter to their
car," I shared.

His mouth got tight.

He didn't know that.

My body got tight too. Or *tighter*.

Then his mouth relaxed. "Another fail," he stated. "And as
you can see, they won't do anything like that again."

Another truth. A big one.

I kept my eyes off the slaughter sharing a room with me so
I could keep hold on my mind.

"I mean no offense. I'm sure you know this," I began. "But
you don't mean anything to me. Still, this plays out like I know
it will, people I care about will be forced to do things they
don't wish to do. They're good men. But this won't stand." I
carefully indicated the floor beneath my feet. "They won't let
it and you shouldn't underestimate them. There's no way you
can win."

"That's where you're wrong."

I stared at him.

He believed that.

Totally.

A chill crept over my skin and I kept trying.

"You won't win, Valenzuela. Seriously, believe me. I've known them a long time. United, the brotherhood can't be defeated."

"Many brotherhoods felt the same and continued to do so until they fell."

I stared into his eyes and I read everything there.

He wasn't going to give up. He wasn't going to go away. He wasn't going to stop. He was weak, with men misinterpreting his orders, facing a woman who could guarantee his time in prison when he was caught and I testified that he'd ordered the murders of two men.

He still wasn't going to stop.

Not until it was over however that came about.

There was something scarily wrong about that. He was a man with every chip in the pot, holding weak cards in his hand.

But he was acting like he had an ace up his sleeve.

"You need to be careful," I whispered.

"Ah, Millie, your concern in touching. But don't you worry. I'm being *very* careful."

"No," I returned. "What I mean is, you hurt him, you hurt High, you hurt any of them, I'll hurt you."

He found that amusing, so much so it was incredibly insulting.

While smiling big, he tipped his head to the side. "You're threatening me while I hold a gun?"

"Wrong again," I told him, shaking my head. "It's insane but I'm trying to save your life. Seriously, you should get out of town."

"I will not fall to Chaos," he said with utter confidence.

"If you don't leave and you also don't fall to Chaos, you'll still fall."

"Chaos gash comes after me after I bring that Club low, that's business I'll be forced to take care of too."

Gash.

He'd said that word before.

It wasn't nice.

It also pissed me off.

I straightened my spine and squared my shoulders, sharing, "There'll be only one storm mightier than the one your men unleashed today. You don't mess with an old lady. You definitely don't mess with an old lady's man."

He was still amused. "After I claim all of Denver, that'll be an interesting challenge."

He might hold the ace.

But his cards were still weak.

"I see your weakness," I told him.

That amused him too. Greatly.

He lifted his brows over dancing eyes.

"I have a weakness?" he asked in disbelief.

"You don't think gash have brains," I shared.

"You're not difficult to look at, Millie, but you aren't being very smart, where you are, how you are, speaking to me the way you are."

"You don't think gash have brains," I repeated. "So you can't know we have them and we also have hearts. And if you don't know any of that, you also don't know we hold a mean grudge."

"I know this," he said in a way that made my skin tighten all over my body. "I ordered the dispatch of two of my soldiers. I did it with a witness. I did it knowing Chaos has gone pussy, taking their twat asses to the cops. So I know you'll share with Mitch Lawson and Brock Lucas. And I don't fucking care."

That was crazy.

My voice was rising high when I asked, "You believe you're untouchable?"

"I believe I get Chaos out of the way, I'll be running Denver. And if I have to put down Chaos, along with Lawson, Lucas, and Delgado to do it, then that'll get done."

Delgado?

Hawk Delgado?

Elvira's boss?

What did he have to do with all this?

I didn't ask that.

I remarked, "So you're gonna leave me alive."

He tipped his head to the side and asked, "What did you see?"

He knew what I saw since it happened five minutes ago and I didn't think it was smart to remind him that I saw it but I had a feeling he had an agenda and that agenda was not further harming me, so I said, "You told your man to shoot them and he did."

"I wasn't anywhere near here and that man doesn't exist."

Both were wrong but I had a feeling he could make it so they were right.

He kept speaking.

"In fact, later today, there will be a man who will come forward, confessing to these killings. He'll have the gun used. And he'll share all about how he did this in retribution for what was done to you."

I stared at him some more.

I'd heard about things like that. Saw it on TV. A bad guy paying someone to take the fall, maybe promising to take care of his family, doing it huge to make it worth the sacrifice.

"Anyway, Millie," he carried on. "A win isn't really a win unless there are losers left standing."

"So you're gonna leave me alive," I repeated.

"Yes," he confirmed.

Okay, I was more than a little done.

"Could you do that about now?" I requested.

He grinned before he creeped me way the fuck out by saying, "You know, I think I actually like you."

"I'm totally showering for three hours when I get home," I muttered.

He burst out laughing.

I didn't move a muscle.

He stopped laughing, lifted his gun, and I remained immobile, my eyes locked to his weapon as he wagged it at me.

"Yes, I like you. I get Judd. Those two uppity bitches who're leading Allen and Kincaid around by their cocks, I don't get. But you might be fun."

I didn't say anything because I couldn't think of what to say.

Though I thought perhaps I should keep him talking. I figured the more he played with me, the longer he was hanging around, I knew Logan, Chaos, and more than likely Chaos's cop buddies were tearing Denver apart looking for me, so they might find us. If he wanted to be standing around having a conversation when they did, it wasn't me who was going to stop him.

Though I wished I hadn't dropped the ice. My eye was hurting like a bitch.

"No comeback?" he prompted.

"My eye kinda hurts and this conversation is definitely getting boring," I replied.

"Then I'll leave you," he said.

I tried not to look excited as I contradictorily tried to think of ways to get him to stay and do that without moving him to murder me.

"Would it be foolish to ask that you wait ten minutes after I leave before you make your call?" he requested.

"Yes," I declined his request.

That amused him too.

God, I fucking *hated* this guy.

"When this is over, if you want to fuck a winner, I'll be sure a line's opened to you," he offered.

Okay, now I was going to have to shower for four hours.

I didn't reply.

He grinned his disturbing grin. "Until then, Millie."

I stayed silent.

He moved, walking to the door like he was just walking to the door. Not like he was walking through two corpses with half their heads blown off.

I swallowed bile and looked away from the bodies. I didn't like Pedro and Carlos much but I preferred to see them shackled and breathing, not this way.

The door closed.

I didn't run to it to lock it. I wasn't going anywhere near there.

Instead I jumped to the bed, crawled on hands and knees to the phone on the opposite side, and reached for it. I took it with me as I turned my back to the carnage, curling into myself.

I didn't have Logan's number memorized because I had it in my phone and I could just press the screen to get him.

I was memorizing it later that day *for sure*.

I called 911.

I reported my emergency.

I made it through giving the operator my name, the motel, the room number, my location, and the fact I'd just witnessed a double homicide before I dropped my forehead to my knees and dissolved into tears.

In other words, I held it together through the important stuff and fell apart only when no one was watching (even though the 911 operator was listening).

Like any good old lady should.

*   *   *

I was standing outside the motel room on a walkway exposed to the elements, surrounded by uniformed police officers, squad cars glutting the parking lot below, folks everywhere. Out of their rooms and standing outside the police barrier that an officer was now rolling out to span the parking lot.

When the first unit had arrived, they'd thankfully not wasted any time and even more thankfully the brawnier one picked me up and carried me out of the room so I didn't get anything on my bare feet that would never mentally wash off.

An added plus to this was I got to shove my face in his neck so I didn't see anything more than I'd already seen even if what I'd seen was burned into my brain.

I didn't need more.

I'd barely been out there five minutes, only long enough for them to get a blanket to wrap around my shoulders and pull a chair from another room so I could sit on it, I was trembling so badly. I'd just begun to share what happened when I heard the roar.

My head jerked so I could look over my shoulder and I saw them roll in in formation.

And I was not surprised to see that Tack wasn't leading the crew.

Logan was.

Like he had Millie Radar, he rode in, eyes up and on me.

"Mizz Cross, I know you're Chaos but I need you to stick with me," the officer said quickly.

I didn't stick with him.

I jumped out of my seat and ran, sprinting down the walkway, the blanket falling from my shoulders, my eyes glued to Logan who had parked his bike outside the police tape and he was dismounting.

I was going so fast down the walkway I had to throw out a hand to grab the post holding up the landing by the stairwell.

My body went flying to the side, but I held on tight, forcing its momentum toward the steps.

Then I dashed down them watching Logan race my way.

We collided two steps from the bottom and I didn't know how Logan didn't fall to his ass when that collision included me throwing myself bodily at him, wrapping my arms around his shoulders, my legs around his waist and shoving my face in his neck.

I drew in deep breaths, audibly sucking in air to hold it together as his strength became real all around me, he held me tight, and I tried to keep my shit together.

But I couldn't stop the shaking.

"The girls?" I forced out.

His arms held tighter.

"Big Petey got a call. They know you're good," he replied, his voice, low and harsh, scratching into my skin.

I nodded, my body bucking painfully as I fought back a sob.

"You're good, Millie. You're here. I got you. You're good, baby," he whispered, gliding a hand up to tangle in my hair.

"I'm good," I whispered back. It was shaky and uncertain but I said it anyway.

"Hold on," he ordered.

That I could do.

So I did it and Logan held me back.

That gave me the strength to pull it totally together, and after I absorbed enough of it, I lifted my head to look at him.

His gaze immediately went to the swelling around my eye and a scariness that was exponentially scarier than that day he'd charged into my office and then dragged me around my house to show me the alarm system he'd set up snapped into place over his features.

"I'm okay," I assured him hurriedly.

He stopped looking at my eye to look into both of them.

"Yeah," he muttered. It was not shaky but it was skeptical.

I dropped my forehead to his, holding his gaze.

"Chaos has a problem," I shared quietly.

"Think we know that, babe," he replied just as quietly.

"No, Snooks," I went on. "He's planning something. Something he thinks means a guaranteed win. I don't know what today meant. I just know he's convinced he can't lose."

Carefully, still holding me close, Logan jiggled me so I knew to drop my legs. He put me on the step in front of him so we were still eye to eye but he didn't let go.

"He'll be convinced otherwise," he announced.

I moved my hand to curl it on the side of his neck, rolling up on my toes to get closer to him.

"You need to be ready for anything," I warned. "You need to be ready and you need to be smart. He has something, Low, an ace up his sleeve. He's determined to use it to bring Chaos down and I don't think he means to harm anyone physically. I think he means to force you to do stupid shit that would end the Club." I pressed even closer. "And I can see it in your eyes, baby. You're fired up to do stupid shit and if he brings you down, he takes you away from me. From Cleo. From Zadie. And, Snooks, you gotta be smart because you cannot let that happen."

He studied me without replying and in the middle of this, we heard, "Sorry, High, but gotta get her statement," and Logan's eyes went beyond me.

I looked over my shoulder at the officer who had begun to question me and looked back to Logan when I felt his hold on me loosen. He nodded to the officer as he took a different hold on me, wrapping his arm around my shoulders and moving me around so he could guide me up the steps with him.

We followed the officer, and with Logan guiding, I could look behind me.

Chaos was standing there.

All of them.

I shot a weak smile in their general direction.

I got no smiles back.

Not even a lip curl.

They'd been nudged.

A different kind of fear started slithering through my insides as I looked away to make the turn on the first landing.

One could say I'd not had a very good day. If the kind of day I had happened to someone I cared about, I'd be pissed in the extreme. I might even consider doing something crazy.

And I wasn't a biker.

That meant it was up to me to stop them from doing anything stupid.

The brothers did what the brothers had to do and any good old lady let that happen.

Except in circumstances like these.

This meant I had to rally the troops. I had to do what I could with my Chaos sisters to be certain the brothers stayed strong.

I had to.

And I was going to.

Like any old lady should.

*   *   *

There were a variety of cars wedged in my courtyard when Logan took me back home after I'd done what I'd needed to do with the cops.

Mitch Lawson and Brock Lucas had showed. I'd also gotten to meet Elvira's boss, Hawk Delgado.

It was lucky I met him then, after seeing Zadie with Valenzuela's men, getting punched in the face, being kidnapped, and then witnessing a double homicide. If I hadn't, with the Chaos boys, Lawson and Lucas, the addition of Delgado would have been hot guy overload and I might have spontaneously combusted.

As it was, I just gave him a handshake, said hey, memorized his dimples when he gave me a small smile so I could take that memory out later and savor it, and Logan carried me (I had bare feet, but I probably could have negotiated the parking lot, though he didn't let me) to a truck delivered by Roscoe (who was riding Logan's bike back to my house).

"Don't get out," Logan ordered before he even stopped in my courtyard. "I'm carryin' you in."

I didn't get out. He wanted to go over the top taking care of me, I'd let him.

Instead, as he parked wedged in with the other cars, cut the ignition, and angled out, I planned the rest of my day.

Make sure the girls were okay. Call my sister, Kellie, Justine, Ronnie, and get their asses to my house so I had my personal sisterhood close to prop me up so I could continue holding it together. Take a shower that might last a decade. Get out, call Tyra, and get her to set up an emergency Chaos sisterhood meeting.

Then spend the rest of the day attempting not to have a nervous breakdown.

Logan came to my side of the car, opened my door, and lifted me out. With me in his arms, he shut the door and stalked to my back door.

He was still pissed. Then again, he'd stood close throughout the whole story I'd told to the police so he wasn't actually *still* pissed. He was *more* pissed.

Not good.

We were several feet away when the door was opened by Big Petey.

He gave Logan a look I tried to ignore, then turned a relieved smile to me as he vacated the door so Logan could carry me in.

He also shut the door behind us as Logan walked me to the edge of the bar and dropped my legs to put my feet on the ground.

Through this, I saw I didn't have to call Tyra because she was already there. So were Lanie, Tabby, and Carissa.

It was a minor relief to tick that off my to-do list but I didn't really get to feel that feeling.

This was because I was suddenly hit by a small force that, although small, sent me slamming into Logan.

I looked down and saw Zadie with her arms around me.

Okay, maybe my shower wouldn't last a decade.

Maybe I wouldn't take one at all.

And I definitely wasn't going to have a nervous breakdown.

I already knew a kid's hug had healing powers beyond the beyond.

But getting that from Zadie was beyond anything.

I put my hand to her hair as her hold spread warmth through me.

"I'm okay, sweetie," I whispered.

She jerked her head back, giving me a red face, wet eyes, and an agonized expression.

"They said they were Daddy's friends!" she cried. "They said they had something special for him!"

I struggled against her hold to crouch down in front of her. When I got into position, I took her in my own hold, not loose, not scary tight.

Just safe.

"We all, every one of us, make mistakes," I said gently. "We trust people we shouldn't. And it makes us feel dumb." As she took a hiccoughing breath, I smoothed her hair away from the side of her face. "That's not right," I went on. "Someone does something wrong, it's *their* bad. Not yours." I moved my face closer to hers. "That doesn't mean you shouldn't be smart. But you also gotta stop beating yourself up. You didn't do wrong. *They* did."

Her damp eyes went to the swelling on my face. "They hit you."

"*They* did," I reminded her. "Got my arms around you, Zadie. Am I here? Am I home with you and your sister and your dad? Am I okay?"

She drew in another hiccoughing breath but didn't answer.

"I am, sweetie," I answered myself (though it was a kind of lie, I wasn't exactly okay, but I wasn't going to share that).

"I was mean to you," she whispered.

"Sometimes, learning how to do right isn't the easiest lesson," I told her. "And you were feeling a lot for reasons that were real, darling. There's nothing wrong with wanting your family together. I get that." Her lip quivered and her bright eyes got brighter so I cupped her soft cheek in my hand, stroking it with my thumb. "But you saw your daddy happy. You saw your mom was good. You didn't handle the situation right in the beginning, Zadie, but if you get there in the end, that's all that matters." I gave her a small smile and asked, "Are you there?"

She took in another broken breath and nodded.

"Will you be my friend?" I asked.

She nodded again, this time more decisively.

No, definitely no nervous breakdown.

With that, no matter what happened to me that day, I was all good.

Everything was all good.

So I gave her a full grin and shared that.

"Then we're all good."

I saw Logan's hand reach beyond me to cup the back of his little girl's head.

"Love this sweetness, Zadie, but you gotta let your old man take care of his woman," he said gently.

She looked up to her dad, her chin trembled, then she nodded and let me go.

I started to straighten but didn't get there because the second Zadie stepped away, Cleo hit me hard, wrapping her arms around me and holding on tight.

"Glad you're okay, Millie," she whispered, her voice frail.

To combat that, I curved my arms around her and gave her a tight squeeze to let her know I really was okay.

When I started to release, she pulled away and moved directly to her sister to guide her deeper into the living room.

Pure Cleo, taking it on herself to do anything she could, great or small, to help out her dad.

I gave her a wink and as Logan guided me firmly to the hall, I turned my gaze to the women in my living room. I tried to give them a look that said *we have to talk*.

I wasn't sure if they got my message before I had to look away to go down the hall.

We were in the bedroom when I asked, "How are you gonna explain all this to Deb?"

Logan kicked the door shut with his boot, kept moving me into the room but did it giving me his eyes.

"What do you need? Rest? Coffee? A shot of bourbon?"

I stopped in a way it stopped him. Then I turned in to him and wrapped my arms around his waist.

"What are you gonna say to Deb, Low? You have to tell her because if you don't, the girls will, and she's gonna freak. That could mean she won't want the girls—"

He lifted his hands and put them to either side of my neck.

"Deb did not spend our marriage in a vacuum, Millie," he stated. "She knew what I was when she met me, when she took my ring, and when she shared my bed. She knew how Chaos changed. She knew our activities after we changed. I didn't lay all of it out for her but I told her what she needed to know. She isn't gonna like this. She's gonna freak. Then she's gonna trust in the brotherhood. It might take her time to get there. But she'll get there."

I found this hard to believe.

"Are you sure? Today was extreme," I pointed out the obvious.

"She never bought into the biker life, babe, but she lived a long time connected to Chaos. She knows us. She wasn't into it because she wasn't into anything. But that doesn't mean she doesn't *know* us. She'll get there."

I found this easier to believe but not by much.

I decided not to pursue that.

Even so, I didn't get a chance before he declared, "And if she doesn't, the gig we got goin' that's workin' good will stop workin' good. No one is gonna keep my daughters from me for any reason. It just is not gonna happen. She tries, she'll learn quick she shouldn't have. But she knows that too. So she ain't gonna try."

That I could believe.

So I nodded, suddenly feeling exhausted.

"I think I need a shower," I told him. "Then I wanna call Dot and—"

"Unh-unh," he denied.

I blinked up at him.

He saw it and tipped his head so his face was closer to mine.

His tone was firm, but gentle, when he stated, "You got a big family. That family is yours, all of it, but that don't mean the bottom line is that you really got *two* families. You know the gig, too, baby. This is Chaos. You got your sisters in Chaos. You need them, they're right down the hall. Other than that, no go. This stays in Chaos, and it fucks me to lay down this law after the shit that went down with you today, but that's the end of it. Hear?"

"Dot won't—" I began.

He cut me off, "Alan will."

I shut my mouth because he was right.

Alan would.

He'd totally lose his mind.

"Hear?" he prompted softly.

I thought of my Chaos sisters in the living room. They'd descended, probably immediately, to look after Logan's girls.

I didn't know them all that well. I just knew I liked them. I trusted them.

And I was Chaos, in this situation, they were all I had.

As well as Logan, that was.

So it was good that was nothing to sneeze at.

With no other choice, because I'd already made it years ago when I chose Logan, I did what I'd been doing all day.

I nodded and whispered, "I hear."

Like any good old lady should.

I knew it was the right thing to do even before I did it.

But when Logan's hands slid up to my jaw and he used it to pull me up to my toes so my mouth could meet his and he could kiss me light, but long and wet, relieved but determined, that knowledge was confirmed.

Tack

It was dark.

There was only one light lit in the room.

Tack sat at the head of Chaos's table.

Hound was standing, his back to the wall opposite the door.

But Tack had his gaze on the Chaos flag under the Plexiglas in the middle of the table.

"High told us what Millie said," Tack told the table.

"Yup," Hound replied.

Tack stared at the flag.

But his mind was filled with hearing High's voice over the phone earlier that day when he'd first gotten the call.

He felt deep what he heard in High's voice. The anger that hid the fear.

He knew how that felt. He knew how it felt to know your woman was in the hands of a madman. He knew how it felt not to know where she was or how to find her. He knew how it felt to know you'd give anything to get her back safe.

Even if it meant giving your life.

Even if it meant that would take you away from her, your kids.

You'd do it.

Without a thought.

He knew exactly how that felt.

And hearing it in his brother's voice, remembering it in a way that cut like a blade, knowing he had to do everything he could to stop High from giving everything he was, after years of that feeling being gone, it again haunted him.

He looked from the flag to Hound.

"You're on this," he ordered.

Slowly, Hound grinned.

"Alone, Hound. You got that?" Tack asked.

The grin didn't waver. "I got it."

"No blowback, brother," Tack ordered.

Hound lifted his chin.

The door opened and both men looked to it.

Tack straightened in his chair and felt the alert coming off Hound when they saw who walked in.

Keely Black.

Every time Tack saw her, the wound of losing his brother, a wound that never closed, opened wider.

And every time he saw her, he thought the waste of the end of Black's life carried on.

The woman was beautiful. Years had passed and that beauty matured along with her. Throw in her being sweet as candy and funny as hell, the way her life ended when her man's did was a tragedy. She had a lot to give in ways that goodness couldn't be given just to her sons.

Tack thought, over the years, all that goodness bottled up, it'd explode and she'd find her way out from under the blanket of grief that was smothering her.

She never did.

And with eyes that were dead even if they were shining with anger, Tack reckoned it never would.

"Keely, darlin', you know, the doors are closed, this room—" he started.

"Fuck what I know," she bit out.

As asked, earlier that day, she'd hightailed it to Millie's to look after High's girls.

But the minute Pete got there, she took off.

It wasn't his first choice to ask her to step in. Fuck, he'd never ask her to step in unless the situation was what it was and High needed his brothers around, and fast, to contain him.

Clearly, she hadn't liked it.

"What we asked today, honey, we won't ask again," Tack told her quietly.

"Damn straight, Tack," she returned, moving into the room and slamming the door behind her. "'Cause, in case you didn't get it *the last time* shit went south. And then the time before *that* and the time before *that*. You should get it now. For God's sake, they took *Millie*."

"You shoulda stuck around to see she was good," Hound told her, and her eyes shot to him.

"I didn't because I know Millie. Happy for High she's back. Took forever and it's good that shit is over. But if she sees me, she'll be all up in my shit to *heal* me. I had enough of that from Pete. From Beverly. From all you all," she returned. "Only reason Bev's still around is because she stopped that shit."

Bev was Boz's ex. She and Keely remained tight.

And it wasn't lost on Tack that was the reason.

"Keely—" he began.

Her eyes snapped to him and she ordered, "Pull back."

"Woman—" Hound tried.

Keely didn't look from Tack. "Whatever it is you boys are stuck in this time, pull back."

He shook his head. "That's not possible."

She crossed her arms on her chest. "It's not possible because your pride is at stake. The Club's pride is at stake. But other, more important shit is at stake, too, Tack, and you're far from dumb. You know it. Whatever this lunatic wants from

Chaos that's making him get into it with old ladies, give it to him and *pull back*."

"Babe, you've got a place deep in my soul, straight up," Hound said, and Keely looked to him. "But bottom line, you don't know what the fuck you're talkin' about."

"I know why you two are here," she returned, lifting a hand, finger pointed, to indicate him and Tack. She dropped her hand. "I know you, Hound. I know when you're called in."

"And you know I get the job done," Hound replied, his voice soft, even tender, and Tack narrowed his gaze on his brother's face when he saw the same reflected there.

Fuck.

That was a look in all their years as brothers Tack had never seen from Hound.

And that was not a look a man was giving the widow of his dead brother.

Fuck.

"It gives me no joy to say that at least when this asshole takes you out, Hound, you're not leavin' anyone who loves you more than the breath they take behind," Keely shot back.

Tack watched the nearly imperceptible flinch strike Hound's face.

Fuck.

Tack drew her attention to him. "Keely—"

"Do not call me again, Tack," she demanded.

His mouth got tight.

She looked to Hound and everything about her changed. She went from pissed and belligerent to sad and defeated.

Seeing that, it also cut like a blade.

He remembered her. He remembered her young and in love and so fucking happy, she walked into a room attached to Black, or walked into a room Black was in, that happiness would warm every inch of the space.

Just like Millie was with High back in the day.

But Millie could get hers back.

Keely never would.

"Be careful," she whispered to Hound. "Be super fuckin' careful, Hound. Because you might not have a woman who loves you more than her own breath, but you still got folks who love you. So please, God, be careful."

With that, she turned, her hair flying, yanked open the door, stalked out, and slammed it behind her.

Tack looked to Hound.

Hound was in control. His face neutral.

But his eyes were glued to the door.

"We done here?" Tack asked, and Hound cut his gaze to his brother.

"Yup," he answered, pushing away from the wall.

Tack watched him walk around the other end of the table. He waited until Hound's hand was on the door before he called his name.

Hound looked back at him.

"You know," he said carefully.

"Know what?" Hound asked.

"You know you don't go there."

Hound's brows drew together. "Brother, you call me when you got somewhere to go no one else can go. What the fuck?"

Tack shook his head but did it with his eyes locked to Hound's.

"You know you don't go there. She's Black's. Dead or alive, she's Black's. She can move on. I hope to fuck someday she does. But she can't move on with Chaos."

That got him something.

Hound looked pissed.

But his voice was quiet when he replied, "You think I don't know that shit?"

"I know you know," Tack returned. "Just remindin' you."

"Don't need a reminder, brother," Hound grated out. "Lived with that for years, bein' in love with a woman I can't have."

Without hesitation, after delivering that, he threw open the door and prowled out. When he slammed it, it was louder and the door shook.

Tack stared at the door.

Then he leaned to the table, put his elbow on it, and bent his neck to run his hand through his hair.

He'd curled his fingers around the back of his neck, the wood of the table all he could see, when he finally muttered aloud, "Fuck."

CHAPTER TWENTY-FOUR

Hear?

Millie

"No Carissa, she's too young, too new to the fold," Tyra declared. "And no Tabby, because she's too pregnant."

"Hear you," Elvira muttered.

"Agreed," Lanie said.

I sat with my back to the arm of the couch under the window of Tyra's office at Ride's garage, my neck twisted to look out the window.

We were having our powwow as called by me through Tyra.

It was Tyra's decision that it was only Lanie, Elvira, and me.

She was the president's old lady. There was a hierarchy even if she did not one thing to demand it, so I knew that was her call.

Even so, I agreed with her decision.

"Millie?" she called.

I tore my gaze off the enormous forecourt outside, bikes parked in front of the Compound, our cars parked in front of the office, the noises muted coming through from the garage, and looked to Tyra at her desk.

Elvira was sitting on the couch with me, Lanie in a chair opposite Tyra.

It was three days after the incident and it had gone down like Valenzuela said it would.

Even though I'd reported to the police he was there and I'd witnessed all I'd witnessed, as Valenzuela said he would, a man came forward and confessed to the crimes.

He had all the timings right. He had all the activities right (not including Valenzuela and his assassin being involved, but he corroborated the Pedro hitting me, Carlos making the decision to kidnap me portion of my story).

He also had the gun used in the murders and gunshot residue on his hand.

Nevertheless, Valenzuela was collected, questioned, but he'd alibied out.

Not a prostitute.

His girlfriend, a woman by the name of Camilla Turnbull, said on record that he was with her the entire time.

They'd also found the prostitute I'd described and she'd said she was there but she'd also said the confessed shooter told her to leave prior to the macabre festivities, confirming all I said that went down. But she also confirmed the lie, that the guy who gave the confession was there, not Valenzuela.

Furthering Valenzuela's story, there was nothing to indicate he was there.

It was a motel; the place was rife with fingerprints and DNA. None of it belonged to Valenzuela.

Canvassing motel guests brought witnesses to me being

forced up the steps and into the room. The prostitute's attendance. Carlos and Pedro being there.

And the confessed killer was identified.

Dozens of witnesses to folks coming to and going from the motel, and no one reported a positive ID on Valenzuela or mentioned any other man being present.

Logan had refused to allow Zadie to be questioned. She was handling things okay and Logan was not fired up to let anything harm that.

Deb agreed. She was not fired up about any of this and not in a super good mood. But Logan had not been wrong. She didn't get ugly about it. She looked after her daughters. She'd called and asked after me.

But she obviously knew the way of Chaos and knew her ex-husband.

She was no longer an old lady.

She was still toeing the line.

Anyway, Zadie couldn't confirm Valenzuela's involvement because he wasn't at my house. So she couldn't give any more to the story than what they already knew.

Valenzuela was careful. He'd totally covered his tracks. In fact, the totality of this was both eerie and scary as shit.

"Millie," Tyra called again.

I jerked and focused on her.

"Sorry," I muttered.

"Girl, you gotta get yourself some help," Elvira encouraged softly, watching me closely. "You need to work things out in your head. The shit you experienced was extreme."

I drew in breath and shrugged.

She was right, of course. I'd been kidnapped and witnessed two men murdered.

I was an old lady but I wasn't made of steel.

But I was also handling it.

"Is it messing with you?" Tyra asked.

I nodded. "I wake up at night." I then shook my head. "Actually, not sleeping great at all."

"Is High taking care of you?" Lanie asked.

"Yeah," I said quietly, because he was.

I knew there was rage burning in him down deep.

But in order to take care of me, he was burying it.

I didn't see it. Not at all.

If I woke up in the middle of the night, he acted like his only reason for being was beating back the demons that woke me. Even during the day when I could control the flashbacks, he was watchful, careful, tender.

It was a balm that was soothing.

But even as potent as it was, I knew there would be a long wait to healing.

"Talked to Malik about this shit," Elvira declared. "He says as good as the support you have around you is, in every case he's dealt with, professional help is the only way to go."

I feared if I admitted I needed a counselor, the wrath Logan was banking would start to blaze out of control.

I slid my eyes to Tyra.

She got me, knew my dilemma, the limited answers to solving it, and gave me a soft smile.

I looked back to Elvira.

"It's sweet you're worried but it'd help if we could focus on the task at hand," I told her.

"I'll do that. Sure," she returned. "Only if you promise you'll consider lookin' after yourself the way you should."

I could give her that so I nodded.

"Right, what we need to do isn't gonna be easy," Tyra declared.

She was right.

Meddling in the affairs of the brothers was tricky business. If those affairs were dangerous and they were dealing with them the way they felt they had to, it was a no go.

But if Logan was banking his rage, I knew his brothers

were too. That was what they did. What one felt, the others reciprocated. What one endured, the others endured with him.

And when vengeance was earned, the others were there to mete it.

And I worried that Valenzuela knew just that.

"Millie, are you sure you're in a place you can be in on this?" Lanie asked.

I leveled my gaze on her.

"Just consider living twenty years without Hop, then getting him back. No matter what happened to you in the meantime, would you ever allow yourself to be in a place where you might lose him again?"

"No," she answered quietly.

"No," I repeated firmly. "So, yes, I'm in a place where I can be in on this."

"Okay, then," Tyra butted in, and I looked to her to see her looking at Elvira. "I think our best bet it to start with Hawk."

"Hawk ain't gonna let us wade in on this either," Elvira replied. "Valenzuela don't like me much after I did that undercover shit with his business. Hawk's also in his line of sight. He gets wind we're wadin' in in whatever way we could do that, he'll shut us down to the point I wouldn't put it past his ass to kidnap *all* of ours and lock us down in one of his safe houses."

Every time he was mentioned, Hawk Delgado got more and more interesting.

"I don't mean asking for his help, Vira. I mean finding a way to find out what's going on," Tyra said. "If we try to get anything from our men, they'll figure it out."

"You think Hawk keeps files on shit like this?" Elvira asked.

"I think you can find out if he does or if he doesn't," Tyra answered.

Suddenly, Elvira grinned. "You'd think right."

Tyra sat back in her chair. "We'll start with that. It may

not come to anything but the more information we have, the better. In the meantime," she looked to Lanie and me, "work your men. Go cautious. Be smart. And I'm not talking about pumping them for information. I'm talking about making sure they get what they'd be leaving behind if something disastrous happened."

"I think they already know that, Ty-Ty," Lanie noted, and Tyra looked to her.

"I know they do. Just make sure they don't forget," she replied.

"I get you all. I get you're freaked," Elvira put in. "Valenzuela is a threat. But Chaos has never gone stupid. Do you honestly think this guy is gonna get the better of the brotherhood?"

"A man took me," Tyra reminded her, "and Tack walked through a hail of gunfire to get to me." She lifted a hand and indicated me. "Valenzuela took Millie. Do I think Chaos would do anything stupid?" She shook her head. "Do I fear that emotion, which is all that guides the Club, love, trust, family, protection, brotherhood, could cloud things when they're up against an insane but worthy opponent? Yes."

"Mmm-hmm," Elvira mumbled, visibly mulling that over in her head before she agreed. "I hear you. I'll see what I can get on where they are."

My eyes drifted back out the window.

"Millie?" Tyra called.

I looked back to her.

She tipped her head to the side. "Honey, you sure you're good?"

I wanted to believe that Chaos had one last battle to win before they were clean and free forever and they were going to win that battle.

But Benito Valenzuela was a man who would go after what he wanted in a way he wouldn't be stopped.

Unless he was *stopped*.

And as crazy as he was, that was a black mark I didn't want on any of their souls.

"Tack'll protect you, High, all the brothers," Tyra said when I didn't reply. "I hope you know that. What we're doing, it's just helping him accomplish that."

"Logan followed a dark path," I told them. They all looked at each other and from the way they did, I guessed they knew a bit about that path so I didn't need to get into that and kept going. "It was because of me even if it wasn't. I don't want him on that path again, because of me, even when it isn't."

"Keep 'im off it, then," Elvira declared. "Man's gettin' more than his fair share of blowjobs, gonna have his mind on his woman's mouth, not on some motherfucker with a screw loose."

A giggle erupted from me because that was the truth.

They laughed with me, theirs I could hear filled with relief that I was laughing at all.

And with that, I decided we were done. Not because I didn't like spending time with them, but because I didn't want to think about this anymore.

Not to mention, I had to go oversee some Christmas decorations being put up in an office suite.

"I gotta go," I said, pushing up from the couch.

They all moved. I put on my coat, grabbed my bag, got hugs and another prompt from Elvira to think about talking with someone to get the tools to deal with what happened.

I took off with a heavy heart, wishing in all that was promising with Zadie coming around before I got kidnapped that we were still on that trajectory of a life of budding happiness that would bloom to carefree.

I knew it wouldn't always be a trip through the tulips.

But the quick taste of having just that that weekend with the girls was sublime.

Hence, I got where Logan's rage was coming from. I got it was about Valenzuela taking me, what happened, what I saw.

It was also that he took that away from all of us.

I just hoped we could get it back.

All of us.

Intact.

Elvira

The door closed behind Millie at Tyra's office and Elvira looked to her girls at the desk.

"We all know you bitches can't wade into this," she stated.

Lanie and Tyra didn't say anything but Elvira knew they knew. They were doing what they thought they had to do for Millie right now. But they knew their men would lose their minds if their women gave a hint of interfering.

"I'm callin' in Shirleen," she declared.

She didn't expect an argument.

She didn't get one.

"Agreed," Tyra replied.

Elvira didn't delay. She dug in her purse and pulled out her phone.

There was one person on this earth outside Millie and the members of the Chaos brotherhood who would stop at nothing to keep Logan "High" Judd clean, free, and alive.

So Elvira called her.

She didn't expect Shirleen would decline her invitation.

She was right.

Millie

The next afternoon, I was sitting at my desk in my studio, my eyes to my computer screen, my fingers entering figures for a budget that would deliver a doable bar mitzvah for a kid whose parents wanted me to pull out all the stops but they didn't exactly have the funds to pull that off when my door opened.

Speck, my protector for the day, stuck his head in and stated, "He's good."

Then he pulled his head out and a large black man so beautiful, I completely forgot how to breathe, walked in, smiling at me.

As he continued to walk in, my head tipped farther and farther back until he stopped at the other side of my desk.

At that point, my mouth was hanging open.

I did not care.

I knew this man was used to women making fools of themselves at the sight of him.

And anyway, I still hadn't regained bodily function.

"Millie, it's good to meet you," his deep, smooth voice said. "I'm Elvira's man, Malik."

Ho...

Lee...

Shit.

No wonder she wanted her ball and chain on him.

"I...uh...I..." I swiftly got up and shoved my hand his way. "Malik, I can't tell you what a pleasure it is to meet you."

He took my hand and smiled at me again.

I licked my lips.

He let me go and stated, "It's come to my attention you're planning my wedding."

Damn.

Fuck.

Shit.

"I...uh...I..."

I stopped talking because I had nothing more to give to that statement.

"Don't worry," he said, his voice deeper, smoother, like a lullaby. "I just have one thing to ask."

He could ask anything, so I nodded.

"You plan a wedding that'll make my baby happy. But

before you do that, you plan a night where I ask her to spend the rest of her life with me that she'll never forget."

Instantly, I forgot how beautiful he was when I felt my eyes fill with tears.

"Really?" I whispered. "You're gonna ask?"

"You help me do that right, yeah."

"Oh my God," I kept whispering. "I'm so happy."

"Glad to hear it, sweetheart, but do me a favor and make Elvira happier."

I nodded madly, now choked up but also grinning like a fool.

"Good we ironed that out," he stated.

I kept nodding like a crazy woman.

And grinning because my girl was going to get what she wanted, I got to plan that, and it was going to be *sublime*.

He grinned back and again offered his hand.

I took it. He squeezed mine, let me go, pulled out his wallet, and said, "My card. You got a plan, call me."

He handed the card to me.

My fingers closed around it. "Will do," I promised.

He gave me another smile. I got happier that Elvira was going to have that for a lifetime, then he said, "Sorry this is short, but I got things to do."

I nodded again.

He turned to the door and I moved around the desk to follow him.

When he made it to the door, he stopped at it and looked down at me.

"While you're plannin', one thing you could do to keep my woman in a good place is find help."

I stopped smiling.

His voice dipped back to lullaby range but it was different this time.

"I know Chaos closes ranks when shit goes down. I know they take care of their own. I get that. I also know my woman is worried about you and I don't like that. But the thing I hope you get is that no brother chooses a woman for old lady that he doesn't wanna hand the world. You need it, High'll want you to have it. That's guaranteed and you know it. They also don't choose women who aren't strong enough to live their way of life. Which means they don't choose women who are too weak to ask for help. Not dissin' you, sweetheart. I get the need to try and con yourself that you can make it on your own. I'm just sayin', why do that if you don't have to?"

I felt my eyes narrow. "Did you come here to ask me to help you plan a pop-the-question night that will exceed Elvira's wildest dreams or did you come here to deliver a lecture because you're sick of hearing how your woman is worried about me?"

"Two birds," he replied.

Elvira.

And her man Malik.

I liked her but I was beginning to realize she could be a pain in the ass.

"Just because you felt free to come here and lecture me, I'm not asking my florist for my usual discount on the *suite* full of roses at the Brown Palace that I'm gonna book for your proposal," I declared.

"Sassy," he said through a smile. Then decreed, "Old lady."

"Damn straight," I returned.

He kept smiling.

Then he quit.

"Get help," he whispered.

"I will," I whispered back.

I didn't know him at all but the relief I saw in his handsome face was not about his woman's peace of mind.

"Thank you," he said, and before I could reply, he disappeared.

I stared at the door he closed behind him.

Then I smiled at the door.

Because I knew Elvira caught herself a good one.

And she was *so* going to get the *best* proposal in *history*.

High

High parked his truck and moved up the dark, deserted lane.

He didn't carry a flashlight. It had been a while, but he knew his way.

The shadows in front of him moved but he just kept walking toward them.

It was no surprise, as he got closer, that Shirleen formed through the darkness.

This was their meeting place. This was where they went when bad shit was going down. This was where he got his briefings when she needed him to take her back. This was where he gave her hers when he needed that returned.

None of that had happened for years.

So her calling him there was a surprise.

And not a good one.

He stopped two feet from her and barked, "Talk to me."

She did.

And she did it to bark back, "Do not fuckin' blow it."

"What?" he clipped.

"Boy, you got redemption. Do you know how hard it is to do good deeds, a hundred of 'em not comin' close to erasin' just one of the bad? Don't answer that 'cause I know you do. You're on that path. Do not stray."

He threw out a hand, pissed, surprised, and blindsided, none of which he liked.

"What the fuck are you talkin' about?" he asked.

"Your woman was taken. That is not good. She was found safe. You hold on to that and you bury the burn of vengeance so you don't blow it."

He got it.

And what he got took him from pissed to ticked.

"You keep outta this shit and you keep Nightingale out of it. It's now all Chaos," he warned.

It was.

Mitch, Slim, and Hawk were history. Tack had them on a string so they wouldn't cotton on, Rosalie still in play, so as far as they knew, Chaos was keeping their shit and it was all still a go.

But Tack had sent Hound in.

So in the end, it would be all Chaos.

Shirleen got in his space and he didn't move, staring down his nose at her.

"It is. No other way it could be. But *you* guide that, High. You guide it so the bounty you got when you got your woman back does not suffer. I know what happened. I know what she did. I know why she did it. Do not make decades of sacrifice all for nothing."

He stared into her eyes through the dark, then he lifted his gaze and looked over her head.

She stepped away, murmuring, "You get me."

He looked at her again. "What he did cannot stand."

"No. And a hundred good deeds don't erase one bad. You got enough bad, High. We both do. You take him down, you do that shit right. You're never gonna have a golden soul, but your woman has one. Don't tarnish it."

He clenched his teeth, feeling a muscle jump in his jaw.

"Not gonna surprise you to know, she's scared as shit what you're gonna do," she informed him. "Not gonna surprise you to know, she isn't the only one. Your women make an art of standin' by their men. Your job is to make that effort worth it."

God, the woman was fucking irritating when she was right.

"You done?" he gritted.

"I get in there?" she shot back.

He said nothing.

She stared at him.

Then she whispered, "I got in there."

"I'm done," he replied.

She said nothing.

He turned around and started to walk away.

She called after him as he did.

"When I had nothin', I had you. I'll never forget that, High, and you got my love until my last breath for givin' it to me. I want everything for you. Now you got it. Just need you to do one thing. Keep hold."

He was ticked, cold, outside Denver, which meant far away from Millie, and he had a black woman bossing him around in the dark.

He did not want to give her anything.

He couldn't do that.

Because she had his love too.

So he did what he had to do.

He kept walking but he did it lifting an arm and flicking out his hand.

*   *   *

He opened the door, walked into the house, heard the beeping of the alarm but stopped dead.

The kitchen was a disaster.

And Millie was at the stove.

"Do not freak out," she ordered, not turning to look at him. "Things are not going great and when you know what I'm doing, you're gonna walk right out and hit a Chipotle. But I want you to bear with me because I figure when I get this going, it's gonna be out of this world."

He closed the door, locked it, and turned to the alarm panel just in time to punch in the code before it sent a signal to dispatch.

Then he walked through the kitchen, seeing the remains of vegetables, bowls filled with a bunch of shit, all of it looking healthy, packaging and wrappers everywhere, what looked like wet, torn paper tossed aside and a glass of wine that had seen spillage so there were stains on the counter.

He stopped behind Millie and saw three pots bubbling, the stove splattered and smeared, and she was bent over a skillet with boiling water in it, a piece of paper also in it that she was poking with some tongs.

She must have felt him because she said, like she was concentrating on something else, not speaking to him, "I just gotta get *one* of these fuckers in the water and out of it in one piece so we can stuff it and maybe eventually have dinner."

"What the fuck is it?" he asked.

She glanced over her shoulder at him, then back at the skillet.

"It's rice paper."

"What?"

"*Rice paper*," she repeated in exasperation, grabbed an edge carefully, started to draw it from the water, reached out her other hand to take hold with her fingertips, and the thing tore down the middle. "*Motherfucker!*" she yelled, lifting the paper in her tongs and snapping it toward the counter where it splatted against several others of its kind and there it remained.

She reached immediately to a package and pulled out a round, thin, white thing, which she carefully slid into the water.

"Babe," he called over her shoulder.

"What?" she asked, poking at the new piece with her tongs.

"What *is* dinner?" he asked.

"Homemade spring rolls," she told the water.

He stared at her profile.

It was set and determined.

He took a slow step away.

Just as slowly, he turned his head and looked around the kitchen.

She was not working.

She was cooking.

The kitchen was not tidy.

It was a total, goddamned mess.

He looked to her.

She was not in high heels, a tight sweater, and a tighter skirt—sexy, but all class.

She was in loose-fitting pants that hugged her ass, girl slippers, and she had a thin sweater on.

Her hair was piled high on her head. It was not carefully arranged. It was slipshod and cute, curls escaping to brush her neck and cheeks.

"Babe," he called.

"Hang on," she said.

"Millie."

"Hang on," she repeated, and he saw her making another attempt to extricate the paper out of the skillet.

"Hallelujah!" she cried, whirling his way, intact paper dripping water to the floor between tongs and fingers.

The minute she stopped, it ripped down the middle.

She glared at it and shouted, "*Goddamn it!*"

High burst out laughing.

"This is not funny, Low. That's like my *seventh* try! We're never gonna eat at this rate."

He kept laughing even as he declared, "I'm never gonna lose you."

Her head jerked and he kept laughing since she was still holding the broken paper in her hand, looking adorable, her sweater from the front cut low, a vision he liked, as she asked, "What?"

"Never, baby, not ever. Never gonna lose you. Never gonna do shit to take away what I got back. Never gonna do shit to make it not worth it, all you gave to me. I'm not gonna go back there. That path didn't feel right from the start. You at my side, it's all kinds of wrong."

"Low," she whispered.

Top to toe he saw it written all over her.

She got him.

So, still chuckling, he got close to her and swept her (and her paper) in his arms.

It was wet against his chest.

He didn't give a fuck.

"Stop worrying," he ordered.

She stared up at him.

He let her go with one hand to take the paper and tongs out of her hands and toss them to the side.

The tongs clattered.

The paper splatted.

He just wrapped his arm back around her.

His Millie.

His girl.

The only woman he'd ever loved, the only woman he'd ever love.

He'd take her tidy, washing out her wineglass at night, getting cats who matched her house.

And he'd take her like this, cooking shit he probably did not want to eat and getting ticked as all hell doing it in a kitchen that was a disaster.

He'd take her however she came.

He'd take anything from her.

What he would not do was do shit that might make him lose her.

"Walked into a party, fell in love with you. Walked through fire when I lost you. Got you back. Nothin', Millie, nothin' will make me lose you. Hear?"

Her eyes were warm, but her question was hesitant. "Did someone...*say* something to you?"

They did.

She didn't need to know that.

"The brothers are gonna do it right," he told her.

They were, once he had words with Tack.

She studied him, doing it closely, taking her time, then she relaxed in his arms.

"Okay, Low," she said quietly.

"Also not gonna eat fuckin' spring rolls," he told her.

She gave a slight jolt in his arms before her eyebrows drew together.

"It's only partially healthy, Logan. The rest of it is all meat and sauce."

"I hate spring rolls."

Her brows stayed drawn. "It's impossible to hate them. Everything in them is good."

He looked to the side, then looked to her. "Sprouts?"

"They're all water. They don't even taste of anything."

"Bullshit."

"Logan—"

"Turn it all off. We'll clean it up later. Now, I'm starved. We're goin' to Chipotle."

"Logan!" she snapped. "I've been cooking for an hour."

"Eat it for lunch," he replied.

"You need to eat healthier," she declared. "We both do."

"Why?"

"Because it's good for you and it's a good habit to teach your daughters."

"Think Deb's got that covered, babe."

She shut her mouth.

He had her there.

He let her go but grabbed her hand and dragged her to the door. "You got some tennis shoes or somethin' to pull on?"

"Do I look like a woman who owns tennis shoes?"

He stopped and looked down at her. "You wanna get healthy and you don't own tennis shoes?"

She looked to the wall.

He had her there too.

He started laughing again.

She looked back to him but only to glare.

"Babe, get some shoes," he demanded.

"You go get Chipotle. I want spring rolls," she replied.

"Get some shoes," he repeated.

"Seriously, Low. This might be a disaster but it also might be really good," she returned.

He pulled her close, bending his neck to get his face in hers.

"Get some shoes."

"This is the bossy part I'm not fond of," she announced.

He leaned back and lifted his brows. "You gonna send your man out in the cold alone to get his dinner?"

"And this is the heretofore unmentioned hot biker manipulation I'm not fond of."

He again started laughing.

"Fortunately for you, I'm fond of that," she said while he did it.

"What?" he asked, still laughing.

"You laughing."

He stopped.

Then he remembered.

And once he remembered, he did something about it.

Because he'd come home but he hadn't greeted his woman properly.

So he tugged her hand hard, felt her body hit his, and he saw to that.

When he was done, he was fighting going hard and had to keep doing it when he saw her face dazed.

"Turn off the shit, baby, get some shoes. Let's go get dinner. Hear?"

"Hear," she whispered breathily. Then she held his eyes and something drifted into them that, along with the sudden tightening of her body, made him brace before she said, "I found a counselor. I'm gonna go talk to her about what happened with Valenzuela."

"You let me know when that shit goes down," he stated immediately. "I'll drive you."

She relaxed in his arms.

She got tight again when he went on to declare, "You gotta know, we're movin' and we're doin' that soon."

"We are?" she asked.

"Your neighbors suck."

He'd told her about her neighbor witnessing her being taken and doing nothing about it.

So when he declared that, she relaxed again and added a smile.

"House hunting," she murmured. "Fun."

If she thought that, she was nuts.

He didn't share that mostly because she rolled up on her toes, touched her mouth to his, then pulled out of his arms to do as he'd asked.

So they could eat it warm, they ate their burritos at Chipotle.

It was cold outside.

But the best she could do was flip-flops.

It was cute.

It was Millie.

And it had made him laugh.

EPILOGUE

Today's No Different

High

"You sure you wanna play it that way?"

Standing alone with Tack and Hound in the Common Room of the Compound, when Tack asked that question after High told him how he wanted things to go down, High only nodded.

Tack studied him for a beat.

Then he said, "Your call, High."

High looked at him, then he looked at Hound.

It was done.

So he said, "Gotta go look at a house."

He said it like he'd rather voluntarily be bolted into an iron maiden, which was to say he said it how he felt it.

Tack's lips twitched.

Hound grinned straight out.

"Later, brothers," High muttered, and jerking up his chin, he walked away.

Tack

"We gonna play it that way?"

Hound asked this question the instant the door to the Compound closed behind High.

Tack took his eyes from the door and looked to Hound.

"Your call, Hound."

"They got to Zadie, they took Millie." Hound told him something he knew.

Tack didn't reply but he knew where Hound was leading.

"They feel pain," Hound said low.

That was where he knew Hound was leading.

"High has chosen the righteous path. It's the right path. But I know you, brother, your path has always been your own," Tack returned.

"Our world, wrong done to our own, righteous takes a different meaning," Hound told him.

Yeah.

Hound's path had always been his own.

"I get you," Tack replied.

"I'm maverick on this, Tack. Club stays clean."

Tack turned fully to him, shaking his head. "No, brother. We're always at your back."

Hound held his gaze a beat before he whispered, "Not this time."

Before Tack could say a word, Hound walked away.

He was uncertain if that was good or bad. Knowing what he now knew, he wondered if Hound enjoyed riding the edge because it made him feel something when he knew what he wanted to feel, what he wanted to have, he couldn't feel and he'd never own.

What Tack was certain of was that Hound was wrong.

He could think he was maverick.

But Hound's brothers would have his back.

He took a stool by the bar, pulling out his phone.

He made some calls.

And he made that so.

High

All his girls in the truck, High slowed to a stop at the curb in front of the house that Millie had found on the Internet.

He bent and looked through Millie's window and up the incline to the monstrosity sitting obnoxiously proud on its huge lot in Denver's Highlands, overlooking the city.

Jesus.

No fucking way.

"It's like...like...*better than a castle*," Zadie breathed from the backseat.

Shit.

"It's *amazing!*" Cleo cried, also from the backseat.

Christ.

He heard their doors open, sensed his girls jumping out eagerly, but his attention was caught by Millie, who had been inspecting the house but now she was slowly turning her head his way.

He caught a look at her face, the face he fell in love with over two decades ago, a face now shining with excitement.

Fuck.

Without a word, she turned back to her door, threw it open, and practically fell out of it in her hurry to get out the door and up the walk to where the real estate agent was standing on the fucking *veranda* waiting for them.

High sighed as he angled out of the truck, moved to the hood, and stopped to look back up at the house, now with an unadulterated view.

Millie had showed him the listing. It was bad enough in photos. It was worse in reality.

But he knew the house had been built in 1903 and in the past two years, roof to foundation restored.

It had a wraparound veranda with Italian tile. It had five bedrooms. It had six baths. It had a living room, a massive kitchen, a buttery (whatever the fuck that was), a dining room, family room, study, and a fucking library. It also had a reno-vated carriage house at the back where Millie could put her studio. Further, it sat on a huge lot that would require him buying a riding lawnmower because no way in fuck he was gonna push a mower across that lawn. It'd take him two days.

It was majestic. It was classy.

It was ostentatious.

It was *not* where a biker lived.

No way in fuck.

His eyes went from the house to his daughters racing up the steps toward the agent, his woman following them, her ass swaying with her excited strut on her high-heeled boots.

He watched Millie make it to the terrace and shake the agent's hand.

Then he watched Clee-Clee latch onto her on one side, Zadie grab her hand on the other, Zadie so out of it with joy, she was jumping up and down, jarring Millie as she took his woman with her.

Millie didn't mind. She just smiled down at his baby girl so huge High could see it all the way to the street.

Oh yeah.

Fuck.

He looked back to the house.

His girls could each have their own bedroom, Millie could have a guestroom and also her junk room.

The basement was finished, so High could also have space of his own.

Further, it had a three-car garage, room for his truck, hers, all his bikes plus plenty of space to park the RV.

And the yard was so damned big the Club could party there with his entire family coming from Durango for a 4th of July bash.

Not to mention, he'd been to dinner at Dot and Alan's. They had a four-bedroom ranch, which was far from shit.

But it wasn't a turn-of-the-century Denver mansion.

When Alan saw this place, High wouldn't need to make the man eat his words.

Alan would have no choice but to choke on them.

On that thought, slowly, High felt his lips curl up.

Slower still, he rounded the hood of his truck and walked up the path to the house.

No.

Not to the house.

To his girls.

The next day, they put Millie's pad on the market.

Two months later, Logan "High" Judd moved his girls in to what Denver had to offer as a castle a mile high in the sky.

Millie

The buzz of the needle sounding, I lay curled on the reclining seat with Logan, watching the ink penetrate his skin.

Logan and I had agreed to a different placement of the tat because Logan wasn't big on shaving and he didn't want my ink obscured in any way.

So it wasn't being inked into his throat.

It was being inked curled around the base of it.

The artist wasn't all that thrilled with me being up on the seat with Low. To be able to be close to him, I'd promised him I wouldn't move and I wasn't.

This was partly because I wanted the tattoo to be perfect.

It was mostly because I was too overwhelmed with the feelings I was feeling, watching me tatted back into Logan's skin.

The... *only* was done when Logan muttered, "Break, bud."

Without a word, the artist wiped him down, rolled his stool away, and took off.

I watched him do this, sliding my hand from where it was resting on Logan's bare abs up his chest. I moved my eyes to his.

"You good?" I asked.

"Fuck yeah," he answered.

I tipped my head to the side. "Then why do you need a break, Snooks?"

" 'Cause it's time to do this," he replied, his hands moving, one circling my wrist at his chest, the other one going from around me and into his jeans pocket.

When I saw what he was doing, my breath hitched and my chest started to burn.

This continued as Logan slid a heavy ring with a large solitaire diamond encased in a solid rectangle of filigreed white gold on my finger. The sides leading up from the band expanded wide at the rectangle. One was embedded with an infinity symbol inside which was an *M* and an *L*. The other side had the stem of a rose entwined with a snake.

It was specially made.

No.

It was an engagement ring especially made for the old lady of a biker.

Primarily, *me*.

In other words, it was perfection.

I looked from the ring to Logan and I did it not breathing.

"Best moment of my life was lyin' beside you, watchin' you ink me into your skin while you did the same with me," he stated softly.

When we'd done it together, he'd felt the same as me.

But of course he did.

My whole body bucked as my breath caught and his hand closed around mine tight, the weighty ring digging into my finger.

"I fucked that up," he whispered.

"Low," I whispered back, shaking my head.

"So I'm fixin' it." He held my gaze. "Marry me, Millie."

I stared into his eyes until I couldn't see him anymore because he'd washed away with the unshed tears.

Then I dropped my face and buried it in his chest.

He cupped his hand on the back of my head even as he kept hold of my other one, doing this tight to his chest.

He gave it a few moments before I heard him rumble, "That mean yes?"

Was he crazy?

My head jerked up, my fingers closed around his, and I replied, "Fuck yes, that means yes."

His body started shaking with laughter.

Mine didn't.

I got closer, pressed deeper, and kissed him hard.

He finally let my hand go so he could wrap both his arms around me and we could make out in a tattoo chair.

We did this until the artist called, "Dude, you go at your babe much longer, I'm gonna need a different kind of break."

This meant we broke our kiss with both of us laughing.

Yes.

Perfection.

Logan's laughter died first as he slid his hand to cup my cheek.

"Love you, Millie," he whispered.

I drew in a deep breath through my nose.

I let it go, replying, "Love you, too, Snook'ums."

He grinned.

I settled back in.

He looked to the artist and jerked up his chin.

I finished watching him get inked with me alternately staring at my kickass engagement ring.

After he was done, we celebrated that tat and our engagement in the back of his SUV in the parking lot of the tattoo parlor.

Because that was the way of a biker.

And the way of his old lady.

Tyra

"Crap, High!" Boz yelled from the pool table in the Common Room, looking disgruntled. "Now I got *all* your girls kickin' my butt in pool."

Sitting at the bar with Lanie and Elvira, I heard Zadie giggle, so I looked that way.

She had a pool cue and was leaning into Millie, who was giggling with her as Cleo lined up her shot.

Cleo let fly and pocketed the six.

"Shee-it," Boz grumbled.

That was when I heard a rough chuckle.

I looked across the bar to my husband, who was standing at the back of it with Pete and Hop. He had eyes to Boz and a smile on his handsome face.

I liked that look, had always liked that look, but I didn't spend time taking it in. I knew I'd get it back. Frequently.

So I looked from my man across the space to one of the couches at the back of the room.

There, I saw High sitting alone, a bottle of beer held to his thigh, his other arm spread across the back of the couch, his feet up, ankles crossed, resting on the battered coffee table in front of him.

He was watching the action at the pool table, a smile playing at his lips.

He was sitting alone but he was not doing it as a loner.

He was doing it as a man watching a live action dream play out in front of his eyes.

He was doing it carefree.

He was doing it happy.

The way I'd noted he was a lot these days.

In fact, always.

I felt something and looked back to my man to see he was no longer chuckling and his eyes were on me.

I read what was in his eyes so I knew I'd never make him say the words. That wasn't how we worked.

But he was telling me I'd been right.

I knew that already, but it still felt good to get it from him.

I gave him a small smile, slid off my stool, and wandered

across the room as I heard Millie say to Zadie, "Your turn, darling. Show Boz all we Judd girls can bring it."

"You got it," Zadie replied.

I didn't look their way.

I made it to High, watching him tear his eyes from the action and bring them to me.

I took a breath and sat down on the couch, close.

I barely had my ass to the seat before he curled his arm that was on the back of the couch around my shoulders.

Then, casually, like we'd done this countless times before, he lifted his beer and took a tug.

I let out my breath, slouched in beside him, lifted my feet, and rested them on the coffee table.

We watched Zadie miss.

Her face fell with disappointment.

"Boz is so totally gonna blow it," Millie declared. "You'll get him next shot, sweetie."

Zadie's face brightened as she looked up at Millie and smiled.

"Thank you," High whispered.

I pressed my lips together.

Then I relaxed into his side, his arm curling tighter, and I whispered back, "You're welcome."

Boz missed.

Millie sunk her ball.

So did Cleo.

And after that, Zadie won the game for the Judd girls.

High

"Holy crap!" Kellie shouted, pushing through the door in front of them. "This place hasn't changed a bit."

"Shots!" Justine cried, following her.

Veronica turned eyes over her shoulder to him and she muttered, "Taxi night."

But she already knew it was a taxi night.

This was because the ride most of them came in was not the ride they'd go home in.

High just grinned at her as he guided Millie through the door after Veronica and Justine, hearing Elvira say from behind him, "This used to be Chaos?"

"Oh my God, this place is totally seedy," Lanie replied. "I love it! We finally have a local that's not the Common Room even if it's miles away."

They all moved in, expanding into the nearly-devoid-of-bodies space.

High did it holding Millie close and the instant they were inside, his gaze went to the bar.

Reb was staring at them, eyes big but face tight.

He bent to his girl's ear.

"Grab a table, babe," he muttered there. "I'll get the booze."

She looked from Reb to him and nodded.

She disengaged, glancing at Reb again, then following her girls to the table, her Chaos sisters, Tyra, Lanie, and Elvira following her.

Tack, Hop, and Boz followed High to the bar.

Reb met them there.

"Rumor's true," she said bitchily to High.

"Yep," High replied.

She looked from High to Millie and back to High.

When she got his eyes, she declared, "You are one lucky motherfucker."

Apparently, rumor wasn't only true, it was thorough.

"Yep," he repeated.

She glanced among them and announced, "Inflation didn't escape Scruff's, assholes. So don't think I'm a cheap date."

"Eleven beers, bottle, whatever's cold, eleven shot glasses, and a bottle of tequila," Tack ordered.

"Don't got table service," she warned, starting to pile shot glasses on the bar. "You boys are gonna have to cart this shit to your women."

"Just serve the drinks, Reb, without the attitude, you got that in you," Boz shot back.

"You lose your memory?" she returned.

"You don't got that in you," Boz surmised on a mutter.

Reb didn't reply. She turned to the shelves at the bar's back and nabbed a full bottle of Patrón.

They hadn't asked for top-shelf Patrón but none of the brothers stopped her.

"What's takin' so long?" Elvira called.

When she did, Reb frowned at Boz before asking, "What's that about attitude?"

Boz decided not to engage.

It was a good call.

The men carted the shit to the table.

The women drank, babbled, and cackled.

Kellie hit the jukebox.

Roscoe showed with a biker groupie. Pete showed alone. Snapper showed, also alone. Malik showed to join his woman. And through this, Reb's meager regulars hit the joint.

Millie had been right. She needed Chaos back. It was plain to see.

Justine took her turn at the jukebox and the women lost their minds and sang Bon Jovi's "Livin' on a Prayer" at the top of their lungs while the men grinned and Elvira glared, mumbling, "One a' you boys needs to get a sister up in this joint so I can counter Bon Jovi with some Fiddy."

It was then, feeling it, High turned his attention back to the bar.

It was not a surprise Reb had her eyes on him.

She also had a shot in her hand.

She lifted it his way, then she threw it back.

After that, she set the glass aside and moved, frowning, toward a man at her bar.

She was happy for him. For them. That was what she was saying and that was all either of them was going to get even if it was Millie who talked High into taking Chaos back to Reb's dying bar.

High turned his attention back to his girl. She had her arms thrown around Lanie, who had her arms thrown around her. Millie's head was thrown back and her mouth was open, loudly shouting the words to a song whose popularity, after decades, never died.

He spent the night only getting loose while his girl got hammered.

But High didn't need booze or anything else.

All he needed was the high of watching Millie let it all hang out in her classy sweater, her tight jeans, her high-heeled boots, all of this in a shady, run-down biker bar that was owned and operated by a bona fide bitch.

And when he'd had enough and she definitely had, he took her home.

Kind of.

Once there, he got blown but she didn't swallow. He finished after he made her come, watching her ride his cock.

They slept tangled up.

He woke getting blown.

She didn't swallow that time either. He fucked her on her knees, his eyes glued to his mark on her back, drawing it out as long as he could, wishing he could fuck her until his last breath, which brought the bonus of forcing two orgasms out of her while he was at it.

Then, once they cleaned up and spent some time cuddling, she sat next to him in his RV as he drove them home from Scruff's parking lot where they'd spent the night.

* * *

"Gonna go up, see if it's safe to return," High muttered as he put his empty beer bottle on the table beside him with all the others (not on a coaster—they had them for the fancy furniture from Millie's old pad that was in their new living room; they had them nowhere else in the house).

He got out of the recliner that was angled toward a now blaring TV to commence what he knew from practice felt like a yearlong journey to get to the kitchen, and he did this as Alan, in the other recliner, muttered back, "Don't get lost."

He felt his lips twitch but he didn't say anything as he moved to the door that led to the stairs.

"Logan."

High stopped and turned back to the man, a man who had not called him by that name since he told him not to do that shit months ago.

The instant Alan got his eyes, he lifted his bottle of beer.

"Proof," he stated.

"Proof, what?" High asked.

Alan swung his bottle around before his gaze went to the ceiling and back to High.

"Proof you're real."

The words were quiet and they were few.

But they said a lot.

Enough he'd let the man get away with calling him Logan.

He didn't reply. He just nodded and left the room.

Alan was there because the women were over. They'd showed two hours ago. When they did, he and Alan immediately absented themselves for reasons that were obvious.

But now he was hungry.

He was a fuckuva lot hungrier by the time he hit the kitchen.

Even so, once he got to the doorway, he stopped.

This was not because Freddie had shouted, "Pink stinks!" and when he did, High made a mental note to bring the boy with him and his father the next time this crew got together.

No.

It was because the huge-ass space was a mess. Plastic

tiaras scattered everywhere. Feather scarves. Crumbs and spent wrappers mingled with half-eaten cupcakes. Glow sticks snapped and glowing. Wineglasses. Wine bottles. Pop cans. Opened bags of chips. Sprinklings of pink and white M&M's.

It was like Cleo's thirteenth birthday was happening, not like the women were planning it.

High saw Chief picking his way across the top of the kitchen table with no one grabbing him to put him down (as usual).

Poem was sitting in Veronica's lap, being stroked, looking like she was asleep.

And Logan was taking Poem in as Katy declared, "I want a pink birthday too, Aunt Millie."

"Aunt Millie gives you one every year, honey," Dot returned.

"Well, I want another one," Katy told her mother.

"You can have whatever you want, sweetheart," Millie told her niece.

"Millie," Zadie called, and his woman looked to his baby girl who was wearing a tiara and had a feather thing wrapped around her neck. Then again, so was Millie. "On my birthday, I wanna be queen."

"You're always queen," Deb muttered, grinning at her daughter and sitting across from Millie at their huge-ass kitchen table (also wearing a tiara and a feather thing).

Zadie turned to her mother. "I wanna be *more* queen."

"Do not deviate from that dream, sister," Kellie advised, smiling at his baby girl. When Zadie looked to Kellie, she finished, "Live for it."

"I already do," Zadie informed her.

High swallowed a grunt of laughter.

"What Kellie's saying is, you can have whatever you want, too, darling," Millie told Zadie.

Zadie gave her attention back to Millie and beamed.

Millie beamed back.

Seeing that, High no longer felt like laughing.

No, looking at his daughter and his woman, he backed out of the doorway.

He retraced his steps down the hall, but this time, he did it looking at the walls.

Walls Millie had covered with the pictures she'd had in her pad in Cheesman.

Pictures that now mingled with framed photos she'd unearthed from that crate. Photos of him and his woman from years ago.

There were also photos of him and his woman now. His girls. His brothers. All of them together. Even photos from back in the day of Keely and Black.

He moved up the stairs, the walls there also covered with photos.

At the top of the stairs, he turned to his and Millie's bedroom.

He walked straight to his side of the bed.

The very first night they moved in, he got in bed beside his woman and when he did, he saw she'd put it on his nightstand.

A blown-up eight-by-ten in a silver frame.

It was a picture of them at a Chaos cookout years before, Millie sitting on a picnic table pressed into him, High standing beside her with her in his arms.

He remembered that shot. It was the first photo she'd placed in the first album of them she'd made.

It was the first picture of them ever taken.

He looked across the bed and saw another frame, this one crystal.

In it was also another eight-by-ten.

In it was High sitting on the couch in their living room with his girls piled on him, his arms wrapped around all of them. Millie in his lap. Cleo in hers. Zadie on top. Cleo had hold of Poem. Zadie had hold of Chief.

They'd been horsing around, so none of his girls were looking in the camera. They were all too busy giggling.

High was looking into the camera.

He was not laughing.

You didn't laugh when you held a living dream in your arms.

It was the last photo of them ever taken since Elvira had snapped that shot a week ago.

As ever, when Millie wanted something done and done right, she didn't fuck around.

The picture was in its fancy-ass frame and sitting on her nightstand the next day.

High looked from frame to frame and as he did, he knew he'd gotten it wrong.

His Zadie had it right.

Never give up.

Never quit dreaming.

Because dreams had a way of being.

You just had to keep hold.

Millie

When the boat stopped, the girls jumped up from their seats and moved toward the exit as I called, "Hurry! It's gonna happen any second. I don't want you to miss it! We'll catch up!"

They didn't need to be told twice.

Cleo and Zadie dashed ahead.

Logan and I, his hand wrapped warm around mine, followed them slowly.

We'd already been there that day because I'd wanted the girls to see the blooms on the trees.

But, of course, we also had to get there in the night.

We sauntered off the boat, Logan and me, hand in hand, and I knew he was keeping an eye on his girls as I did the same.

We got there in time. We stopped underneath. The girls were roaming, eyes up, waiting.

Logan didn't roam.

He pulled me into his arms.

I didn't lift my eyes up as in *up*, but I did lift my eyes.

To his.

"Today's no different," he murmured, his voice low but also scratchy.

Responding to his tone, I pressed closer, wrapping my arms tighter around his back.

"What, Snooks?" I asked quietly.

"Today's been fuckin' great, love givin' all my girls a spectacular spring break, but it's no different."

"Different than what?"

"Different than all the rest."

I tilted my head to the side, confused.

"All the rest of what?"

"All the rest of days, every one, every day since I first laid eyes on you. Today's no different. Fuck of it was, even when I didn't have you, I felt it. Which was why I never let go. And today's no different. No different from every day I had from the first day we met. Waking up in love with you. Day's almost done, gonna go to sleep more in love with you."

My breath caught.

My heart skipped a beat.

My arms convulsed.

My eyes filled with tears.

And my throat felt funny as I forced through it, "Ditto."

He shook his head, grinning. "You are such shit at that."

I was.

But it didn't matter.

With his flowery biker goodness, he made up for it.

And anyway, I had other ways of telling him I loved him.

So I did that, rolling up on my toes as he dipped his head, and in between, our mouths met.

I saw sparks on the backs of my eyelids just as they did.

It wasn't (all) Logan's kiss.

It was the Eiffel Tower above us bursting into beauty.

Tabitha Allen grew up in the thick of the Chaos MC, and the club has always had her back. But one rider was different from the start, and now Tabby wants more than friendship with the one man she can't have.

Please turn this page for an excerpt from

OWN THE WIND

"I Dreamed a Dream"

HIS CELL RANG and Parker "Shy" Cage opened his eyes.

He was on his back in his bed in his room at the Chaos Motorcycle Club's Compound. The lights were still on and he was buried under a small pile of women.One was tucked up against his side, her leg thrown over his thighs, her arm over his middle. The other was upside down, tucked to his other side, her knee in his stomach, her arm over his calves.

Both were naked.

"Shit," he muttered, twisting with difficulty under his fence of limbs. He reached out to his phone.

He checked the display, his brows drew together at the "unknown caller" he saw on the screen as he touched his thumb to it to take the call.

"Yo," he said into the phone.

"Shy?" a woman asked, she sounded weird, far away, quiet.

"You got me," he answered.

"It's Tabby."

He shot to sitting in bed, limbs flying and they weren't his.

"Listen, I'm sorry," her voice caught like she was trying to stop crying or, maybe, hyperventilating, then she whispered, "So, so sorry but I'm in a jam. I think I might even be kinda... um, in trouble."

"Where are you?" he barked into the phone, rolling over the woman at his side and finding his feet.

"I...I...well, I was with this old friend and we were. Damn, um..." she stammered as Shy balanced the phone between ear and shoulder and tugged on his jeans.

"Babe, where are you?" he repeated.

"In a bathroom," she told him, as he tagged a tee off the floor and straightened, waiting for her to say more.

When she didn't, gently, he prompted, "I kinda need to know where that bathroom is, sugar."

"I, uh...this guy is...um, I didn't know it, obviously, but I think he's—" another hitch in her breath before she whispered so low he barely heard "—a bad dude."

Fuck.

Shit.

Fuck.

He nabbed his boots off the floor and sat on the bed to yank them on with his socks, asking, "Do I need backup?"

"I don't want anyone..." she paused. "Please, don't tell anyone. Just...can you please just text me when you're here? I'll stay in the bathroom, put my phone on vibrate so no one will hear, and I'll crawl out the window when you get here."

"Tab, no one is gonna think shit. Just give me the lay of the land. Are you in danger?"

"I'll crawl out the window."

He gentled his voice further and stopped putting on his boots to give her his full attention.

"Tabby, baby, are you in danger?"

"I...well, I don't know really. There's a lot of drugs and I saw some, well, a lot of guns."

Shit.

"Address, honey," he urged, and she gave it to him.

Then she said, "Don't tell anyone, please. Just text."

"I'll give you that if you keep me notified and often. Text

me. Just an 'I'm okay' every minute or so. I don't get one, I'll know you're not and I'm bringin' in the boys."

"I can do that," she agreed.

"Right, hang tight, I'll be there."

"Uh...thanks, Shy."

"Anytime, Tab. Yeah?"

He waited, and it felt like years before she whispered, "Yeah."

He disconnected, pulled on his last boot, and stood, tugging on his tee as he turned to his bed. One of the women was up on an elbow and blinking at him. The other was still out.

As he found his knife in the nightstand and shoved the sheath into his belt, he ordered, "Get her ass up. Both of you need to get dressed and get gone." He reached into the nightstand and grabbed his gun, shoving it into the back waistband of his jeans and pulling his tee over it. "You got fifteen minutes to get out. You're not gone by the time I get back, I will not be happy."

"Sure thing, babe," the awake one muttered. She lifted a hand to shove at the hip of her friend.

Jesus.

Slicing a glance through them he knew he was done. Some of the brothers, a lot older than him, enjoyed as much as they could get, however that came, and they didn't limit it to two pieces of ass.

He'd had that ride and often.

It hit him right then it went nowhere.

He'd never, not once, walked up to a woman who looked lost without him and became found the second she saw him. Who leaned into him the minute he touched her. Who made him laugh so hard, his head jerked back with it. Whose mouth he could take and the world melted away for him just as he made that same shit happen for her.

And he would not get that if he kept this shit up.

He jogged through the Compound to his bike and rode with his cell in his hand.

She texted, *I'm okay*, and Shy took in a calming breath and turned his eyes back to the road.

She texted again. This time, *I'm still okay*, and, getting closer to her, Shy felt his jaw begin to relax.

A few minutes later she texted again. This time it was *I'm still okay but this bathroom is seriously gross.*

When Shy got that, after his eyes went back to the road, he was flat-out smiling.

She kept texting her ongoing condition of *okay*, with a running commentary of how much she disliked her current location, until he was outside the house. He turned off his bike and scanned. Lights on in a front room, another one beaming from a small window at the opposite side at the back. The bathroom.

He bent his head to the phone and texted, *Outside, baby.*

Seconds later he saw a bare foot coming out the small window and another one, then legs. He kicked down the stand, swung off his bike, and jogged through the dark up the side of the house.

He caught her legs and tugged her out the rest of the way, putting her on her feet.

She tipped her head back to him, her face pale in the dark.

"Thanks," she said softly.

He, unfortunately, did not have all night to look in her shadowed but beautiful face. He had no idea what he was dealing with. He had to get them out of there.

He took her hand and muttered, "Let's go."

She nodded and jogged beside him, her hand in his, her shoes dangling from her other hand. He swung on his bike, she swung on behind him. A child born to the life, she wrapped her arms around him without hesitation.

He felt her tits pressed to his back and closed his eyes.

Then he opened them and asked, "Where you wanna go?"

"I need a drink," she replied.

"Bar or Compound?" he offered, knowing what she'd pick. She never came to the Compound anymore.

"Compound," she surprised him by answering.

Thank Christ he kicked those bitches out. He just hoped they followed orders.

He rode to the Compound, parked outside, and felt the loss when she pulled away and swung off. He lifted a hand to hold her steady as she bent to slide on her heels, then he took her hand and walked her into the Compound.

Luckily, it was deserted. Hopefully, his room was too. He didn't need one of those bitches wandering out and fucking Tab's night even worse.

"Grab a stool, babe. I'll get you a drink," he muttered, shifting her hand and arm out to lead her to the outside of the bar while he moved inside.

Tabby, he noted, took direction. She rounded the curve of the bar and took a stool.

Shy moved around the back of it and asked, "What're you drinking?"

"What gets you drunk the fastest?" she asked back, and he stopped, turned, put his hands on the bar and locked eyes on her.

"What kind of trouble did I pull you out of?" he asked quietly.

"None, now that I'm out that window," she answered quietly.

"You know those people?" he asked.

She shrugged and looked down at her hands on the bar. "An old friend. High school. Just her. The others..." She trailed off on another shrug.

Shy looked at her hands.

They were visibly shaking.

"Tequila," he stated, and her eyes came to his.

"What?"

"Gets you drunk fast."

She pressed her lips together and nodded.

He grabbed the bottle and put it in front of her.

She looked down at it then up at him, and her head tipped to the side when he didn't move.

"Glasses?" she prompted.

He tagged the bottle, unscrewed the top, lifted it to his lips and took a pull. When he was done, he dropped his arm and extended it to her.

"You can't get drunk fast, you're fuckin' with glasses," he informed her.

The tip of her tongue came out to wet her upper lip and, Jesus, he forgot how cute that was.

Luckily, she took his mind off her tongue when she took the bottle, stared at it a beat then put it to her lips and threw back a slug.

The bottle came down with Tabby spluttering and Shy reached for it.

Through a grin, he advised, "You may be drinking direct, sugar, but you still gotta drink smart."

"Right," she breathed out like her throat was on fire.

He put the bottle to his lips and took another drag before he put it to the bar.

Tabby wrapped her hand around it, lifted it, and sucked some back, but this time she did it smart, and her hand with the bottle came down slowly, although she was still breathing kind of heavy.

When she recovered, he leaned into his forearms on the bar and asked softly, "You wanna talk?"

"No," she answered sharply, her eyes narrowing, the sorrow shifting through them slicing through his gut. She lifted the bottle, took another drink before locking her gaze with his. "I don't wanna talk. I don't wanna share my feelings. I don't wanna *get it out*. I wanna *get drunk*."

She didn't leave any lines to read through, she said it plain, so he gave her that out.

"Right, so we gonna do that, you sittin' there sluggin' it back and me standin' here watchin' you, or are we gonna do something? Like play pool."

"I rock at pool," she informed him.

"Babe, I'll wipe the floor with you."

"No way," she scoffed.

"Totally," he said through a grin.

"You're so sure, darlin', we'll make it interesting," she offered.

"I'm up for that," he agreed. "I win, you make me cookies. You win, you pick."

He barely finished speaking before she gave him a gift the likes he'd never had in his entire fucking life.

The pale moved out of her features as pink hit her cheeks, life shot into her eyes, making them vibrant, their startling color rocking him to his fucking core before she bested all that shit and burst out laughing.

He had no idea what he did, what he said, but whatever it was, he'd do it and say it over and over until he took his last breath just so he could watch her laugh.

He didn't say a word when her laughter turned to chuckles and continued his silence, his eyes on her.

When she caught him looking at her, she explained, "My cooking, hit and miss. Sometimes, it's brilliant. Sometimes, it's…" she grinned "…*not*. Baking is the same. I just can't seem to get the hang of it. I don't even have that"—she lifted up her fingers to do air quotation marks—"*signature dish* that comes out great every time. I don't know what it is about me. Dad and Rush, even Tyra, they rock in the kitchen. Me, no." She leaned in. "*Totally* no. So I was laughing because anyone who knows me would not think cookies from me would be a good deal for a bet. Truth is, they could be awesome but they could also seriously suck."

"How 'bout I take my chances?" he suggested.

She shrugged, still grinning. "Your funeral."

Her words made Shy tense, and the pink slid out of her cheeks, the life started seeping out of her eyes.

"Drink," he ordered quickly.

"What?" she whispered, and he reached out and slid the tequila to her.

"Drink. Now. Suck it back, babe. Do it thinkin' what you get if you win."

She nodded, grabbed the bottle, took a slug, and dropped it to the bar with a crash, letting out a totally fucking cute "Ah" before she declared, "You change my oil."

His brows shot up. "That's it?"

"I need my oil changed and it costs, like, thirty dollars. I can buy a lot of stuff with thirty dollars. A lot of stuff *I want*. I don't want *oil*. My car does but I don't."

"Tabby, sugar, your dad part-owns the most kick-ass garage this side of the Mississippi and most of the other side, and you're paying for oil changes?"

Her eyes slid away and he knew why.

Fuck.

She was doing it to avoid him. Still.

Serious as shit, this had to stop.

So he was going to stop it.

"We play pool and we get drunk and we enjoy it, that's our plan, so let's get this shit out of the way," he stated. Her eyes slid back to him and he said flat out, "I fucked up. It was huge. It was a long time ago but it marked you. You were right. I was a dick. I made assumptions, they were wrong and I acted on 'em and I shouldn't have and that was more wrong. I wish you would have found the time to get in my face about it years ago so we could have had it out, but that's done. When you did get in my face about it, I should have sorted my shit, found you, and apologized. I didn't do that either. I'd like to know why you dialed my number tonight, but if you don't wanna share that shit, that's cool too. I'll just say, babe, I'm glad you did. You need a safe place just to forget shit and escape, I'll give it to you. Tonight. Tomorrow. Next week. Next month. That safe place is me, Tabby. But I don't want that old shit haunting this. Ghosts haunt until you get rid of them. Let's get rid of that fuckin' ghost and move on so I can beat your ass at pool."

As he spoke, he saw the tears pool in her eyes but he kept going, and when he stopped he didn't move even though it nearly killed him. Not to touch her, even her hand. Not to give her something.

It killed.

Before he lost the fight to hold back, she whispered, "You are never gonna beat my ass at pool."

That was when he grinned, leaned forward, and wrapped his hand around hers sitting on the bar.

"Get ready to have your ass kicked," he said softly.

"Oil changes for a year," she returned softly.

"You got it but cookies for a year," he shot back.

"Okay, but don't say I didn't warn you," she replied.

He'd eat her cookies, they were brilliant or they sucked. If Tabitha Allen made it, he'd eat anything.

Shy didn't share that.

He gave her hand a squeeze, nabbed the bottle, and took off down the bar toward the cues on the wall.

Tabby followed.

*   *   *

They were in the dark, in his bed, in his room in the Compound.

Shy was on his back, eyes to the ceiling.

Tabby was three feet away, on her side, her chin was tipped down.

She was obliterated.

Shy wasn't even slightly drunk.

She'd won four games, he'd won five.

Cookies for a year.

Now, he was winning something else, because tequila didn't make Tabitha Allen a happy drunk.

It made her a talkative one.

It also made her get past ugly history and trust him with absolutely everything that mattered right now in her world.

"DOA," she whispered to the bed.

"I know, sugar," he whispered to the ceiling.

"Where did you hear?" she asked.

"Walkin' into the Compound, boys just heard and they were taking off."

"You didn't come to the hospital."

He was surprised she'd noticed.

"No. I wasn't your favorite person. Didn't think I could help. Went up to Tack and Cherry's, helped Sheila with the boys," he told her.

"I know. Ty-Ty told me," she surprised him again by saying. "That was cool of you to do. They're a handful. Sheila tries but the only ones who can really handle them are Dad, Tyra, Rush, Big Petey, and me."

Shy didn't respond.

"So, uh . . . thanks," she finished.

"No problem, honey."

She fell silent and Shy gave her that.

She broke it.

"Tyra had to cancel all the wedding plans."

"Yeah?" he asked quietly.

"Yeah," she answered. "Second time she had to do that. That Elliott guy wasn't dead when she had to do it for Lanie, but still. Two times. Two weddings. It isn't worth it. All that planning. All that money . . ." she pulled in a shaky breath ". . . not worth it. I'm not doing it again. I'm never getting married."

At that, Shy rolled to his side, reached out and found her hand lying on the bed.

He curled his hand around hers, held tight and advised, "Don't say that, baby. You're twenty-two years old. You got your whole life ahead of you."

"So did he."

Fuck, he couldn't argue that.

He pulled their hands up the bed and shifted slightly closer before he said gently, "If he was in this room right now, sugar, right now, he wouldn't want this. He wouldn't want to hear you say that shit. Dig deep, Tabby. What would he want to hear you say?"

She was silent then he heard her breath hitch before she whispered, "I'd give anything..."

She trailed off and went quiet.

"Baby," he whispered back.

Her hand jerked and her body slid across the bed to slam into his, her face in his throat, her arm winding around him tight, her voice so raw, it hurt to hear. His own throat was ragged just listening.

"I'd give anything for him to be in this room. *Anything.* I'd give my hair, and I *like* my hair. I'd give my car, and Dad fixed that car up for me. I *love* that car. I'd swim an ocean. I'd walk through arrows. I'd *bleed* for him to be here."

She burrowed deeper into him and Shy took a deep breath, pressing closer, giving her his warmth. He wrapped an arm around her and pulled her tighter as she cried quietly, one hand holding his tight.

He said nothing but listened, eyes closed, heart burning, to the sounds of her grief.

Time slid by and her tears slowly stopped flowing.

Finally, she said softly, "I dreamed a dream."

"What, sugar?"

"I dreamed a dream," she repeated.

He tipped his head and put his lips to the top of her hair but he had no reply. He knew it sucked when dreams died. He'd been there. There were no words to say. Nothing made it better except time.

Then she shocked the shit out of him and started singing, her clear, alto voice wrapping around a song he'd never heard before, but its words were gutting, perfect for her, what she had to be feeling, sending that fire in his heart to his throat so high, he would swear he could taste it.

"*Les Mis*," she whispered when she was done.

"What?"

"The musical. *Les Misérables*. Jason took me to go see it. It's very sad."

If that was a song from the show, it fucking had to be.

She pressed closer. "I dreamed a dream, Shy."

"You'll dream more dreams, baby."

"I'll never dream," she whispered, her voice lost, tragic.

"We'll get you to a dream, honey," he promised, pulling her closer.

She pressed in, and he listened as her breath evened out, felt as her body slid into sleep, all the while thinking her hair smelled phenomenal.

Shy turned into her, trapping her little body under his and muttering, "We'll get you to a dream."

Tabby held his hand in her sleep.

Shy held her but didn't sleep.

The sun kissed the sky and Shy's eyes closed.

When he opened them, she was gone.